PRAISE FOR COMPOSITE CREATU

"With a feline inscrutability, *Composite Creatures* exerts a compelling hold on the imagination – Ray Bradbury meets Sally Rooney. Deliciously creepy!"

Chris Riddell, three-time winner
of the Kate Greenaway Medal

"Hardaker's nuanced prose and great sense of character ground the story as it delves unabashedly into the surreal, consistently catching the reader off guard with eerie imagery and delightful twists on expectations... A tale that is as thought-provoking as it is chilling."

Publishers Weekly

"The writing is wistful and works in such a way you don't realise how wonderfully strange the book is until you are enfolded in it."

RJ Barker, author of *The Bone Ships*

"*Composite Creatures* reads like an ever-tightening garrote. What could pass for the memoir of someone trying to live a normal life on the poisoned Earth of Philip K. Dick's *Do Androids Dream of Electric Sheep*, Hardaker's debut tells the story of sacrifices made in exchange for corporate-sponsored longevity. It is an unapologetic, intimate tale of our shared human fragility, and the deceptions we employ to keep from breaking."

Chris Panatier, author of *The Phlebotomist*

"Set in a future that feels uncomfortably close, Composite Creatures explores what constitutes love, how to build a life when a lot we tak   takes to 'glue together a sp   Ro   osities

Caroline Hardaker

COMPOSITE CREATURES

**ANGRY
ROBOT**

ANGRY ROBOT
An imprint of Watkins Media Ltd

Unit 11, Shepperton House
89-93 Shepperton Road
London N1 3DF
UK

angryrobotbooks.com
twitter.com/angryrobotbooks
Rock-a-bye baby

An Angry Robot paperback original, 2021

Edited by Eleanor Teasdale and Paul Simpson
Cover by Rohan Eason

ISBN 978 0 85766 902 5
Ebook ISBN 978 0 85766 903 2

Printed and bound in the United Kingdom by TJ Books Limited

9 8 7 6 5 4 3 2 1

For Juno, without whom I couldn't have written this.
And for Ben. He's quite good, too.

PART 1

1

There are some things I remember perfectly. I can close my eyes and be there; in school, shaping a stegosaurus with playdough, climbing stone walls and wooden stiles with Mum, or even on the observatory roof, hand-in-hand with Luke, searching through the smog for sparks of life. Even now, I see his face lit green beneath the moon, smiling in absolute awe at the cosmos and proving without doubt that he had eyes only for antiquities. The way things were. The stars were so bright that I could hear them, like glass shattering. They've never shone so brilliantly since.

But the fact I can relive all these things so vividly just convinces me that I've made them all up. Each time I play these memories through, Mum or Luke say something new. It's always something that warms my belly, something that makes me feel better. Only occasionally is it something that hits me hard. But even then, it still strikes a low satisfying note telling me I was right about being wrong, all along. What would you call that?

I wonder if it matters, whether these images are real. It's somewhere to go that's dark and balmy. We all do it, don't we? Where do you go?

A long time ago, Mum told me that in her youth the sky would flock in spring and autumn with migrating starlings, finches, even gulls. Huge grey and white beacons of the sea. I've heard recordings of their calls – somewhere between a lighthouse's horn and a baby's wail. I sometimes close my eyes and imagine how it would sound as hundreds of gulls moved across the blue like shot-spray, all wailing to each other out of sync. Ghosts that swam the sky. I think it would sound like the end of the world.

Over the years, Mum had collected all the fallen feathers she'd found in the garden, on the roof, in the gutter. There was nowhere too low for her to stoop, no mud too deep or sticky for her to squish her knees into and scoop out the treasure. She rinsed the feathers as best she could and balanced them in egg-cups wedged between books on shelves. "Stuff of stories now," she'd murmur as she pointed them out to me one after another, telling me which birds they came from. This one a barn owl. This one a crow. But she might have well been naming dinosaurs – I couldn't picture any of them. All the illustrations in Mum's reference books were completely flat. One time, we were sitting on the garden wall together when a bird landed on a perch above us and made the strangest sound, sort of a low whistle. I'd never seen anything like it, with its fat grey form and striped underbelly, but Mum just laughed at it and clasped my face between her hands. "Are we supposed to think that's a cuckoo? The little patchwork prince. You can almost hear the clockwork." I felt silly then and didn't look back up at the lie, but I kept listening for a telltale ticking that never came. Perhaps Mum could hear something I couldn't.

Still, I continued to stroke Mum's collection of genuine feathers, gliding the silky fronds between my fingers. Something about them always made me want to pull away, but Mum encouraged me to keep going, to know what they felt like. But it was confusing for me. Was the feather still alive, without the body it had been attached to? I wanted to stick their sharp shafts into the skin on the back of my hands and wave them in the wind. "Be gentle, Norah," she'd whisper, "They're fragile, and who knows if we'll find more."

I wished I could see inside her head. I could almost feel them, *her thoughts*, or at least the shape of them. She was my mum. But the things she said, the things she lifted from mysterious drawers – they were from another world. She looked up to the sky for things I couldn't understand, always through her old binoculars; heavy black things, held into shape by stitched skins. She liked to shock me with little facts, things like, "When I was little, the sky was full of diamonds that you could only see at night," and "Me and your Gran used to lie on our backs and watch fluffy clouds go by. You could see shapes in them, and if you asked the sky a question, it sometimes told you the future." The more stories she told, the less I believed her, and would gently push my hands in to her belly and say, "You're fibbing, tell the truth." But Mum would just shake her head so her red curls bounced over her face and promise that it was real, *she'd seen it with her own eyes*. One night, she even told me that, "the moon used to be as white as a pearl." At the time, I didn't know what a pearl was, which seemed to make her sadder. She pulled me to her side and pressed the binoculars to my face. "Keep looking, Norah. Up there in the dark. The birds – they might come back. They might."

I don't know if I believed that. The birds had just disappeared, it was their choice. The news reported a muddle of reasons for it over the years; climate change, lack of habitats, a faltering ecosystem. The fact that the earth and sky are turning plastic. I remember when I was little, seeing on TV the reports about initiatives to encourage the building of bird boxes and custom annexes on business premises. Children's TV shows had segments where the hosts showed you how to build your own bug-hotel or bird-feeder out of an old pine cone, but I didn't know anyone who managed to actually bring anything to roost. Later, after I'd discovered the joy of watching the world through Mum's binoculars, I did ask her when it'd all started, the fading away of wildlife in the wind and soil. But she just looked out of the window and squinted her eyes against the white-grey sky. "It all happened so gradually," she said. "I don't think any of us noticed until they'd gone."

Mum tried to make me believe the miraculous could happen, that surprises were around every corner. But even then, I only nodded and smiled to be nice, to make her feel better. I've never understood why people need to believe in something we can't see.

It's like reality isn't enough – they constantly need wonder, awe. When Art and I were dating, even in the earliest days, he always threw in the unexpected. For our very first date, we arranged to go for a meal at a French restaurant, La Folie. I spent far too long tangling myself up in dozens of outfits before deciding on a pair of rose-gold trousers and a black chiffon shirt, only a bit sheer.

At thirty-one, I wondered if I was a bit too old for clothes that showed so much, or whether I'd come across as desperate. I ran my hands over the shape of me, repeating to myself the mantra, "I do look good, I do look good." Even after I'd committed to an outfit, I couldn't stop faffing. I tried the shirt my usual way of leaving it loose and flowing, but it just didn't seem right. I then tried tucking it in but I couldn't stand feeling constrained. In the end I undid the last three buttons and tied the open panels in a bow. Already the chiffon was sticking to my skin. My hair – a fluffy brown nightmare at the best of times – was unusually coy and submitted to being clipped to the side with a gold triangle pin. I painted my skin in bronze and peach, finishing myself as I would a precious gift. When I caught my reflection in the mirror I hardly recognised myself, and fought the instinct to wipe it all away. Maybe it was good that I felt like a stranger. This was the new me – a new beginning. Perhaps a costume was what I needed.

I took a taxi straight to the restaurant, my cheeks burning at how late I was. At one point I lowered the window to cool myself down and the caustic air stung my nostrils. It was so much worse in this area of the city. How could I forget to wear perfume? *Stupid.* All I could hope was that the restaurant had plenty of scented candles and a top-notch purifier. I rolled the window back up and tried fanning my face with my handbag, but a quick glance at my watch and I was distracted again. *First impressions are so important.* Though in the end, my lateness probably wasn't a bad thing – my desperation to get there quickly proved to be the perfect distraction from my beating heart, the mounting sense of panic rising up my throat.

I flew into the restaurant not at all thinking about how I looked or whether the other diners would guess why I was there. I spotted Art straight away, sitting at a table in the far corner of the restaurant, a leather portfolio resting between the cutlery in front of him as if he was ready to eat it. The bronze ankh and "E.G." stamped on the cover shone in the candlelight.

I weaved my way between tables crushed with friends and lovers all leaning towards each other, all baring their teeth and spilling wine, and finally reached our table. Art stood when he saw me coming, the fingers of his right hand twitching a little, his right arm pinned down by his left.

"I'm so sorry, Arthur–"

He stopped me short by pulling me into an embrace.

"Don't worry about it, you look beautiful."

My arms wrapped around his shoulders, bending on wooden hinges and dangling on strings. I was conscious that I stood a little taller than him, and my elbows awkwardly sought out the place they would have sat before, which now was empty space. I finally let my arms rest on his shoulder blades, acutely aware of how the expanse of my hands fanned across his back.

We sat, and I saw there was already a glass of red wine waiting for me. I picked up the glass by the stem and took a sip, my tongue shrinking away from its dry and mossy texture. Art picked up his glass and took a long, romantic draft, his eyes on my eyes on his eyes. His hair was cropped much shorter than when I'd watched him in the waiting room. Then, he'd had an early hint of a beard too, but now his skin was shaved so close that his cheeks and chin looked like porcelain. I wondered whether he would break if I touched him. Would everything break? As soon as I sat down, he grabbed my hand and gave it a squeeze. His palm was dry and rubbery, not like china at all.

No, it wouldn't break. I'd make sure of it.

But then the worst happened. Within minutes of me getting there, I didn't have anything to say. My tongue rolled in my empty mouth searching for something, *anything* to fill in this enormous chasm before it got even wider. I'd stalled, utterly and completely. Art's eyes were huge and exposing, and all I could think about was how his skin was even paler than mine, how his hair might feel between my fingers. Bristly, maybe. Not soft. It could've been seconds, it could've been minutes – but it felt like years were spinning by and I couldn't get off the carousel.

Art smiled, showing rows of straight, white teeth with a little gap between the front two around the size of a penny's cross-section. "I thought this might happen." He reached below his chair and on sitting up swung his arm in a flamboyant arc to the ceiling before bringing down on his head a miniature yellow party hat shaped like an ice cream cone, peaked with a cloud of fluorescent pom-poms. "Happy first date day!" he sang, his arms stretching wide in celebration. I laughed, spitting puce across the table and then covering my face with my hands, as if denying I had a mouth at all. He pulled a second hat from beneath his seat, this time shaped like a canoe with long strings dangling from the front and back like a horse's tail. He thrust it towards me. "I thought it might break the tension. Join me?"

Terrified, I took it by the tassel and didn't know what to do. Wasn't everyone in the restaurant already looking?

"I–"

"Come on, put it on!"

In the end, I did it not because I wanted to, but because I thought it might showcase us as a real couple, celebrating a birthday, or anniversary. The other diners would whisper, "Well, they *must* know each other already. Why else would they dare to be so ostentatious?" I grinned back at Art as if it was all for him, only letting a hint of self-consciousness shine though. And you know what? As soon as I pulled the hat over my eyes, something changed. I couldn't even see if anyone was looking anymore, and that slight act of outrageousness overshadowed mine and Art's feeble history. Now, we were set apart from everyone else in a positive way. We were the loud ones, the ones everyone deliberately tried to ignore. It was genius. We had our first funny story. *Remember the hats, darling? Tell them about the hats!*

Art moved his portfolio aside to the edge of the table, leaving it closed, and I didn't even take mine out of my bag. The whole thing felt surprisingly organic, and we moved through the night at the same pace, holding hands through time. He told me a little about his family in Wisconsin, how he'd moved to New York in his early twenties to get away from the crowd he left behind. He was vague about the details, and when I asked him about it he just shook his head and took a drink. It wasn't that he avoided it, but I picked up that he saw his life in the US as a chapter which had very much ended. At this point he'd only been living in the UK for a few months, but it sounded like he was determined to cut ties with everyone back home. He said it was "simpler". So, I was going to be taking on Arthur alone, no extra baggage, which pleased me. Nice and clean.

I watched him all the time. While he talked, he had an odd little tic of pulling on the fleshy bit of his ear as he tied off sentences, and he often looked at me sideways when I talked for more than a couple of minutes. When he ate, he never touched the cutlery with his lips or teeth, and simply dropped the food into his mouth. He opened his eyes particularly widely when listening, as if he heard more with the whites.

Our little table was positioned in front of a huge aquarium, which reached up to the ceiling and across the wall. The glass looked thick as brick, and made a dull *clunk* when Art tapped a knuckle on it. At head height, between the waving reeds, a shoal of guppies flickered with long, flashy tails, and fish with dalmatians' spots cut through the gloom to follow my finger across the glass. We each picked our favourite fish. Art chose a white guppy with a blue sheen which he named Albatross, and I chose the little brown catfish, which snuffled around on the sand with her feline whiskers and otter-like mouth. She was the only one that moved slowly enough for me to make out the tiny stitches holding her together, the bulging seams.

The right time never came to show our portfolios, so we decided to exchange them at the end of the night, taking them home to read before discussing them at our next date. I was even more thrilled about this than I let on, as this seemed like a far less mortifying way to share the inevitable. If only we all could be absent when we're standing in the centre of someone else's room for the first time, naked.

Surprisingly, deciding what to include in my portfolio hadn't been as difficult as working out what to wear that night. Easton Grove had sent me their official protocol list, but I didn't need it. I seemed to just know what would be required of me, and putting this on paper was always easier than living it in the flesh.

I included my CV, which mainly recorded my career history beginning with my teenage job in the bakery and ending with my insurance job at Stokers. I tried to make the most of my responsibilities, keen to make myself seem like a "catch", but it was obvious to anyone reading the facts that I was more of a "cog". Once I realised that, it seemed better to be frank about it upfront after all. My job was to process small insurance claims. I never spoke to the clients myself – my part was to sit in the middle and transform loss into bankable assets – but I sometimes watched their appointments with the suits and ties through the glass walls of the meeting room. Basically, I saw everyone's misfortunes, and turned the gears enough for a few pennies to come out somewhere down the line. Though how much dropped into their purse, whenever it did, was never enough. Their eyes said it, even if their lips didn't.

On its own though, my career history seemed pitiful, so I also included a photograph of the house I grew up in on the Northumberland coast – the rows of houses behind all painted in their pastel colours, prints of two of Mum's paintings (one of me sitting at a little table with a book and the other of a sea, split by the leap of a blue whale), and a USB stick, containing a file of Edith Piaf songs. I had ummed and ahhed about the music, something about it seemed a bit... *pretentious*. But I knew the rise and fall of the melodies by heart, and though I didn't know what the lyrics meant it didn't matter, because the notes made my blood flow in quixotic waves. I hope Art would understand that, even just a little bit.

This all would've been fine on its own, but my portfolio *still* lacked the spark that made me, me. This disturbed me, because the gaps say more about you than what's between the pages. I tried writing something, a poem, a few lines of meaning, but it went nowhere and meant nothing. So after a few increasingly frustrated evenings of scribbling, I scrapped my futile attempt at creativity and instead slipped inside an old photo of a seagull that I'd picked up at an antiques market years before. I wished I still had the feathers in the egg-cups. How significant it would have been to fold something so irrefutable between my pages. But they were all gone now.

By the time I got home from La Folie, the Shiraz was bubbling back up my throat. I locked the door to my flat and threw myself on the sofa, face-down. The room shuddered and swayed, the walls pulsing with the beat of Art's voice, every word he'd spoken. It was late and my flat was silent, yet it was so very, very loud.

I turned on the TV to drown it out, and unzipped Art's leather folio on the coffee table. He'd included his CV, ironed crisp, detailing his journey from his first job as a junior copywriter to full-time authorship. Here was a list of his published novels, and I counted seventeen, including the one currently in progress. Scanning the list, I hadn't read any of them, but I'd heard of one or two of the titles, and could remember one or two of the covers. They were all crime novels, not my sort of thing but the sort of paperback people snap up at the airport for holiday reading. I would never have told him this, but I looked down on them. These were lives written to templates, and it made my skin crawl that the main character – though so flawed in all the usual ways – claimed to never see the ending coming.

But looking at Art's list of successes was still enviable, and with a sickening jolt I realised that he would be looking at my own paltry resumé right now. I let the CV waft back onto the table and picked up one of the two novels he'd included. The title *Frame of*

Impact groaned in heavy blue and black. I turned it over and on the back was a greyed-out picture of Art sitting in a library, the desk in front of him messy with open volumes and stacks of old hardbacks, as if playing a detective himself. He didn't look like the Art in the party hat. This was Arthur McIntyre, who didn't laugh or smile. His eyes were smaller, concealed behind thick-framed acetate glasses that he might've found in a fancy-dress shop.

There was a photo in the folder too: Art when he couldn't have been more than five or six, standing beside a couple wearing the protective green overalls, wide-brimmed hats, and veils of the scatterers. Behind them stood a row of sealed white tents and chemical sprinkler pipes. Above the awnings and half out of shot, I could just about make out the edge of an iron cage suspended in mid-air – a tractor, or harvester of some sort. Through the mesh, the woman grinned from ear to ear with the same straight and square teeth Art had. The same wide, white eyes, but set into a face that had lost a lot of weight. Skin hung loose beneath her chin, her neck a slim column of blue tendons. The man, who must have been Art's dad, stood head and shoulders above the woman, and wore a sharp grimace. One arm pinned the woman close to him, while the other held Art's wrist. Art was half-standing and half-sitting, as if his legs had buckled and the photographer had captured the exact moment he'd started to fall. He was looking away to the right, at something beyond the edge of the snapshot, with his mouth gaping, his eyes angry and small. I propped the photo up against a cup on the coffee table.

Back to the folder. Next up was a pile of letters, folded carefully into envelopes which were badly crinkled at the corners. I knew what these were. Art had been telling me about a pen-pal he'd had in his early teens who lived in England, a girl the same age named Wendy. They'd been matched up by a school programme and written to each other for four years, comparing their day-to-day lives and sharing ambitions that transfigured with every letter. They never met in person. Art said that as the years went by he'd get a thrill when a new letter arrived in his mailbox, and he'd rush straight upstairs to his bedroom to read Wendy's news. But when it came to writing back he'd hit a blank, and end up repeating the same stories, hating himself for his laziness and the banality of what his life must sound like. So he started to make things up, but when he received further replies from Wendy he was surprised to see she wasn't as captivated as he'd imagined she'd be. She just wrote about herself.

His stories became more and more elaborate and unrealistic until he ended up writing stories for himself, rather than Wendy. This way, he could live a thousand different lives without lying to anyone. But he kept Wendy's letters, and when the opportunity came (years later) to move to the UK he snapped up the chance, this being the only other home he felt he knew.

The final piece of himself Art had included in the folio were a pair of purple socks, spotted with red. They were obviously well worn, the heels thin and threadbare. When the voices began to settle and I could raise my head again, I carried the socks to my bedroom, closed my eyes, and threw them towards the bed. They lay at the foot on the right hand side. I stared at them for some time before stripping and crawling under the covers on the left side, trying to forget that the socks were new and convincing myself that having them there was utterly, utterly normal.

2

It seemed that nothing in my own folio turned out to be too horrendous, and Art and I continued to meet up in safe public spaces for "activities". It all seemed so old-fashioned and formal, and there was something reassuring about that. One thing that I did find odd was that Art was often keen to revisit the same attraction or venue over and over again. At one point, we went to see the same film on *four occasions*. It wasn't even a new film. Art talked about that film endlessly; turning what should have been flirtatious after-drinks into a post-midnight panel discussion. The film was about a boy who survives a shipwreck by escaping on a lifeboat, shared with a tiger. After seeing it once, I shared Art's enthusiasm – revelling in the luscious tapestry of the sea, the animals, and the blazing sun. We debated the possibilities: was it all a dream? Was he dead? Was it all a lie? But after the second viewing, I started to see metaphors for all sorts of things, and by the third I started to feel irritated at the obvious flaws in the boy's story. I didn't believe him anymore. Art felt the opposite and sank deeper into the boy's fantasy with each retelling. By the time we went to see the film for a fourth time I didn't want to talk about it further, and just let Art waffle on, only adding in an occasional nod or shake of the head.

One time I wanted to take Art somewhere special *to me*. I picked him up at his flat and drove him to Copsickle Castle, an ungated ruin free to wander. By day, the place was crushed with couples huddled on picnic blankets, families bending their knees awkwardly to all fit in a photo, and outdoor types spearing the earth with Nordic poles and striding across the yellowing lawn with too-heavy boots. It made the castle look like it was built on a sea of gold, so delicate that you could kick it up with your shoes. This was one of the last "unscattered" places, land made up of what land should be. No chemicals turning the earth, no carcinogens creeping up through the clay. And even though it was no longer green, you might still find a worm after the rain, or even a drunken bumblebee caught in a southern wind.

Wanting to avoid everyone else, I took Art to the castle on a Thursday after work. Sometimes community groups projected films on the ruins or acted out amateur plays between the stones at night, when the sky would darken and cast an eerie crimson light across the stage. I wanted it to be about us, so made sure to choose a night where we'd be alone.

We walked in silence, taking snaps of the lilac smog oozing up from behind the monoliths and climbing the ancient steps to halls where lords once sat. My hands shading my eyes from the setting sun, I waited on one crumbling wall while Art leapt across a crevasse to a square of stones with a central hollow, set like a throne. Art sat in it and surveyed his kingdom below. I teased him then, unapologetically goading him for taking the throne before I had the chance (though I never intended to really). He lifted his chin, and snootily replied that the throne was his, but as his queen I could sit on the arm and shine. From the height of our crumbling turret, the remains of the castle foundations stuck up from the ground like bones.

After dates like that, we'd come back to my flat for an extra drink or two, learning to be comfortable with our bare toes nudging each other under the table, our hands in each other's cupboards. At the time, I lived alone and my flat was pure function; a one-room studio, chalked in cheap magnolia. The only real flash of colour was crumpled in a corner beneath a coffee table. A patchwork blanket stitched from mismatched fabrics, with one strip at the end crudely knitted in yellow and shot with holes. I hardly had any knickknacks or anything like that, and instead blue folders blazing with Easton Grove's bronze ankh lay in piles on the floor, contracts and small print spilling from their edges.

The flat naturally felt like a "nook", wherever you sat or stood. The kitchen, living room, and bedroom were all part of the same space but hidden around corners in a horseshoe, with the living room in the centre. The bathroom was the only room with a lock. My only chair - a two seater sofa - was only large enough for one person to lounge or for two people to be uncomfortable. I sat on the floor when Art visited, legs crossed like a child listening in assembly.

The walls were bare apart from a rattling air purifier and two small oil paintings from Mum. One was a likeness of me in blue dungarees, crouching behind a huge plant pot overflowing with trickling ivy. I look like I'm about four or five, but I have a feeling she painted it from memory long after I'd outgrown hide and seek. The other was a portrait of the two cats she'd kept as a child, in the days before people ranked hygiene over hugs. One was a little black lump with a white nose and squinty eyes, and the other was a mix of tawny, marbled like an exotic butterfly. When I was little, I used to stroke the paint with my little finger, imagining what their fur would feel like. Their names had been Bathsheba and Bertie, and most of Mum's bedtime stories to me had been about their antics, whether it was how Bathsheba would shuttle up the doorframe like a fireman down a pole but in reverse, or how my grandad would take Bertie out for a walk with a pink harness, much to the sniggering of the neighbours. Mum said Bertie lived to the age of twenty-eight, but I couldn't see this being true. Twenty-eight is a human age.

Art's flat in comparison was an urban ruby. I'd never seen anything like it. He rented it, a refurbished Victorian office space above an architects' studio. The interior walls were lined in a rich red brick, and the ceiling was a night sky of navy. Unlike my air purifier, which groaned like the exhaust of an old bus, his was tiny and beautiful and silent enough for you to believe it wasn't even there. All his furniture stood very far apart, so if you lifted your arms and spun them at various points in the flat your fingertips wouldn't brush anything. Shelves along the walls supported leafy ferns, glossy banana trees, and succulent yuccas. I couldn't tell if they were real or purely ornamental, even when stroking their waxy skin.

He'd only been living there four months when I first visited, plenty of time to make the place his. It seems naïve now, but the idea of being locked into his flat made my palms sweat. My plan was to head over there after spending a frantic hour after work transforming myself into someone bright and sparkling. I shouldn't have driven, but by the time I realised that it shouldn't be this hard to put the key in the ignition, it was too late to call for a taxi. I practised casually leaning backwards and away from the window, in case I was stopped and needed to dodge a policeman tasting my wine-breath.

I made it to Art's without drama, and as I settled into his leather sofa and waited for my next glass to be poured, I began to scan the flat for clues – nudging aside cushions to see what they covered, flicking through the magazines under the coffee table. But this was a show home and I found nothing to give him away. He could easily have been a spy or an assassin. There were no photographs or magazines lying around, no half-eaten meals or empty bottles. The only thing "in progress" was a pile of papers on the arm of a chair – forms and pre-addressed envelopes with "Visa Exemption" in bold across the top and Easton Grove's blue "sanctioned" stamp over it all.

Art showed me around, pointing out his many, many books arranged in rows on the ledge where roof met brick, but they were too high for me to read the spines. He introduced his bedroom as "our room" and then brought me to the inner sanctum – his study. In contrast to the rest of the flat, this room was chaos – stacked with piles of paper, ring binders, and slippery plastic folders. Post-its stuck to books, the computer monitor, the legs of his desk. The walls were a mosaic of A3 sheets, nailed into the brick. His scrawls looked like hieroglyphics, mixed in with pie charts, line graphs, and tables of names and plot points. So many lives, condensed into cold, hard, stats. Art called this room his "aviary".

I'd brought back one of Art's books that he'd lent me, and I slotted it into the row of paperbacks on the windowsill. I told Art that I'd enjoyed it, particularly the ending when Ben had climbed the wall and told the world to go fuck itself. He grinned eagerly, and immediately handed me another to read, which I dropped into my handbag quickly. I hadn't actually read that first book, I'd only flicked to the last chapter, but if you know the end people don't ever question if you know the beginning.

It was already late, so we sat at his glass dining table to play a board game. During the hour we spent sinking each other's battleships, I waited for the wine to work its way into my blood. I became bold – stretching out my naked feet under the glass for a touch of warm ankle or curling toe. My hands danced the table and I used them decadently, flourishing my fingers as I talked about my week. When I laid them back on my lap between gestures, I could feel them shaking.

Art brought out midnight snacks – cheese and biscuits, grapes, flatbreads and hummus, and though I'd never felt like eating less in my whole life I picked at the grapes, chewing them until I was left with the empty skin. Something about the taste was "off", a bit like rust or damp stone, and I wondered if he hadn't scrubbed them like he should. Maybe all that was different in the US.

At one point when I was listening to Art gush about his recent two weeks in Rome, a small beetle the size of a grain of rice scuttled from the fruit bowl to hide under my plate. A rare little jewel. But when I lifted up my dish the bug was no longer there.

It must have been 3am or so by the time we stumbled to "our room". The curtains were open, and through the window I saw the moon, cold and white, punched through a sky already teasing the pink of dawn. We sat on the end of the bed and pressed our lips together, my hand reaching out for his unexplored middle. I had no concept of Art's dimensions – the width of his torso, or the location of his navel. His body was a vast land for which I owned no map, so I tried to memorise every hill, gully or soft valley, so that I might find my way back.

Art's eyes were closed when our faces met. His lips were thin, *different*, and just as I started to fall into another place I focussed on my breathing, pushing the darkness out with the exhale. Art raised his eyebrows at me, so I brushed off the red rising up my neck as "the wine", and leant in again, this time – starting with my mind's eye already pressed somewhere I'd learned to go.

We sat apart again and peeled off our clothes before climbing into the bed, Art on my right, as if it would always be so. I had removed everything, all trinkets and treasures, and Art had removed everything aside from the blue leather bracelet that set us both apart.

"You should have left that on," he whispered.

We didn't need to touch each other, the inches between us tickled, and I was struck by how much this arrangement (though so organised) felt so erotic. We were turned on our sides facing each other, the duvet tucked around our necks. Art made no effort at all to hold me, and as the room continued to sway like the deck of a ship, all I could think about was how much of me Art could actually see with his glasses sitting there on the nightstand.

I had an early booking the next morning to go through my seventh round of genetic counselling. After a brief few minutes of running my fingers through my curls and smudging a lipstick across the apples of my cheeks, I swept out the door – Art and I following each other's gaze with the same, conspiratorial smile. I travelled to Easton Grove wearing last night's clothes as a mark of triumph.

I drove the forty or so miles to the clinic straight from Art's flat, only stopping to pick up an Earl Grey and victory bagel from a service station. I devoured them in my corner of the car park, each mouthful deservedly sweet and full of life. I didn't care if the heightened sugar levels in my blood would expose my failings.

What did it matter? I'd spent the night with Art, and he was wonderful. And he was mine, all but for a signature on a dotted line. But plenty of time for that if that day ever came. Months, years, perhaps. My head swam with all the possible futures we could have – all the places we could go, and things we could see. Art would open so many doors, taking me with him into tomorrow. And more importantly, he wanted me, he seemed to really, genuinely want me. *Me*. If that wasn't an occasion for cake, I don't know what was.

Easton Grove is such an English name for what it was, a township of small cottage-style surgeries set around a larger central building, housing all the key conference halls, clinics, and laboratories, and fronted by a marble reception where your footsteps echo. Though it couldn't have been built more than fifteen years before, the main building had been built in the style of an old manor house, with high ceilings and rows of windows with crisscross lead hatching.

The whole Easton Grove site was set way out of the city, surrounded by acres of forest and fields which changed colour through the seasons, from spring's yellow stretches of rapeseed to winter's frost-bitten blue. I had never seen greener grass, and it squeaked beneath your shoes like clingfilm. The air there was sweeter – not fresher, exactly, but like the synthetic scent of laundry liquid. If I'd read the label, I bet it would have said "cool cotton" or "flax". Everything there seemed artificially bright, as if the smog between earth and the sun had been sterilised. If it wasn't for the bronze-plated sign embossed with the brass ankh by the front gates, you might've thought it was a secluded country community, protected from trespassers and preserved like a pressed flower. Access to the site was via three sets of gates, manned by Grove staff dressed (in my mind) a little too much like farmers, smiling widely in glass booths, clad in checked shirts and earthy corduroys. Sometimes groups of non-members waited outside the gates, clasping the railings and glaring through into the compound, but today there were only one or two stragglers standing on their own, so I let all my muscles relax.

During my induction phases, the fallow fields and lack of life around the site had left me cold, but that day everything was illuminated. Rooftops shone like hot terracotta, and the stacks of white transporter cartons outside the surgeries reflected the brilliant gold of the sun. Even the ridiculously polished statues of what I suppose were meant to be pheasants and swans beside the path glittered like real silver.

The air tasted *incredible* today, so I took the scenic route to reception. On the way, I passed Grove caretakers wearing forensic suits and carrying their crinkling black waste-sacks, and their faces beamed in welcome and pleasure to see me. Lab coats glowed, like the shrouds of saints. A pair of doctors nodded to me like comrades do in films when no words are necessary. Even the gloomy-looking cottages with no windows that sat beneath the hanging branches of the willows didn't distract me. It was easy to be fooled by them, but as you got closer, you couldn't help but see the peeling paintwork, the chipped wood panelling. They were just painted pre-fabs, the sort you see when there's a pop-up blood donation drive or a polling booth. The doors were always closed, and only staff in white coats or tweed went in and out of them during clinic hours. Today though, the sun bleached out the shadows from the trees, and the recordings of birdsong drowned out the strange clangs and thumps that could be heard from within their walls.

I'd been a delegate of the Easton Grove private healthcare programme for six months at this point, and of the five treatment phases I was on the cusp of breaking into phase four, *Establishment*, wherein my membership would start to actually roll out. This was the point where each patient reacts a little differently. Some adjusted relatively well, taking their new fitness and nutritional plans on the chin, while others reacted with spite. One woman in my focus group – I think her name was Barbara – stuffed her personalised plans straight in the paper bin, bellowing, "This isn't where my money goes is it? Fuck this, I could download this shit off the internet. You might as well give me my fucking tarot card reading, as well." Barbara was marched off to a sealed room by two small nurses dressed in cream tweed and clicking their ballpoint pens, both straining to hide their annoyance behind the smiles (but not concealing it enough). Barbara re-joined the group an hour later, her face flushed, a new plastic sleeve of exercises and food plans rolled in her fist. She didn't speak to any of us again after that, and listened to the professor's toxin warnings and nutritional basics with pursed lips and a chin jutting out like the tip of a sword.

Most patients didn't make it onto phase four, and disappeared without so much as a sad little wave. It must've been devastating to get this far into the programme and then not make the cut, to be relegated to fight for a hospital bed. Some people waited months or even years for a slot to open, and then were told that their initial test results weren't compatible or their body type just "didn't fit the strict criteria". Easton Grove had received plenty of criticism over the years for its inflexibility and unwillingness to admit members from different areas of society. I did think to myself that the exclusivity wouldn't last – they surely couldn't keep accepting so few people while the world watched and wilted? Those who didn't make it into an intake saw the rest of us as withholding some genetic secret, but the truth was that we had no idea why we were chosen.

In the early days of phase one and two we were all treated the same, and went through identical blood tests, cardio assessments, ultrasounds, invasive extractions, musculo-skeletal exercises, psychological exams and genetic analysis. Some left you sore, and almost all left you feeling strange. We attended the Grove in gangs of forty, sitting together in conference halls with freshly-brewed coffee and piles of fresh fruit. We each held a numbered ticket, and waited until our number was called on one of the mounted TV screens to go in for our next trial.

It warmed your insides, having so many professionals buzz around you, wanting to know exactly who you were. Two consultants asked about Mum, and though their questions made my throat tighten, each of them squeezed my elbow and made me a sweet milky tea, which did help. It was an acquired taste, that tea. Thick with sugar and cream, but once you'd had a few cups it felt like an instant hug. I'll never forget how Fia, my ovum organi consultant, tipped her head and smiled as she offered me an embroidered handkerchief to wipe away my tears. "Keep it," she'd said, so softly. But after our time in the consultation room was up and I returned to the waiting room, I felt alone again. Out of balance. Even though I could still taste the sugar on my lips, I was bruised and longed for my name to be called again so that the next doctor would piece me back together.

We were encouraged to chat and get to know each other between assessments, but because all the candidates were desperate and no one knew the judging criteria, everyone pressed their truths to their chests and kept neighbours at arm's length. All the while, consultants dressed in their tweed drifted around the perimeter, swiping on their tablets and occasionally clicking their ballpoint pens as if distracted.

I didn't do well, being watched. I clammed up, my mind going completely blank when another applicant asked me a question, even when it was as innocuous as, "How was the road for you, getting here?" Every time I stammered or didn't follow someone's thread the consultants tapped their screens and gave me a little smile. In the end I decided to not talk too much and just try to look like I wasn't panicking. Loosen the jaw, eat a plum.

Not everyone wanted to be there of course. During one day of assessments, a girl who looked fresh out of school slouched low in the chair opposite. I had been reading a handout entitled *"The Greying* – How to be Clean, Inside and Out", but couldn't resist watching her. She wore a black leather coat and pink Dr Martens, and hid her eyes behind a sweep of glossy chestnut hair. If she did look up and catch my eye, she'd flick her face away before sinking down to face her bony knees, lost again in whatever thought held her. She constantly fidgeted with the studs on her jacket, then a zip, then the loose threads dangling from the conference chair.

Her name tag said "16: Jane", and whenever "16" filled the TV screens she'd stare at it motionless for a good twenty seconds or so before dragging herself upright by the hips, as if her head and torso were more reluctant than her legs to leave the chair.

But over the course of the day, I think I got the measure of her. She'd have been funded through the programme by her parents, and for some reason was rallying against it. Maybe they'd chosen to fund her membership to the Grove rather than send her to university, or probably more likely Jane was *used* to being funded and was just damned ungrateful. In a lot of other programmes Jane would have been one of the first to be weeded out, after all there were thousands of people who would slip into her empty chair with no fuss at all, lips buttoned shut. But as is the way of it, Jane lasted the full course, and never for one moment did she look happy about it.

Jane wasn't the only delegate at the Grove who exuded the musk of secret wealth. Prospective members had to jump repeated financial hurdles to even get onto the programme. First there was the non-refundable deposit to enter the lottery, and then another upfront cost if you were selected for testing. If after this you were lucky enough to be accepted onto an induction (phase two), you started to pay a monthly fee. Graduating to each phase meant another lump sum, and another adjusted monthly fee. This would continue until you graduated from phase five and became an outpatient member of Easton Grove, and then you just paid your monthly fee indefinitely. There were rumours that the Grove did a lot to help members in financial crisis, but I never met anyone who didn't exude the comfort that comes from a life without money worries.

I stuck out like a sore thumb amongst those people. I had no family to raise me in a queen's chair or a cash-cow career to fall back on. I'd been upfront with the clinic from the start about my financial situation – I was there because of a gift. My funds were finite.

After Mum's funeral, I'd started to sort through her rooms, sectioning her life piece by piece into boxes labelled "Keep",

"Charity" and "Bin". I remember dropping off the donations at the charity shop, the white plastic bags freeing their nicotine musk when the volunteer peered inside.

I should have been bereft. I was saying goodbye to the dresses and coats I still pictured her in, but all I felt was embarrassment at the smell, and I left without a word.

The "Keep" box was no larger than a shoebox, around the size for storing knee-length boots. The more stuff I placed in the "Keep" box the heavier I felt, and so I only packed feather-light memories; photographs of us together, letters, even a few scrawled shopping lists she must have written in the early days of illness. I also took her binoculars, her palette – still smeared with a Monet of watercolours – and her table top easel. Finally, I chose one of the feathers from amongst her bookshelves – a soft black thing, about six inches long, shining iridescent blue along its edge. I considered taking her perfume, but the bottled oil smelled like a funeral.

And then the loft. Stacked behind a tower of cardboard boxes sagging with stuffed toys and plastic games, a pram without its wheels, and steel cases of rusted bolts, screws, and tools, I discovered over forty of her paintings and miniatures, all wrapped in old bedsheets.

I looked at them all, one by one, holding some for a lot longer than others. There was no theme to them, unless the theme was "Mum". The Northumberland coast that she loved, the Yorkshire moors. Animals. She used reference photographs to paint wild things where wild things should be. No dead earth. No lilac sky. There were three portraits of me when I was a toddler, and one of Aubrey and I in Mum's back garden, sitting on the wall with our arms interlocked and our eyes on the sky.

At first the find felt like treasure, but quickly I felt trapped by it. Anchored by a collection that would fill up my flat and be impossible to hide from. I couldn't face the still eyes of Mum's self-portrait, the loose strands of curly red hair dried into the paint, or accept that the world was as colourful as she saw it.

Of the forty or so paintings I kept only the smallest two. Mum wasn't famous in any degree, but she did have a regular cohort of collectors. I could only imagine that these paintings were hidden up there because she thought they lacked something, or she hadn't considered them finished. Sometimes she'd bring out a landscape from years before and start dabbing on more oily layers, her face inches from the canvas. Mostly the added layers were making it all darker, not better, but she'd bat me away, telling me that I didn't know what I was talking about and that she'd changed, so the picture should too.

Mum hadn't produced any new work in at least a year before she died, so her collectors were eager for a last piece of posthumous pie. I pulled out of all negotiations, waving off the canvases to the agent without as much as a word. Only a fortnight after emptying the loft of oils and watercolours, I received a letter from the agent with a cheque for more money than Mum had ever earned while living, even with the agent's fees removed. I hadn't expected to inherit anything – her cottage was rented, and I hadn't been surprised to discover that she hadn't much in terms of savings. There had just been enough to cover a funeral, the price of white roses, and several plates of sad crustless sandwiches, sausage rolls, and Victoria sponge.

Those paintings paid for my future with Art.

Art wasn't there in the initial assessment days of my programme; he came into my focus group during phase three. At this point patients arrived and disappeared weekly, and you got used to keeping a distance.

I was in the waiting area, drinking from a bottle of mineral water when Art first walked in. He wore a forest green velvet jacket and bright mustard trousers, and darted through the clinic's duck-egg like a greenfinch. The world didn't dim around him, my heart didn't skip a beat, but I felt as if I *could* know him, and could anticipate his nature if only I knew his voice. He sat directly opposite me on a plush red chair, and after a single scan around the waiting room, picked up a copy of *National Geographic* and started to read. I knew who he was, even if he didn't immediately know me. Art was at once a mystery and a map.

Once I'd passed the medical checkpoints and signed yet more paperwork, our focus groups were brought back together to learn about the Grove's current research into the biomechanics of the ovum organi. Most people weren't interested in that bit so much, but the doctors seemed to have anticipated that so they kept it brief and discharged us all with an information pack and instructions to carry on with life as normal while they compiled the results of our assessments and made their final decisions. The doctor's face was expressionless as he said it, but you could tell that he knew that his words were empty. How could we just forget it, when the email from them in my inbox might mean life or death?

I opened up the information pack as soon as I got home. The bulk of the material was bound in a single guidebook as thick as my thumb. I'd seen the poster-image on the cover before, in doctors' waiting rooms, on TV, glossy sponsorship banners at airports. *"The Art of Self-Preservation"*, written in gold under a bronze ankh. An instantly recognisable garden with the violet heather, golden buttercups, *everything wild and lush*. A crystal-clear lake in the foreground, a man and woman sitting beside each other on the bank. Both intent on something deep beneath the surface of the water, and grinning at whatever their secret was.

Tucked into the back of the book was a small envelope stuffed with a twelve-page confidentiality agreement, typed in the tiniest black font. Clipped to the agreement was a pink leaflet apparently detailing "The Potential for Member Reconditioning", but the writing was even smaller and – frankly – terribly photocopied and completely unreadable. In fact, focussing on the words made me feel nauseous, so I flicked to the back page and the dotted line, where again they'd included the lakeside photo. Finally, a business card tumbled from the envelope with the details for my personal legal representative at Easton Grove, if I needed a "reassuring helping hand to guide me through the unlikely complications of membership".

There was one other envelope, white and labelled with my membership ID. I took three deep breaths before peeling it open and unfolding the single A4 sheet. A copy of a copy, signed by Fia Ostergaard. My vital statistics, blood type, genetic profile – the black and white of what I was. Towards the bottom, I found something that made my lower stomach heave so I folded the sheet into eighths and pressed it into the back of the guidebook. I didn't want to know more.

When I look back to those days, I can't help but cringe at how ignorant I was. How I was sure I understood everything, but in reality, how lightly I walked through the assessments and training. It wasn't that I hadn't prepped. I had. I read all the material meticulously, asked all the right questions, showed all the right signs. I was the one with the shining eyes and a hand in the air. I wouldn't have made it through the programme otherwise. But perhaps it was that there had been so many papers to shuffle, sites to trawl, clinic appointments every week – and of course, Art – that neither of us had time to really digest what we were doing. We wore the facts like badges, never looking down at the truth we'd created.

Because before Nut arrived I had no idea. Like everyone, I spent all my time listening, not truly thinking. I've seen it in others time and time again – relying on that instinctual stab in the belly to tell them something's wrong before the misfortune slaps them in the face. But the gut can be distracted by other things, and in those instances the stomach-twist never comes.

And then it's too late.

3

My graduating from phase four synced with Art and I moving in together.

Moving Art into my flat was out of the question. It hardly had enough room for me, and Art needed an office. Art looked into extending his contract but the landlord replied with a clear and definite "No", never elaborating on why and refusing to meet. Art asked again, even offering to up his rent voluntarily, but the landlord stopped replying to his emails, and instead issued an end of contract letter for his tenancy, signed and predated.

We started looking at rental properties just out of the city, so I wouldn't be too far from work and Art could look out to the green belt, with its stretches of seeded earth and the scatterers treading up and down the rows in their overalls and sprinkling the dead soil with good numbers. To me, they looked like the pictures of old beekeepers you'd see in books, but the green of their overalls was almost bleached white from the hip down. Sometimes they'd be driving some sort of tractor that sprayed the fertilisers from a chute at the back, but most kept their practice primitive – walking slowly up and down the furrows, often coughing into their elbows every few feet. A horrible job. And even though the city air clung to my hair and stung my nostrils when leaving Stokers, I still preferred it to the fertilisers when caught in a crosswind. Whatever they were, they burned deep in the chest. But Art said the cleaner air would help him think, so we started searching for a place that would fit the two of us comfortably and that felt like a "step up" from our apartments. Somewhere cosy, with room to grow.

But the main priority was that the house would need a sizeable, soundproof loft that could be easily accessed and securely sealed.

We viewed three properties before we found our house on Dukesberry Terrace – a slim, two-bedroomed red-brick with a little yard at the front (for show) and a decent-sized creamy lawn out the back. From the front windows you could watch the terraces coil like a snail shell, dotted with little figures hurrying from A to B. Everyone's curtains were either closed or obscured by netting, which made me wonder whether they were hiding too. Even if their circumstances weren't like mine and Art's, they were all blocking off the world, *the light*. Perhaps if they knew what we were doing they'd understand. The estate agent turned out to be far more open-minded than Art's landlord had been, blithely telling us that people here kept to themselves, and that there were other couples just like us across the street and a few doors down. He said there was a community drive to pick up litter every fortnight but taking part was optional, and a fruit seller set up shop on the corner two streets down every Saturday.

I loved how the house sat propped by its brothers, as if being backed up in a fight or leaning together against a cold wind. Despite the house technically having three floors, the building was still a little shorter than its neighbours, which had additional conservatories, annexes, and extensions built on all the available sides. What were once probably front gardens were now all paved over, with plastic gnomes replacing what would have been flowers. I suppose it was easier than fighting the losing battle every day. Cleaner than coating your front step in fertilisers.

Our front door was painted purple with fine white streaks through it like the petals on a primrose. We had two ground floor windows and two on the first floor. The house looked like a child's drawing of what a home should be. There was even a chimney, which I imagined would puff white clouds from its lips.

We decided to make the place ours before moving in. We painted a room each evening after I'd finished work at Stokers. We'd start out full of chatter, but by the time night came we'd be side by side, stroking the French grey and earthy olive up and down in meditative, easy silence. While painting I sometimes thought I heard the doorbell go, but Art never looked away from the walls so I ignored it too.

When he wasn't looking, I watched for little things that Art did that might give his game away. Like when he dropped paint on the hardwood and tried to rub it off secretly with his fist in a sock. How he kept giving me only half the sugar I asked for in my coffee, and never explained why.

We'd usually lie on the sofa for an hour or so after giving up the brush. When he was absorbed in watching something on TV, he'd rest his head in the spread of his hand and squeeze his scalp. One night we were watching the news, and afterwards a sponsorship clip came up for Easton Grove. He perked up in his chair, his eyes wide and white, when the man and woman began to laugh into the lake again. The woman's fine gold necklace glittered impossibly.

"That'll be us next year, lover," he whispered, shaking my elbow. "Me and you."

In an effort to wake the house up, I went through a phase of buying spidery ferns, trees, and fertilisers at a garden centre after work nearly every day, dripping the compounds they needed onto the roots with love and lining the windowsills with life. Part of me did it because Art had had so many plants in his old flat, and I thought this might help to make the place feel like home. When he saw me carry in the third batch, he let out an "Ohhhhh", as if he'd only just realised something, and told me that the greenery in his apartment had been artificial and already there when he'd rented it.

Art wanted to set up his new "aviary" alone. He painted the

walls in beetle-shell green, and spent long nights after I'd gone home mounting shelves and ordering his books and papers first one way, and then another way, stacking them up from the floor and along the windowsills. He placed his desk, a square slab of polished oak, in the centre of the room so if you walked in you'd be facing him, sitting in his leather chair.

I left him to it, and spent the time packing up my flat into boxes labelled "Keep", "Donate", and "Bin". I didn't want to bring anything that reminded me of the life I'd had, which didn't leave me with much. Frankly, it was horrifying that I could disappear so easily into a few cardboard boxes. What would Art think when he saw my lack of substance? He'd only been in the UK a few months and already he had awards, certificates, *validation*.

I found that most things I didn't know what to do with lived in the top drawers of cabinets that I never opened – thin rolls of sticky tape, plastic keyrings from museums, cinema tickets, birthday cards. To anyone else it would look like junk. I left this drawer until last, but there's no avoiding these things forever.

I poured a glass of wine down my throat before I set to work.

In the front corner of the drawer was a small wooden box that used to contain an ammonite. You know, the fossil that coils in on itself? It wasn't lost; I could picture exactly where the ammonite was – sitting in a top drawer in another flat with darker walls but more light. Perhaps being lifted from its secret home by hands that loved old things. Hands that'd once felt like warm butter on my skin and smelled like vanilla.

On autopilot, I reached to the back and pulled at a plastic bag which clinked as it slid towards me. Inside the bag, the shattered glass shone invitingly like diamond. I *knew* one of the faces in the photo beneath the glitter was mine, but it looked rounder, or maybe the hair was shorter. Anyway, she wasn't me.

I stroked my finger around the edge of the gold picture frame before pressing a fingertip to a spike, holding it there until a dome of red bloomed. I couldn't feel a thing. I wiped the blood over the two faces with their cheeks pressed together, then stuffed the orange bag and wooden box in the kitchen bin. After that, the rest of the drawer was easier.

As Art and I spread our haul of new furniture and soft things around the house, it turned out that there wasn't a lot of room left for memories anyway. We placed our photos side by side on the dark wood mantelpiece in the living room, placed our towels tight together on the bathroom rail, and stacked mugs on the branches of our new mug stand, which twisted up and out from its base like a family tree.

I was careful to only put my things in the left side of the bedroom, and not be presumptuous. I squished my clothes to the left of the wardrobe, left him three empty drawers, and plumped up the pillows. I brought up the patchwork blanket, and, sure that Art would hate its tastelessness, rolled it up tight and stowed it under my side of the bed where it wouldn't be seen.

Just as I was finishing the bedroom, something fell through the letterbox with a heavy thump. I leapt down the stairs to find a slim blue box with "Arthur and Norah" written in iridescent bronze ink. There was no postmark or address, so I pressed my face to the living room window to see who had dropped it off, but the street was cold and still.

I sat with the box on the bottom stair. Art was at the market, picking up some bits to see us through. I knew that the Grove would want us to open the box together, to bond, but I couldn't resist the temptation of some kind of head start. I opened the box gently, so it could be closed seamlessly again afterwards. Inside the nest of tissue were a pair of bronze keyrings, a long and shimmering "Welcome Home" banner, a pair of envelopes – one addressed to each of us, and a window sticker for the front of the house, which read "We are the future". I pocketed the sticker straight away, *almost sure* that Art wouldn't want to broadcast our lives either, but it was easier to not give him the option. Next, I opened the envelope with "Norah" handwritten across the sleeve. Inside was a long list, entitled "The secret persuasions of Arthur McIntyre", such as spontaneity, banoffee pie, clocks that don't tick, Indian head massages, and crisp white shirts. I folded up the list and placed it back into the box. *No*. Wouldn't it be better for both of us if Art shared those things with me naturally? Besides, without context, what did they even mean? I couldn't imagine Art wearing a crisp white shirt, so did it mean I should wear one? I wished I could read the list they'd given Art, but I couldn't think of a way to open the envelope cleanly enough to reseal it convincingly. I didn't even remember telling the Grove what I liked or didn't like. How could they know?

When Art came home, we "discovered" the box on the doormat together. When he read through the contents of the envelope with "Art" swirled on its sleeve, he nodded sagely and winked in my direction. I played along of course. Rather than curl up on the new sofa, we spent our first full night sitting on the kitchen floor, playing *Battleships*. The house was a home and not a home, and it felt too soon for me to act like being there was routine. Once we finished playing, we headed up to bed together, and I spent the dark hours watching his chest rise and fall, and acclimatising to the sound his breath made against the pillow. I was an explorer, studying a wild beast, with daybreak as his backdrop.

As a gift to us, and as a much-needed break from decorating and unloading boxes, Easton Grove had booked us a morning session with a portrait photographer, so we could have some decent pictures of us together to put in frames around the house. They would also keep one or two on file, ready in case any press-worthy stories came up in the future.

We both dressed in the least creased outfits we could find amongst the chaos of cardboard boxes, and made our way there – only a little bit self-conscious about the prospect of showing our best faces to each other and a complete stranger.

The photographer was a short, greasy-looking man with stringy hair that clung to his cheeks. He seemed totally out of place in the pristine studio, but as we walked in, he sat with his legs spread and shoulders relaxed, as if he belonged there more than anywhere in the world.

He showed Art and I through the racks of backgrounds Easton Grove had approved, and we sniggered and gave each other plenty of side-eye as we pointed out the worst ones – an empty beach, lined with palms, the plaza in front of the Leaning Tower of Pisa, and grassy banks, peaked with the giant heads of Easter Island. We settled on a mottled blue background with spray-on clouds – like the background in an old graduation picture. It seemed the least ridiculous.

The photographer had us sit next to each other on a box draped with a blue sheet, and then asked us first to look at each other's eyebrows, then at an imaginary pool between us, and then at his finger floating – here, then there, then there. Each pose was as difficult to navigate as the last. Art obviously wasn't sure how much he should touch me, and even when he did pull me close I barely felt the weight of his arm around my shoulders. My hands lay fidgeting in my lap with nothing to do.

"Try something else. Breathe. Breathe. In through the nose, out through the mouth, lips apart, like this." The photographer's nostrils flared obscenely on the inhale, and his jaw dropped as he let out one long exhale. It didn't look particularly photogenic. "Relax-the-FACIAL-MUSCLES."

We both tried it. I took a sneaky look at Art and he was doing it all wrong – tensing his brow, pushing on the outbreath, pursing his lips. The photographer rubbed his red face and got us to stand, bounce on our knees, flap our arms. Then we tried posing while holding hands below the frame and out of shot, both of us looking at our fingers intertwined.

Eventually the ordeal ended, and the photographer beckoned us over to a screen to see a preview. He scrolled through rows and rows of thumbnails and stopped on one somewhere near the bottom of the file. He pointed at four near identical photos in a row.

"I think this is the best you can do," he said. "Sorry. Definitely the best of a bad lot."

He gave us the four prints in a sleeve to take home, and when we got back to the house we spread them on the table, both of us grimacing at how awkward we looked. In each of them I was looking at Art as if about to say something, my top lip flattened on the cusp of the letter "B" or maybe "P". Art was looking at something past me off-camera, his eyes blurred by a half blink.

I stood one up against a vase, muttering under my breath, "And this is the best we could do."

Even though the process had been excruciating, I was still glad of the terrible photo. All that time spent decorating and primping and plumping before we moved in made moving-in-day feel like I was stepping straight into someone else's life. Even my own stuff took on an uncanny, alien feel in its new setting, and I avoided touching any of it. At least with the photo it looked like I actually did live there.

The only space we hadn't already refurbished was the loft.

Having the loft was part of the tenancy agreement, and we were given free rein to ditch or re-use whatever we found. Most of it was junk; depressed sofa cushions, shoeboxes full of old papers and faded bills, grubby toolboxes rattling with loose screws, and charity bags full of old sheets and Christmas decorations. We hired a skip and poured all of it away, leaving a long cavernous space which seemed somehow larger than the floorplan of the house.

The loft was flanked by two long wooden benches, the kind older kids sit on in school assembly, and these were the only bits of furniture we kept. We discovered beneath the dust that the wood flooring we'd been promised was still in good condition, though deeply scratched. I crawled on hands and knees, cleaning, polishing, and disinfecting it, while Art danced away from the wispy cobwebs following in his backdraught.

When the place was clean, we painted the walls and ceiling a deep plum, and replaced the yellow light in the roof with a daylight bulb. There was a little skylight in the far corner, and I scrubbed at the glass until soft lilac shone through.

With the lights switched off and the water pipes thrumming, the room became a hollow womb, only escapable by the small opening to our first floor. We kept the loft stripped of accessories and anything that could snag or catch, apart from a cardboard box stuffed with a plaid towel, an old chintz bedspread (folded into quarters and pressed into the corner of the loft) and a plastic fruit crate lined by a green fleecy jacket that Art never wore anymore. Finally, we placed an oblong plastic tray in the far corner as instructed, and sprinkled in wooden pellets that smelt of pine. Even after the loft was finished, I took up the paint tins late at night to smooth on further coats of plum, until I was sure that the space was ready for its new occupant.

We'd been in the house for a fortnight. I picked out a dress printed with black willow trees, and painted my face with sophisticated taupes and tan. I reached for my old starling necklace, but instead picked up a chunky silver choker. Already the weight of it pulling at my neck annoyed me, but I kept it on because it matched. In the bedroom mirror I looked like me and not like me. A dream version of me. All grown up, now. I pressed a cold glass of water against my neck to cool the red petals of anxiety blooming up my throat.

Art sidled into the room, already in tweed trousers and a blue paisley shirt, buttoned tightly to his neck.

"I'm excited. Are you?" he whispered, leaning in behind me and pressing his chest against my back.

"Petrified."

"Maybe this'll help. Close your eyes."

His hands squeezed my shoulders and I tipped back my head, bathing in the rhythm of his fingers. After a moment or two he let go, and I swayed in the darkness, all alone.

"Turn around."

I spun on my heel and reached out my arms to find him again, but Art was gone. When I opened my eyes, he was kneeling on the floor. I knew straightaway what was happening but I was so taken aback that I couldn't speak. Art laughed, and reached up for my hand. "Don't worry, it's alright. Norah, will you?"

I feel ashamed of the way I reacted now. But shocks are exactly that – shocks. Fight or flight. I staggered, knocked off balance. "Art, who told you to do that?"

"No one. This is all me. And you, obviously."

My left hand wrapped around my now crimson throat. Married? Us? "Arthur and Norah". We'd already committed to an entwined life until the end, so why did this feel so different? I suppose I thought we'd talk this sort of thing through and decide together, like we had with everything else. I thought I'd said goodbye to spontaneity, and I'd made my peace with that. Now Art had pulled a stick of dynamite and was wiggling a match dangerously close. Good explosion, or bad explosion?

"Is that a yes, wifey? And then we can arrive in the New Year in style?"

What else could I do? I nodded, dumb as a shop mannequin. Art brought my hand up to his face for a kiss, and then retrieved a red box from his pocket. There it was.

"Call me paranoid, but I didn't want to get this out until I knew you'd say yes." He pulled open the box and inside sat a gold ring, set with a white stone flecked with scarlet and green. It looked like stained glass.

"It's a fire opal. You deserve something different to the norm. *We're* different."

Art slipped the ring down to my knuckle, and twisted it side to side to get it past the bone. I looked at my new hand, the nucleus shining like a nugget of sky and the skin around it bulging as if about to explode. It might have been my imagination, but I could swear that my finger was already starting to go numb.

"It's beautiful."

And then I started asking myself all the questions. You know the ones. Did I feel different already? Would I have to take his name? Would I be spending my evenings practising my new signature, as Norah McIntyre? And oh God – what would everyone say when I told them? We'd only just moved in, and we'd only known each other for eight months. None of my friends had even met Art yet, and tonight was meant to be the night he'd charm them, ease them into what we were, and introduce them to the new me at the same time. *And now I was going to have to tell them that we were engaged, too.*

It probably sounds like I wasn't happy about it. I know, I'm prone to worry. I *was* happy. Here I was – having just moved in with the wonderful, lovely, talented Art – and already engaged. Before now I'd never even lived with a man, and now I had someone willing to sign on the dotted line and promise himself to me romantically. In truth, I was bent between elation and worry, neither sense completely taking over the other.

Downstairs in the kitchen Art opened up a bottle of something pink with gold glitter inside. He poured out two flutes and we chinked them high in the air. I drank the glass in one go.

"My God, Norah, at that rate what the hell are the desserts going to look like?"

Blackberry pie was the last thing on my mind. Luckily I'd made the artichoke dip and batch of Gruyère gougères earlier that afternoon. Art was in charge of the jackfruit casserole.

Before I had time to flap, Rosa arrived wrapped in a thick black duffle coat which (even with the hood down) almost cocooned her whole head. As soon as I opened the door, she swooped over the threshold and escaped her layers like a hatching from its shell. After kicking off her shoes, she lifted her arms around my neck and rested her feathery head on my shoulder. She turned her face up to my ear. "Happy New Year's Eve! It's going to be brilliant. Let's make this brilliant."

I could have kissed her.

She thrust out a bottle, and stood on her tiptoes to get a first glimpse of Art, standing behind me with his hands in his pockets.

She grinned and swept towards him, arms outstretched, and they sank into each other; I can only guess with relief that both were happy to play the nice game. The pair headed off to the kitchen, Rosa chirping and Art mirroring her as best as he could in his singsong drawl.

I'd broken one person in, only two more to go.

I needed to be ready so stayed in the passageway, though the longer I hovered there the more I felt the attention in the kitchen drift in my direction. I was just starting to give in to propriety's gravitational pull when the doorbell rang. I wished the front door had a peep hole.

I stumbled to the door and opened it, only for it to jam sharply. For a moment I was completely stumped as to why the door would only open a few inches, and so I shut it then heaved it open again and again, blindly. A voice from the darkness outside: "You've got the chain on." And then I saw the brass shining right in front of my eyes. Why did I put the chain on?

"Sorry, I'm an idiot."

I opened the door to Aubrey and Eleanor. They huddled closely, like they'd already spent time together somewhere warm. Eleanor smiled her tiny smile, her eyebrows raised under a jagged black fringe. Beside her, Aubrey was utterly unreadable, her face as soft and expressionless as sleep. I was shocked at how short her hair was now, shaved to her scalp on the left side. It made her look both vulnerable and fearless.

I avoided her gaze and waited for Eleanor to pounce on me like Rosa had, and when she didn't it left the trench between us seem impossible to cross.

Eventually Eleanor did break the stalemate. Through chattering teeth, she muttered, "Can we come in? It's fucking Baltic out here."

I swept up my arm and invited them into No-Man's Land. She stepped over the precipice and flicked off her leather coat and patent black heels as if doing a jig. She hissed in relief and rolled her eyes back in her head.

"Why the fuck do we do it to ourselves, Noz?"

I ignored the water pooling around the bottom of the shoe pile. "It's a no shoe world in here. No foot-binding required."

"Thank fuck. Right. Where's the man himself? This man who hath tamed the Norah-creature?"

I waved Eleanor through the kitchen and faced the music. Aubrey. She'd gone from watching me constantly to scanning the coat stand as if inspecting the scene of a crime. It had been eight months, the longest I'd ever not seen her, and here we were, neither of us willing to break the wall. She should have been happy that I'd invited her, that I'd been willing to accept her into my home, but she showed no sign of appreciation. Just, curiosity.

I'm not ashamed to admit that I'd been terrified when Eleanor had said Aubrey was coming, but when I'd seen her in the doorway, huddled against the cold with her ears and nose red from the cold, something had melted away. A tickle of joy, even. Considering everything that'd happened, it was remarkable. Some friends are their own time warp.

But still, in that hallway, cold or no cold, we couldn't blend. Oil and water. But I had to do something. What could I say to her that was safe? That didn't raise questions? What if she talked to Art about Luke?

Be general. Be dull. "Did you both get a taxi together?"

Aubrey nodded. "We went for a drink first. Elle said she'd had a bad day, and wanted to burn it out before… this."

Maybe they'd been talking about me? They probably had. I was the juicy news. I kept my hands tucked into the pockets of my dress. "Come and get a drink, and then you can catch up with me too."

I strode to the kitchen, hoping she followed behind me. Eleanor was sitting on a stool, holding our photo from the studio session, her head cocked at something Art had said. I knew it must have been an Art-joke, as Rosa looked confused and Art was standing with his legs astride, practically doing jazz hands.

Eleanor spluttered, then: "Oh my God, she didn't? Fucking hell."

My entrance. *Play the part.*

"Is that me, by any chance?" I stepped into the dining room, holding out my chin like a battle sword. *En garde.* But this isn't how it should go. Art and I were a team, on the same side. We had to show them we were on the same side. Art skipped around Eleanor and wrapped an arm around my shoulder.

"I'm just telling them about the time you pretended to read my books but didn't."

"I did read some."

Eleanor purred, "Noz is good at pretending. Well, I'd love to borrow one sometime. Or maybe just recommend one and I'll buy it. Support my local bookseller and all that." She held up the photo to me with her eyebrows raised, "And by the way – *cringe.*"

I became very aware of Aubrey, still standing silently in the passageway just outside the dining room. Right then I wanted to snatch the photo from Eleanor's hand and burn it. Instead, I spun Art on his heel.

"This is Aubrey."

I'd told him a bit about Aubrey, but not all of it. The old stuff. He didn't question that the stories stopped when Art and I met, or that I hadn't seen her while he'd known me. I'd told him that we'd made different choices, which was true, and that we hadn't fallen out, which wasn't true.

He knew she'd be the most difficult to melt, so he reached out for her hand rather than her whole body in a bear hug. She took his hand with a stiff smile, inspecting him like a mannequin in a ghost train or a fun house, one that might all of a sudden jump into motion. I'd seen that look before. She watched him like he was an animal.

Art didn't seem to notice. "I've heard lots about you, more than these losers."

Eleanor tutted dramatically, sipping her wine with a pinkie outstretched. Rosa's head flicked left and right between Art and

Aubrey, biting her lip so hard that she'd turned it white. For a moment we were all caught in a freeze-frame, waiting for the drama to break. Aubrey let out a sharp little breath. "I've heard lots about you too. I've brought you a present."

After a "blink-and-you'd-miss-it" glance at me, Aubrey handed Art a purple gift bag with a dangling "New Home" tag. Art delved into the bag and retrieved a little potted plant with fat pink leaves which sat spread-eagled upon the soil.

"It's an echeveria, a succulent," Aubrey said. "They're the hardest houseplant to kill apparently. No stress."

Art handed me the plant and embraced Aubrey, "Sounds perfect." She let him hug her but she didn't move a muscle, as unyielding as an oak. In my hands the cactus called out for water with a shrill little cry only I heard. I prodded the dry and crispy soil. To distract myself from the lurching feeling in the pit of my stomach I headed to the sink and turned on the cold tap, thrusting the plant beneath it. Over Art's shoulder Aubrey spotted what I was doing, and pushed him away.

"No – don't water it too much, they like to be dry."

Crap. I quickly pulled the pot from under the tap but the soil was already soaking. I couldn't believe what I'd done. How could I be so stupid as to assume I knew what to do? Perhaps I'd already killed the thing, and I'd only had it a matter of seconds. Art pressed at the dirt with his fingertips. "It's fine, it just needs to dry out. Stick it on the windowsill and let's go for a tour. I'll be the guide."

"Just give me a minute. I'll fix this." I turned the pot over, squeezing out every drop of water I could with my fingers, as water began to leak from my own eyes. The four of them had already left me behind. One of the fleshy pink leaves fell with a soft thump into the sink.

I placed the cactus in the middle of the kitchen windowsill and dropped the lost leaf in the composting tub. I turned back to the empty kitchen, wiped the smudges from under my eyes, and listened to Art's laughter in the study upstairs.

* * *

By the time Art brought everyone back to the dining room, I'd set the table with my homemade starters and lit some candles, the sort that burn with a rose-tinted flame. Everyone looked impressed enough with my hosting skills that I felt a little bit buoyed up again, and I moved around the group, flamboyantly pouring wine from the wrist like a butler on TV. Everyone accepted a top-up except Aubrey who clung to the wall, fiddling with the collar of her shirt.

We sat around the romantically lit table and began to talk in turn. Mostly stories about "work gone wrong", or the minor catastrophes in the lives of friends-of-friends that always seem funny when you're not involved. We kept it light, and skimmed dialogue across the table like pebbles across a pond. I hid my left hand underneath the table, and kept my stones for strategic throws. It seemed like a betrayal of the reality of things to talk about fluff when there was meat hiding beneath the oak.

Aubrey laughed along with Eleanor and Rosa but stayed leaning back in her seat, hands hidden like my own. While I found it impossible to catch her eye, Art tried repeatedly to hook her in, asking her questions about me, how I'd been at university, how I'd been when we'd lived together. Nothing Aubrey said back to him was ever rude, or short or blunt – but somehow she managed to kill each conversation with a few soft words. You had to admire her skill to create an answer impossible to reply to each time, but it also struck me as incredibly unfair. I knew she'd find this hard, but she was being cruel to a man that didn't deserve her bitterness. That was the truth of it, and I tasted her spite on the sharp tip of my tongue.

It would've been too much to share my newest news. I was still in shock myself. The ring had pulled me back to a particular night last spring, and I just didn't have the strength to argue this time. Not with everyone watching. Not on a night when we should all be looking towards the future. A new year, and a new beginning. No. I'd let the snow fall on that night.

I looked up from the table straight into Rosa's pink eyes. She lifted her glass and drained the last few drops between lips that trembled as if she was about to speak. Instead, Eleanor boomed across the table, "So, when's your little bundle of joy arriving?" Almost as soon as she said it she looked... twisty.

I looked to Art for confirmation. "In the second week of January. So, in nine days? We're all prepared, I think. And don't get ahead of yourself. It's hardly a bundle of joy."

Eleanor gave a little nod. "It's joy of a sort though, isn't it? My uncle's never been better since he got his. It's brought him so much relief."

"Relief?" Rosa piped.

"Totally," nodded Eleanor. "Complete relaxation. He's had *the greying* three times now. He worries far less these days, about everything. You never read so much about that side of it. But it's bloody important. He calls it his little matter cow. Odd really."

"Yeah," Rosa chuckled, "Odd. I don't know much about it all, to be honest." She raised her glass. "Maybe I'll do some research."

I wondered what I could and couldn't say about it all. Instinctively I did a mental run-through of all the workbooks, contracts, and booklets. How confidential were the few details I did know? Art looked up at the ceiling and nodded wistfully. "Yep. It's all going ahead, all official now. Norah and I are going to have to work even more at being a fully functioning couple. After all, a little life depends on it."

The rest of the meal went as smoothly as I could have wanted it to, and Art's casserole tasted full and fleshy. Aubrey kept quiet, and my worry that she'd bring up Luke or say something she shouldn't finally started to ease off. I was fearless. I kept catching her eye but she'd always look away, focussing on Eleanor's lips as she spoke, or Rosa's fingers fondling the stem of her glass. I made a game of it, flicking my gaze at her when I thought she'd least expect it. Her expression was unceasingly difficult to read. A lot of the time she almost looked bored.

No one noticed the engagement ring when I dished out each course, or at least they didn't say anything about it. As the night went on, it seemed so unlikely that they hadn't seen it, that I started to wonder whether they had and just didn't want to bring it up. One mountain moved is enough for one night. Every so often I'd catch Art's gaze and he'd raise his eyebrows just a bit, pointing his nose at my hand as if to say, "Is it time? I'm leaving it up to you."

Maybe it was the wine but I'd started to feel a bit smug that I had this secret, and it was a secret that none of the others had experienced yet. Luckily Art didn't push it, he sensed that I was deep in some internal mood-swimming and he bowed out of the race to keep playing Mr Nice Guy.

I kept the wine flowing, but as faces around the table began to flush I kept a close eye on who was drinking the most. I tried to act like Art, who seemed to be in his element and not worried about a thing.

When I came back from checking on dessert with another uncorked bottle in my hand, Eleanor had everyone's attention latched to her. Her own expression was blank, staring into her empty wine glass.

"What made you go?" said Rosa, leaning her head on her hand.

Eleanor craned her neck forward and curled her fingers into claws. "Well, I'm getting on, aren't I? Got to count up those eggs if I want one to hatch."

We all shook our heads and nodded at the same time.

"And," she went on, "I know I've got a few problems. I want to know what they are."

Aubrey reached across and squeezed Eleanor's wrist. "Toes all crossed," she said. "Everything crossed."

Eleanor gave her a wink and then looked across at me. Our eyes met, and then after a second or two she laughed and said, "Does it sound stupid?"

I shook my head. Art was watching Eleanor with a strange little look on his face. I really wanted him to say something to her, to help. Something that I'd be proud of him for saying. But he just sat there, his brow creased, head tilted down. But when I pulled my eyes off him, I realised that everyone else was looking at *me*.

Rosa sighed. "What next?"

"Bloodwork. Ultrasounds. Slowly, slowly, all queues and little movement. NHS, obviously, but still – it's haemorrhaging money. I've burned the surface off my credit card."

"You're born to it, Elle," said Aubrey. "Millions are in the same boat. Even if you did need help, there'll be something they can do. Look at the stuff you see on the news! If they can grow a thumb like a carrot in a test tube, I'm sure they can help you do what you're made to do."

Eleanor puffed out some more air. "It's not the same though, is it?"

The kitchen timer went. The pie was ready.

I got up from the table and consciously made Art responsible for changing the subject. He was good at subtle. At gentle nurture.

Soon after midnight, Eleanor started to say she needed to make tracks. She headed to the hallway to call a taxi for herself and Aubrey, and a moment or two later Rosa followed her out, batting her eyelashes and determined to barter her way into the car share.

I was left sitting in the kitchen with Aubrey and Art, the pair of them stuck in a face-off over crumbs left from the night's feast. I'd normally have said anything to break the awkward silence, but I'd lost interest in peace-making, and almost wanted to see them fight. Besides, it was too tempting to lower my head and cradle my face in my arms. Just for a minute. Maybe no one would notice.

But then it seemed that I blinked and Aubrey already sat in her purple parka, the front zipped up to her chin. Another slow blink and the taxi driver rang the doorbell. Despite the weight, I heaved myself from my chair to help Rosa and Eleanor, who were jostling together by the front door with their coats and fleecy layers. Rosa's hair was caught in her zip, and she squealed one long "Eeeeeeeee".

Once I'd liberated her she hugged me and Art together. Eleanor leant over and kissed Art on the cheek, whispering to me on the way past, "When it all goes down the shitter, tell him to call me. He's a keeper." She winked over her shoulder, and then swaggered into the night.

Aubrey was last to go, and raised a palm to Art as she slipped out the door. She didn't even look at me. I couldn't let her leave like that, I couldn't. Lurching forwards, I grabbed her wrist and pulled her around to face me. She jerked her head back, eyes wide, and glanced between my hand and my face as if I was uncontrollable. *Me*. In that moment I was ready to say anything to make it right, to make it like it used to be. I didn't want her to go and not come back, and I somehow knew that this could be my last chance to make her see.

"I'm OK. I'm really OK. I'm happy. I'm going to be fine," I whispered under my breath.

At first, she seemed to consider what I'd said, and parted her lips to ready a reply. "How's Luke?"

I froze, terrified that Art would hear her from the kitchen. She hadn't even kept her voice down. How could I answer that, here?

This time she lowered her tone. "I saw him, you know. Not long ago."

That knot in my stomach twisted hard, and I felt a flash of something dark. I let go of her wrist and backed away. My hand felt dirty.

I stood there, silent, until she reached across and squeezed my wrist, looking at me in a way that made something in the lower part of my stomach do a sharp flip. She was stoking embers I'd buried under coal, and she knew it. I looked away, but already dreaded being left in the dark.

Aubrey gave a little shake of her head, and was gone.

I've never forgotten how she looked at me then, and how quickly it all changed. How dare she judge me? Us. *She didn't even try.*

I locked the front door and rolled my forehead left and right on the cool wood, letting out one long, deep groan. Behind me, Art's breath tickled my neck.

"Why didn't you tell them?"

There wasn't an answer to this. No answer he would have liked. To be honest, I just wasn't ready to act up to it. I was happy, obviously I was happy, but there'd be questions, then more questions, and I'd need answers, and not instinctual answers that come unstructured. I'd have made a mess of it all, and I'd have let him down. He didn't deserve that. Imagine how it would feel, to have proposed and then for your fiancée to sound unwilling?

I turned, and flashed him one of my finest flirtatious smiles.

"I kind of liked it as our little secret."

I sidled up to him, wrapping my arms around his back. He stood still for a moment before taking my waist. I could taste his breath on the air between us, tinted with wine and Art's unique woody scent.

"There's plenty of time to get everyone else in on it. But for now, it's ours. Our secret."

4

Nut arrived in a small, unmarked white box made from everyday corrugated cardboard. Art carried her in like we'd have carried a new baby in a Moses basket, while I followed behind clutching a rainbow of plastic folders. The house already felt different.

We'd taken down our meagre Christmas decorations the day before (we'd only hung them up so the house looked festive for the party), and though the place felt lifeless now and drained of colour, that wasn't why it was odd. The passageway seemed lighter and the doors further away, as if I was psychically stretching out into every room on alert for sharp things or towers likely to fall. I was a thousand eyes cast across the floor and tingled with electricity, ready to release a bolt.

I dropped the folders at the bottom of the stairs and flung my soaking boots on the shoe pile. Art and I gave each other a look and then began to walk the mile up the stairs, Art balancing the box carefully in his arms. My hand kept slipping on the bannister, and either because of nerves or the cold, I couldn't feel my feet.

When we reached the first floor, I stretched up and grabbed the long white cord hanging down from the ceiling. With a gentle pull, the stepladder swung down and landed with a soft thud on the carpet. Art led the way, hugging the box close to his body, his knuckles bone-white. I followed him, and once I reached the loft placed four interlocking baby gates in a square around the hatch, as I'd practised. Two of the corners snapped into place with extra childproof locks, and as the hinge on the third corner was tested it made a shrill whine, despite the fact it was all new equipment and shouldn't need adjusting so soon.

"At least we'll be able to tell if she makes a great escape," Art whispered. He sat on the polished floor close to the white box, watching me with one hand on his knee and the other fiddling with his collar. I sat beside him and grasped his cold hand for reassurance, though I must admit, my skin bristled with excitement at this new beginning. A huge part of my future, no, wait, *our* future, was curled up inside this oh-so-average box. Nut was going to be a symbol of our life together, our commitment to each other, all wrapped up in a little furry bundle. *Our little bundle of joy.*

"This is it."

"I know. I'm ready."

Art picked up a pair of nail scissors and carefully snipped the safety tab. Stowing the scissors away in his back pocket, he started to slide open the interlocking flaps at the top of the box, releasing the slip of cardboard holding the front panels in place. I crushed my fist in my mouth as the folds were peeled away one by one, until at last the side of the box nearest Art fell open like a drawbridge to a fort.

Silence.

The box was pointing the wrong way for me to see inside and my tongue couldn't form the words, so my eyes were on Art as his face pressed deep into the cave. He sat motionless, staring as if he'd forgotten what he was looking for or as if he was lost.

"What is it? What's wrong?" I hardly recognised myself, I sounded so dry.

Art let out a breath and quickly thrust his hand inside the box, scuttling his fingers along the cardboard base like a spider or tiny man running. He started to make this strange tutting sound that people have always made to animals or babies. I'd done it myself when I'd been to the zoo-museum with Mum. We'd stood there looking at the parrots or the meerkats or the otters (it really didn't matter) and muttered together, "Click click click click click", spitting our tongues from the roof of our mouths. To this day, I can't think of a single animal that made that noise, so I have no idea why we do it. It did attract attention, but has an animal ever done it back? Maybe all this time we've got it wrong. As long as we get a reaction, we don't seem to care. I wonder if Mum did it with Bathsheba and Bertie too. She talked about them like they were *family*.

Instinctively I wanted to stop Art. How did he know that he wasn't coming across as aggressive? I hadn't read anything anywhere about the sounds she might make. But still, his clicking was hypnotic. From inside the box, there was no sound at all.

Art shuffled backwards across the floor to create space. What if she was dead? What if she was already horribly mangled and sick, from only being in the house less than five minutes? What if all of this wasn't going to work? *What would happen to us?*

And then I saw her.

One little foot, no more than a paw, stepped onto the flattened cardboard drawbridge. It couldn't have been bigger than a strawberry; round, padded and soundless as it moved. Another foot stepped out, and there she was, stumbling like a lamb, just born. A second later and a sweet and musty smell, a bit like talcum powder, followed her into the world.

I'd not really known what to expect before Nut arrived. The paperwork said each little one would be different, just as every litter contains champions and the obligatory runt. Nut wasn't a runt, but she wasn't chunky by any means. From my side angle her body was longer than I'd imagined it would be, and from her rear swayed a long, flexing tail, tipped with black. Her back curved into two rumps, like an ant covered in fat. Round, translucent ears protruded from the top of her head, twitching and flicking, listening to the quiet grind of my knees on the wood floor. From head to toe she was covered in a light layer of downy fur, which when it caught the light shone in shades of lavender and dove-grey. She reminded me of something in a museum, something that had been living and breathing once but shouldn't exist now, and immediately I wondered what Luke would've thought of her, how he'd have stroked her head and inspected her toes. How he'd have understood how her heart was just like my heart, and not alien at all. I imagined him pressing his hand against her chest to feel it beat. Frustrated at myself, I pushed him from my mind and shook off his ghost.

This was the first time in my whole life I'd been close enough to touch something *animal*. Nut had four legs, a tail, fur. She was all the cats my mum used to own, and she was all the pets owned by generations of families before the trend died. But now, there were too few chances to encounter something in the wild. Mum used to say that the sky had expanded, the birds were getting lost, and all the land-animals were moving underground to escape us. I believed her for a long time, and while Mum searched the skies for feathers I'd spend hours in our back garden digging little holes with a plastic bucket and spade, proclaiming every twig or tree root to be a snake, a ferret, or a gecko.

But Nut didn't belong in the wild. She belonged to Art and I *together*. She was the only thing that did. We owned separate cars, and our various knickknacks, strewn through the house, all still existed in the singular. This book was either mine or his, not ours. But Nut couldn't be divided.

We'd set up home for her in the loft for the foreseeable, and had kitted it out following all the official advice, guidance and case studies Google had to offer. The gates around the opening meant that she wouldn't fall down onto the landing below but we could still keep the hatch open for fresh air and to keep an ear out for trouble. A food dish and a water dish were parked neatly by the hatch entrance, and other than the litter tray, beds, and long benches against the walls, we kept the room empty. Fewer hazards. Fewer stimuli.

Nut skulked from the box and sat directly between Art and I. Would I be able to lean across and see her properly without frightening her? I shuffled forward, and she flinched – looking up at me with alarm.

Her face.

My God, the first time I saw that face. For a moment I saw nothing else, just her nose, her eyes, the shape of her chin. It was a face broader than it was long, and the look it wore was so deeply familiar that for a moment I forgot what I was looking at. The back of my throat burned, and I suddenly felt very, very cold.

I hadn't known it would be like this. She looked at me like she owned me.

Shit shit shit shit *shit*. Maybe I'd done the wrong thing? Maybe this was all wrong.

Art's palms cupped his nose and mouth. "Isn't she weirdly beautiful? She looks like you!"

"Stop it, Art." Obviously she didn't, but I didn't tell him the truth. I didn't want to say it out loud. "*Is* she a she?"

Art ducked his head to ground level, peering at the tiny gap between Nut's paws. "They said she'd probably be a she. I can't see anything to suggest she's not."

"Does she know she's a she?"

"I think she's just… what she is. I don't think she knows she's anything. She just feels the need to breathe, to eat. She wants to stay alive."

"But do you think she knows what she is? Or how we're different to her?"

Art looked away. "I don't think she thinks about any of that stuff, Norah. She's not human."

He was right of course, Nut wasn't human. But she was alive, wasn't she, looking at me with bright blue eyes and all the whites showing. I tried to shake it off. "She's a lot more petite than I'd expected, is this what you thought she'd look like? Do you think she's… alright?"

Art tipped his head to the side. "Yeah. She'll be fine. Remember that bit in the manual that each set has lots of different sizes and shapes? This one's ours. I think she'll grow quickly. She looks like a fighter."

He tapped her on the head with a finger and she raised her

moon-face to follow it. He wiggled it in the air then tickled her under the chin. She didn't indicate that this was good attention, or bad attention, just continued to stare at his finger, and then at his eyes, watching him watch her watch him. I wasn't sure whether all this touchy-feely stuff was a good idea. Didn't the manual also say that we should stay back? She was so vulnerable and everything was so new, maybe Art would spread bacteria. I thought back to what I'd read in the car.

"Maybe we should give her some space. Turn the lights off, make it relaxing. I'll bring up some food later."

Art was busy rubbing Nut's cheek.

"OK, I think that's what they said to do anyway, didn't they? Keep clear for a couple of days." He looked at her for a few moments, and I could practically hear his gears grinding. "You know, I thought they were being dumb when they said it'd be difficult, but now I know what they meant."

He extended his hand and stroked it slowly down her long, narrow back. She hardly moved, her face still peering up into his face. I couldn't tell if she was trying to understand him or she was inspecting the roof above, perhaps already planning an escape. Art slid his hand along where Nut's spine would be, under the haze of grey fur.

"She does seem a bit thin. I'll bring her up some of that canned stuff now."

He stood, stretching back like a feline, and offered me his hand. I let him pull me up, and as my head lifted the room started to tilt and wiggle, as if I stood surrounded by baking heat. I felt my hand be squeezed, and I was pulled towards the hatch. I didn't look over my shoulder.

"I'll reinforce these gates when I come back up. She's so small, she could slink right through them."

I closed my eyes, thankful that Art and I were still on the same wavelength. I had no idea if she could even think, never mind conspire to come downstairs and encroach on our lives. I'd done a lot more reading than Art had. He'd done everything required of him of course, and read the manual, looked up a few of the websites, even checked into a few online forums to see what other owners were talking about. But I'd gone further, delving deeper and deeper into the experiences people had made public.

Though none of the material strictly addressed self-awareness, it did seem to imply that Nut wouldn't be sentient like you or me, but she would have needs, and therefore consciousness. Consciousness just at the level that keeps the brain from switching to dormant mode and letting the vital parts of the body die. But seeing Nut assess her environment, and then the panic in her eyes when I moved too swiftly showed that Nut wanted to live – just like we did. But even a tree will adapt to survive, won't it? Spreading its leaves to gather in the light and fighting off rival roots where we can't see.

When I'd been really young, keeping animals in the house had been more common, though you never knew more than one or two friends whose parents had time for it. I must have only been six or seven when I last visited a friend with a tame animal. In this case it was a bearded dragon, a dinosaur with skin made of stones and a head which would tilt on a pivot. I'd never seen anything like it in all my life, and Marcia's dad kept it in a huge tank planted with plastic trees and shoots which stretched across the back of the living room. No one ever touched Jambo – his teeth were knives – but he didn't seem to care about that and spent most of his time sitting facing the large lamp in the top corner.

A couple of years before Jambo, Marcia's dad had an old rabbit, a real white one, in a three-story wooden structure in the garden. My mum had told me that if I ever saw a white rabbit I shouldn't chase him, as he'd lead me down his rabbit hole and I'd get stuck there forever. No coming back. I was terrified by Marcia's dad's rabbit, and though there was never a chance of him leading me anywhere, I was convinced that every time I blinked, just before my eyes closed, there was a flash of white.

This rabbit was huge, with long ears that flopped down like strips of suede, and he had a black spot between his eyes. His name was Smudge. Marcia once stuck her finger through the wire mesh to show off. Smudge hopped over and after a brief wiggle of his nose clamped his teeth firmly around her fingertip. Marcia shrieked and leapt back, blood already trickling down the back of her hand. In my terror I started to cry too, while Smudge just sat there like a docile lump of snow. While Marcia was being patched up, her dad explained softly that Smudge would have expected her finger to be a carrot or a stick of celery, and it wasn't his fault. I cried in the car home, not so much for Marcia being driven to hospital for a tetanus, but for Smudge, who would be disappointed that he hadn't chomped down on a carrot after all.

But neither Jambo nor Smudge left me with the stirrings that Nut had evoked. Maybe they never do, until they're your own. I read once about a phenomenon which said that every cat-lover thought their cat was the most beautiful, no matter how wonky-faced or wicked-eyed it might be. And with children, motherhood turns us into lionesses, willing to protect our offspring with tooth and claw. They're our future, the continuation of our bloodline, though it's never a future we'll have much say in.

But I wondered about Nut.

Over the first few days, I watched her through the bars of the baby gate from the top step of the ladder with a cup of tea. The hot air in the house all rose to the roof, which is why we thought it'd be the cosiest place for her. The vast size of the loft also meant she had space to run around, though she didn't do much moving. Twice a day she'd trot around the outside of the room and then flop down in the middle under the skylight, not asleep, but resting with her eyes half-closed in a state of semi-consciousness. We'd been prepared for this, *the muscle-run*, the instinctual desire in her to expend energy and build her strength.

It looked like she couldn't quite work out which sleeping box she liked the best, and went through little phases of choosing one, climbing in, rolling about in it with her feet in the air, and then falling out. First, she chose the plastic fruit crate, and then after a day or two she upgraded to the quartered bedspread, which gave her room to stretch on her back and roll like a fuzzy rolling pin. Though she'd snubbed the cardboard box I didn't remove it, and within a few days Nut's main pastime became chewing on its corners and trying to flatten it by climbing on each of its walls. It seemed harmless enough, as long as she didn't start eating the gnawed-off pieces. She batted the pieces of cardboard around the floor with a front paw before changing her mind again and tearing strips from the box like leaves from a lettuce. She was probably teething.

Art stapled a layer of steel mesh around the baby gates in case Nut tried to squeeze through, but she never approached the bars, at least while I was watching. She didn't seem to question the barriers of her world. She accepted her lot with heart and soul and gut, as if all she needed existed within those four walls. She didn't climb the benches to seek the light, or even sniff for wisps of air through weaknesses in the roof slates (of which there were many). She seemed content, and the more I watched her, the more I felt utter relief that she didn't cry for me, didn't show any signs of confusion at us disappearing downstairs.

A weight was lifting, a weight that had been thrust on my shoulders since Nut first turned her face to me. It was going to be all right.

Of course, Nut wasn't supposed to be happy or sad; my reading so far into the biology had told me that. But the reality was always going to differ from the theory, wasn't it? Nut lived in the immediate present, and didn't question any other moment than the one she existed in. No before, no after. Just Nut, in the skin of Nut. Maybe this is true contentment. The manual suggested it was the presence of a survival memory which humans have lost, which comes with no sense of regret, or loss or anticipation of failure. With that mindset, you could attempt the same feat over and over, and no matter how many times you failed you wouldn't be discouraged.

I made sure there wasn't anything in the loft to provide an education. No predators to dodge, no prey to catch, nothing that might disturb or teach her skills she wouldn't need. Offering a little rubber toy to chew on rather than the cardboard box could be disastrous if the shaping of a mouse or haddock convinced her through learned behaviour that she should be stalking food or hunting for pleasure. As she'd never be leaving our home, there was no way she'd be able to do those things, and I couldn't stand the idea of causing her to want more, all for the sake of a squeezy rubber mouse.

You may think that I was thinking about this far too much, and I'd done far more reading that anyone else would have done in the situation, or more than you'd have done yourself. But you have to remember, animal psychology is an abstract concept, and I just wanted to do things right. The look in Nut's eyes that first day had frightened me backwards, and a single stupid decision could destroy everything.

5

Nut had arrived on a Friday. That weekend was spent hiking up and down the ladder every hour making visits to her in secret, so as to not disturb her settling in. At one point Art suggested that I cover my head with a pillowcase as a sort of disguise, and I did it too, until the Sunday afternoon when he saw me descend the ladder whilst wearing it and he took pity. Turns out he didn't think I'd take him seriously. I do wonder if he'd known for longer and laughed at me for longer than he let on.

It didn't matter anyway. Whether I wore the pillowcase or not, Nut didn't pay me the slightest bit of attention. Most of the time she slept in the cat bed, a faceless bundle of grey fluff. Art took her sleeping pattern as a sign that we didn't need to check up on her so much, she was fine, but it made me need to visit the loft even more – just to make sure she opened her eyes. Before we went to bed on the Sunday, we made a pact that we wouldn't go up during the night at all, that we could "lay off it now", and we'd close the loft hatch in case Nut chewed through the mesh and fell onto the landing. I was convinced that I wouldn't sleep a wink, but Art wrapped his arms around me and I slept like a baby. I don't even remember dreaming.

There was a huge part of me that was relieved to be going back to the office the following Monday. I liked the driving to work, sailing along on anonymous roads that lead to endless places I could get to, if I wanted to. This Monday I felt particularly liberated, but with the luxury of a buried ember to heat my middle. I had a secret, and I smuggled this not-so-secret secret into work with me, hidden beneath my coat. I had a living house to go back to now, a home complete with its own beating heart. This heart was my heart, also. This was the dark and delicious thought that would feed me for the first couple of hours, while being back at work was still a novelty.

Don't get me wrong, I'd struggled to leave her that morning, but I knew that it was better to get used to it sooner rather than later. Besides, Art would be in his study, and he'd promised to get up and check on her every two hours. I asked him to text me every time he did, so I could be sure. It's not that I didn't trust him to keep his promises, I just knew how consumed he became when hammering away at the keyboard or drawing up outlines.

I strode into work with my head held high – feeling a million dollars. And while I shone, the office buzzed around me like a monochromatic hive. I hadn't known it until then, but I was still on high alert. Every microfibre on my cubicle's felt walls tickled, and every sigh or throat being cleared was a shock from silence. My face was red, bloating with all the blood, and I couldn't ignore the feeling that I had a flashing sign above my head. Bodies bristled when I passed by, and yet I couldn't catch anyone's eye. And though in itself that wasn't too weird, the longer I stood at my desk and scanned the office, the more peculiar it became that no one at all looked up. Everyone was completely still. When a woman whose face I vaguely knew from the second floor shuffled by my desk with a stack of folders I offered a sheepish smile, but she averted her eyes and carried on towards the lifts. There was a chance that she hadn't seen me I suppose, but we'd been only inches apart. It didn't seem likely.

I set down my bag and settled into my chair, letting myself sink into the comfort of confined spaces. Though a lot of people complain about them, I liked my cubicle. Because no one could see me, I didn't have to imitate anyone else anymore. All my skin-tugging idiosyncrasies didn't matter. I could sit there twitching, stroking and fiddling all day long like a monkey in a tree. All I was judged on was my output, and *that* I could control. There, it was up to me if I burned myself out or gave myself a day to drift off. And returning to work that morning, fresh from our first weekend with Nut, having my own walls felt better than ever.

On that first day back, I resisted thinking about the house. Work was another planet, but because I was waiting for Art's check-ins I couldn't relax. I felt a crazy urge to scale my cubicle, like Nut would, just to release some tension, my weight folding the walls flat beneath me. Would anyone even look up if I sat amongst the melee, gnawing on a piece of plywood?

By midday I hadn't heard from Art at all and my skin was breaking out in a sweat. Didn't he realise how stressed this was making me? He wouldn't be doing this on purpose… Could something have happened? I broke my silence and messaged him in the most bright and breezy manner I could manage, sticking an extra couple of kisses onto the end to prove my triviality. He replied within a minute with a short message saying everything was fine, Nut had eaten half a tin of feed, and he was having trouble concentrating so was thinking about going out in the afternoon for a drive.

My gut clenched. How could he possibly leave her alone? Sickly sweet, I suggested that tomorrow might be better for that, and that he maybe just needed an afternoon watching a film or two on the sofa. But I suppose the pressure of not writing was too much, and he remained adamant that going out was what he needed. We played message tennis, my coy and pleading messages becoming longer and longer while Art's became shorter and shorter, until he stopped replying entirely. At first I thought he'd taken a break to just do the rounds with Nut but the silence endured for minute after minute after minute, until it'd been nearly half an hour and I still hadn't heard back. For the first time in months I felt utterly alone. What had I done? Had I pushed him too hard, pushed him away already?

No, it was me that needed to get perspective here. It was nearly

2.30pm, he was probably eating lunch. It was long after the time I usually ate it too. I'd normally stay in my cubicle, idly scrolling through articles I didn't read on my phone, but I'd done enough phone watching already today.

I picked up my bag and made my way to the shared cafeteria, a square and windowless room painted in buttercup and crammed with plastic tables. Each table had four silver seats, but because the tables were so small the chairs couldn't be parked beneath and so stuck out in the aisles. I hardly ever went in there; the yellow gave me a headache and the sound of metal chair legs screeching across the tile floor made my skin itch.

Looking around, every table had at least three or four people already sitting there. Most were pale and scowling into their plates, crushed too close to each other to look up without awkwardness. Some tables were so packed with drinks and plates and laptops that the cut flowers in vases had been relegated to the floor. Several had been knocked over by unseeing ankles, and leaked puddles of milky water around sneakers and stilettos.

Sitting at an allocated six inches of grubby plastic wouldn't help, so I returned to my cubicle and opened up a joyless bag of granola. I couldn't bear to look at my phone again for Art's non-existent message, so I worked through lunch, punching at the keyboard one-handed in a far more forceful way than I expect I normally did.

"You should get some fresh air, it's bright outside. All the snow's melting."

My mouth crammed with oats, I looked up into the face of a man I recognised from three cubicles along. Jerry, Joey, Joseph? He smiled down at me and patted the edge of my cubicle before disappearing again behind the waves of wall. Even if my mouth hadn't been packed with nuts, I don't know what I'd have said. He was the first person to have spoken to me all day. He seemed nice. Maybe he didn't know what I was part of, or maybe he didn't care. Some people didn't, but their voices were always quieter than those who objected.

When the day finally ended, I drove home grasping the steering wheel and battling the distant thrum of a migraine. When a man dressed in a tattered jacket and camo pants staggered across the street in front of me with a placard I almost didn't brake quick enough. I skidded to a stop and he bounced softly off the bumper into the middle of the road. He didn't even look, just stood there, stunned, somehow still holding his painted sign aloft;

When you send forth your Spirit, they are created, and you renew the face of the earth.
– Psalm 104:30

After a few seconds he jerked his body and continued to stumble across the road, all the while mumbling something that I couldn't make out, his eyes on my eyes through the windshield. He moved like his legs were wood.

It didn't mean anything. *How could he know?*

I swallowed the lump in my throat and gripped the steering wheel until horns on every side of me were blaring. I shook myself off and started the car, squinting against the too-bright-light. I needed to go. I needed to get back to Art. Would he worry, if I didn't come home one day after work? Would he call the hospitals and rush to my side, or would he assume I was a liability? Sick too soon. Dead weight. I hadn't heard from him since morning. Would he even notice? Perhaps I should bring him something. Should I be apologising? What if I'd ruined things already? What if this was a side of me he didn't like?

As I turned the corner onto our street I couldn't decide if I wanted Art to be there or not. Who would I be for him today? I approached the house, sensing for the heartbeat that had carried me through the morning but the pulse was slow, dull. The door opened without any obstructions, and there – at the end of the hallway – I spotted the point of Art's elbow beneath a rolled-up green sleeve, and the clatter of a plate being washed.

Normal. *Normal.*

Not even a whiff of atmosphere. It could have been the day

before today, or the day before that, a day when we hadn't fought or clawed away each other's skin. *The relief.* He mustn't have heard me come in, as he didn't turn or alter his dance of splash-rub-rotate-dunk-splash-clatter.

I had to make sure everything was alright.

I dropped my bag by the stairs, flung off my boots, leapt the stairs two at a time, and scaled the ladder like a spider up wallpaper. I stopped with my head through the hatch and she was right there, sitting behind the baby gate, this fluffy and perfect grey lump – no taller than the stretch of my hand. Her eyes were a marshland, blue speckled with flakes of gold around the pupil. They were far too big for her face, and in the loft's red gloom they shone, flickering as if on the verge of tears. A little pink tongue emerged and delicately licked the flecks of jelly from her muzzle.

"Hello, Nut."

She didn't move, just continued to stare me down with those bulbous, cartoonish eyes. From beneath the ladder there was a shuffle, and out of the corner of my eye I caught a glimpse of Art standing beneath the ladder and drying his hands on a tea towel, his eyes looking up at me dolefully.

"Errr, no kisses?"

I took a long, deep breath. His cheek felt hot under my lips, and I pushed my beating heart against his to remember the life we shared.

6

And so you adapt. One day bleeds into the next, and though the tide washes in and out, it's the same sea. You've plugged your toes in the same sand. This beach isn't going anywhere.

It took a few weeks before I started to relax into our new routine. I spent a lot of January second-guessing everything around me, from the brand of tinned slush we gave Nut (was this one that would definitely help her grow?), to the posturing of cushions and lamps. Art kept prodding me about why I still hadn't told anyone about our engagement, and each time I answered him with a breath in his ear, a brush cheek-on-cheek. Sensual movements. I flipped reality, squeezing myself into a "truth" where there were fewer questions, more squeezes of my arm. But there wasn't a moment of the day when I didn't feel the weight of that opal, or the treacherous swing of the gold – ready to slip from my finger if I stopped concentrating.

I wondered whether I should get Art an engagement present in return, but nothing seemed right. Apart from his laptop and vast collection of notebooks and novels there wasn't much he prized. Besides, before I had the chance to do anything it was my birthday. Thirty-two this time. It sprung on me suddenly – probably because everything was so different, the world was spinning faster. All those birthdays before, all the drinks clinked in the air by Aubrey, Rosa and Eleanor to commiserate another year gone, belonged to another lifetime. This time there had been no build-up, and when

I'd spoken to Eleanor by text the week before, she hadn't even mentioned it. It was as if with Art and Nut in my life, perhaps I wouldn't get any older at all.

But when March arrived, I awoke to the sound of trumpets.

"HAPPY BIRTHDAY WIFE-TO-BE!"

I pulled down the duvet to see Art at the foot of the bed, not actually playing a trumpet, but holding his phone in place of a saxophone, bouncing his knee to the rousing tune of "Congratulations". I sat up in a bed of petal spray in bright shades of red, plum, and violet. Some were so silky that I could hardly feel them between my fingertips.

"They're beautiful. Are they real?"

"Does it matter?" Art slid one across the duvet with his thumb. "They're all for you. No half measures today. *Drink!*" He thrust a small glass of something pink and chemical-looking between my eyes. "Just in case you can't see it, you know, with getting older and your eyesight failing, n'all."

I took the glass and took a swig, crossing my eyes as I did it for good measure. The fizz hit my empty stomach immediately, and I felt a strong urge to eat whatever the petals were just to soak it up.

"Still want to marry an old maid?"

"Not sure. It wasn't part of the deal that you'd turn thirty-two."

"May I remind you that you're thirty-eight?"

"But with the face of an angel. I mean – look at this skin."

Art pushed his cheeks together between his palms and fluttered his eyelids. *Disgusting.*

"As long as I don't end up looking like a devil in comparison."

I imagined myself thin, wizened, bald apart from a fuzz of grey around my face. Chin too, most likely. And Art beside me, looking like my adopted grandson, looking up at me with those saucer eyes.

Art was often met with surprise when people learned his age, particularly at conferences. I didn't see it, but then again I woke up with the stubbled Art and went to bed with the Art with shadows beneath his eyes. Everywhere else, he was paid to be perky, paid to grin with his short white teeth.

I'd watched online videos of Art answering questions at book launches and events and it always struck me how incredibly earnest and open he looked. When asked a question, he'd pause for a second or two and then open his whole face to answer. It lit up the camera. The audience hung on his every word like he was telling them their futures, their cards pulled from his mysterious tarot. Maybe you had to be there, but listening objectively, I didn't think he said anything particularly insightful. Perhaps it was the way he said it, or that the audience was already in love with the idea of his words and he didn't need to do all that much at all.

It did make me wonder whether I had it in me to hypnotise like he did. After all, Art and I were compatible, two side by side pieces of a wider jigsaw. Maybe I just hadn't found my niche yet. To have one person hanging on your every word… I've never even been close. Even I get distracted when I'm talking.

A week or so before my birthday, after I'd been back at work for almost two months, I'd told Art a story about a conversation I'd heard through my cubicle wall. Joyce, my neighbour, was crying. She was on the phone and I could tell by the voice she put on that it was someone she didn't really know. She enunciated every syllable, and repeated the alien-word "Yes" every few seconds or so. I listened to this woman on the phone every day and she never said "Yes". Usually, she'd say "Yeah," or "Aye". Joyce then asked if he was going to be OK, what could she do, where was he. I couldn't help it, but I immediately pictured her son, David, (he was twenty-five or twenty-six at the time) crushed in a car accident, or her husband, thin and curled like a weed, receiving some test results.

As the call went on, she would let out little gasps between yeses that faded to soft whimpers. I couldn't even make out her final few words before the call ended. The weirdest thing about it all was that though the call seemed to end badly she didn't get up, she didn't leave. She stayed at her desk until the end of the day, and considering that call happened before lunch this seemed like a crazy amount of time to sit on such bad news.

At the end of the day, I tried to catch a glimpse of her as I pulled on my winter coat. Her desk was a snowscape of crumpled tissue, some spotted bright red. I don't know if she registered that I was looking at her or not, but she was staring up at me regardless, her whole body frozen and her eyes a dead void. The skin above her lip was flecked with dried blood. I quickly picked up my bag and turned away, my palms sweating and my breath coming out in ragged gasps.

Art was in his study when I told him about it, and he just sat there listening, his face blank. While I was talking he fiddled with his pen, spinning it like a baton. After I finished, I asked him whether he thought I should've done or said anything but he just pouted, tapped the pen on the table, and said he didn't know. He looked so thoroughly uninterested that I was convinced he hadn't listened to my story at all, and had phased out halfway through, but nevertheless he was quiet for the rest of the night. He ate dinner in his study, and I didn't see him again until I collected him to come to bed. As he climbed under the covers, he reached out and grabbed my hand, rubbing his thumb along my wrist. "It's hard, but there's nothing we can do for people like that," he whispered. "We have to forget that we're different to other people."

Maybe it did stick with him, now that I think about it.

Above our heads, I could make out the soft *thump, thump, thump* of Nut's nightly exercise around the loft. She was getting heavier, her body filling out with blood, and it wasn't easy to ignore her steps while the rest of the house slept.

"Norah." Art squeezed my hand tighter, his eyes desperately asking. "You would save me, wouldn't you? You would help me?"

"Of course," I whispered. "I promise."

Art was right, of course. We can only help people like us. If I'd said something to Joyce she'd have known I didn't have a clue what she was going through, so how could I have understood what she needed? Joyce didn't know what had happened with my mum, but that was a different life. Anything I'd have said would have been flaunting my fortune in her face. So I'd headed home as fit and agile as a cat, still with all nine lives intact.

Through the ceiling, the padding stopped, and for a split second I wondered if Nut would dream while she slept.

Art leaned towards me and slapped his hands on the duvet cover, causing the petals to flutter up in the air before coming to rest again. I took another slurp of the pink fizz and the bubbles tickled my throat. I don't think I liked alcohol that early.

"Come on, Milady, your main gift's downstairs."

My head still woozy with sleep, I let Art lead me by the hand down the dark stairs, lit only by the eerie flush of dawn. I passed a scatter of blue envelopes on the doormat bearing my name and the bronze ankh, and was puzzled for a second at how early the postman must've been to deliver them.

Art dragged me on down the corridor to the kitchen. Against the dining table stood an easel mounted with a stack of A3 paper. One of the dining chairs sat in front of it, and on the seat was a stack of watercolours, oils, chalks, pencils… *Colours and colours and colours.*

"Oh, Arthur."

Sliding open a box of oil pastels and running a finger along a shaft of indigo, I picked up an old heavy scent met by fresher outdoor air – afternoons in the sun, my head on Mum's shoulder, my fingers playing with a coil of rusty hair. Feet resting in cool patches of clover. But instead Art was beside me, his eyes on my eyes.

"Happy birthday," he whispered.

I inspected the packs one after another without letting go of a single one. So much joy from something so simple. Each one took me back to somewhere else; the musk of Mum's art cupboard, the waxy membrane inside the drawers. Wrapped in Mum's coat on the moors. All those years dipping paint-soaked brushes in water to watch the colours bleed, learning to smudge away blunders with a blunt thumb. Why hadn't I thought about picking up the palette knife myself? In seconds I was back there, and all it took was a rainbow.

Art pointed at the boxes in my hands. "Choose your weapon."

It had to be the watercolours.

Art swept the others to the side and placed the pack beside the easel. Pressing my drink back in my hand, he pushed me down by my shoulders into the chair. With a flamboyant wave of his arm, he sidled behind the easel and started to tear open the paints, winking conspiratorially around the edge of the mounted paper. A satisfying clunk and splash, as several brushes were plunged into a jar. A few glassy taps later, Art began sweeping the pad in wild abstract strokes. He obviously hadn't used watercolours before, as the paper wasn't taped down. I watched as the crisp edges became warped, unbalanced, curling in on themselves.

"You do know you don't use watercolours like that, you idiot."

He peeked over the top of the paper, and tilted his head this way and that to find my best angle. I lived up to it, turning my head in profile. My eyes are little, and I forced them open so much that my left lid flickered with the effort.

Art pointed his brush at me. "I'm the creative here – I can use them however I want, *Muse*."

"How do you know I'm not a creative genius? *I'm* the daughter of a famous artist. You're an Arthur, and 'author', not an 'art'."

"You throw the word 'Art' at me fifteen times a day, it's about time I lived up to it, don't you think? No one ever called me that before you."

Was that true? I was sure he'd introduced himself as Art when we first met. I wouldn't have just started calling him that, surely?

While I puzzled over that, he continued to paint in eclectic flourishes, fired up by the challenge. I rubbed my twitching eyelid with a knuckle.

"What are you even doing?"

He let out a huge sigh and dropped the brush back in the jar with a wet 'plop'.

"I'm recording you for future prosperity. I'm going to capture you, Norah, right here and now, on your birthday morn. And I'm going to do it for as long as I still have fingers, and you still have a face."

"Why stop then? I doubt the result would be different if you held the brush between your toes."

"How dare thee."

"And if I don't have a face? Doesn't say much for your capturing of my inner soul, does it? Sexist pig."

Art closed his eyes, and bowed his head gravely. "Hmmm. I wouldn't want that, it's not good for publicity." He sliced a pointed finger through the air. "Alright. Let it hereby be said that I'll continue to capture you, even if my arms end in stumps and your face slides right off your skull."

"Deal."

I leapt from the chair to plant a kiss on Art's forehead. "And then I'll paint you afterwards."

He shook his head. "No. You have to wait until my birthday next January. That's the tradition. We paint each other on our birthdays. That way it means something."

That was almost a year away. I felt guilty. It had been Art's birthday six weeks before and I'd only given him the study lamp he'd asked for.

"Then I'll get some practice in."

"Nope, this is spontaneous soul-catching. No cheating, no practising." He winked and flicked me back to the chair with his finger. "Don't want you getting better than me."

I sat back down in silence, my chest a little bit tighter than it was before. Looking down, my knees were spotted with splashes of green watercolour from Art's palette. I licked my thumb and rubbed the marks until my skin drank them in.

We spent the rest of the sitting in quiet, me trapped in time while Art swept his paint into the blank corners. I had no idea how such bright and violent strokes could possibly mirror this still and silent me. Art finished his masterpiece by swearing at the paper, one hand still clutching his paintbrush and in the other... a roaring hairdryer.

On announcing that the portrait was finally completed, he asked me to close my eyes while he spun the easel. At the press of his lips on my nose, I saw myself.

Art had painted me from the waist up, wearing my cotton robe. I had been right – he wasn't an artist. My hair was wild, coiling like a tangle of hazel branches. My face was an egg – a blank and milky oval which could have belonged to anyone, crisscrossed with pale blue and green, a pursed little mouth, and a pink blob for a nose. The eyes weren't mine. Mine squint, but Art had made them bright almonds, almost feline in their curves. He had the colour right though, a muddy brown. The sweeping abstract strokes must have been the background, which he'd filled in with wide emerald stripes, a bit like ferns. The portrait had the shape of me, but I couldn't help but think Art had tried to show something I wasn't. I didn't mind though. I wanted to be those colours.

We left the portrait on the dining table to dry, taping down the corners to halt any further warping. The rest of the day was spent in a semi-doze. I went up to the loft to visit Nut every few hours, refilling her food bowl with jellied vitamins and tinned slop, clicking and tutting under my breath to prick up her tail and send her galloping towards the food. Art retreated to his study again, only returning to watch me blow out the candles and cut the cake when night came. We sat for a calm and lovely twenty minutes together, legs entwined on the sofa, stuffing our faces with three-quarters of a cake meant to serve eight. All the while we sniggered under our breath like schoolchildren at what Easton Grove would have thought of our greed.

As Art padded back up the stairs, I burrowed down beneath the blankets, still smiling. So much had changed for me in the last year. I'd met Art, and he'd brought out a side of me I'd never imagined in a million years to be there. *I was interesting.* I had moved into a house, a grown-up house, on a street shared by established families and successful couples. You never saw an unhappy face. I felt safe, and for the first time I had back-ups. I was now a member of one of the most exclusive healthcare systems in the UK, and with that came assurance that I was fit and healthy, with a long time yet ahead to find my place. The staff there had my back, and cared about my every movement in case I took a step wrong. And of course, there was Nut. Our shared little creature, a fluffy grey comma, every day growing bigger and connecting mine and Art's hearts.

It was past 10pm when I picked up the box of acrylics. I arranged the glorious palette on my left and a fresh jar of water to my right. The brush rolled between my fingers and I wondered if this was how a pen sat in Art's hand, or if this was how my mum had fiddled with her tools, between the middle digit and thumb. Jutting her chin and biting the tip of her tongue until it bulged like a cherry. Her hair streaked with crusty paint in all the colours of nature.

She loved landscapes the most.

Most of my memories were of her looking out of a window with a sketchpad, or taking me to a part of the countryside with (to my young mind) nothing in it. Low hills of stubborn rock and yellow heath, skinny trees sticking up between stones like broken fence posts. No flourishing copses or snow-peaked mountains like in magazines. I'd sit next to her with a book or a game, not able to understand why she picked those scenes to paint. She didn't even look happy when she worked at it, and she'd correct invisible mistake after invisible mistake, all while sighing and tutting and muttering under her breath as if disappointed with the view. In the end, the finished painting never looked anything like the land. Sometimes she'd look between the two and cry, but when I clutched her arm and asked her to tell me why, she wouldn't. She just squinted up her eyes and wiped my face as if I was the one weeping.

Surely much less difficult, I was going to paint my own portrait.

If Art didn't want me practising his portrait I wouldn't – I'd work on myself, an entirely different shape. I kept the paints quite dry for added control, and started from the outside, working in. I drew a dark circle then stopped – the brush hovering above the paper. When it came to my insides, I didn't know where to start. I started to pile on paint in sloppy layers. My hair became an amorphous cloud, and the colour I mixed for my face made me look like I was on the verge of a heart attack. I had to give it to Art for his attempts to add dimension with blues and greens. To me, I was as flat and formless as a magnolia wall.

I didn't stick at it long, and put away the paints in a fit of misery. Absent-mindedly, I picked up my phone and (already irritated by various notifications on the screen) I swiped them away without opening. I'd read the names before the messages cleared – Eleanor and Rosa. Nothing from Aubrey. She wouldn't have missed my birthday, I was sure of that, so maybe by staying silent she was trying to make some sort of point. It didn't matter anyway. Any of it. I had more on my plate than they could understand right now, and I needed to focus on this house, this space. Art. Nut. Myself. I switched off my phone and left it on the arm of the chair as I stood tall and took one long deep breath.

Earlier, while we'd been eating cake, Art had mounted his crispy portrait of me in a wooden frame. I held it in front of this wall and that wall, seeking a home for this version of me. But everywhere felt wrong, as if I was laying myself bare for surgery, each wall a sterile and fluorescent-lit operating table.

7

Mum was always a painter.

That's how I remember her now. Overalls streaked with irreversible oils, hands calloused, fingernails packed beneath with powdered colour. She took parts of reality and mixed them together to her own recipe, creating a world for me to grow up in.

I don't remember Mum having many close friends before she died, but that didn't seem odd at the time. She had me, and she had enough arguments in her head to listen to. I sometimes caught her talking to herself in the shower, or when sitting at the dining room table sketching out a new painting. If she caught me spying, she'd chuckle and say, "Keep on the right side of yourself, my lass. Everyone deserves a bit of sweet-talking sometimes."

It never bothered me that Mum didn't surround herself with like-minds, because it never bothered her. It's natural that you see friends less as you get older, anyway. Life becomes more about *you*, and your small body swims a constant sea of commitments. There's so much more to *do*. So much more to *think about*.

It was so much simpler before. At university, the little flat Aubrey and I shared in second and third year was the whole world.

In those days she wore her blonde hair down to her hips and shooed off any suggestion of having it trimmed, though the ends lay brittle on her back. We'd connected over shared loves of bloated haggis, horrible soap operas and books set before we were born. We split ourselves open and then stitched ourselves together, sharing everything in that parasitical way only students do. We were crawling the world's ladder, side by side, each of us so confident of our individuality that (unknown to us at the time) is fed to us by our friends. We hung up fairy lights, stuck up the "People or Planet?" and "Earth's Eviction Notice" posters we'd all been given by the Students' Union, and made up for lack of furniture with cushions and cheap fleece blankets.

The truth is, I lost interest in other people, and when our course mates were heading out to house parties or the uni's monthly safeguard socials, my planet shrank. In a sea of greying skin and worried voices, *I'd never felt more alive*. When Aubrey's personal tutor reprimanded her for not attending a free cancer-prevention seminar she was furious, bursting through the front door and shouting, "What does it matter? It's in us now – we're breathing it in every day. If I'm a fucking Jack-in-a-box, I'm going to live like one." And then she stuck her head out the window and screamed "Boo!" down into the street in one long howl.

Aubrey always wanted to do the thing she wasn't doing. "What's the use of sociology, really? It's fucking people skills, isn't it?" she'd moan. She'd want to go back to the beginning and try English literature, or run her fingers over her face and say it should've been biology, or even music. She played acoustic guitar every day, singing hoarse and husky country songs about love and firemen and French toast. She'd sometimes say they were her own songs and then laugh at me for believing her. But she'd often leave notebooks open on the coffee table scrawled with black-inked lyrics, covering everything from her ex-boyfriend's sexual habits to the texture of her favourite cheese (always brie). I'd sometimes sing along, mumbling old mantras to her new tunes.

Renting a two-bedroom flat wiped out our student loans almost straightaway, so we engaged with the world through TV. In choosing between diluting our dynamic with more students or poverty, we chose poverty. Together, we guffawed at the ridiculousness of made-for-TV movies, pointed and gasped at old nature documentaries, and watched the news the day the

National Health Service publicly signed with a private institute to make up for lost funding. I can still remember bits of the NHS Chief Executive's speech, spoken with sad eyes and quivering chins. "Today, we mark our professional honesty by opening our doors to innovation," followed with something like, "We are in a needs-must scenario. Life has been handed an eviction notice. This contract," here he gestured at the paper he'd signed, "will save lives. Design. Inventiveness. Entrepreneurialism. This is what will save the NHS. We all deserve to be saved." And then the head of an unnamed private institute, a clean-shaven man in tweed who looked too young to be there, stepped up to the microphone.

Aubrey looked at me then, a lock of yellow hair between her teeth. "Isn't he the one who makes the squirrels?"

The man in tweed smiled down at the press. "Not only are we committed to restoring the National Health Service to its former glory, but we're committed to sharing our resources to a better end. So each man, woman and child born today enters a world where they can win."

It all seemed like the sort of stuff that happened to other people. I'd never even had a broken bone. Though I would never have admitted it to Aubrey, I was still a child, soft and sticky. There was nothing in me that wanted to win any race. Happiness was on the sofa, raising an eyebrow at satirical soap operas and eating cheap pizza. The future could wait.

Aubrey was more outward-looking; she'd already planned out several lives for herself. In typical me-style, I hadn't fixed my mind on anything, but it didn't worry me. Loads of my other friends were in a similar position, and even though they never said it aloud, I could tell they half-willed their parents to absorb them into their businesses. An easy life with instant monetary payback.

I played with the idea of moving back home after finishing, doing a bit of painting with Mum, helping her with her equipment on trips to far-flung landscapes. When I told Aubrey about it she started to imagine herself enacting them too.

Even before she met Mum, she loved the *idea* of her and her big red hair and ability to swear in French, German, and Chinese. The first time Aubrey came home with me, she was so quiet and red-faced that Mum asked what I even saw in her – so sure was she that I'd latched on to the first person who was nice to me. But like a sunflower Aubrey soon followed the light, even playing her guitar one night in the garden. Mum sang along with made-up words in an order that didn't make sense and slapped her bare knees to an irregular beat, always with a smouldering cigarette clipped between her fingertips. It was hard to be embarrassed for her when she was having a far better time than anyone else. Mum always did have this uncanny ability to make you embarrassed about your own normality.

That was the night we stayed out in the dark and thought we saw a vole, burrowing through Mum's back fence towards the bog which used to be a river. We stood around it like three mountains, not breathing, holding on to each other to be still. It had wedged itself between two stones, flicking its tail up and out of the crack like a tentacle.

"Is it still alive?" I asked. "It doesn't look right."

Mum leaned in, hacked up a ball of phlegm, and pointed a stubby finger at the tail. "It's not natural. Look, the line up the tail." She stood up straight and coughed into her palm. "I know they're doing it to repopulate, but any idiot can tell they're not the same."

Between second and third year I earned a few extra pounds working in a café in York, mostly spilling drinks and charging the wrong prices, so I didn't go home all that much. I spoke to Mum on the phone, of course, but my attention was elsewhere and frankly so was hers. Our calls ended quickly, and our conversations often dried up before they began. It had always just been the two of us, but now I was enjoying my freedom. As the phone calls became further apart, Mum's voice on the line became quieter and quieter, as if she was already travelling away from me at great speed. I took her for granted, and assumed that when the time came for me to settle down, I could catch the same train as always, sit with her, and it would be just like old times.

During third year, I decided to make a surprise visit home in the November. It'd been eight months since I'd seen the house.

I'd spoken to her earlier that week and she'd told me she was having a quiet week in, no stress, just enjoying the view. But that Friday night when I rang the doorbell and she answered it, reality turned inside out. Mum was a wraith, leaning on the doorframe with a purple hand. She swayed side to side as if drunk, and all the soft flesh around her cheeks had melted away. She was both small and childlike, old and sharp-boned. *The greying.* She stared at me like I was a stranger, a spirit visiting from a long-forgotten past. Without speaking, she turned away and walked into the dim light of the house, leaving the door ajar.

I felt sick.

As I followed her over the threshold, the house smelt different. The air hung thickly, still and cloying. I found her in her living room, sat on her usual yellow chair, her head bent low over her knees.

She said it started with feeling like she had a cold.

When it went on for more than a couple of weeks she wondered if she'd developed hay fever from all the days out on the moors. She stocked up on over-the-counter medication but when they didn't help and she'd started to cough up phlegm, she decided to sit it out in the comfort of her armchair. It took her another month to phone for an appointment. Once she found out that she had stage four lung cancer she went back home to that velvet armchair and hardly ever left it. She just sat there, enjoying the view.

She didn't consent to a day's worth of chemotherapy or any other treatment, determined to let her body do what it wanted to do. She was adamant that she wouldn't spend the rest of her days "vomiting into the kitchen sink", and would do as she "bloody well pleased". We fought. I couldn't believe that she'd kept it from me all this time, and she was furious that I felt free to tell her how to live her life after (in her own words) "hardly seeing the world outside your shell at all". And throughout it all, as I screamed and she bellowed back, wheezing, she never dropped that cigarette. She never gave up on the thing which killed her. I tried to knock it from her hand and she leapt away, hissing, "Are you trying to kill us both?"

I returned to university two days later, just as I'd planned to. She didn't even try to stop me. She wanted me to go. I left her in bed on the Sunday afternoon, reading a pile of magazines she'd had delivered for as long as I remembered, but never before had time to read.

She waved me out the door with a careless flick of the wrist, "Go, I'm finally enjoying myself. I'll speak to you in the week."

But she didn't ring me. And I didn't ring her. She had kept this huge secret from me, and in my own way I was releasing myself from the problem by letting it be her secret again.

Aubrey was there for me those next months, listening, helping, and researching the outlook for lung cancer, even though Mum had already told me what would happen. But you never believe it, do you?

She died the following June, at home with her carer, Moira, by her side. Mum had needed a permanent shunt to drain the fluid build-up, and as time went by she needed help with everything, from making her morning porridge to lifting her head. Short and wiry Moira was militant, her hands thin and deft as blades but they always moved softly, slowly, as if trained to sweep through a flock of birds without frightening them.

I spoke to Moira on the phone a lot towards the end, but never saw her in the flesh until I went back to the house to see Mum before being taken away. Seeing Mum in her bed, she wasn't her. There was nothing of the body that held me when I fell down, when I needed comfort. Her hair was streaked with white, and her skin had burnished, as if she'd spent her last weeks sunning herself in the garden. Looking down at her, I remember thinking *this isn't her. This isn't her. Where's she gone?* And Aubrey held my hand and sobbed beside me. Moira wrapped her arms around Aubrey first and only then seemed to notice me standing there, and moved over with a sheepish drag of her feet.

It's the natural way of it, for a child to see their parent die. But it's cruel, isn't it? It's the death of a place, a time. When she leaves, a mum takes a part of you, the part where you're still young and full of potential. That's the version of you that could turn out to be anyone. She takes memories only the two of you share, and without anyone else to share them they may as well be made up. What you're left with are all the things you've done on your own, which for some people might be a great load of good things. But me – I was fresh from the egg. I hadn't done anything other than reading, studying, and staying in with Aubrey. I'd only lived through a thirty-eight-inch screen. I had no idea where I was going to go next or what I was going to do. Mum had always been the sun and I a body in her orbit, finding my way by her light, no matter how far I'd strayed.

The summer Mum died, I found a little flat to rent near her cottage so I wasn't too far away to sort out the paintings and belongings before the landlord rented her property to someone else. He gave me three months to do this on account of Mum having lived there for twenty-two years.

Once everything had been sold or donated, I got myself a job as a waitress in an Irish pub for a few months before being taken on at Stokers. It was the perfect time for it to happen for two reasons; one being that I had been truly terrible at waitressing; messing up orders, dropping glasses, and regularly phasing out. Sometimes I'd come to after a rough shake of my shoulder, and I'd find myself staring into the kitchen's sink or at a readied order, already going cold.

The insurance job, though just an admin role, had the appeal of being steady hours, a steady wage and a steady stream of three or four simple tasks on loop every day. It didn't even occur to me that this might not suit everyone until two of the new intake left after the first week without telling anyone, and the remaining three stayed on for another month but did so with their heads bowed in misery.

Between the restaurant and starting at Stokers, I didn't see Aubrey for a few months. She moved home to Inverness, just as I'd hoped to do with Mum. She still messaged me every day, but it was a relief that she wasn't around. My days were full of doing, doing, doing, and the thought of stopping to talk it all through was unbearable. Just not possible. Besides, the tone of her messages had changed so that they didn't always sound like the Aubrey I needed. She often sent me quotes from strange political websites and questions out of the blue about animals and souls and even artificial intelligence, but if I'm honest I just didn't care. What did those things matter now? From a distance, a squirrel in a tree is just a squirrel, whether it's stitched together or born. It's still out of reach. Aubrey was blurring reality with science fiction and I was too frustrated to draw the line for her, so instead I tried to be polite, filling my replies with the quizzical emojis I thought she wanted. But as time went by, it was easier to mark her messages as unread and store my phone somewhere out of sight.

By Christmas that year, the hills and lochs had offered all they could to Aubrey, and she wanted to be part of the world again. She found a flat to rent a ten-minute drive from me, and bagged a full-time job in a music shop, one of those little places often found down some steps, where they sell old LPs and second-hand record players. She settled right into it, even bringing her guitar to work sometimes and tuning the strings behind the counter.

At first, she wanted to meet up a lot but I hadn't the time, and it took many requests from her and firm answers from me before she started to respect my balance. Still, it was never the same. Aubrey was different. I don't know if it was those few months in Inverness or what, but she seemed so much more pushy, always getting at me to try new things, meet new people, and "move out of my comfort zone".

One time she even booked a last-minute weekend away for us in Edinburgh without telling me. The hotel, the train. Everything. While there, we'd be going zorbing, where you roll down a hill in one of those inflatable bags of air. When she told me, I just sat there, spaghetti sliding off my fork. After a pause in which she grinned and (I'm sure) self-congratulated, I told her there was no way. It was too last minute, and I had plans that I couldn't cancel. She shook her head and went anyway, taking another friend in my place. I spent the weekend in the flat, hearing from no one. It was delicious time for me to be alone, scheduled in fair and square.

Aubrey's reckless activities worried me a bit. She focussed so much on the peripheries that she never could see what was in front of her. But believe it or not, I sometimes got the feeling that *I* frustrated *her*. I never saw it coming until I'd already done something that she deemed to be wrong. It always happened when we trod old ground.

"Have you visited her?" Aubrey said, her voice slow. "Out there?"

Mum's ashes were mixed into sand on the Northumberland coast. I'd gone alone, and after watching the tide creeping in in its subtle way over the wet slick, emptied the canister unceremoniously over the side of a dune. Within a few seconds I already couldn't tell where the ash stopped being ash and became sand, dead shells, and broken glass. I'd pulled Mum's last feather from my pocket and rolled the shaft between my fingers before releasing it. Rather than it lifting on the wind like I thought it might, the cold gust dragged it slowly across the beach, never quite out of sight. I turned away and headed back to the car anyway.

"No," I replied. "She's not there. All the good bits are gone. I only scattered the parts that killed her."

The bereavement staff never told you where the tissue donations went, just that there was some good to come out of the horror of death. Not to think of the body, but to think of how smiles and love would carry on. But the folders of information that you went through weeks, months later, gave guarded hints that the vast majority of donations didn't go to people in need. And by then the NHS was deep in service to some early iteration of Easton Grove and hungry to benefit from the offal of its research.

Aubrey read this paperwork before I did. She had them all spread across the floor of my flat while she crouched on her knees, squinting in the low light. Her face was squeezed between her fists as she stared at the words, and I saw her lips silently mouth "Fuck."

I was on the phone at the time to Mum's landlord, and when I started to say the things you do to get someone to hang up, Aubrey began piling up the papers and stuffing them into a brown envelope. This she put into a shoebox with other letters and forms to store. She gave me the brightest smile when I hung up, and it was for that reason I needed to see what had disturbed her enough to lie.

After she'd gone, I pulled out the envelope and discovered that not one piece of Mum was still helping anyone. All the parts, roughly scooped from her middle, were sent to private institutes for genetic research into DNA manipulation. There was no mention of investigating cancer, *the greying*, or even anything else that could save a life. The last letter in the pile was a copy of the agreement I'd blindly signed to not follow up on the donations, and to trust that Mum's last act was to further the same technology that had been used to synthesise natural creatures, and feed original research into longevity, living batteries, second chances.

Surprisingly, the idea of Mum's parts not living on in someone else didn't upset me. I was relieved. A warm tingle ran down my back. It felt good to know that Mum's kidneys weren't working to clean out a stranger's mistakes, or that her eyes weren't looking at things in new ways and betraying their history. I preferred the sterile, neater option. It felt more like an end. *Like freedom.*

My quiet disturbed Aubrey, and so it was probably a strategic move to introduce me to Rosa and Eleanor. Fresh faces, open me up. So imagine her shock when I actually enjoyed myself. I loved that I was a complete unknown to them. When the four of us met, we talked in a vacuum. Everything we discussed only mattered at that table and would never shake the world. This was extremely comforting. Whatever I said, I could predict the response to the degree that I could direct dialogue to hear that which made me feel better.

This birthday with Art, my thirty-second birthday, was the first time I hadn't been asked by any of them to go for a meal or a drink. Aside from Aubrey's recent hostility, I could only imagine that I hadn't heard from Rosa or Eleanor because I had Art, and maybe even Nut. Rather than feel sad, I felt surprisingly emancipated, and for once in my life I wasn't answering the call of others. I called the shots.

Soon after my birthday, I dreamed that Art and I were digging a hole in the middle of the back lawn.

As our shovels met the earth, the ground started to sag and give, sucking us into the deep soil like quicksand. We threw aside our shovels and scrambled against tumbling rock and stone to escape, pulling up clumps of turf in our fists. When I turned to check that Art was safe; I saw that he'd climbed onto the opposite side of the sinkhole and we were now separated by an expanding chasm. Making a megaphone with his cupped hands, he shouted at me to jump across to meet him, presumably because his side of the garden was the one with our house in. Though he must have been no further than ten feet away his voice was distant and echo-y, as if he was calling from across a vast lake.

Just as I was considering making the impossible leap, the sinkhole retched, and regurgitated the nose of a huge, moaning white cow. Her head ducked and bobbed as she worked herself free, her nostrils snorting out lumps of soil and long, sticky worms. With one last heave, her enormous frame emerged from the wet earth by the strength of her spindly legs.

Standing sidelong, she took up the whole width of the lawn and obscured my view of Art completely, her deep huffs masking the sound of Art's call. Both terrified and entranced, I longed to touch the oily hair that fell in loose curls around her eyes and under that expansive mud-stained belly like a waterfall. The cow rocked on her heels before turning slowly towards the far end of the garden. I pressed my back against the fence to let her pass, and as I watched her go it occurred to me that I couldn't see any udders. This felt so completely wrong that I had to question whether this cow was a cow or some other animal in disguise.

I turned back to Art to alert him to this but he'd vanished, and the only explanation I could think of was that he must have tried to rescue me and slipped into the sinkhole. But looking into the deep, I could only see old pieces of trash; a broken washing machine, a kettle, three worn out shoes. No trace of Art. I fell to my knees and cried, the heels of my hands already sinking into the soft and yielding mud. Entirely weakened, I let myself be taken, and my last sight before being consumed was of our house, red against a blazing blue summer sky, and the silhouette of Art through his study window, working with his head down at his desk.

I awoke as the mud slicked over the world.

It wasn't yet day, and there was no sign at all of the sun. I reached over for Art's reassuring warmth but my hand grasped at a cold bedsheet, nothing more. There were still a few silk petals on my pillow from yesterday.

Next to Art's side of the bed the door stood ajar. I pushed away the bedcovers and picked up my dressing gown. Wrapped up tightly, I padded to the landing, lit only by a strip of yellow under the closed bathroom door. The house was in utter silence. I stood outside the bathroom for some time before turning back to the landing, my focus now on the loft hatch. I pulled on the cord and quietly coaxed the ladder onto the carpet. I climbed it on all fours and stood with my head above the parapet, squinting as my eyes adjusted to the dark.

It was even blacker up here than down below, the glow of the moon not making much of an impact through the skylight. Reaching through the bars of the gate, I flicked the switch of the portable lamp Art had positioned near the hatch. As the loft slowly illuminated, I spotted Nut sitting at the far end of the space, awake, ears pricked and tail madly swishing in a figure of eight behind her. She was staring straight at me, her body quivering in high alert.

In those two short months she'd grown a lot, at least trebling in length from nose to hind. Her slender shape had become thicker, coated in a layer of fat which shifted in waves when she ran, and a little pouch of it hung below her midriff. During the day she'd gamble around the loft at quite a pace, running in circles around the space and leaping over any crates or baskets in her racetrack. Her legs had started to become more refined, the twists of muscle more apparent, and where she stood, her elongated toes spread confidently across the wooden floor.

But that night she'd given up on running, and her attention was all on me. Some deep instinct told me I shouldn't stay too still. Isn't that what a predator would do; skulk and stare? To make sure she knew I wasn't hiding, I lifted my arm and drummed my fingers on the edge of the wooden floor in a repeated tap-tap-tap, tap-tap-tap. Nut immediately skulked towards me, her head lowered and black pupils dilated. Now she stalked me like I was the piece of meat, and ignoring the nagging voice that so often told me I was wrong, I continued to dance my fingers on the wood. Nut came to a stop in front of me and flopped down passively on her soft belly, crossing her eyes as she pressed her nose against my fingers.

As I considered how much she might be able to pick up about where I'd been the previous day or what I'd eaten by my smell, I felt a strange gritty sensation across the back of my thumb. Through the bars of the baby gate, Nut was stroking her tongue slowly across my knuckles, her eyes closed in what looked like bliss.

Oh, Nut.

This was terrifying. New. It had said nothing in the guidebooks or prep material about this. And always, that little voice, screaming at me that I shouldn't let this happen.

Could she taste something on me? Was she hungry? Was she trying to get a better sense of me? The thing is, it felt *so caring*, this soft working of my hand. As if she was using the most intimate means she could to communicate. I imagined myself licking her back, dragging my tongue against her fur, each of us scratching each other's inner itches.

I didn't want her to stop.

I scratched behind her ear with my other hand and she rolled her neck to press the back of her head hard against my fingernails. Without words, she was talking to me, telling me that she wanted me there.

Nut shouldn't be doing this, she shouldn't be aware of pleasure or seeking it, not here, not living in this red loft. I had had no warning. It was me that sought her out for comfort, not the other way around.

I should check the manuals, I should check the manuals again just in case.

I pulled away and retreated down the ladder, giving one last look to the little round face peering down at me from the darkness. Art was still in the bathroom but the door was now ajar. I tapped it open with the tips of my fingers until there was enough space to stick my head through. I kept my voice low, soothing.

"Arthur?"

Art stood in front of the sink, staring down at something I couldn't see in the basin. He didn't turn or show a sign that he knew I was there.

"Arthur."

There was the slightest movement as he let out a sigh. He shook his head slowly, side to side. "It's OK, just g- go. S'fine." He stuttered on the "g", and I felt a sickening lurch.

Hold onto the doorframe, deep breaths. Be present. Don't go back.

I didn't believe that everything was fine. Art was lying. But I left him there and returned to our bed to slip into memories of the cow-dream I'd risen to escape from.

8

It wasn't until early summer and we'd been living together six months or so that the signs of moving were permanently hidden. But even then the dust hadn't quite settled.

Art and I were both on edge, with each other and the house. I'd spent most of my twenties in my own flat, and it had been far easier then to live in balance with my environment. I'd put things in a certain place, and they'd stay there until I moved them again. I had secret drawers and cupboards for the scissors, the sewing kit, the egg timer. I have a good memory for places.

But in Dukesberry Terrace, trinkets and treasures migrated around the house. Art would decide that there was a better place for something, or he'd use the scissors and never put them back, instead tidying them away to some dark corner only he knew about. Sometimes picture frames moved from one end of a ledge to another, and Art would be adamant that he hadn't touched them. It was always my treasures that were on the move, while Art's things stuck out amongst the stampede, immovable as mountains. I couldn't help but feel like these walking memories were playing some cruel emotional game I didn't understand, so I focussed my attention outdoors.

The house opened up at the back to a long lawn which tapered to a point. The effect was such that the far fence looked further away than it actually was, and only by walking from the back door to the shrub at the end would you discover the truth to the distortion. The lawn was patchy and uneven, bordered by shallow troughs of pale and dusty earth.

Despite how dead the soil looked, it was still punctured by sprigs of creamy weeds, tiny leaves, and sickly-looking clovers. The only green thing of any substance was a huge shrub at the garden's apex. The leaves were dark jade, stiff, the edges curling like the watercolour paper before we taped it down. It looked like a holly bush, apart from the tiny white berries which were starting to cluster at the end of each branch. All in all, the shrub stood up to my shoulder, and underneath the matrix of twigs, the bush-stem was thick and gnarled through many years of weathering storms.

A wooden fence protected the garden from anyone looking in, and I wanted the space to be a sanctuary. I could just imagine myself sitting on a cloud of lush green to the sound of trickling water over stone, and the soft breeze sloughing through red Japanese maples. I researched how I'd go about creating my own zen garden, and then when I discovered how much this would actually cost I moved onto a cottage garden, then a Mediterranean garden, then a modernist garden – complete with clean lines and evergreens. I looked at the lawn from all angles to work out what I could do with each section, even getting an aerial view through the study window while Art watched me from behind his desk with one eyebrow raised.

I wrote page after page of Latin botanical names until the words blurred together and the lists lost all meaning. At one point, I started to draw the layout of a pond, working out where its banks would lie, and what I'd plant in it. I imagined Art and I sitting by its edge with homemade lemonade, looking deep into the water for signs of life. But after spending too long crossing out all the plants that I'd been sure I'd wanted just to make room for the trench, I suddenly realised that I didn't even want a pond. The whole idea was ludicrous. We hadn't the room and the prospect of a gaping chasm in the lawn made me nauseous. And what would I do, get some bioplastic ducks to float blindly on it? A few mechanical koi to swim in endless circles? *Stupid.* I brought out yet another new piece of paper to start again, but by then my mind had gone blank, and I'd forgotten what I'd wanted in the beginning.

One Saturday morning in July, I piled up all the papers, stuck them under the Easton Grove manuals on the end of the kitchen counter, and didn't look at them again. I drove to the garden centre and returned home with four crates of plants and bulbs I didn't know the names of, all wrapped in orange netting. Art showed a bit of interest, reading some of the labels and picking his favourites. A few of them he'd heard of, and he told me that they'd grown in his parents' garden in Wisconsin. He smiled wistfully as he said it, and I wanted to ask more but his attention was already on the next plant, the next label. The moment had passed.

Art helped me carry them into the garden and lay them out on the grass. We arranged them along the dusty border, reading the labels as we went to check if they preferred sunlight or shade.

My houseplants, though I'd been meticulous with neutralising the soil and making sure they had the best of the sun, were all in varying states of failure. Despite the fact that they were all similar species, each had developed completely different problems. Some had gone flaccid, their soft and fleshy stems bending under the weight of their leaves. Some had shrunken back, their stalks dry and bone-like. Some had lost their green and were turning grey, like ghosts. All of the others were dropping leaves at a pace I couldn't match, and I went from room to room, watering and feeding them with the feeling that I was sending them to their doom, but watering and feeding them anyway. Only Aubrey's succulent seemed to be doing OK, holding tight to its plump, lavender petals.

I took photos of where the plants would go in the border, and asked Art to return the pots to their crates. Probably humouring me, he did it without saying anything and carried the crates into the kitchen one after another.

Before planting, I needed to purge the soil of all the roots sapping what meagre nutrients it had left. I started at the wall nearest the back door, thinking I'd work around the garden clockwise, meeting the mega-shrub in the middle, and then keep going clockwise until I met the house again. Once I'd cleared a space, I'd sprinkle on the good numbers and neutraliser to do its work before planting the new flowers. Art pulled up a deckchair on the lawn and curled up within its arms with an old hardback. I couldn't see the name. He didn't look up, other than to occasionally say, "You should be wearing a mask, doing that."

It didn't bother me that he wasn't helping, I hadn't asked him to after all, and in a way I wanted the garden to be *mine*. Just how I wanted it. And the only way to make something truly yours is to make it yourself. It would have been nice if he'd offered, but this way the flowers would grow where I buried them. These memories would be staying put.

But weeding was tough work. Pulling up twisted nettles and dandelions was easy, but the soil was littered with thousands of sickly buds as if attacked with spray paint. And Art was right about the mask. Soon, my throat was so raw that every breath rasped, but still I wouldn't stop. I needed to see it through. Art suggested just using a big shovel and mixing it all in but then the roots would have still been there, deep in the mix, and would sprout again in search of light. I couldn't have that, so I spent an hour or so each evening after work with a tiny trowel, digging out each offender by the stalk and placing it in a glass bowl. Even Art couldn't deny that the patch of soil I was working on looked pretty flawless. Every so often he'd touch my shoulder, and remind me in a soft voice to head inside and sterilise my hands. The gardening gloves weren't helping all that much anymore, and my hands were burning beneath the latex.

After layering on balms and new gloves I persevered, but by the time I reached three-quarters of the way around, the yellow spray was already starting to reappear at the beginning again, the tiny stalks already bending under their weighty heads. So I went back to the beginning, tearing out the new-borns before heading back to the three-quarter point. I was putting out little fires everywhere. Every time I turned around, another flame had sparked, and so

I couldn't catch my breath, but kept digging, until eventually I threw down the trowel and rested my spinning head on my knees.

All the time this was going on, the prickly shrub was growing, looming over the house, the berries luminous white, like fat little moons. Frustrated with the endless tending on all fours I went at the bush with shears, hacking it as far back as it would go, right to the bare black bark. While I swept up the branches Art came out of the house to see what I'd done. It was the first time I'd seen Art show real distaste. He clicked his teeth and twisted his face as if he'd tasted something rotten.

"It was too big, Art. You'll have to help me dig it out."

But he didn't help me; instead he bluntly reminded me of the four crates still on the kitchen floor. Abandoned and suffocated by their tiny pots, they'd already started to wilt and dry. By that point I was short-tempered, I know I was, and I told Art to "Bring them out then if you're so worried. Bring them out." He did it without a word, dumping the crates onto the lawn and stalking back inside, slamming the kitchen door behind him. I wondered if he was still in the kitchen, quietly seething at what I'd done or whether he'd gone back up to his study to sulk. I couldn't see any movement through his study window, so maybe he'd headed up to check on Nut, whispering to her about how I don't have it in me to nurture anything.

Having sat on the kitchen floor for over a week, the plants in the crates were showing many signs of neglect. Some had turned a sorry shade of yellow, and others looked like they'd been executed, their blossoming heads decapitated from skinny bodies. I dug a hole in the border at random and picked up the first plant I could reach. I thrust it in the hole and squeezed the earth around it without even checking that the stalk was level.

I continued in this way with all four crates, planting a wild and unconducted chorus of orange, rose, violet, and inky blue amongst the speckled soil. Finally, I took a canister of fertiliser and dowsed the earth all along the border before standing back to survey my handiwork. Somehow, even though I'd planted around thirty-five little plants, they all seemed so small and indistinct in the grand scale of things. Sometimes it's better to not get perspective, to not be faced with the cold, hard truth.

And then, something moving. Stirring beneath the red petals of some unnamed plant. I teased away the leaves and stalled, unable to move a muscle.

"Art!" And then louder, "Arthur!"

He must have only been in the kitchen, because in seconds he was by my side, peering down with me into the border. Stretched out beneath the fall of scarlet lay a green, shining frog. I'd never seen such a thing. Its limbs shone like plastic twine, a wide bowl of lump-encrusted back-skin split along a deep spinal ridge. Its eyes were black and glassy, and stared eerily to both the left and the right.

I could practically hear its skin sizzling.

We stood there motionless for some time, all three of us too afraid to move. I didn't need to look for a seam, a flaw. The frog was indescribably *actual*, as if it was somehow more than itself. Vibrating too quick for our eyes to see.

After some minutes Art leant over and whispered in my ear that he'd go and get a bowl. He ran off at a pace, returning with a shallow saucer of cold tap water. But by the time he set down the dish, the frog had gone.

9

I woke up so many mornings that summer convinced that the frog had come into the house and was now squatting next to my face on the pillow. I'd be in a dream, and then the plug would be pulled and the world would swirl around me until I hit the bed with a jolt. Face deep in sheets. For weeks I met the day confused and dizzy, sure that there was something wet and sinewy hiding around a corner.

I'd only seen a frog once before, but it had been dead for a few days. Luke had brought it home in a plastic Tupperware box. As a taxidermist, Luke already knew how to capture life in a curled lip or curious eye. Whenever the police got a report of a fallen sparrow or rabbit caught under the wheels of a car, a museum got the cadaver. If it was something unusual, it'd go to a research institute then a national museum, but if it was a species they already had in the archive, the remains went to a regional museum. And so Luke became a precious thing, a keeper of the secret way to open up a skin, clean out the rot and swell a belly.

By the time the bodies were brought in, they were usually already in a pretty bad state of decay. Being frozen stopped them getting worse, but whenever Luke laid a stiffened corpse under the lamps on his dining table, I had to turn away. No matter what the species, they were always dark and twisted things. So I'd turn to the TV's latest breaking news on genetic chimeras or the natural history books on his side table, bright with the beautiful illustrations I preferred to the rotting things he cut, stuffed and stitched.

Luke was always baffled by this, and I think he thought (wrongly) that it was death I didn't want to see. He'd beckon me over, saying, "Touch something real, Norah. This bird came from a bird. Once it's behind glass, that's it." And so, once he'd worked his magic, I'd stroke the blue jay's feathers for him, or the shafts rising from a hedgehog's back. Those feathers felt different to the ones I'd caressed as a child. Never as smooth. Congealed, tacky, and when I pulled away, oil clung to my fingers.

These finds were so few and far between that each one could've been the last, and we both revered and dreaded the bodies laid on his altar. Years later, I'd wonder how few years in the grand scheme of things Luke's hands had left to give life, and who else would be left to do it with as much love.

The frog in the garden reminded me of those cadavers. Beneath the duvet I pressed my clammy hands against my sides and tried not to blink in case I saw it again.

I did tell Art that I couldn't stop thinking about it, and whether the fertilisers could've killed it, but he just smiled, and said, "Don't worry about it. The company wouldn't make something that helps one thing and hurts another, and then give it to us in a spray bottle." When I kept worrying, he suggested I go looking for it between the pansies and marigolds, if that's what I wanted to do. If I found it, I could drop a jar over it, bring it inside and check it over. We could even draw it together with our birthday gear. He grinned like it was a game, so I shrugged back with an air of coolness, with a slant of the lips to say, "If I come across it again, I'll come across it. If it's meant to be." But I watched through the kitchen window anyway, clutched my mug of tea and pressed it hard against my lips.

The green lawn wavered like a hallucination through the pillars of steam. As I stood there, I looked ahead to weeks, months, and years of rooting around between the leaves with my trowel, pulling up tangles through the routine purge, utterly focussed on the functions of a life elsewhere. And then, without seeing, slicing through soft green flesh concealed between leaves, hearing the snap of little bones splintering under steel. Or perhaps I'd be sitting on the grass, palms flat to the earth behind me, and I'd feel what felt like a twig by a fingertip. I'd look down and find the frog dried, fossilised, limbs stretched and straining as if mummified just before leaping. What would I do then? If life ended in my square of earth to tend? It would be my fault, and I'd never know what more I should have done to help it survive.

I hoped the frog was gone. I wanted it to have disappeared to die elsewhere, in someone else's garden. Where it came from I couldn't even guess, but I couldn't see how it would have long left. The sun was burning. Art had left a terracotta bowl full of cold water by the back step to lure it close, but he forgot about it as the days passed, and I stood by as the cool surface retreated to the bottom of the bowl, the last few glimmers of life soaking into its parched, orange skin.

Art lay in late, and usually slept through my waking. One Saturday I woke with the usual jolt, my hands in a lattice around the back of my neck. I opened my eyes, letting the light between the blinds bleach any dream-shapes still drawn on my eyelids. Art wasn't there this time; he'd gone to London to deliver an afternoon lecture at a literary festival. One of those events arranged by a publisher to showcase their portfolio, just as much as their authors. Five days of talks, seminars, and schmoozing afterparties, everyone sucking in someone else's story and twisting it to be their own. Finding a hook and reeling in an audience at all costs.

I'd heard Art's script a few times through the wall of his study as I lay prostrate in the bath. Though muffled, it sounded a little like he was singing. His sentences dipped and rose in hypnotic rhythms, full of confidence. He seemed to be able to use his voice to mask everything else going on underneath. Listening to the words rounded with perfect clarity, I couldn't hear Art at all. He was a stranger from another world, a secret society I wasn't party to, one that sent me further and further from myself like a bullet from a gun.

I sank deeper and deeper into the water. Art's voice must have had the same effect on Nut, as the soft thump-thump-thump of her nightly pacing above slowed, slowed, and stopped. I could almost sense the air of expectancy weighing down through the ceiling.

While Art was away, I had the weekend left entirely open to do whatever I liked, with whoever I liked. I could embrace the single life again, or I could hide away, re-reading Nut's manuals and guides for the millionth time. The world – or rather, the house – could be both my oyster and my clamshell.

I'd thought about it all week, what I might do. Time alone was so rare. But now that Art was gone I was already rattling around the place. Mutely I moved from room to room without a single thought in my head, picking up Art's odd socks and old mugs, moving small relics from shelf to shelf. It was the first time I'd been alone in the house since we'd moved in and I couldn't focus. Well, obviously I *had* been on my own briefly before, but it's not the same when you know someone's going to walk in the door again at any moment. It's that that keeps the air electric. It was so stupid; I'd lived on my own for years before this house, and never noticed the air feeling so emaciated.

I made myself a pot of tea on autopilot, sifting in five teaspoons of sugar, and sat with a bowl of muesli at the dining table. I ate slowly, each clunk of spoon on bowl chiming obscenely loud, and sipped at the tea but it made my teeth sting.

What the hell was wrong with me?

I still had all my faculties. Maybe I should have offered to go with Art to the festival, but then again he hadn't asked me to. Would it have been appropriate? How would that have felt – hearing him talking to the room like that, with authority? What would I have said, if someone had approached me as his fiancée? Or for God's sake, why hadn't I arranged to meet Eleanor or Rosa like a normal person? My phone rested in my palm like an alien device. I hadn't spoken to either of them since the party at New Year, and now it seemed like I just couldn't remember how to do it or to make it look casual. Also, there'd be so many questions about everything – Art, the programme. I looked down at the engagement ring, still tight around my finger. Was I ready for that? No. No.

How would I have spent a Saturday alone before Art? There weren't many of them. I always seemed to be joining meals out with co-workers for an endless stream of birthdays, anniversaries, and all the rest. A treat used to be driving to a museum out of town, usually one of those stately homes, half mocked up in period-style with little interpretive panels. Museums to lives, rather than things. I'd have gone with Luke, who planned those trips like a boy writing his Christmas list. When he got really excited, he'd brush back his curly fringe over and over like it annoyed him. It'd flop down again sweetly over his eyes again every time, but he always kept it long. He used to twist those curls and mine together, marvelling at how they held fast even though they coiled in different directions. He couldn't resist playing with my hair whenever I laid my head on his shoulder, and no matter where we were, the tickling of his fingers on the nape of my neck were far more vivid than history or promises.

And of course, before those days I'd been to museums with friends and with Mum when I was smaller, but it was always better to go on my own. With Aubrey, I was her shadow as she ricocheted from room to room, my eyes only on the things she pointed out. And even with Mum, I was led by the hand from gallery to gallery as she picked out her favourite pieces, pressing a finger against the case to point out a bone, or stitch or fraying feather. Her favourite parts then became my favourite parts.

But that's not what these places are about. Like how a church should feel, you should lose yourself in the threads of weave. Only on my own could I walk from room to room and really comprehend that these were lives just like mine, once. Every empty glove held a million ghosts, and every portrait spoke to me of the painter, just as much as the painted.

I could have gone to a gallery or museum while Art was away, sure, I could have. But it was different now. How could I lose myself if I couldn't even feel myself enough to let go?

Around mid-morning I pulled on a T-shirt and shorts and rode my frustration with the Hoover in my hand, then the duster, and then disinfectant and a surprising number of cloths of every colour and texture found beneath the kitchen sink. I had no idea where such a range came from – I certainly hadn't bought them – but an even deeper root around revealed an even greater host of cleaning tools still in their packets. It was like discovering treasure.

Whenever I had to stop, I filled a glass from the tap, drank my fill, emptied the glass, and washed and dried it immediately. I went through each motion without thinking about all that much, mechanical in both movement and mentality. I used up the entire collection of cloths just from wiping the grime and build-up from the windows. I can't remember what time I finished, but the light in the house had dimmed, dulling all the shining surfaces with renewed grey lint. It hardly looked any different.

I laid myself as straight as an arrow on Art's side of the bed, staring up to the ceiling, and relaxing my muscles one by one. I'd been to a guided meditation session years before, where you squeezed and relaxed each set of muscles from the toes up. On that bed I hardly had to do the tensing part – I just focussed on letting myself go limp, piece by piece. The house was still silent, apart from a soft shuffling from the loft above.

I rose again, and opened the cupboard, rooting around behind the shoeboxes and bags for the wide tin of sketching pencils I'd hidden there. Prising open the lid, I saw that the pencils were still as sharp as needles, never having been broken in. I took one of these from the tin and slid the huge art pad out from behind Art's portfolio folder.

Tucking it under my arm, I headed to the landing and heaved on the ladder pull, stepping out of the way as it swung down in a creaking arc. I crept up the steps, and then crouched with the baby gate at my back and the paper on the floor in front of me, all the while scanning the room for Nut's face. There she was in the far left corner, peeking from behind the long wooden bench. Her face tipped sideways and an ear twitched, flicking its funnel towards me curiously. I started to make that tut-tut-tutting noise, reaching out towards her with an open right hand, rubbing together my fingers and thumb. *Come on, little girl.*

Nut crept from her corner stealthily, eyes focused on my fingers. Her soft, cushioned feet padded the floor with a soft and graceful thump, thump, thump. She stopped in front of me, flopping down her backside with a sound somewhere between a grunt and a chirrup. Her tail swished behind her, and she faced me brazenly with her wide, moon-like face.

I picked up the pencil and pad of paper and started to sketch her outline, working from the outside back in towards the heart. For some reason I thought that'd be easier, but Nut ended up shapeless, formless. It occurred to me that if I started from the outside, I wouldn't get the features inside right – they'd all be the wrong size, and it wouldn't look like Nut at all. I was sure that I had to get the face right, but no matter what I drew it looked either ugly or alien, and I became angry with myself.

I spread my discarded attempts on the floor to try to assess where I'd gone wrong. As I scanned my eyes across the scribbled leaves, I noticed a few interesting things. One was that Nut looked completely different in all of them. If someone had walked in there was no way they could've known that they were doodles of the same creature. This drawing looked a bit like a wildebeest, this one a little like a lion – a plume of tawny crowning around a scowl. Some sketches looked like nothing in particular but I could still pick out features I recognised. I'd drawn Art's eyes on her face there, and in this one I'd given her the uncommonly rosy budded lips of a cherub in one of those Renaissance paintings.

I piled the papers up carelessly, my mission unsuccessful and results frankly a bit weird, and scratched Nut behind a twitching grey ear. Even though I hadn't anything to show for it, I felt pacified, as if I'd switched off a little part of me and everything had gone quiet. A nice quiet.

Just then, I heard the phone ring downstairs, so I made my way to the kitchen to answer it, leaving all of my materials upstairs with Nut. I picked up the receiver, stuttering a little on my "hello". It was Art, checking in after his lecture.

"How did it all go?" I asked. *Breezy. Breezy.*

"It was incredible – they sold every ticket! I ended up there way longer because everyone wanted me to sign their stuff. But the festival was pleased with that, so they're taking me out for dinner shortly."

"Oh right. Who are you with?"

"Just Kelly right now. Paul was here too but he's had to leave for another lecture. So we'll just find somewhere close." Art trailed off, his voice shrill on the line.

"Who's Kelly?"

"Ah, she's quite new, first time I've met her in the flesh. She's the publisher's new Talent Support Coordinator, Officer, whatever, so she's here for the whole two weeks."

"Say hi from me."

"I will. You'd love her. She's so easy to talk to. And she really buoyed me up before the lecture. I had a wobble, and if she hadn't physically pushed me on I don't know how I'd have done it. So weird. I don't usually wobble. Anyway, what's going on with you?"

I felt self-conscious then, and told him that I'd been to town to meet Eleanor. I'd come home, tidied a little, and was now going to make a dinner with various tapas bits I'd bought while out. Mature stiltons, sun-dried tomatoes, zucchinis, mushrooms, and homemade bread shot with black olives. He made all the right appreciative noises, and then abruptly changed tone.

"Anyway, I should go now. Kelly's waiting, and we need to leave soon so we can find a table somewhere. So–"

"OK, Art. Send me a message later maybe, before you go to bed."

"I will. Love to you."

I placed my phone on the table top and placed my hands flat on either side. I had this really weird feeling in the pit of my stomach, somehow tight and heavy at the same time. I made my way to the fridge and not surprisingly at all most of the shelves were empty. No answers there. I'd have to restock before Art came home.

I spent half an hour grilling half a tofu fillet left over from the day before with a couple of wilting asparagus stalks, and boiled up a handful of rice. I plated them, squeezing a few drops of lemon juice over the tofu before heading to the living room.

Art wasn't eating alone. So why should I?

I did a one hundred and eighty degree turn at the living room door, and grabbed a tin of Nut's feed from the kitchen. I headed up the two sets of stairs to the second floor, setting down my dinner next to the baby gate. Nut was sitting on the paper pad, holding the pencil in her mouth like a moustache. I pulled the pencil from her jaws with the gentlest of coos, and then spooned some of the gelatinous slop into her dish. Grey and formless, it looked awful, but at the sight of the jelly, Nut bumbled over and pushed her face deep in the bowl. Little satisfied slurping and grunting noises filled the air and I relaxed back into my position by the baby gate. As I chewed, I watched Nut's long tongue lift the jelly into her mouth greedily, and each mouthful she ate nourished me, too. This was just what I needed, after that phone call.

Then, almost without thinking, I lifted a piece of my tofu and offered it to her on the palm of my outstretched hand. Nut's face flicked up immediately and she ambled over, peering down at it with eyes fixed on the prize. She sniffed at it slowly and suspiciously. I held my hand firm. Nut's self-restraint was a revelation. The way she'd been guzzling her own food had seemed so desperate that I couldn't understand why she hadn't torn my hand off to get at something new and illicit. After a pause, Nut leant forwards and lifted the tofu from my hand with large, flat, gleaming white teeth.

I pulled back my hand sharply. I hadn't realised her teeth would be so, well, like that. *Already*. They beamed bulb-like between her lips, a crush of pale pearls, far too big for her. She had a gap between the front two. I pulled my cardigan around my shoulders, shivering. Were those teeth uncomfortable for Nut? She was so young, and still teething. Forcing such oversize lumps through tender gums was a horrible thought. I pressed my tongue to one of my molars, and flicked it off one sharp corner.

Nut licked the floor for any juice she'd dribbled before turning back to her own bowl, unmoved and unthanking. I was pleased. I scooped up the plates and cutlery and headed down the steps, locking the baby gate behind me. I cast a quick look over my shoulder to see Nut sitting in the same spot, watching me over her shoulder, eyes half-closed, tail arcing slowly from side to side.

In the kitchen, I dropped the plates on the table and picked up my phone. I typed Aubrey's number from memory and held the phone to my ear, breathing slowly – in through the nose and out through the mouth, just like in meditation classes. The line rang. And it rang. And it rang. And I didn't hang up.

When the time came to go to bed, teeth brushed and body showered, I pulled out the patchwork blanket from beneath the bedframe and spread it across the duvet. I looked at it for a while, tracing my fingers over the chaotic stitches holding the pieces together. As I ran my hand across the knit, my engagement ring, the stone having swung to my palm, snagged on a loop of yarn, and as I pulled away I made one of the gaping holes in it worse.

I cursed under my breath and tried to weave the wool back through so it looked like it did before, but I didn't know what I was doing. I turned away, and decided that I'd sleep with the blanket on the bed, and put it away again tomorrow before Art came home.

Only once I'd decided this, did I click the red "end" icon on the phone. I stared at the screen for some time after it had switched to darkness. I rose from the bed and switched off the light on the landing, totalling the house in the same void: empty, black.

10

It wasn't long after that when Art and I had our first joint appointment of the year at Easton Grove.

Knowing us both as they did, I felt sick at the thought of telling them about our engagement. Crazy really. For them this was ideal. How much more stable and committed to the programme could we possibly be? We were perfect press release fodder. But there was still this little niggling feeling that I wasn't ready to share our story. Perhaps it was that I was still digesting it myself. Once I'd done that I'd be ready to wear the veil of a blushing fiancée, but for now it all was too raw, the bridal shroud a storm cloud.

Art was excited to tell them, and on the drive to the clinic he rolled down the windows so the radio played out loud and melodious on the summer roads. He bobbed his head side to side and sang along, raising his pitch whenever he looked at me to join in. I tried my best, but I didn't know the words to his music and made do with silent miming. I don't think Art noticed, he was too busy shouting the lyrics to himself.

At one point my phone buzzed, and as I pulled it out Art gave me a sideways glance. "Put it away," he sang. "Today's about us, remember?" I swiped away the message from Rosa and dropped the phone in the glovebox. He was right – I needed to focus.

As we approached the triple gates, a larger crowd than I'd seen in a long time were crowded around one of the security booths. Through the raised hands and placards, I could just about see the tweed-wearing guard behind the glass shouting into a black mobile phone. Some people were banging their fists on his window, while others rattled the fences or sat holding their heads in their hands in the squeaky green grass. A crude white banner was tied to the fence with string;

All life matters. STOP PLAYING GOD.

One of the woman finishing off the knots raised her head and my stomach clenched. Her platinum hair was shaved down one side. *Was it her? Was she here?* But then she turned and her face was wrinkled like a crumpled paper bag. I released one long breath and sank low into the passenger seat.

"Let's just take the side exit, eh?" Art spun the steering wheel and we headed down a narrow country lane towards a set of painted white gates. The security guard there looked just as rattled as the one in the front booth, and scanned our ID bracelets and paperwork with shaking hands. Then, a quick and husky "Thank you", before opening the gate just long enough for the car to inch through the narrow gap before locking behind us with a clang. We pulled into the car park and sat in silence for a few minutes. Art's face was grey and I could see all the whites of his eyes, so I reached across and held his hand. He looked down at it, his lips tight. "It gets a bit fucking much sometimes. Why won't they just give it up?"

We were early, so had a little walk around the wooded grounds before hunting down the phase five clinic. It felt like when we visited a stately home in our early days, but of course this time all of it was new – the trellises, the trees, the turf. Some saplings looked like they were struggling for light between the larger, artificial oaks. On those, bark sparkled like it was newly coated, but it still peeled in the midday sun. On one wooded avenue I picked up a pinecone to inspect the tight fit of its armour. I used a thumbnail to separate the layers, and discovered that the inner was constructed from corrugated cardboard. I pressed it back together and returned to the grave before carrying on walking.

Further back into the deeper woodland were the clinics reserved for the full members, in phases four and five. These were larger buildings built of stone, perhaps converted old barns and farmhouses. They couldn't all have been though; there were too many, and they stretched on far between the trees. As we made our way up the gravel walk, we made a game of guessing which buildings were genuinely old and which were fake, judging them on the colour of the stone, the slates on the roof, the window frames. But as neither of us could work out the truth, our game ended without any sense of closure. There was no winner, and instead we just tailed off, each of us lost in our own thoughts.

It wasn't long before we reached the area with the painted pre-fabs, beneath the willow trees. The speakers in the branches were blasting out the kind of deafening coos and hoots that I would never have associated with a feathered thing. Art pointed to the central hut. "You know, once I heard the strangest thing coming from there, in a pause in that crappy soundtrack. It was like a shout, but it wasn't words. Just vowels, really."

I didn't want to think about it, I wanted to be away, but Art started to drag me over the grass towards the door, crisscrossed with metal bars.

"Stop," I said. "This bit's not for us. It's private property."

Art twisted his mouth. "Private? We're members now. Nothing's hidden anymore."

I yanked my wrist from his grip, but not before I was close enough to read the small bronze sign low down beside the door handle: "The Core: Detention and Reconditioning". Art stared at the plaque for a few seconds before turning back to me, his eyebrows raised, his cheeks ashen. I grabbed his hand and pulled him back towards the path with one thought in my mind. *We shouldn't be here.*

We continued along the gravel in silence. What was there to say? We didn't *know* what was inside the pre-fab for sure, but I couldn't stop wishing that I'd used a magnifying glass to read all that small print in those first information packs.

After a few more minutes we realised how utterly lost we were. We'd given ourselves plenty of time to find the right building, but by now we'd definitely wandered too far. We stood for some time, looking back and forth along the trail for a clue or a signpost, both of us growing increasingly panicked that we were going to be late. It seemed to me that the place was designed to lead you off into the wild without any signage to guide you home, and I knew deep in my heart that it was deliberate. Nothing at Easton Grove was ever accidental.

"I can't say much for their user experience," Art muttered into my ear.

To our left was a three-storey stone building painted in duck-egg blue, with a sign by the door which read "Surgical Recovery", and just opposite, a huge white behemoth marked up as "Organ Auxiliary Centre". Beside that was the entrance to a long, low-lying complex which stretched back into the trees, so I couldn't see how big it really was. There were no windows, and the stone-effect exterior made it look more like a bunker than a medical centre. Art wasn't looking and drove me onwards, but before we passed by completely I craned my head to read the sign: "Ovum Organi Genesis Centre". Strange glassy clangs and thumps could be heard from within, and I quickly turned away and focussed on the squeaking green grass, the daisies that never died.

If how deep you went into the grounds reflected how long you'd been a member, we'd definitely come too far.

We headed off back in the direction of the entrance, but all we met were closed doors, and white signs plugged into the grass: "Ovum Organi Recovery Unit 1.2", then "Ovum Organi Rehabilitation 1.1", then "Stem Cell Regeneration Centre". Where was everyone? At least from the flow of buildings, we could tell that we were finally heading in the right direction. I became aware of how tightly I'd clasped Art's hand and I loosened my grip to match his own.

When we eventually found the right outpatient reception, we signed in at the desk and were shortly invited into one of the consultation rooms in "Area F". It was the first time we'd been to this part of Easton Grove and I have to say, it was pretty underwhelming. I'd expected it to be an upgrade from the previous clinics, after all – we'd upgraded too. You pull out all the stops for *family* visiting, surely?

Area F lacked the light from the other clinics' open-plan architecture; the bright windows, the bouquets in glass bowls, the bright and grinning staff members. Area F had the feeling of being underground, with dull grey walls and navy-blue plastic seating oddly spaced with huge gaps between chairs. There were flowers on the tables but they weren't the glorious summertime bundles we were used to. Those had been replaced with crooked spider plants, their spindly leaves drooping in the fluorescent light. The overall effect was of tiredness and still air, no dynamism at all.

We were called into the consultation room by a young man I hadn't seen before. Underneath the long white coat he was excessively lean, and held out his elbows at odd angles as if he'd only just realised he had joints there and wasn't sure what to do with them. His mouth quivered a little as he called our names, and his neck flushed at the sound of his own voice. As I passed him in the doorway he gave me a wide, toothy smile.

Sitting in the room already was a face I'd expected to see, Fia, the consultant from my early days of assessments who'd given me the smile and the handkerchief. She'd signed on to continue as our joint mentor, and oddly she looked younger than I'd remembered, or maybe I just felt older. She definitely had fewer greys, and the self-conscious curve of her shoulders that I'd related to before had flexed back elegantly, her spine as straight as a catwalk model's.

Fia would be our main contact to coordinate between our lifestyle mentor, physicality mentor, psychological assessor and ovum organi advisor. She'd seen both Art and I through phases three and four, and I was relieved that we wouldn't have to tread any old ground.

She offered us tea from a pot newly brewed, and when Art asked for a black coffee instead, the young man (who had stood by the door the whole time) dashed out of the room to make it. While we waited, Fia acted as if we weren't there and started typing, even pulling up the leg of her tights where it had gone wrinkly at the ankle. The silence was almost physical, and I had to fight the urge to break it out of sheer awkwardness. I took a sip of the tea, and the sweet milky tonic made it better.

The moment the young man returned with Art's coffee, Fia perked up and addressed us both, still typing with one hand.

"I hope it's OK for Nathan to sit in with us. He's on a placement and is keen to see how joint-members transition through the phases. Is it alright for him to listen and take notes? It's all confidential."

We agreed that it was fine. "Nathan will also have some access to your early induction notes as part of his project," Fia continued. "He might use some of it as a case study but he'll anonymise it completely. He's been given the highest level of clearance access to our records, but we still have to get permission from you if he uses anything… *personal*. I trust that's also fine? If so, we'll proceed."

We nodded, but the idea of some unknown man trawling through my backstory gave me a queasy feeling. He didn't know me, he wouldn't understand the decisions I've had to make every day. Inevitably he'd make judgements based on black and white, but what right did he have to decide whether my shade of grey leaned into the light or the darkness?

Fia stopped typing and swivelled on her chair to face us. "So, this is just a routine check-in as we see it. We want to know how you both are getting on. So, how've you been since moving in together? All's well in the bird's nest?"

Fia clapped her hands together and leaned forwards as if eager to be let into a secret.

"All better than you might have guessed." Art reached for me and thrust my left hand towards Fia. There was nothing I could do. As soon as she saw the gleaming opal she looked up at Art with the oddest expression. The only way I could understand it was that she was looking at him conspiratorially, as if he'd done something slightly cheeky but would get away with it. "You didn't wait long, we thought that might take years." She laughed, peering in at the ring for a closer inspection. "Why didn't you tell us first?"

Art squeezed my shoulder. "Why wait? You have to seize the day, right?"

Fia nodded sagely, her eyes closed. "You do. My, we've taught you well. Norah, you must be thrilled."

I smiled, a trickle of laughter making it out before I was interrupted by Art. "We're keeping it between us for now. No parties or shindigs or gloating. We're sitting on it like a warm egg."

Fia looked thoughtful and released my hand. I pulled my sleeves down over my knuckles.

"Very wise. You often see couples get so wrapped up in the celebrations that they don't think about what they're actually doing. And when it's all over, they're left with a reality they're not prepared for. It's sad really, but there you go."

I reached across and grasped Art's hand, it seemed the right thing to do. He grinned at me with what felt like honest love. Fia sat back in her seat.

"You're both making it too easy, I feel like my work is almost done."

In the corner, Nathan scribbled notes into his book. Fia tucked an escaped lock of hair behind her ear. "You're both about to go on a journey together that will make you grow in so many ways. And we're glad to be a part of it. Your next visit – we'll bring champagne, not coffee." She took a grandiose slurp from her mug. "In fact, this deserves something better. How about more tea? Nathan, do you mind?"

Nathan nodded and left the room. Fia folded her hands across her belly. "And how are your vocations going?"

Art went first. "Not too badly. I was just part of a sell-out festival, and I have another book coming out at the start of next year. I'm now fully into the big one."

"Are you pushing yourself too hard?"

"No, I'm careful not to."

"Good. I'm sure Norah's doing all she can to support you too," Fia glanced at me from the corner of her eye. "After all, it might be your big success that funds the pair of you in the future. Like a good old-fashioned married couple."

"I hope so," said Art, squeezing my hand.

"And you, Norah? How's your work going? Stokers, isn't it?"

I said the words, I smiled the smiles, all the while knowing that Fia's ear was trained for lack of substance.

"How long have you been in that position now?"

I pretended to count. "Ten years or so, ish."

"Don't you ever want to move up the ladder? Be influential to the company as a whole?"

"It's not the sort of place with a lot of progression."

Fia tipped her head and pouted irritatingly at me. "But isn't that *frustrating*?"

I tipped my head too, and imitated her singsong tone. "Not at all, Fia. I make a difference in little ways. I like that."

"But you'll be so experienced at that now. Don't you want to be held up for loyalty?"

I imagined myself hoisted on the shoulders of giants, all for the glory of processing insurance claims.

"I think it's unlikely."

Fia didn't reply, and Art's shuffling caught my eye. He was looking at his knees, flicking at a spot on his trousers. When the room went silent he looked up at me like I was a stranger. Was what I was saying so odd? Why was he so surprised that this was the language I was fluent in?

There was still a need to present ourselves as a united front so I laughed, shrugging my shoulders as if throwing off a heavy cloak. "But I'm still finding myself, aren't I? My niche."

The door opened and Nathan came in carrying a tray, and handed Art and I a blue mug of steaming tea each. It smelled even sweeter than my first cup, like hot cream and something else, cloves, maybe? I wrapped my hands around the mug and felt my body relax.

Nathan sat back in the corner and smiled at Fia, who was still staring at me with her face puckered to a pout. She obviously wasn't convinced by what I'd just said, but it was easier for me to concentrate on the heat of the mug, the steam on my face, than play games with her. Finally she turned back to her laptop to tap away on the keys. "We might need to give you extra support with this. You're in your prime and we need you to do well. For the programme. You're both such perfect advocates. Young. Approachable. Attractive. Accessible. But you must make an effort to show a holistic approach to wellbeing, here. Don't mix with anyone that'll drag you down, Norah. Have you seen your friends recently?"

I told her I hadn't, and she seemed pleased enough with that. Art looked at me quizically and I suddenly remembered my lie from when he was at the festival. That I'd seen Eleanor. I gave him a quick smile and then focussed all my attention back on to Fia. *Don't say anything Art, please.*

Fia pointed at my tea and I gladly took another sip. She continued to type through the remainder of our session, making notes after every answer we gave. She asked Nathan to measure our blood pressure and take a small sample of blood from each of us as a routine health check. Nathan was gentle, moving my arm into position as if I was a china doll that might shatter if he moved me the wrong way. I watched him closely as he pressed his thumb pads in the crook of my arm to identify the vein and then slipped in the needle. He smelt woody, like drying bark, but also a little herbal, like eucalyptus or rosemary.

Fia booked us in for another joint appointment in six months' time, and pressed upon us another folder of updated guidelines for self-care management. By the next appointment the snow would be back and we'd be ringing in another New Year's Day. But rather than see that as something to look forward to, I felt nothing. The appointment had knocked me hollow, and I dashed out of those sterile grey halls as quickly as I could without looking like I was running. Art skipped along beside me, seemingly unaware that the cold that had descended on me hadn't yet thawed.

If anything, I felt a bit stupid, and as always a hundred better retorts than the ones I'd actually given Fia and Nathan revealed themselves to have been in my head all the time – but inaccessible. *Surprise.* Traitorous brain. No chance to say them now.

So what if I'd been in the same job for a while? Is it a crime to continue doing something after you've mastered it? No one would say that to a scientist, to a potter, or to Art. No one told him he should be writing film scripts or Christmas jingles. Surely it's a bad thing to skip from position to position, never becoming an expert in anything?

And why, despite the sad, soft looks, did their offer of help feel like a threat?

I tossed the folders onto the back of the car and slid into the front passenger seat. Art leapt in the driver's spot and turned on the ignition. "Obligations over. Let's go, shall we?"

It had been my idea to make the most of getting out of town. Since Art had been away, I felt like we hadn't quite clicked back together as comfortably as we had before. Admittedly I'd built this afternoon up in my head as a chance to really get back on track with intimacy, but I'd sold it to him as simply an opportunity to enjoy the country. Less intimidating that way.

Luckily it was a blazing hot August day, and I'd prepared a picnic, all wrapped up in a red fleecy bundle, and mapped out a route to an ornamental garden around an hour's drive from Easton Grove.

The air conditioning filter in Art's car was on the blink so I wheeled down the passenger window to feel the wind on my face. Every so often I'd take a deep draught and the air would catch on my throat. Even though we were out in the middle of nowhere, and the only sign of life was the slow tread of distant scatterers on the horizon, you could still taste the tang of pollution – like licking the handle of a knife.

At one point, we drove past a wide body of water trapped in a grassy valley. On the bank nearest us were two men and a boy of about eight or so, dressed in identical waxy-looking clothes and yellow rubber boots that went up to the knee. Each was sitting in his own deckchair with a fishing rod balanced beside him and his eyes on the point where his line met the lake. They were very still.

"That's cruel," said Art. "I bet they've told the kid he'll catch something."

I wasn't sure. The three of them were perfectly focussed on *something*. But part of what Art said was right – the boy wouldn't have known a day when just anyone with a rod could catch a fish. Perhaps there was another prize to be won from fishing in the toxic soup.

We reached the gardens early. Thinking it wouldn't be all that busy, I'd expected a quiet afternoon where we could both recline with only the whisper of wind through leaves to keep us company. But it was a Saturday, and I really don't know why I thought my great picnic idea wouldn't occur to everyone else in the local area too.

The ornamental garden was in fact a long, stretching lawn behind an old stately home called Crawcrook Hall. The grass, violently green with too many stimulants, was bordered by a fence of ancient trees, gnarled and half-fossilised, the type that have seen and weathered everything. Their arms twisted up towards the sky and down again, all elbows and wrists, like they'd been dancing and then entombed.

That day, the rolling lawn was a patchwork of blankets and people, spreadeagled and shining. Couples sprawled together in knots, their limbs tangled together, while parents chased excited toddlers and children from straying too far into the woods. Babies lay on their backs under lacy parasols, weighted to the earth like washed-clean pebbles.

So many people. All those lives just… happening. And everyone so happy and free, their laughter falling like water down a mountainside. I wondered if they could tell we weren't like them. I felt as though we moved like automatons.

It had been a long time since I'd last crushed into a picnic ground like this. The last time would have been with Luke a year and a half before, and while it wasn't at Crawcrook it was at a similar stately home called Hibiscus Hall. I remember it like it was yesterday. Luke had surprised me with a basket bursting with tasty bits for afternoon tea – cupcakes, pastries, cheese, berries, beer – and we ate it all sitting on the lawn. At no point did I need to smile to show him how I felt, he just knew. I was wearing shorts and the grass tickled the back of my legs, as if I sat on the fur of a shifting creature. We hardly spoke but lay there for hours, all people and places outside the park as distant as a bad dream.

Later, I'd remember both picnics but only one would feel like a fiction. Though what was the difference, really? Luke and I had definitely been there, just as Art and I had. I could remember both afternoons. Both versions of me. How I remember it all, well, that's more to do with me making sense of it all. And I don't mind that. It's somewhere I can go, not say anything, just watch the clouds roll above me like I'm watching time from an untouchable place.

Anyway, Art and I weaved through the sea of bodies and finally found a grassy spot just past the recycling bins. Complying with the rule of all picnics I'd packed far too much, and after laying it all out on the grass it was official that I'd brought an obscene amount of food for two people. It was mostly stuff Easton Grove would have approved of: leaves, fruits, berries and veg, but then I'd also brought some naughtier crisps and cookies, and I'd baked some little cocoa ball-things which immediately melted into one solid lump under the midday sun.

Whether it was the warm light on my skin or being free from the appointment with Fia and Nathan, I felt lighter than I had done in a long time. Art looked brighter too, and I was struck by how much I wanted him. It was like we were back in our dating days, when every touch was a thrill, a question. I loved him. There wasn't a doubt in my mind about that. But it's an odd feeling to have a thing, and to want that thing, but to still feel like it's not quite yours.

After we'd finished our feast, Art removed his brogues and socks, then wriggled his toes. They looked absurdly naked sticking out at the end of his chinos. He leaned across and slowly pulled off my sneakers so we matched. He pushed himself backwards and pressed the soles of his feet against mine so we were walking our feet together across empty space. I bent my knees, and leaning forwards slotted the fingertips of both my hands through the gaps between his toes, wiggling them gently. Art let out an awkward twitch and recoiled with a sudden "What was that?" I'd lost myself for a moment, and I forgot that not everyone likes their feet fiddled with.

I pushed our soles back together again on the blanket, balance restored. We didn't speak all that much for a while but I was content to watch Art as he watched the families around us, a little smile flickering across his face. Before long though I realised he wasn't watching them as I thought he'd been, he was elsewhere, somewhere his imagination had taken him and where I couldn't follow. That wasn't the deal.

"Where are you?"

He turned to me and smiled; he couldn't have been too far away. "I was in my book."

"What's it about, this big one?"

He sighed, leaning back on his elbows. "It's hard to explain."

"Try, we've got all day." I threw a strawberry into his lap. He looked at it before retrieving it, this bright red blossom falling between his legs.

"Well, it's about a man. A man looking for something he can't find."

"What's he lost?"

"He doesn't know." Under his breath he let out a little laugh. "The problem is I've started it without knowing what he's looking for myself, so I've hit an impasse. But also, the more I work on it, the more I think it's about me."

He bit into the strawberry, sucking out the juice. This revelation didn't seem all that bad or surprising to me. "Isn't that OK?"

He shook his head, his brow furrowed. "This is the first time

I'm trying to do something important. Every book I've written before has been all plot, action, clues, suspense. A little guy on a journey. I do it because they do well, people buy it. But this, this is supposed to be the one that makes me. My legacy. A story that'll last longer than me, one that I'll leave behind."

It seemed to me then that Art hadn't realised that *that* was the reason why he was writing about himself. Maybe it's different when you're the one pouring out the words and every character boomerangs back.

I bent my knees just enough so that I could stroke his ankle. "It's always going to have a bit of you in there, Art. Maybe that says something good about it."

"No. I shouldn't be in it at all. I should be the voice above it all, outside of it. It's meant to be a modern-day parable, it's meant to change everything. My other stuff is crap, it goes from bestseller lists to bargain bins in a week. No one remembers them. But this, this is meant to be timeless. Who'd care about another fucking memoir? Especially from someone like me, right now. It's too risky."

I let my nail scratch his ankle as I pulled my hand away. He was right. Though Easton Grove wanted us to be delegates, what if people found out where we lived through Art's books? Would we then have those same desperate protestors at our door, their placards pressed against the windows? We both knew it couldn't work, and it would be stupid to contradict him on it. I could see Art's mood had plummeted, and the only way to salvage our afternoon would be to soothe him.

"Maybe it's about time we set a date."

He didn't seem to hear me, and was still inspecting the half-eaten strawberry.

"Do you want to set a date, Art?"

At his name he looked up at me again, quizzically. "What are you going to do about work, Norah? Are you going to look for something else?"

So, he'd turned to sparring? I wasn't in the mood to defend, and laughed it off. "I'm sure something'll come up. Aubrey always thought I was made for customer service."

Art smirked. "What does she know? The problem with Aubrey is she can't share. She doesn't want you to move ahead of her. She doesn't want you to do better."

"Maybe I should write my own memoir. Perhaps one day I'll be the one making waves with my artistic side."

Before Art had the chance to reply his phone rang, and he answered it with hardly a glance at who was calling. I sank into my own thoughts as he chatted, my conversational cogs churning away in preparation for the moment he was back with me. He hung up after a minute or two, biting his lip. "I'm sorry, I forgot I had a Skype chat with Kelly booked this afternoon to go through a contract. We'll have to go now if I'm going to make it at six."

We packed up the empty packets and bottles in silence. Art was mouthing words to himself, likely preparing what he'd say to Kelly. But when every trace of our being there was consigned to the basket, I didn't get up from the blanket.

"Let's do something."

Art looked down at me, his brow furrowed.

"Let's go somewhere. Let's go somewhere you like but you've never been for a long time. You can get me drunk, if you want."

His eyebrows raised at that, and he looked at me like he was inspecting something new and amusing. A dog doing a trick. "I said I'd be back…"

"There's a lifetime to be back. Kelly can wait. Come on, take me somewhere."

I didn't really expect him to change his mind, but as soon as I'd said the words his eyes lit up. He drove us to a bar an hour south of the picnic ground, and all the while I smiled – knowing that he was choosing to take me somewhere rather than answer Kelly's call.

As we climbed out of the car, he told me that he'd read about the place on a referrals site when he first arrived in the UK and driven all the way here just for a drink. It was the first place he found that he felt at home, and he came here once a week or so before he met me. It did seem strange that he hadn't told me about it before, but then it was just a bar. It was hardly a representation of his heart and soul. But still – in those early dates of showboating ourselves through little adventures around the north, why hadn't he taken me there?

Called the Red Room, it wasn't what I'd expected at all. From the outside, with its glass windows and rustic oak signage, I expected it to be a hipster hangout spot, but inside the place was set up like an old public house from the 1940s and was inhabited by men in twos and threes who were a fair bit older than we were. All the tables and seating seemed just a little bit smaller than in a normal pub, and the walls curved inwards towards the ceiling as if we were beneath the canopy of a circus tent. Most of the furnishings were blood red or a deep purple, the wood all dark and glossy mahogany. Art led me to a two-seater table in the corner towards the back, and grabbed a drinks menu from the next table.

"If I'm to get you drunk, let's do it in style." His finger skimmed down the list of cocktails.

"No, my idea, my treat. I'm paying."

"Oh. Well in that case." Art chose a bottle of some dark brew, and after he promised that he'd let me try a sip when it arrived, I stuck to wine. When I returned to our table, Art was tugging on his ear self-consciously, perhaps suddenly bashful that he'd chosen such an odd place to take me to. I don't blame him, I would never have matched it with Art at all. But as he reached the end of that first bottle his fires were stoked again, his voice now loud enough to rouse some of the older people who were sitting alone from staring at their beermats.

Without asking me, Art bought us the same two drinks again. I sipped at my wine as he told me the story of his first few months in England. I'd heard it all before of course, but this time he told some of the details differently. In one, he'd seen a woman get mugged on his second day in the UK, but in this latest retelling it was a young girl who was mugged, and it was Art who called the police. Some of his stories I didn't remember so well so I couldn't be sure about those, but others I did remember – having heard them two or three times already. The way he told them in the Red Room you'd have thought he was on stage, giving a reading from one of his books. But he was so obviously enjoying himself by this point that I didn't raise it. What's the harm in his trying to entertain both of us?

Art picked out a different beer for his third, and I chose a diet coke, but asked at the bar for it in a spirit glass. We raised our glasses to ourselves with a customary chink. I was already feeling a bit light-headed, but the cool weight of the soft drink helped a little. Art kept at it, downing drink after drink like a starving man with water. His mood peaked and dipped and peaked again between victor and underdog, his rollercoaster ride entirely self-driven.

This out of control Art was an alien creature to me, an animal to study behind a pane of one-sided glass. All I needed to do was sit back in my seat, and watch him break himself down in that superficial way drunk people do, dissecting his deepest self with blind eyes, forgetting first to remove the skin.

Art's fingers prodded his chest clumsily, and he leaned forwards conspiratorially, breathing hot beery words in my ear. "You know why I really like this place?"

Keeping my eyes wide I shook my head. "Remind you of somewhere?"

He twisted his face. "What? No. Like where?"

"I don't know, you're the one making me guess. Somewhere back home?"

He looked like he was laughing but no sound was coming out. "No. I don't want anywhere to remind me of back home. Ever."

Art had never spoken to me about the photo I've seen after our first date. "I liked seeing your parents' faces. In your portfolio. They looked... nice."

Art stared back at me. "I don't remember putting that in there."

I shrugged. "Well, it was. You were only little. On a farm? Are they scatterers?"

Art coughed, but kept his lips pinned shut. "They were, yeah. They're dead now. The usual. They *greyed.*"

"Oh." Shit. Why did I bring this up? I should have known. He said he didn't want to talk about the topic, so why did I pursue it? Stupid stupid stupid. There was nothing to say, so I reached across to brush my fingers across his knuckles. He didn't move. "OK, so it's not back home. Why's this place so special?"

He stared out at the bar as if he'd forgotten what he was going to say. He looked sad, smaller, and I wished I hadn't said anything at all. Everything I did was wrong. He took a swig of his drink and shook his head as if dusting off a dream.

"It's because everyone's *so fucking old.* No one comes in here if they're younger than sixty. Everyone looks at you because you're fresh and different. I even move differently to them. They're weighted down whereas I'm free as a bird. Free and light." He waggled his fingers at either side of his head like fledgling wings. "It's like I'm immortal."

It felt like a long time before Art's stomach began audibly rumbling and he tired of drinking. He didn't finish his last beer and instead proclaimed that we needed to "go on the hunt for sustenance."

Arm in arm we stumbled to the car and I helped him fall into the back seat. He didn't even try to sit up, and instead curled on the pew, his hands covering his face. I could see the soles of his brogues hadn't fared well with the chemicals on the lawn. I'd have to make sure he didn't touch them while on the back seat, and I'd check both our shoes for boot-rot when we got back.

He lay silent for the whole three-hour journey home. From the front I couldn't see if he was asleep or thinking, but either way he was mentally far, far away from the car. I didn't mind, and my thoughts flocked around my own head for a while. I thought about tomorrow, when Art would wake up with a sore head and worse, and likely not be able to write at all.

The thought made me smile.

After all, if it was all about perspective I had plenty of time, didn't I? Whatever sickness might be thrown my way I'd beat it. I had a backup. I had ten backups, a hundred backups. And I had all the help I could ever need to use that time well.

It took a while to get Art out of the back seat and through the front door. With each step he gathered himself, until he flopped down on the sofa with a high-pitched giggle. He grabbed my arm, his eyes wide and white.

"Norah – it's all going well, isn't it? You'll always be here for me? No matter what happens?"

"Yes," I whispered. "It's all fine."

He patted me on the wrist, all doe-eyes and honesty. "Well be a dear, and get this old flake a slice of toast or, what do you call it, a Cornish pasty? If I must go without food a moment longer I may faint where I am lain. Oh, the hunger."

I kissed him on the forehead and left to forage for something filling. I called back to him, "I'll just be a minute. Your mini-me needs vitamins too."

I grabbed a tin of jellied feed and jogged up the stairs to the landing. Once I'd sorted Nut out and made sure Art had something to eat, maybe I'd coax him to the bedroom. Sit with our feet touching again. He didn't like the fingers through the toes, but I'd find another gesture, another caress he did like. Despite the state of him, spending more time with him had opened me up to Art in a way I'd forgotten since the house had settled. Hopefully he too felt warm towards my touch.

I stuck my head through the hatch entrance and scanned the room for Nut. I couldn't make much out, the bulb in the lamp would soon need replacing. I heaved myself up through the trapdoor and stepped through the baby gate, still creaking with that slow wail. Nut's cardboard box was empty, as was the fruit crate, and though I couldn't see her right away I knew she was here, as if a sixth sense told me so.

And then I spotted her. Silent. Still. Flat on her side as if captured in a snapshot of a hare, running.

PART 2

11

We were never supposed to name her, you know. Nut. They told us this when they made her.

Names lend significance to things, meaning more to the giver than to the receiver. To me, I'm just "me", but to everyone else I'm a foreign body with a face and a feel. They say my name and hear its song. And you can't shake it. You might strive against it your whole life, shortening it or changing it completely. Or you might love your name. You might have hated it in childhood but as an adult you embrace it in its weirdness or hide within its insipidness. A name can conjure anonymity, too.

It's the same with animals. I don't know if they named each other in the wild; I doubt it. It'd be smell or markings that set them apart. But when we give an animal a name and repeat it to them day in and day out, we're giving them something to respond to. They might not understand "identity" as we do but when you call their name and they come running, they must know that they're needed, and they're needed by *you*. They run to you, in love or in servitude, it doesn't matter, and it's never obvious which it might be.

But what about us? What happens to us when we decide on a special name?

It was me that chose the name Nut, and I named her after the way she'd curl around and into herself, cut with ripples through her fur like a walnut. It started off as a bit of a joke, a code name for her between Art and I, but it stuck. It became a far less clinical name for us to use with the curtains drawn. Even when she stretched out to near half a metre long, she still looked to me like a Nut. Maybe I'd have felt different about her collapse if she hadn't had a name at all.

On finding Nut cold and still, Art had bolted back downstairs on Bambi-legs to call Easton Grove's emergency number while I'd stayed with her, trying frantically to remember my training; check her airways, listen for a heartbeat, feel for breath.

Nut was stretched out on her side as if leaping, her paws contracted inwards as if pulling the shape of her into a protective round. I rubbed her sides vigorously to bring life back whilst also trying not to recoil at her rigid muscles, the stiffened skin. It wasn't like touching Nut at all, it was touching something wrong, something alien. A terrifyingly real doll, stuffed inside Nut's membrane.

From the far end of the tunnel, I could hear Art on the phone and shouting up at me to check her mouth for a foreign body. Pulling my sleeves over my hands, I tried clumsily to turn her head, but her neck was unbending, locked back in a tight arc. I tried to bring her back by saying her name over and over, as if she'd hear me and come galloping from sleep just for another lick across my knuckles.

This is why all the material tells us not to give names. It means we can't call them back when it's time for them to die. Lest we forget, Easton Grove's ethos is *the art of self-preservation*.

I have to give them credit, the staff at the Grove are militant.

After hanging up, Art scaled the steps and in one silky motion lifted Nut like a serving platter and carried her to the car in his arms. Without a word, he climbed into the back seat with Nut across his lap. I slipped into the driver's seat, my hands shaking on the steering wheel. My mind blank, I had no idea how to start. I couldn't connect.

A hand gripped my shoulder. "Turn the key. I can't drive. We need to go."

All the way to the Grove I couldn't look away from the road, and every few minutes was convinced that I could see creatures darting from the dark to cast themselves beneath the wheels. I couldn't have stopped for them anyway and whenever I remembered to breathe, the air tasted bitter like medication.

Four staff in white coats were waiting for us at reception, and next to them stood a metal gurney, like one of those stainless-steel trolleys tea ladies used to wheel around office buildings, only longer. A man with a red tie took Nut from Art and laid her on the tray. A flock of white coats swooped around us, each applying his or her own instrument to Nut like synchronised swimmers. One consultant stepped forward out of nowhere and offered us milky tea, her voice soft and slow. I noticed that she was wearing a lot of make-up, badly concealing dark half-moons under her eyes. Her face looked sticky. I was still standing in the waiting area when the tea arrived, steaming, in a bone china teacup painted with miniature pink posies.

By now it was near midnight, and the other members in the waiting area all seemed to be in a similar state of shock. A man in a leather jacket opposite us was twitching his head left and right, his hand squeezing his thigh in short sharp bursts. A few seats along from him a middle-aged woman in a tired-looking brown suit spent the entire time staring at the ceiling. She'd taken her shoes off, and was repeatedly running her hands through her hair, giving her the look of someone that had spent time hanging upside down. Above our heads, the ceiling was painted with the most ridiculous caricatures of birds that I'd ever seen. All the wings were stunted, and their long necks twisted in ways which weren't natural. Some were almost tied in knots. It made me feel sick to look at it.

Art was sitting with his head in his hands, trying to massage sobriety into his scalp. But what frustrated me most was the slow, floating walk of the staff passing through as if they had all the time in the world.

It felt all too familiar even with distance, the standing and sitting dead. But the time before, that waiting room was dark, with threadbare curtains and chairs backed with sackcloth. A bowl of scentless potpourri on a coffee table. A magazine from three years before, with "*The Greying*: Pollution's Wife, and Our Inescapable Fate?" written across the cover in bold black. A dark wood door to the old hospital chapel, abandoned and forgotten.

That night Aubrey was there, squeezing my hand a little harder each time I tried to let go, and working hard to meet my eyes whenever they looked up. I was desperately cutting myself off because as soon as our faces met she peeled me open. She would say with those eyes, "I know what you're feeling, I understand", but she didn't know. Not all of it. That if it hadn't been for her, maybe I'd have noticed what was happening with Mum before she was already half-gone. And I could have stopped it. I could have bought Mum more time.

But after Mum's death I was still lost in Aubrey, I needed the warm cocoon of her skin, and I curled up into her like a snail in an old shell, disappearing completely. That day, Aubrey was my voice, answering for me and calling me back whenever I started to sink. She pointed at the dotted lines I needed to mark to claim Mum's personal effects, and she fought a fight I hadn't the stomach for when it came to the advanced donations – extracting the entirety of the bone marrow for storage. While I sat scanning the same words on the pages over and over, I heard her flat out "No," and then further away, "She doesn't want it. She needs to move on."

But I did sign the paperwork in the end, and that was the confirmation Aubrey stuffed in the shoebox, later. The staff must have snuck the form into a pile of other things, desperate to move the whole thing on with as little fuss as possible. I don't know what I'd have done at the time, if I'd known what I was giving away. It was a different time then. Mum was what Mum said, and did and made. She wasn't something you could grow in a jar. And that's just how I pictured it; faceless men in white coats and latex gloves growing a stomach or a kidney just because they could. Making it pulse and dance in a vat to see how long it twitched after they'd stopped feeding it. Mum's parts would be born predisposed with an appetite for peat smoke, whisky, turps, and with fingers itching to hold a brush, to plunge into paint and smear dye.

It was such early days then, for all this.

How things change. Back in the waiting room surrounded by Grove veterans, I'd have taken any of their hearts, livers or tracts to piece together Nut, if it would end with the three of us going home together. I didn't care from where the parts were sourced – Nut had always been worth more than the sum of her components.

It took forty-five minutes before the same tired-looking consultant returned and invited us into a private consultation room. Once we were in there, she dragged her chair closer to us as if she knew us well. Art leaned forward as if he knew her too. God, he looked terrible.

"I'm sorry, Fia isn't on call tonight so I'm stepping in. I hope that's OK?" The consultant's name tag read "Zoe". She seemed familiar, but I didn't think I'd had an appointment with her before. Perhaps she was one of the consultants assessing us during the early interactions?

Her voice was soft. "So firstly, it's awake, so don't worry, you've done nothing wrong." She smiled, one hand on my wrist and the other on Art's arm. She spoke the next part very slowly. "These things happen sometimes, and I wanted you to know that neither of you did anything wrong."

But would Nut be OK? Zoe hadn't said explicitly that she'd be OK. If she wasn't going to be alright, we must have done something wrong. It's cause and effect. Art spoke up.

"What happened, then? Is there something physically wrong with her? It?"

Zoe squinted and ran her tongue along the edge of her teeth. It only lasted a second before she switched to a smile, shrugging her shoulders in a way that struck me as inappropriately casual.

"Not necessarily. We're looking for the cause now, so we're going to keep it here for a while. Best guess is some kind of seizure; hence the spasms and rigidity. It can seem like a body isn't breathing at a time like this, when really it is. But the source of the seizure we don't know yet. It could be a fault with the biology, true, or it could be something else entirely. We'll look into it. It might be that if we find there's some flaw we can't fix, we'll switch it for another. Another ovum organi that won't be at risk."

Switch her? Nut was ours. Made for us. How could they consider replacing her just like that? And if Nut reacted so violently, did that mean there was something wrong with us? I looked to Art for reassurance, a sign he felt differently, but he was lost in thought.

I sat forward on my chair and braced my shield. "But she's been fine – not acting ill at all. I'd have seen if something wasn't right, I know I would have."

Zoe gave another irritatingly apathetic shrug. "It's sometimes the case that non-human matter hides its weakness if perceiving threat. It might be that it was sick all along."

Did she think I wouldn't have noticed this? I knew Nut. For starters, three simple reasons why this couldn't be; one, that for this to be true, Nut would have to consider us as predators, despite us being her only contact with a living world. Two, that Nut would have to understand her own illness and the sense of consequence to come from it if discovered. And three, that this meant she was *pretending* in order to survive, and that she could deliberately manipulate her own behaviour to manipulate ours in turn. Each of these meant that Nut was a thinking, feeling being, and this wasn't what Easton Grove had prepared us for.

Next to me, Art shook his head furiously. "But how the hell did this happen? How didn't you realise that it had a flaw at the beginning? It's fucking substandard."

That was it, turn it against her. Fight slander with slander. Besides, he was right. As part of the relationship with the Grove you offer up your trust to them completely. To give us Nut, a real living creature as a promise of our future, and then miss something in her physiology as vital as this? It beggared belief. It wasn't just jeopardising our mental wellbeing but our physical health too. Imagine what would have been if this had happened when we hadn't been there to check on her?

I reached for Art's hand and squeezed it. It was cold and clammy. "Thank God," he said, "that this happened sooner rather than later."

"Sometimes these things can't be detected in pup stage, and anomalies occur as they grow," Zoe nodded. "We'll do everything we can to save your ovum organi, but only if it's viable."

Zoe told us that they'd keep Nut in for a week or so to monitor her in quarantine. She assured us that we could visit in the evenings between 5pm and 8pm if we wanted an in-person update, but there wouldn't be much to see.

It was around 3am by the time we were free to go, but I wanted to see Nut before we started the drive back. Zoe showed us to the quarantine tank and then scuttled off back to pass some notes to reception. Nut was up and trotting about as if nothing had happened, pacing the length of her incubator with long strides and investigating each glass corner with her twitching nose.

This was the first time I'd seen Nut properly out of the loft, and in such stark light she looked *magnificent*. It was the only word for it. Her body was this full moon, round and bountiful, coated in thick, fluffy fur the colour of storm clouds. Her ears no longer stuck out like handles on a cup, and in fact had grown very little while the rest of her had swelled. Four paws, wide and hefty, gripped a green fleece, each digit capped by a long, black claw. Tubes trailed around her chest, roping through to a white box which flashed with red numbers, as if Nut was the power source for an engine. And her blue eyes – they looked at everything, drinking the light.

Before we left, Art made one last trip to the men's room while I stayed with Nut, mouthing her name through the layers of glass. She either heard me moving or caught sight of my hand on the window and came plodding over, lifting her frame onto her hind legs and pressing her paws against the glass. She knew me, and while she'd seemed happy enough in her tank before, she now pawed at the glass restlessly, agitated that she couldn't break through the barrier.

Of course, this was the other side of the coin. Not giving Nut her name would perhaps have protected her from us, too. I watched her blood ooze through a loop of plastic and pressed my fingers to my wrist. Was I feeling what she felt, on the inside? Was her heart thumping, just like mine was?

I owed it to Nut to visit her every evening after work. Art came with me the first couple of days, standing silently by my side, not sure what to say. But once he was assured that Nut was comfortable and there being no change in her status he chose not to come again.

At first, the receptionist had looked at me kindly and patted my hand when I checked in. She even made sure I knew how to get home when I left in the late hours. But as the days went on she spoke to me less, and then began to greet me tentatively, as if I really shouldn't be there but she didn't quite know how to tell me to stop. I'd brought Art's fleece from the loft, and now it lay scrunched up and unused at one end of the incubator, Nut having kicked it to the side. She'd look out for me visiting, and when she saw me open the door to quarantine she'd roll over and spread a wide paw on the glass, showing me her life line, heart line, head line. I'd lift my hand to meet hers, and repeat her name to comfort us both. Nut was always silent, but I knew she was glad I was there.

Each time I visited, Grove staff would repeatedly follow me into Nut's room to tell me that it was fine to go home, they'd update me if there was any change. One night, near the end of visiting hours, a pale faced consultant came in and tried to schedule me in for a genetic counselling session. I wasn't scheduled to have another one for months so I told her I was fine, I'd wait. By the way she watched my face I could tell she thought I was avoiding her, but the truth was I just hadn't the time, and if Nut was going to need extra attention when she came home I'd have even less of it to waste talking. She didn't insist.

Someone at the Grove must've been in touch with Stokers,

because they were far better about my being distracted than I'd expected. I even made a few stupid mistakes when punching in numbers. Markus – my manager – pulled me into his office to let me know that if I needed time off for extra appointments I could take the time off in lieu, an out of the ordinary generous offer from him. As I left, he called out my name, and I looked over my shoulder to see him attempt an awkward wink. "Great things happening for you soon, kid." It was disturbing.

It took thirteen days for the clinic to say they'd run all the diagnostics they could and couldn't find anything wrong with Nut. She appeared to be the picture of health, still viable, and the consultant made sure to tell us that while she'd been in the clinic's care she'd gained "a meaty two and a half kilograms".

Before we could bring her home, we were to come into the clinic together that weekend for a scheduled recap session on her care and be given instructions for how to monitor her in the weeks ahead. Art and I sat in the consultation room, hands clasped. Even though I found the idea of a "care recap" session incredibly patronising, I was so eager to get her home that I had forgotten to wear my usual Easton Grove armour. In fact, I was happy to accept every critical blow sent my way if it meant I could take Nut with us when we left.

To my surprise the consultant that joined us was the same Zoe we'd met on the night Nut was admitted, though this time she was almost unrecognisable. She was wearing a cast of make-up and a sunshine yellow tea-dress under her tweed blazer. I wondered if the colour was somehow supposed to help put me at ease. She pulled out some sheets of paper from the printer and scanned them slowly.

"It looks like a few temporary changes are in order but nothing too severe. I'm contracted to ask, though, if you've reconsidered the ovum organi in-patient option? I can see you turned it down during your early phases, citing..." Zoe looked at us under lowered brows, *"financial reasons.* So it's not part of your current fee, but just in case circumstances had changed I thought I'd mention it."

Biting my tongue, I let out a long, deep breath. "Our circumstances are the same."

Zoe nodded, one hand raised. "That's fine, I'm just obliged to ask. Sometimes people find the funds later – inheritances, family assistance, that sort of thing – and decide that letting us take over maintenance is the easiest option. Out of sight, out of mind, and all of that. And the option is always there for you, in case anything changes."

"That's fine."

Giving the paperwork a quick scan, I could see that most of it was a record of Nut's vital statistics; weight, length, blood type. The last page was all bullet points, each one a short line or two of instruction. Zoe tapped her fingers on the paper.

"You'll have to keep a closer eye on your ovum organi for a couple of weeks. I understand it has the run of your roof space at the moment? It's too much. It needs to be in more confined quarters, still with space to pace of course. Maintenance will be far easier this way. Do you have another secluded space or annex that you can doctor?"

I shot my answer at her like an arrow. "Yes, we've a room that'll be perfect."

"Excellent," said Zoe. "Keep the house heated between twenty-four and twenty-six degrees, too. It'll be a bit uncomfortable but it's only temporary. If only this had happened at Christmas!" Her laugh was shrill and shot through my head. God, the room was bright. Zoe pulled a white plastic bottle from the top drawer of her desk and checked the label. "These are for you too. It might be unenthusiastic about swallowing them. Grind them into its food, or if that doesn't work you may have to tag team. Arthur, you could hold the body down while Norah – you'll press one of these down its throat with your finger. Twelve hours apart. That's two a day, for the next ten days."

"What are they?" Art took the bottle, peering in close to read the tiny type. I could just about see mine and Art's names there and a barcode.

"Mainly a multivitamin and a dose of lysine. It'll help with any stress from the move between locations. Nothing to worry about, really. But what we do need to do is arrange a home visit for a few weeks' time. Evenings best for you?"

Art stared at the pill bottle and fiddled with his ear. I nodded and smiled, nodded and smiled, determined to push any issues I had with this to the back of my head for now. Definitely problems for later. Not today. Today was a good day. Nut was coming home.

Zoe brightened, and began typing into her laptop. "Excellent. We'll send you an appointment letter once we find a slot."

The door to the consultation room opened and Nut was brought in in a grey carry case with a netted fabric front. A clump of grey fur stuck through the mesh as if she was crushed inside. The relief I felt at seeing her, packed and ready to go, flooded up from my diaphragm. All was well. All would be well. We'd be back to the status quo soon enough.

But there were things we were going to have to deal with, and the drive back wasn't one of our best journeys. We were both tense, though I don't know if my reasons were the same as Art's. If we were meant to be of one mind, the mind was splitting and hiding its parts around corners. I sank into the passenger seat and shielded my eyes from the shocking flashes between trees.

"Why did you lie to them?"

I didn't know how to answer. I knew the answer, but it wasn't what he'd want to hear.

"I just wanted to get back to normal. We can make a room for Nut somewhere, it'll be fine."

"They know where we live, Norah. They'll know when they do a home visit that we don't have a spare room for her. What's it going to look like if you start lying to them?"

"I didn't lie. I said I had a room in mind, that's all."

"Fuck's sake, Norah." Art gripped the steering wheel. "We're on the same side here, you know. That's what we're paying for."

"I didn't like the assumption that we're not good enough because we don't have money for another custom annex. She has our files, she knows we don't have the big house, the cash to flash like the others. It was inappropriate. The same with asking us about inpatient residency for Nut. Where did that come from?"

"She's just doing her job, Norah."

"It's something we're never going to do. So why bring it up?"

"Hey, you never know what'll happen with us, we might get a windfall at some point. My book might make a mint, or you could scale the ranks at Stokers. Anything's possible. Everything we've got gunning for us now, it's a *positive* thing."

I didn't want to talk about it anymore and was frustrated that Art had chosen the wrong side. Easton Grove had done all they could for Nut, I'd give them that, but they were teasing us – holding us close then pushing us away. Why would they do that when they're supposed to be looking out for us? I didn't speak to Art again, and Nut stayed perfectly silent in her carry case on the back seat. The stalemate wasn't broken until we were only ten or so minutes from home.

"So where *are* we going to put her then?" Art asked. "Maybe we'll have to cordon off a bit of the loft."

"No, Zoe said we need to keep a close eye on her. It needs to be somewhere we can sit with her."

My idea involved using our bedroom for the next two weeks. It was a small and safe space, we could close the curtains and turn up the dial on the radiator, she'd have the run of it during the day, and she'd hopefully be asleep at night anyway. It seemed to be the most sensible solution. Art protested at first, but when I reminded him that the only other suitable room was his study he soon relented and went up to the loft to bring down Nut's sleeping crate, litter tray, and her food and water dishes.

Nut hadn't seen our bedroom before, so we needed to introduce her gently. We left the door to her carry case open and left her alone in the room with the door closed, thinking it would overstimulate her if we were there too.

Art coughed into his elbow and then pressed his ear to the bedroom door. "Do you think we need to buy a lock?"

We made sure the door was properly shut before heading downstairs for some breathing room. My hands shook with the same jitters I'd had on Nut's first day. We sat in silence in the kitchen, both of us not saying anything but listening for the creak of floorboards above.

12

Sometimes it's the silence that wakes me. It penetrates the void, louder than sound. My first thought is always, "Please be here. Please don't be gone. Please don't have died secretly in the night. How can I lift your body when I'm soft as butter, as weak as milk?"

But as autumn began to burn, Nut would always be there asleep under the bedframe, the curve of her back a mountain of heather, rising and falling between me and the light of sunrise.

Our new system worked well, at least at the beginning. Art would check on Nut during the day when he went to the bathroom or to grab something to eat, and he said her routine had hardly changed from her loft-days. Sleep, pace, eat, sleep. We kept the blinds closed so she couldn't be seen by the upstairs residents across the street, and lit the room with a daylight lamp. Whenever Art opened the door a crack and peeked inside, Nut would be either lounging sidelong on the floor or cleaning her flanks with long, sensual licks of her tongue. Every few hours or so she'd snap, and run around the room as if chasing a scuttling creature he couldn't see.

Every morning, Art would heave Nut onto the bed and pin her there while I vacuumed the thick minky layer of hair coating the carpet. Now that Nut was a juvenile, she didn't need it anymore, and even though we'd known this would happen I still couldn't help but check again with Art (as I went over the floor for the second time that day), "Is this definitely normal? Should she be losing this much at once?"

The only damage I could see from Nut having free run of the bedroom was that she'd started to pull up the carpet by the door so she could gnaw the floorboards. One morning, she'd pulled out the patchwork blanket from under my side of the bed and dragged it halfway across the room. Art picked it up by one bedraggled corner.

"Where did this come from?"

I sat up in bed and made my face go soft. "Aubrey made it for me when I moved into my flat. It's pretty old now."

Art's face twisted as he turned it this way and that. "Why's it so... mad? Didn't she know what she was doing?"

"She started off knitting it, see the yellow? But it took too long, so she sewed her old jumpers together to make the rest." I could still see her sitting in lotus position, finishing one row on her needles then punching the sky in victory.

Art was still staring at it, seemingly at a loss for words.

"I think she wanted to see my face when she gave it to me. If she'd kept on knitting it, that day would never have come."

"She never struck me as the future-facing type."

"She can be. Sewn together this tight, that old rag might even outlast you."

"Hmm." Art rolled up the blanket and thrust it on top of the wardrobe where Nut wouldn't be able to reach it again. "Not sure I'd be so proud of that, if I was her."

Anyway, pulling out what I stashed beneath the bed was small fry, considering how big Nut was getting. I never caught her doing anything she shouldn't, and by the time I went up to bed at around 11pm she'd already be curled in her crate, good as gold. She wouldn't even stir as Art came in and undressed an hour or two later. She'd sleep through our morning alarms, and only stirred at the clink of her food bowl being filled.

But this peace didn't last.

Perhaps it had been the stress of her time in the Grove that'd temporarily subdued her, but as the days went by Nut's sleeping pattern became disjointed, and she began to rise earlier and earlier each morning. She started to take her morning run at just past 3am, stomping around the space regardless of what stood in her way. At first, when she got to our bed she'd run beneath the frame, but soon she became emboldened (or wanted a challenge), and instead of scrabbling underneath, she'd vault onto the bed and leap over our heads in one terrifying arc.

It was impossible to sleep like that, and we moved our pillows half a metre down the bed so Nut had a clear runway and we'd avoid being crushed by her night-time stampede. I was exhausted but didn't want to let on, so painted on more lipstick and cream blush. Art looked terrible, and whenever he did drift off he mumbled incessantly. "What's she saying?", "Shhhh", "Too loud." Maybe no one else would have noticed, but standing side by side with him in front of the bathroom mirror revealed how pale he'd become, how his hair had darkened with oil. His lips were practically white.

I still couldn't concentrate at work. My eyes couldn't read the numbers fast enough, and shot side to side painfully in order to keep up. If I could just see this though, keep my head down, try to not make any more mistakes, it'd be OK. Every so often Markus would stroll past my cubicle and give me that same strained wink, his lip twitching in a way I'd never noticed before. Even he looked more tired, kept awake by some phantom.

A letter from Easton Grove arrived with instructions to book a home visit for the following Tuesday. I emailed them straightaway to say that Art and I wouldn't be around that day, and I didn't suggest a new date. I left it in their hands, my head buried deep under the dunes.

One night as Nut began her nightly parade, in a fit of desperation Art stood bolt upright and swore at the ceiling before opening the bedroom door and wedging it at the bottom with a dirty sock. He stomped across the landing, slammed the door to his study closed and climbed back into bed without as much as a word. He turned away from me and huddled beneath the covers, still and silent as if in a deep sleep. Had he just given permission for Nut to roam the house? I continued to feign sleep, dead to the heave of the bedframe, the catch of Nut's toenail in my hair.

At first Nut didn't seem to notice the change, and looped the room a few more times. But after a few minutes the pounding of her feet stopped, and she padded off onto the landing to investigate this new terrain. A whole new world for her to explore. Pinned between fascination and fear, I was desperate to see what she was doing but I was still pretending to be asleep. I'd committed to it now. Besides, maybe it was best if I wasn't the one to find her fallen down the stairs, or choking on a misplaced hairpin.

Despite all my wild imaginings, unbelievably I did nod off. And when I awoke, Art was already up and Nut was lying stretched out full-length on the bed, just where Art should have been.

We never talked about what Art did that night. I think he saw what he did as a chess move he couldn't retract and for better or worse he'd have to see it through.

Nut now had the run of the house. Every room was her domain except Art's study, the door to which was always closed. He said it was his inner sanctum and he needed quiet. This wasn't a bad thing – the room was a death trap – piles of heavy hardbacks and slippery plastic folders everywhere. Swallowable paperclips and pen lids. It wasn't the place for a curious creature only starting to learn the dangers of the world.

It was odd how easy it was to sleep with Nut running free around the place. It's a funny feeling, to just accept that calamity could technically occur at any time. It's not easily at home with me, that one. But maybe I just trusted her, or at least trusted her ability to handle what might harm her.

I wasn't as bothered about the house itself, even when on her mad runs she'd knock into table legs or the coat stand, causing relics of life to fall and break. Art didn't find it so easy. He continued to look worn out, as if his skin was stretched tightly across his cheeks and stitched beneath a tense jawline. He had the look of someone coming down with something, but whatever bug it was never materialised.

One night, after falling into bed, he whispered, "Do you think we should get Nut back into the attic soon?" I touched his face, shocked at how cold his cheek was. "I don't think we can do that now, Art. It's too late."

He didn't bring it up again, but continued to lose weight. Sometimes I caught him rubbing furiously at his temples and on either side of his nose. I asked him if he was perhaps allergic to Nut's shedding fur but he shook his head spasmodically. I suppose with growing up on a farm he'd know that already. Perhaps it was all this self-imposed pressure he put on himself to perform. He hardly left his study other than to eat or sleep, and even then he only stopped for a silent few minutes before running back upstairs with his plate and his mouth still full. Whenever I asked him to stay with me downstairs and talk for a while, he snapped at me, and accused me of not taking him seriously.

After Nut had had free rein of the house for around a month, I needed to do something to stop the shift I could see happening. Outside, the sky was getting darker, igniting with that autumnal red that lit the trees. I'd just been channel flicking in the living room, Nut curled up by my ankles, when Art ventured out of his study to the kitchen. I followed him and dragged him to the sofa by his wrist. He watched me do it without a word, and didn't even show the slightest spark of a fight.

I sat him next to me, making sure as much of our thighs were touching as possible. I kissed him fully on the lips and whispered, "Do you like that?" The whites of his eyes grew and his lips parted. The tip of his tongue flicked off a tooth. I kissed him again, and pushed him back into the sofa, straddling his lap. "What do you want to do now?" I crooned, coiling his hair around my fingers.

Did I look as desperate as I felt?

Art looked up at me, apparently speechless. I leaned forwards so our faces were enclosed within the dark curtains of my curls. "I'm kidnapping you."

He looked genuinely terrified. It was a game. *Just a game.*

He pushed me off and sat upright, his hands held in front of him as if to say "Wait". It took him a minute to frame his words before he spoke.

"I'm not myself, Norah. I'm sorry, I can't." He tucked my hair behind my ear. "I don't feel all that good today."

He looked beaten. I felt victorious. *It wasn't me.* He grasped the back of his neck. "I can't think. I'm hearing two voices all the time and I don't know which one's me, I don't know which one's right. I can't concentrate on anything and it's hurting me."

A giggle bubbled up my throat, but I gulped it down and furrowed my brow. Listening is bonding too. I'd bring him back. I stroked his hair and it felt soft and faint, not greasy like I'd expected at all. I guided his head down to my lap, and he sank into me, forgetting that I was another person and not part of his body. All the while, I wore my worried face, and a little piece of me tried to work out why I didn't care. It was sort of nice to have him limp and semi-conscious across my knee. All I wanted to do was make sure he didn't fall *too* ill, so sick that he needed official intervention. I could handle this. Hot broths. Blankets. Vitamin C. Ibuprofen. Easton Grove couldn't know.

If they caught wind of this, everything would go wrong.

I wonder now how things would have turned out differently if I'd just talked to him, or dragged him by his hair from that study, even when the door looked so firmly closed.

When the world was quiet, I sent Art up to bed while I turned off the lamps. The last room to do was the kitchen, and as I emptied our glasses down the sink I took a good hard look at the houseplants I'd arranged on the windowsill before New Year. They were dry as straw, their leaves emaciated and dark. The trunk of my yucca plant had become a thigh bone. Maybe the fertilisers hadn't been enough. Chemicals on chemicals. Fire on fire.

In the centre of the row, Aubrey's succulent still held her petals though they were in significantly lower numbers than last time I checked. Art must have thrown them out without telling me.

I looked past the boneyard into the garden beyond. The light from the kitchen only reached so far, illuminating the funereal bluebells. The far end of the garden was a void, but I swore I could still see the outline of the berry bush by the far fence, its branches stretching towards the house like arms. No matter how many times I went out with the hedge-trimmers, those limbs kept returning – reaching out into space for something solid to grasp onto.

13

Trash TV became my friend. You can trust the fair-weather faces of actors and news presenters to tell you the truth, and even a pre-written, cold script can warm the heart. It's selfish pleasure, guzzling it down because we don't have to give anything back. No pretending.

From coming home from work to going to bed I never switched it off, and yet never watched a single show all the way through. I couldn't lose myself in it like I used to. The characters seemed artificial, hollow, and I found myself picking my nails, pulling at loose threads on my clothes. Sometimes the TV schedule changed without notice and regular shows were replaced with feature length films featuring case studies of Easton Grove. A year earlier and I'd have guzzled these down, I might've even taken minutes. But now the only mental notes I made logged the glazed eyes of the "star", the way their hands sat clasped tight and white on their laps. And the things they didn't say. Whether there looked to be chains beneath the table, or a shadow of a puppeteer overhead. Whenever the show's focus moved to the ovum organi I switched over. I couldn't stomach it.

No. The only programme which had a chance of waking me up was the news.

One night that November, I was watching a "breaking news" bulletin on the sofa while I massaged Nut's shoulder blades. The announcement had been really built up, with teasers during the ad breaks all evening. When the time came, the newsreader could hardly contain her glee. She grinned from ear to ear, her finger scrolling through her tablet as the story unfolded. "A new development in the gifting of life", she called it. Her voice oddly clucking, she continued to explain that a new programme had launched officially today, and now older people with incurable illnesses could offer to donate their organs to the young as replacements or spares. These "persons in prime" had to be a blood relation and compatible, and in return the older donors received a premium to fund their funerals and settle their affairs. If the donation was a life-terminating one or they died within six months after the procedure, they also received an additional premium to go to a recipient of their choice.

This system had been in and out of the news for a few years but it wasn't until then that the law had finally been passed. The breathy newsreader cut to an interview with a flushed governmental official and a weak-chinned NHS senior manager, before showing footage of cheering families standing outside of their local hospitals, the blazing, unnatural sun making their skin glow. The report didn't say if the hospitals behind the young people reaching for the sky were regional branches of Easton Grove, or whether they were newer organisations springing up around the country, but I'm sure I caught the odd gleam of bronze pinned to the most crisply pressed lapels.

I tasted bile.

Though I could appreciate the sense of balance between the old and the new, what frame of mind must you be in to relinquish your life like that? Even if you'd been told your end was coming, what must it feel like to be willing to just give up?

In amongst all the officials and happy families, they interviewed one woman in her sixties who had campaigned for the law to be passed. She didn't look sick to me. Straight to camera, she said clearly, "This is an opportunity for us to pass on something truly valuable. Some of us might not have had children of our own, and this way a little bit of us will continue to do good even after we're gone. Who knows what great deeds we might accomplish? We can only hope that what we pass on is used wisely, and that we're remembered for it." Behind her I could see a placard bobbing up and down, with "Taking Back Control" painted in red letters. The interviewee looked straight into the camera lens and said, "*We* are not the vulnerable. *We* are the strong."

I leaned over and pushed my face into Nut's back, half-bald and still moulting. She'd lost nearly all the fur on her flanks by now, and you could see her thick pink skin glowing beneath the lingering fuzz. Since Art had told me he didn't feel right, I'd taken to keeping Nut close to me and periodically checking her soft fingers – newly broken through the buds of her paws – and her toes for missing digits, and running my hands along her back and belly for stitches, or scars. I combed my fingers through her coat, pulling out a grey clump between my fingers. We were both changing, growing into each other. She looked up at me with Art's eyes and I kissed her on the forehead.

Nut was my main source of companionship those nights. I used to go out a lot before this life; birthday nights, leaving dos, anniversary parties, or post-work catch-up coffees. I can't pinpoint the day it all changed, when all my intent curled back on itself so radically. Where had all those friends gone? How hadn't I noticed them slip away?

Before Art, I hadn't really thought about what "love" was, or what it meant. But this doesn't mean I hadn't experienced it. I suppose this is where Luke comes in. Luke's smile lit up a room, drawing people to him because he looked like someone who could make you feel better about yourself. But when they came to him he stuttered, too shy and self-conscious to understand why they would love him. He was tall and carried his head low, hiding beneath a fringe of curls. Words fell from his lips in gusts, as if he pushed his heart (still beating) painfully into the world just to reply to you.

He didn't stutter with me. Ever.

Even that first conversation we had at the bar. Brazen with too many margaritas, I stumbled up towards his friends, made sure I was close enough for him to see me, and danced with my arms in the air in my best attempt to mirror his shine. His friends turned and laughed at me before he did. He watched me with a straight face, hiding behind his hair. I danced harder, flicking my wrists and tipping my shoulders one after the other. I didn't care where my friends were or who was watching – all my drive was focussed on proving to him I was an equivalent flame. Slowly he started to smile, as if he'd finally understood something. I felt like a beacon in a lighthouse: "I'm here, I'm here". The next part I remember like a scene in a film; his finishing his drink, placing it on the bar, walking through the crowd, holding my hand. His eyes on my eyes all the time, letting me see through the curtains to where he kept his secrets.

I didn't feel like I'd won a prize, I felt like I'd opened a door. And the whole room, dark and dingy with dirtied posters and peeling paint, burst into colour and life. Tingles in every bump from a dancing stranger, in every crack of broken glass beneath our feet.

I don't know how long we stood like that, just opening up, but eventually he leaned down, pressed his forehead against mine, and whispered, "Do you want to go somewhere?"

Now, I wonder whether he didn't stutter because he didn't feel afraid of me. Or maybe he didn't love me as much as all that after all, and he didn't care enough. I could believe that. I can't imagine approaching anyone like I did in that bar now – how do I know what they'd do? Or say? How do I dance?

Luke wasn't a dancer. He was gentle, uncoordinated and long of limb, but he had the steadiest hand I'd ever seen. Hypnotised, I'd watch him paint his little figurines of soldiers and monsters and things long into the night. Even though his hand wouldn't appear to move at all, each figure would bloom with colour like a flower creeping open at dawn. I suggested once that the littlest ones must be goblins so he should do them green, but he just laughed, gave me a wry little smile, and told me that they weren't goblins, they were just children. He painted those with the most care of all.

I found him and everything he did lulled me into a deep sleep-state. Sometimes we'd just lie on his sofa for a whole weekend, dozing and fiddling with each other's fingers and toes.

Those were different days. The sister-me. Luke broke my heart, and even now I hate the day I met him, for life would have been without so much hurt if I hadn't known he existed. Years later, when I knew he must be long dead, I still felt the blow he struck me.

But anyway, even in those days I still had my own life outside of Luke. Life flickered by, yet I fit so much more in. But life with Art... no more invitations. Though I sometimes still heard whispers across the office about the same nights out, the same get-togethers. But no one told me about them anymore.

Later that month, after eight consecutive nights alone on the sofa without sight or sound of Art, I finally dared to break his law and open the door of his study. Just to ask him to the cinema. To see a film I knew he'd like. One evening contrived totally to his pleasure, whether I enjoyed it or not. How could he be angry at me for that?

"Don't, Norah. I need to get this. I need to get this right. Please."

His face was grey, the words croaking through a dry throat. In my opinion he shouldn't have been working at all, he was exhausted, but still – he *pleaded* with me to leave him alone. At least he didn't make a thing of me breaking into his study.

Screw him, I thought, and headed downstairs to look for Nut. She trilled when she saw me, and bounded over to rub her cheeks against my calves. I didn't want her to see me at such a loss. Here I was, depending on Art for entertainment when really I should have my own, right? Unfortunately, though the garden had started as a hobby it had become a manacle, a fight I couldn't win. I needed something else.

It wasn't that I couldn't think of anything to do; the world was full of things that would be fun to try, in theory. I just didn't want to be alone. Without a friend to point out the colours, I couldn't see them.

Paints. I'd paint it out.

The birthday art equipment was still in the kitchen cupboard. I dug them out and made my own "aviary" in the corner of the living room, setting the easel in front of our floral armchair. That's how my mum used to paint, by sinking into an armchair, with drinks, snacks, cigarettes, and all her comforts within arm's reach. Not that she touched them. When she painted, it was the only time she didn't need her vices. And now those pictures were hanging in hundreds of homes around the world, all alive.

My skin prickling, I pulled the patchwork blanket from the top of the bedroom wardrobe and wrapped it around my shoulders. Seeking grounding, I poured myself a scotch from a dusty bottle in the cupboard – my mum's favourite drink – and downed the entire glass in one blistering swallow. After settling in the chair, I began splashing the watercolour onto the page in wet flourishes, filling the paper with swooning blues, skin-pinks, and merry yellows. But I wasn't painting anything in particular, I was just covering up the blank space.

I dropped the brush into the water jar and noticed that I'd already managed to get paint on the patchwork blanket. My stomach lurched and I rubbed it between my fingers, adding a splash of water to dilute it and then cursing, because that water wasn't clean either. It was just typical of me to ruin it, within seconds of being independent. I took another swig of the scotch and tried to deaden the strange ticking that echoed in the back of my head.

I cast my painting on the floor and set up a new piece of paper, and with a pencil in my hand started to sketch the outline of my shape. Mum always sketched the top of the head then the feet, filling in the middle and then the background. But where could I be, in this imaginary space? I drew myself standing, but it could've been anyone. I sketched in a mane of curls down the front of the body so the figurative me could be looking at something in the distance. But what? Should I draw Art beside me, or Nut?

Before I put pencil back on paper the phone rang, a sound it took me a few seconds to recognise, muffled beneath a pile of unopened and unread post.

"Hello, lovely," Rosa said, her voice breathy and thin. "How... how are you?" She sounded quiet and far away. A stranger.

A sudden wave of guilt flushed up my neck. "I'm OK, y-you know how it is." I couldn't even get those few words out without stammering and I squeezed my eyes shut to hide from myself. *I needed to hold it together. She needed to think that I hadn't been alone all this time since New Year. That I was happy. That everything was perfect.*

Rosa jabbered on for a few minutes about her day at the university and I listened as best as I could, but the flood of words was overwhelming, and all the while I pressed my hand hard over my mouth to hold in the fireworks. By the time she stopped talking, it became even more awkward as it was now blindingly obvious to both of us that I hadn't even been listening. The silence fizzled. If she was waiting for a reply I wouldn't be able to help her there, so I desperately tried to think of something perky to say. But it'd been so long since New Year. It was almost winter again, and my world had changed as much as the seasons. Why had Rosa stayed away? In all this time she hadn't even called to ask about Nut.

Rosa went on to tell me that she and Eleanor were going for dinner that Friday night, and *"if I wanted to come"* we could make it a bit of a belated birthday night. *Very belated.* She said it in that same breathy whisper she'd greeted me with, and as we talked, I kept my ear open for clues to her detachment. She'd already made it seem so easy for me to say no, to wheedle out of it, even though she'd been the one to mention my birthday so many months earlier as a reason to join them. I would never have had to have a reason before, but I supposed everything was different now. This was the new world – split, some of us on one side and some of us on the other. Something in the way she spoke to me made me feel like I'd have to fight to accept the invite and cross the divide. That the whole phone call was "obligation".

But maybe I was being touchy. She was still my friend. We hadn't fought, we hadn't anything, in fact. No. I'd go, and work out the truth. I'd meet them at the restaurant straight after work – as I likely wouldn't get out until after 7pm anyway. I'd face them, and I'd face them smiling.

After hanging up the phone I packed away the easel and paints, and crushed my self-portrait into the recycling. My skin tingled, and I felt more awake than I had done in weeks. Those brief minutes of talking – *this* is what I needed. This.

The next day, I went to Stokers dressed for night. My nerves were like date-night nerves, the sort I used to get when Art and I would meet in the early days. In the afternoon, I jotted down some topics on a scrap of paper I could use as conversation starters, safe stuff, in case I dried up. Art's lecture, the garden. But when it came to Eleanor and Rosa's lives I had no idea what was going on, so I couldn't think of anything to ask. Any question would be broad and impersonal. Had it always been so complicated? I hadn't asked Rosa for any news while she was on the phone. Perhaps her sheepish tone was because she was hiding what she wanted to say, too.

From around 4pm my skin was prickling and my throat was blossoming. A frantic glance into the bathroom mirror showed me that the rash had bloomed up the sides of my face. I smeared on a stick of concealer, thick and chalky, powdering on a rosy flush to soften the camouflage.

As I was switching off my workstation, Markus stuck his head out of his office door and beckoned me with a curling finger. He wore the clichéd half-smile of a Bond villain. All these gestures and side-winks in the last few months, it was all new. I was in the infantry and he was in the white tower, and he'd always loved it there, you could tell. Our exchanges had only ever been one or two words as our paths never even came close to crossing. Lately, I was sure he'd even avoided me, sidestepping my cubicle to ask one of my neighbours for a figure or data file he needed. This had always been fine with me. In fact, I welcomed the ease that came with indifference. I never had to look him in the eye, as he never looked into mine.

But something about Markus was changing. Before, he'd stride, but now he shuffled with little urgent steps. When talking to colleagues in the middle of the office he'd tweak his nose, and sometimes scratch the side of his neck until it raged, red and angry. He kept his head down in the office until he came right past my cubicle and he'd shout "Good morning Norah," loud enough for everyone to hear, grinning from ear to ear. What made it particularly odd was the way he'd never wait for a response, but would continue on in his mad shuffle, still watching me out of the corner of his eye, and then lock his office door behind him.

Anyway, I dropped my bag back on my chair and followed Markus into his office. After a quick glance to see who was still in the wider office, he closed the door behind me and gesticulated in the direction of the seat in front of his desk. I hardly had time to sit before he started to talk in a strangely shrill voice:

"How are you doing, Norah? You're here late on a Friday."

"I'm OK, I was just finishing–"

"Here's the thing, Norah, I've been watching you for a while and frankly, you've been overlooked."

"I don't think–"

"I have to apologise for that. No, I want to apologise. You get your head down and you work, you're solid. You don't shout up but that's to be commended. The hardest working people do the work, after all. I'm going to look into how I can improve things for you. I'm sorry. I'm so sorry."

Markus had been standing, but once he'd finished speaking he sank into his leather chair. Slumped low and fiddling with the edge of the desk, he didn't meet my eye.

"Do you accept my apology?"

I hardly knew what else to say other than a quiet "Yes." All of his colour drained, Markus took a deep breath and pushed himself up in his seat. He waved his hand towards the door, regaining a little of his old dismissive style. "Go on, go home. You shouldn't be here so late anyway."

It was such a weird interaction. It was as if he thought I held him to account, and I certainly didn't. And even though he grovelled, I knew that he didn't care. What did he mean by "improving things" for me? They were fine as they were. Maybe a bigger cubicle would be nice, or a pay rise. But otherwise it didn't seem an exciting prospect that my work-life would change. In all this time it hadn't even crossed my mind to wonder how the different departments worked where I wasn't involved, or to try to work out what Markus' job actually was. Like most of my faces, Stokers wasn't my life, it was a means to an end.

14

In the taxi, I couldn't shake off the peculiar, creeping feeling Markus had left with me. Through the window, a dance of young girls in their glittering dresses mingled with couples hand-in-hand, trussed up tightly for each other in coordinating jackets. My outfit already felt tired and ready to be changed, and for the length of the journey I tried to iron out the creases with the flat of my palm.

We were meeting at a little Japanese place near Eleanor's estate agents' office. I loved that restaurant. It wasn't huge or flashy; it was actually quite small and always dimly lit by antique yellow lanterns on the walls, even on the sunniest of summer days. The light hardly made it through the front windows, so most people passing probably thought the place was closed and didn't come in. But that's why I liked it. It felt like a secret den. I'm not sure I'd have made those aesthetic choices myself, but I liked the fact that management had sacrificed success for atmosphere.

The restaurant's speciality was a menu of over a hundred types of cultivated sushi, all listed in a little paperback book on each table. Some of them just *had* to be made up. Each little dish had a name and price, and a description of how it was made and the provenance of the ingredients. The back page was reserved for whatever real fish dishes were available that day. Usually there'd only be one or two, usually peachy salmon or snapper, and the cost was enough to make my eyes water. I sometimes wondered what the flesh might feel like on my tongue, slipping around like it was still living.

Before, while Aubrey, Rosa and Eleanor always debated the menu and ordered something different each time – sometimes the four of us breaking down with laughter at how horrendous most of them turned out to be – I always ordered the same thing. They'd usually berate me for that, Aubrey being the first to say, "But Norah, you've had that a million times. It's dull!" Prompting me to remind them all that I wasn't willing to pay extra for something I didn't understand and probably wouldn't like. Nonetheless, I loved seeing the mysterious little plates being carried from the kitchen. It was a huge part of the place's appeal for me, and though we'd been to the restaurant countless times I still felt like I saw something new and colourful every time.

But it wasn't just the dishes that fascinated me, it was the way people approached eating them. Some would be straight in there with chopsticks, expertly breaking the structure down into perfect-sized morsels containing a little piece of each ingredient in every mouthful. But then some people didn't know what to do, and those were my favourites. They'd start with the chopsticks and try to pull apart this unknown thing to understand it, as if dissecting a model heart in biology class. They'd taste the mystery lumps and stalks one by one, pulling the oddest expressions as they worked out whether they liked it or not. And then others, after failing to lift a single mouthful between the sticks at all, would then migrate to a fork – and stab at the sushi with renewed confidence. As if none of their previous embarrassment even happened. They were all children exploring new toys. I think some parts of us never grow up.

On entering the restaurant, I spotted Rosa straightaway, her shoulders draped in a thick orange shawl she'd probably made herself. She stuck out like a sore thumb amongst the tables of sleek black dresses and crisp shirts, and on seeing her my stomach did the oddest little flip. She'd spread her belongings across our favourite corner table, owning it like a falcon would her nest. Rosa stood up when she saw me and wrapped me in her arms.

"Eleanor's just in the loo. Sit, stranger."

I dropped awkwardly onto the chair opposite and saw there was already a glass of wine sitting there. I started to move to the next chair along but she stopped me. "No that's for you. Happy birthday." I thanked her, and said that I'd wait for Eleanor to return before I celebrated with a slurp.

After Eleanor swooped back in and sat next to Rosa, my skin really started to prickle. Sitting side by side, they assessed each part of me like an interview panel, their eyes scrutinising everything from the flyaways at the top of my head down to the thread dangling from a loose button on my velvet shirt. My clothes felt tight and twisted, and I desperately wanted to fiddle with my hair but instead clasped my hands together on the table behind the wine glass. Had I changed that much since December 31st? They looked at me as if waiting for me to reveal something, something they couldn't ask outright. What did they know? Had they spotted the engagement ring, perhaps? I slipped my hands beneath the table ledge and asked the innocuous question, "How's Aubrey these days?"

Eleanor raised her glass to her lips. "Oh, she's alright. She's been having a tough time of it at work. She thinks the shop's closing. Imminently. And quite predictably, too."

Rosa chipped in: "Really? It was packed out last time I was there."

Eleanor shrugged. "Meh, it's just what she said. She's having a rough time of it anyway. I'm seeing her next week at some point."

So, though they'd both seen Aubrey, they hadn't seen her at the same time. They likely had different ideas about how she was. Neither of them seemed to want to pursue it.

"She's been asking after you," Rosa said. "What you're doing, when we're seeing you."

"Did you call me because she'd told you to?" I spat it out, the anger already building. Aubrey wasn't even there, and she still had the ability to make me fume. She'll have been spying on me to find out if I'd admitted making a mistake, and was now having to live with what I'd done. In other words, that I knew that she was right.

"Don't be bloody stupid," Eleanor scoffed. "You're letting yourself down here, Noz. Stop it."

"Well it seems a strange coincidence, doesn't it? Aubrey wanting to know if my choices are working out, a phone call out of the blue–"

"Norah," Eleanor's voice was low, bristling. "It's *you* that hasn't been in touch with *us*. We've both tried to message you, but you've never replied. So don't blame us, OK? It's insulting."

Beneath the table, my hands gripped my knees. The three of us had only been together five minutes and already it was all going wrong. It had been fine at New Year... OK, not brilliant, but fine. So why was it falling to pieces now? If Art had been here he'd have helped to diffuse the situation, but this time I was alone. I lifted my glass of wine and in two swift gulps finished it off. Eleanor sighed and topped it back up. I took that as an apology from her, so thought I'd take the high ground and move the conversation along. Something I could control. I'd talk about work. That would do.

I was about to speak when a squeal ripped through the air. All three of us turned to a table by the window, at which a couple were cooing over a swaddled bundle on the table. They'd moved aside the plates and glasses, and were inspecting the exposed face like a precious specimen. All the while, the bundle twisted side to side like a caterpillar.

"Have you been back to the clinic, Elle?" asked Rosa, quietly.

Eleanor hissed slowly through her teeth. "Just once. I'm hardly a priority though, am I?" She fluttered her arms up and down her body. "Poor and mightily single as I am. Back of the queue."

"Have they mentioned any treatment," I said, "for whenever the time comes?"

Eleanor looked at me and I caught a brief but violent flicker of annoyance. It could only have been a microsecond, but I felt its tail like a whip. She blinked and it passed as quickly as it'd appeared. "No, not yet. Besides, it's going to take a long time to save up, anyway."

Rosa sat back and pursed her lips. Eleanor obviously didn't want to go into it, and I was happy not to. Happier things. *Light and airy.*

"What did you think of Art then?" I said. "I never had the chance to ask you what you thought since the party – if you can remember." I tried to laugh.

Eleanor pouted. "Audaciousness, that's what I remember. He was… audacious." She took a sip of wine and leaned forward conspiratorially. "But honestly, I hate him. I hate you both. You're both so extremely attractive and yet extremely unavailable. Typical."

"Just your luck." Rosa prodded Eleanor in the arm.

Eleanor waved to the moustachioed waiter behind the bar and pointed to our wine bottle, already down to the last inch of red. "Fucking cheek," she smiled. "Hopefully I'll get one of you so drunk tonight that I'll have my way with you anyway."

"Cheers to that." We clinked. More like it.

Rosa leant forward across the table. "And we didn't know he was some sort of famous writer. You kept that one quiet."

I felt the need to play this down. "He's not all that famous. But he wants to be. Or at least, he wants to do something famous."

"Hasn't he done that already? Now that I know what to look for, his books are everywhere."

"It's true," Eleanor added. "After I got home from your party, I realised I'd had one on my shelf for who knows how long. All this time. Seems I've known him longer than you have, Noz."

"Ah," I pointed my finger in the air. "But have you read it?"

Eleanor smirked and raised her glass. "No."

"That's it, though," I laughed. God, I'd missed this. "Neither have I. And from what I can tell even people who have read them forget what they're about straightaway. That's what Art says. But commercially, it works. People don't retain the plot, so they buy another. And it doesn't matter how similar the stories are because no one remembers. The only inkling you get that you've read it before is a nice cosy sense of familiarity, and that doesn't sound bad at all."

They both nodded. "Well," Eleanor replied. "He's got his head screwed on, hasn't he?"

"And is he, you know," Rosa whispered, "rich?"

I thought about it. We never discussed our personal accounts apart from when we worked out bills and expenses. Art's earnings were a mystery to me. He was never ostentatious with money, but then if he really did earn a lot from his work then surely he wouldn't have needed me. We wouldn't have met, and we definitely wouldn't be together. That there was the cold, hard, truth of it. He wouldn't be sharing this life with me. If his parents were scatterers, they wouldn't be able to help him. Art was on his own. Perhaps it was no surprise that he kept a close watch on his statements, in case he ended up wearing the same bleached overalls, his skin beneath them burning.

I smiled at Rosa. "Question mark, I'm afraid. We each keep something private. Though I don't think the bards of this world ever set out to be the richest."

Eleanor looked confused. "I don't know. If he's already got his name plastered over every bestseller list in the country and he's not bothered about money, then what does he want? What's he keep pushing himself for?"

I shrugged. "Now he wants to write something that'll last. He hardly tears himself away from his laptop."

"Let him. We all need our little hunts. As long as the money keeps rolling in, he's taking care of you." Eleanor's merciless conclusions were usually right.

They thought he was taking care of me, so I'd show them, I'd prove to them he was. I pulled out my left hand from under the table and held it out for them to see. They both stared at my hand like owls; all bulbous, unblinking eyes and pursed bills. Claws perched on the table edge.

"He asked me to marry him."

Rosa was the first to break their paralysis with a squeal and a flap of her hands. She leapt up to my side of the table and wrapped me in her arms, stamping her feet at the same time. Eleanor smiled slowly, and though Rosa was draping herself all over me I kept watching Eleanor. She was thinking, churning something over in her head, and though I wanted to get drunk on Rosa's enthusiasm, a well-considered response was far more valuable.

Eleanor reached across and took my hand, stroking the opal with the pad of her thumb. "It's beautiful," she whispered. "And you're happy?"

Rosa plonked herself back in her chair. "She must be. Oh, it's a freaking fairy tale."

Eleanor kept her eyes on me. "You're definitely happy?" She held me in her sights, not letting go of my hand. Rosa looked from Eleanor to me and back again. "Because this is serious now. This is the big game."

I pulled back my hand. "I know that."

"And this is definitely what you want? You're sure? This is totally different to, well, all the other stuff."

"Yes."

"You love him, now?"

"Yes, I do."

"And he loves you? As he should, for this?"

"Yes. He wouldn't have asked me otherwise."

Rosa took my hand from Eleanor, seemingly to look at the ring but I could tell she was trying to diffuse the tension. This was her way but there really wasn't any need – you had to expect this from Eleanor. In one conversation she could swoop from elation to fury in a matter of seconds. She was very much alive, Eleanor, and her passion was infectious. I've never felt so angry at injustice or at politics that I hardly understood than when I was with her. And if, poor you, you became the focus of her wrath, you'd fold up at a mere look, shrinking until invisibility owned you.

Eleanor let out a heavy sigh, and smiled, as if she'd conceded. But I didn't want it to be over quite yet. "Don't you believe me?"

She fiddled with a napkin, rubbing it between her fingers and thumb. "I just think it might be too soon. Don't you agree? And don't you think it's extremely convenient? I mean, it's fucking perfect, but it's also fucking unlikely. Don't you think it's all a bit much?"

"Why do you have to think about it at all? It's *my life*. Can't you just be happy for me?"

"I'm fucking delighted for you, Noz. I just want to make sure this is right for you. It's not our world that you're living in. I just need to be sure that this isn't something you're doing to impress. When I know, we'll get even more drunk to celebrate. That's all."

"You've made that clear. Let me work out what's good for me."

Rosa had given up trying to break the strain, and was staring at the table top, her lips puckered in a child-like pout. Her purple lipstick had smudged across her cheek. Eleanor leant over and wiggled her fingers in the fur of Rosa's shawl as if scratching a cat. "Don't worry, kitten. I'm done. Obligatory friend-care-taking done. You can get back to planning your bridesmaid dress now."

Looking back, I suppose I'd have said the same if our situations had been reversed. She was just looking out for me, though she'd acted cruelly, backing me into a corner like that. I don't think she realised that she'd stabbed me somewhere delicate, and that her knife was so shrewd that I couldn't heal. Hidden in those deep nooks there were secrets even I didn't want to face.

Eleanor reached below the table. "I'd brought you this as a belated birthday present, but it can be an engagement present too, now. Merry birth-engage-day." She pulled out a parcel wrapped in shimmery green paper. I took it reluctantly, on edge as if this was a trick.

"Open it."

I peeled back the foil and found within the folds a paperback. It was clearly old, and smelled like I'd imagine bones to smell, somehow dry and damp at the same time. It reminded me of school trips to libraries that had their own special taste on the air. It was like something seeped from people into the books. On opening a cover, it was perfectly acceptable to see stains, maps to someone else's skin.

This book could have been an antique, but it still held itself together with some stability. It felt heavier than it looked as if the pages were lacquered, and the front was embellished with swooping illustrations of seagulls. The title in big white letters read, *Common Birds of the British Isles*.

Flicking through the pages, each bird had its own double-page spread of sketches showing the bird in flight from the ground, the head in profile, feather markings, and nesting habits. It might have been from when Mum was young, when it was easy to spot birds at the coast or over gardens.

"To match your mum's binoculars," Eleanor said. "You might not spot anything soon, but it doesn't mean you should stop looking. And this way you won't look like a pervert hanging out of your bedroom window."

In lieu of an embrace I squeezed the book between my hands, taking comfort from the strength of its binding, the physicality of it, anchored in time and place. *This was from a time when the air didn't taste this way.*

I don't know what Eleanor meant by giving it to me. It was a really thoughtful gift, but it filled me with a sorrow I couldn't quite fathom. Rather than gain a present, it was as if I'd lost something. I thought back to the feather I'd taken from Mum's house, where it had been collected so carefully and stored up high – where it belonged. Even though Mum must've told me a hundred times what bird it came from, I couldn't now remember the name. I flicked through the pages looking for a creature that looked similar but they were all little unremarkable brown things, not black or blue. I pushed the memory from my head.

The thing was, the chance of seeing any of the birds in the book were so few and far between I could waste my life with my eyes on the sky. Rather than a guide for the present day, the book was a relic of a time that would never return. I didn't want the others to see this, so I clutched the volume to my chest, thanking Eleanor with honest tears in my eyes. She leaned forward and gave me a wink. "The future's bright, kiddo. The birds might come back one day."

By the time we wrapped up the evening, I'd lost the feeling in my legs. I only realised how much I'd had when pulling on my coat seemed more difficult than escaping a straitjacket. When I tried to stand up, I managed to knock over the empties with the swing of a padded sleeve. *Strike.*

As ever, despite her tiny frame, Rosa managed to hold herself together with the most decorum. I've never understood the biology behind that. Maybe it's nothing to do with size, and Rosa had just been born with the innate ability to fight toxins with efficiency and finesse. Easton Grove would have liked that.

Rosa cajoled us into our taxis, before calling her current boyfriend to pick her up. I hadn't yet met Mike, but then I rarely ever met any of Rosa's boyfriends. You almost didn't need to, they were always the same – poetic, usually bulky, and a little on the sullen and protective side. Not the best sense of humour. It's like she was deliberately seeking her opposite, to balance herself out.

By the time the taxi reached Dukesberry Terrace I was starting to feel sick. Even I could hardly make out the incoherent vowels I gurgled to the driver, so I signalled for him to stop at the end of the street by gesticulating – pointing at the floor and then to me. He seemed to get it without even needing to turn his head, and when he pulled to a stop I quickly flashed my plastic over the card reader and scrambled out onto the pavement.

The nausea subsiding, I felt more alive than I had in months. The sound of my breath felt obscenely loud in the metallic drum of sky. I'd lived here with Art heading for a year exactly, and I still wasn't used to the taste. I leapt over the cracks between paving slabs as if they were gullies, ravines, canyons. I'd never moved so fast, so ferally.

The street was silent, lit only by a few orange street-lamps, and above, the purple sludge of space hung low, almost close enough to touch. How long had it been since I thought I'd seen stars? Mum would watch from the kitchen window, binoculars glued to her face, and even when I pulled at her elbow she wouldn't look down. I thought I'd seen them with Luke once, through the observatory roof, but I don't know. Maybe it was just rain on the glass. But still… The smoky canopy above the street was like the velvet in the lid of a precious box, so I swung my bag around me like a moon in orbit – stretching out my arms into the soft space above, the thick, warm hug of it. Like water. Freedom. The aching in my feet was gone, my whole body full and whole. I felt like a god, like the world was full of possibility, blessed with time, and it was mine to seize while everyone else slept. I thought back to Mum telling me that she used to ask the clouds for a sign and they'd tell you the future. Even when I was no taller than her elbow I'd shaken my head and rolled my eyes. But here I stood, in what felt like a fallen cloud, all damp and magical lilac, and what could be more fortuitous? I looked up into the sludge and didn't ask for a future – I thought of Art and *commanded* it. But what image came into my head instead? Nut. I shook off the rush of feeling and twirled, owning the street, the world – all on my own. Here, loneliness was a virtue, not a drain. I could be the god of loneliness.

Too soon I reached our purple front door, and I leant against it with both palms to centre myself before going inside. I had my key in my hand for some time before I stuck it in the lock. Beside the front door, the living room curtains were drawn, but around them cracks of light shone gold. Had I left the lights on since morning? No, I don't think I'd even gone in there. I imagined Nut turning on the lights for herself, and settling down on the chintz chair with a cup of tea and a flapjack. I chuckled at the front door and turned the key.

But it wasn't Nut. It was Art, stretched out on the sofa with a pizza box across his belly, a beer in his hand, and a car chase on

TV. Out from the dim light of his study, I was seeing him for the first time in weeks. He was so thin that his shirt collar hung down in front of his chest, and his one visible hand looked practically blue. All white-knuckled and flaking skin. His eyes were sunken, the whites dull.

But still, the worst of it – *how many nights* had I waited for him to come out of his study? How many nights did I ask him to join me, how many nights did I sit alone while he lost himself within himself upstairs, like a glutton? And here he was, taking the first opportunity when I wasn't there to sit in our living room like it was an absolutely normal thing to do. He'd even ordered food.

He lifted himself up on his elbows and looked at me up and down, smiling wryly.

"Well hello there, wifey. Good time?"

"What the fuck, Art?"

I needed him to think I wasn't drunk so I leant backwards on the wall. Art flicked his head from me to the TV and back to me. "What? It's not porn."

"Why are you here? What are you doing?"

"I thought I'd take a night off, get some space. It was your idea. My editor's going to kill me anyway."

No. No. He'd broken the rules. My skin hurt. The weight of my necklace on the back of my neck, the pinch of my dress at my elbow, my hair sticking to the sides of my face. I wanted to tear it all off and stand there on fire and scream, *This is who I am. This is who you're assigned to.*

But I didn't. If this was all a game to him, I'd roll the dice. The tiny part of me that could still think thanked the god of loneliness for the booze in my blood. I needed its venom.

"What's happening, Arthur? Where've you been? Don't you want to be with me?"

Art raised his eyebrows and flattened back into the sofa. I suppose in all the distance we'd come, I'd never spoken to him so bluntly. After a few seconds he regrouped, and spoke in a low and level tone, like a teacher to a student. "Are you changing your mind?"

I stood there, too furious to say "No" but terrified to think he thought I'd say "Yes".

"'Cause you know," he whispered, stretching his arms wide, "none of this should be a surprise. You knew what I wanted. When I signed on that dotted line, you signed too. Partnership."

So that was it? If he wanted officiality, I'd give him officiality.

"Partnership?" I spat the word back. "Where *is* my partner? I never see you – and the only time your show your face is when I'm not here. You have to make a fucking effort, otherwise what's the point?"

Art pushed himself forward, colour rushing up his neck. "An effort? I *am* making an effort. You *know* I've struggled to work since all this started. If I can't make this work, that won't only be the end of my career but the end of all this," he gestured at the walls, the ceiling, me. "I don't have an inheritance to chip away at. I got nothing. I have to make more, all the time. Do you want me to stop earning? Is that what you want?"

Obviously I didn't, but I'd be damned before I'd let him see it. He deserved nothing.

"Norah," he reached out a hand to me, palm open. "I'm just doing what we set out to do, together. It's *you* that keeps changing the rules."

Oh, really? It was as if I'd stepped out of my body, just for a second, and watched myself clinging to the wall like a great sucking leech. Was this why Art looked so thin, so exhausted? Was it my fault? No, he was different, and he was trying to save face, surely. He asked me to marry him. *Marry him.* That doesn't sound like a business partnership, that's love. And as you both grow, and progress, your love grows and changes too. It has to, otherwise, it shatters.

Art stood up and wrapped his arms around my waist. His hair pressed against my cheek and the salty tang of chemicals filled my head. Despite myself, I started to feel warm, and stroked my hands up his back. Fights were healthy. Fights were productive. Fights cleared the air. We'd promised to always be honest to each other about what we wanted, maybe *this* would be our real beginning? Lately we'd hardly spoken to each other about anything other than Nut. What about *us*?

"Where's Nut?"

"Hmm?" Art whispered into my ear.

"Where is she?"

"Not sure. I haven't seen her in a bit. Probably in a boat off to Paraguay or something."

"I'll go find her. I'll come back and we can finish this." I pressed my lips against Art's cheek and began my tour of the house, trilling and tutting and calling her name. She was nowhere to be found on the ground floor so (only slightly concerned at this point) I continued my hunt upstairs while Art lounged into the sofa and glued his eyes back on the TV screen. As I stumbled my way upstairs, I hoped Art was still thinking about what had just happened. I hoped it worried him.

"Nu-ut!" I called for her in a sing-song tone, as if we were playing hide and seek. After a few more minutes of searching I called down to Art. "Arthur, where is she?"

I heard the TV go silent and Art appeared at the front of the stairs. "I don't know, somewhere around the house, I suppose."

He wasn't being flippant, but I gritted my teeth as I responded, "I can't find her anywhere."

He looked up with a baffled smile and impassive eyes. "She has to be somewhere. I've not even been outside today." Art shuffled to the kitchen, and I heard the creak of cupboard doors being opened and slammed and kitchen chairs being dragged across the floor. I waited on the landing, desperate for him to prove me wrong. He emerged from the kitchen and leapt the stairs two at a time, sticking his head in the bathroom and finally our bedroom. We were both silent as he followed the steps I'd just taken, checking everywhere Nut had access to.

She couldn't have vanished.

Tick tick tick tick tick.

A thousand scenes were streaming through my head one

after another, and in all them Nut appeared prostrate, trapped in cupboards, crushed under the wheels of a car on the motorway. She'd never seen the world; she wouldn't have a clue. She wasn't made to understand a world of threats. She was pliable, personable. If she got into the wrong hands, or if Easton Grove found out about our negligence, we'd be excommunicated. Or worse. I pictured the detention centre, the windowless bunker. We didn't know what happened inside. Why didn't we ever ask?

My head was light and fuzzy, the world fading into black and white. If I'd been out only one night and something had happened... *What had we done?*

"I can't believe this." Art held his head in his hands as if trying to unscrew it from his neck. "I haven't been anywhere, she has to be here."

I leant back against the wall, my hands spread across the paint and listening for the reassuring heartbeat-like thump-thump-thump-thump of her feet. Perhaps if I pressed my ear to the paint the house would tell me, whisper to me what happened to our little life.

"You don't think," Art blurted, "that when you came in just now you let her out?"

No, no, I'd have felt her. That round, voluptuous body would have knocked me to the side if she'd passed by. Nut was not a creature to slink. By now she stood thigh-high, her back the width of a coffee table.

"Norah, did you leave the door open?"

Was this me? My fault? *My head. My head.*

"I'm not stupid," I croaked. But still – I glanced at the front door. She could just be on the other side of it, sitting to be let back in, but if she was there it meant it was my negligence, not Art's. If I looked, I'd be admitting it.

Art reached for his cardigan and snatched the keys from the side-table. While Art went into practical mode, I clung to the bannister with both hands like an old coat.

Losing Nut meant we'd lose everything. We'd have violated

our contract with Easton Grove. There'd be no replacements. Everything we had would be meaningless, and everything connecting Art and I would disintegrate. And worst of all – the most plunging feeling deep inside my gut – was that Nut would be alone and suffering without me, thrust into a selfish world she wasn't made for.

All my fault.

But just as Art stuck the key in the door, there was a thump on the landing. Art flipped his head around, and I followed his eyes to see Nut gambolling down the stairs as if greeting us home. I fell hard on my knees and buried my face into her fleshy middle, the full and hot roundness of her belly overwhelming my face, my hands, my chest.

Behind me Art thumped his elbow against the wall and let out one long breath. "Thank fuck. Where the hell was she?"

I didn't care and pushed myself under her skin, breathing in her hot musk. Art reached down and pushed the heel of his hand hard across her spine and she flexed against it, grunting with each bump. I sat back into Art's legs, between my two lifelines, finally able to think.

"No." Art stepped around me and started up the stairs. Looking up I saw that the door to his study was ajar. It had been closed before, it was always closed whether Art was in there or not. We hadn't checked the room for Nut because there's no way she could have got in there.

Art pushed the door open gently and stepped inside. Still holding Nut, I called up to him. "What is it?" The house responded with silence.

"Art?" I pulled myself to my feet and followed him, clicking my fingers at Nut for her to stay by my ankles. Art was standing in the middle of the study staring at the floor. At first, I couldn't see what he was looking at and the room looked very much like it always does, a jumble of ideas and chaos. Stained mugs and plates with dried-out crumbs were stacked along the windowsill, and the surface of his desk was so full of papers and notebooks that there wasn't an inch of wood visible. In its own way, the study was the whole house, condensed into one room. A world, poured into a womb.

"Look." Art pointed at the floor. I stood beside him and followed his gaze to a hip-high mountain of books. This pile wasn't a random stack like the others; the books had been stacked horizontally, the angle of each adjacent book just so that the wall of the structure curved around. Between each row of closed hardbacks there were stuffed paperbacks or pages of foolscap. The more I looked at it I couldn't see how I'd assumed it was just another of Art's hoards. It was an igloo, complete with a small opening at the front.

"She did this," Art whispered.

"No." I knelt at the foot of the mountain. "How?"

Art remained stuck to his spot. His face was grey, his lips cracked. "I've dreamed of a fort like this. It's made up of all my favourite places to go. It's a good dream."

Nut hadn't followed us in, and was sitting in the doorway, her tail swishing proudly behind her. Peering into the igloo's chamber I could see a nest, made of torn-up paper. But it didn't feel right to stick my arm in. It would be intrusive. Art didn't seem to think so, and kneeling in front of the hole thrust his arm inside. After a few seconds of fumbling he sat back up, clutching what looked like wet ribbons, ragged and bright. They were paper streamers, half-chewed and torn, and flaking with red and blue and brown, drifting from them like dirty snow.

Art leaned further into the den, sweeping his arm across the floor to gather the shreds. He started to move pieces around as if assembling a jigsaw, but an infuriating second-hand jigsaw that you discover to be missing half the pieces after you've committed to it.

As the pieces shifted it began to dawn on me exactly what it was that Nut had dragged back to her cave. All of Art's paintings of me from my birthday, clawed apart and half-consumed by our first-born.

15

Shocks, jolt.

Though the walls are the same, our clothes are the same, we eat the same food, we speak in the same subtle accent we're deaf to – the world is a different place. Colours and abrupt sounds shock like a defibrillator, just as we think our hearts are settling. New fears lurk around every corner, the stick ever-raised to whip again.

Never before had I been so utterly responsible for another living thing, a creature that was as unable to articulate its needs as a new-born. What sort of person was I if I couldn't look after her? Sometimes I'd be doing the dishes or watching TV, and suddenly need to know exactly where Nut was, or I'd be at work and imagine Nut loose in Dukesberry Terrace, hanging out of an upstairs window by a single claw, or lying prostrate across some dark corner, locked in a second seizure. I'd text Art and he'd reply so quickly that I can only guess that he had been sitting with her all that time. Perhaps she was in his study, curled around his ankles or sharing his lunch.

Mistreatment of your ovum organi was an offence resulting in termination of membership, and expulsion from all the benefits that came with it. And where would I end up without the guidance of my mentors? You never heard about anyone this happened to, which made me wonder where they went. Were all we members really as pliable as that?

Losing Nut due to something as stupid as not looking when I opened the door would definitely be seen as negligence, especially since I'd lied about her having her own secure room. There was no way I could return her to the loft now, now that she bumbled around the house like it belonged to her. It would be like removing a child's favourite toy.

But more than that. Nut had a soul. I could see it now. And when she balanced on my thighs with her hands on my chest, she'd smile and I'd smile back. Her little face brightened a room, and the world was made a better place by her being in it. *If only there could be more of you*, I'd whisper in her ear, *each one helping me to be better.*

This was a new kind of love. But if Easton Grove got wind of what had happened they would take her away. And what would happen to her then?

Two more letters arrived in November, each one requesting a house visit. The last one was posted in a sickly salmon-pink envelope, like a jury summons. But with Art working all hours, Nut needing more and more entertainment, and all the purging still to do in the garden it was easy to find legitimate reasons why we couldn't squeeze in a visit.

Art never noticed the letters on the doormat, but would stare into the recycling before dropping something into it. He'd pause on the way back to his study, watching Nut and I curling into each other like yin and yang, his lips as dry as chalk. He never said anything, but sometimes I thought I could hear him speaking to someone in his study, his voice low, worried. I could never make out the words, even with my ear pressed against the wood.

As the first frost was starting to settle that November, the ringing of the doorbell began. The first time it happened, I quickly ducked down beneath the windowsill, craning my head to see if it was a face I knew. But I didn't recognise this one, with the thick black glasses and shaved head. But I knew the tweed, the blue folders. I knew what that meant.

I waited for him to leave before letting my muscles relax, one by one, my eyes squeezed shut. A few seconds later, Art's cool hand was on my shoulder. "How long can you keep this up, Norah?" he whispered.

The same man came back three times over the next two weeks, always in the evening when I'd finished at Stokers. The final visit came late one night, when I was rinsing the toothpaste from my mouth. I peered out of the bathroom shutters to see the man pressing his face against our living room window. Beside me, Nut rubbed her flank against my hip. *She knew.* "Shhhh," I mouthed, as I stroked the skin behind her ear. Just then, Art opened the door to his study and my head flicked round, my finger pressed to my lips. He stood, stock still, his eyes wide and luminous in the dark. "Don't," I whispered. "You can't."

Two days after that night, the final red letter arrived. No more than ten minutes later, I was in the porch with a screwdriver and scissors, cutting the wire connecting the doorbell to the electricity.

I stopped carrying my phone around, leaving it in different rooms and under cushions. It was easier to swipe and clear the missed calls from withheld numbers than to hold the caller in the palm of my hand. Besides, no one else was trying to contact me. Apart from one night shortly after my birthday meal when I'd had three missed calls from Eleanor, my phone felt like it'd become a single frequency radio to Easton Grove. Eleanor hadn't left a message or even followed up with a text, so I didn't call her back.

The ground froze that month, tipping each blade of grass like a little silver sword. The soil was solid coal, shot through with the tiniest green shoots. I'd have admired the weeds for their sheer bloody resilience if it hadn't meant that I'd have to spend hours in the dark, crouching on the bitter earth, pulling them out with stinging fingertips. Gardening gloves were useless for finding the little weeds so I went at it naked, picking at the earth by solemn torchlight.

Afterwards, I'd sit at the dining table, peeling away the broken nails one by one. Nut would usually leap up at this point in a rare show of athleticism, pushing her face in close to inspect the little pile of milky crescents.

I'd grab the nail and cuticle wax and take in the glorious lemon scent – I can still smell it now – then take a generous scoop and massage it gently into Nut's nails. Her claws were sharp and black, with a golden ridge tracking from root to tip. They took a lot of wear and tear, those nails; they were designed for it.

Nut's instinctive hour-long runs were as speedy as they ever were despite her increasing bulk. I never put her on the scales like I was supposed to, but she must have weighed in at least thirty pounds. Maybe more. Hold your hands in front of you at hip width, swivel them out around forty-five degrees, and that's about how long she was at that time. I called her "my Chunky Nut".

Each time Nut finished her habitual run she'd flop by my ankles or scramble onto the back of the sofa to sniff my hair, making sure I was still me. I learned which ways she liked to be touched, the meanings behind each little tilt of her head, and what she did with her body when she'd had enough and wanted some time to herself. I fed her titbits of my dinner, and discovered that her favourite nibbles were peas (offered one at a time on the palm of my hand), little prawns, and cheese, particularly feta. She wasn't keen on fruit, and would wrinkle her entire face when taking in its acidic spray, her round eyes disappearing behind thick, fleshy pink folds. She hated tofu and would turn away in total disgust when I offered it to her on a palm. She sniffed my steaming cups of chai tea and milky coffee curiously, but never took a sip.

More to entertain myself than anything else I started to teach her tricks. I tried "sit" first, pushing down her back end as I repeated the word, but as her main position was on her rear or flopped on her side she didn't seem to catch on. I had a little more success with "come", by coaxing her to the opposite end of the living room with a pea or mini carrot. She'd amble over and push her face into my palm for her reward, and I'd rub her about the ears and reach underneath to tickle her belly. I'd repeat the process over to the other side of the room but by that point she'd have sniffed out some crumb or my plate of leftovers and would be helping herself. I'd flail my arms to get her attention but she'd just look at me over her shoulder and roll her eyes before turning back to her new discovery. I could never tell if she was too clever for the game or too stupid, but, ultimately, she always got her own way.

It wasn't until our neighbours started to illuminate their dark bricks with Christmas lights that I started to relax a little again with Nut. Yes, I still felt the aftershock, but I had started to accept that nothing had actually gone wrong. Nut hadn't escaped, she hadn't fallen ill again. Our days just continued. We'd had her almost a year, and life had developed its own routine. It was a relief to let my body fall into that rushing stream without having to swim, or paddle, or fight. Finally, I could shut out the light and let the water carry me from shore to shore without fear of drowning. All I had to do to float was keep breathing, keep saying yes, keep being amenable. Yield.

This was to be our first real Christmas in the house. Last year we'd been too busy making sense of existences crammed into cardboard boxes to think about dressing the place in baubles and twinkling garlands. I had a few festive bits and pieces from my old flat, and even though the artificial green fir and strings of multi-coloured pompoms didn't sit right with me anymore, I still brought them out and strung them loyally around the living room like the Ghost of Christmas Past. Some of them had been Luke's, but I only realised once they were already pinned to the walls. I told myself that it didn't matter, they were only things. Art twisted his face at the sight of them but having come across from Wisconsin with only two modest suitcases he had no heirlooms of his own. His Christmases were to be sketched on a clean slate.

The idea of festooning each room with only my outdated tat made me feel too naked, so I suggested that we make some new decorations. Art bought into this idea massively, ditching his desk to research homemade baubles. Not long after, I started to find small crumpled pieces of ruled writing paper in every room of the house. At first, I assumed it was Nut running off with Art's notepads, but when I picked one up and noticed that the paper was too precisely folded, I realised what Art was doing. Every time I found one after that, I took care to open up the ball and turn it this way and that to work out what it was supposed to be. Sometimes I thought I had it all worked out and would mutter "Ah, a penguin," or similar, and other times I'd have to admit defeat, shrug it off, and drop it in the recycling with the rest of the animal farm.

The sheer volume of paper-folding failures made me wonder if Art had given up writing entirely. I sat watching him one night at the dining table as he painstakingly cut the paper and pressed it with the flat irons of his forearms. Something about the way he forced his fingers down onto each fold had the same effect on me as fingernails down a blackboard.

He attempted robins, angels, snowmen, Christmas trees… None of them looked quite right to me, but I smiled encouragingly at each one he finished, finding a home for it on a mantelpiece or windowsill. This was Art's concentration face; brow creased, the tip of his tongue peeking from between his teeth. I wondered if this was the face he wrote with, in those intimate moments I wasn't allowed to see. I'd only ever seen the wide-eyes of surprise or the downturned mouth of concern when I interrupted him. Did I like Art's concentration face? I wasn't sure.

Sadly, neither of us saw the flaw in our new paper-crafted decorations until later. The impetus of Nut's runs sent them wafting behind the TV or in some cases out through the window, even if it was only opened a crack to let the air in. Before long we stopped picking them up, and Nut would trample them, only occasionally stopping to chew on the corner of a snowflake or pin an angel beneath her hands as she ripped it apart with her teeth. Once Art realised that his creations were simply toys for

Nut and would never last, he stopped making them altogether, disappearing back into his private engine room.

Our brief sojourn together ended, I dressed the rest of the house alone, decking the walls and surfaces with my old garish greens and ruby reds. At first, I'd felt oddly sheepish, as if I was dressing a stranger in costume without asking her permission. So, while I wrapped her in cheap, flaking gold, the house held her breath, looked away, and remained aloof.

But I saved the best for last. A set of four vintage silver-foiled baubles from Mum's house.

They'd been one of the few knickknacks I'd salvaged from the clear-out. At the time I hadn't thought too much about why I was keeping them, I was just aware of the fact they outdated me and Mum, and it would have been a crime to dump them in a skip. What right had I to destroy history? I hung the baubles from the curtain rails, and at night the light from the streetlamps reflected across the walls like moonlight on surf.

To Nut, each room had become a funhouse. Imagine it – extra obstacles to vault, shiny curiosities with foreign scents to sniff, loud and crinkly textures to investigate under tentative claws. She'd sit for a good hour in the centre of the living room, just watching one of the antique baubles spinning in the air current. What she saw in it I have no idea, but I thought the effect on the walls was hypnotic. I sometimes stood there too, humming softly, imagining how it would be to float on the sea.

There had been a few times like that, where Nut had imitated me. I'd be watching a film on the sofa with Nut stretched out on the floor beside me, only half-aware that both she and I were chewing on our lips. It was a tic Art had pointed out to me only a few months before. Life repeats, doesn't it? Chewing on her top lip was Mum's thing. It was just what she did. It meant she was digging deep into some thought, nothing for me to be concerned about. But I saw collectors and dealers misread it as impatience, and give a little to her demands. I wonder now if she knew that and played on it.

So with me Nut chewed her lip and tilted her head, but even more obvious was her growing obsession with Art's study. She'd nap outside the locked door, perking up immediately when she heard shuffling from within. The lower three feet of the door was scored with deep furrows, curls of white paint scattered on the carpet like frosting. If Art came out to go to the bathroom or kitchen she'd slither inside, lithe as a snake, and set up home under his desk. She pulled books from his shelves, her fingers now dextrous enough to turn pages. She'd become more vocal than ever, and often mumbled a series of low grunts whenever Art spoke.

She'd also started to look like him, really look like him. Her face was one thing, but there was a certain confidence in her walk, an elegance in the bend of her elbows and knees which reminded me of how Art moved on stage. Sometimes I caught myself just before I talked to her like I would Art.

But this confused me. Nut barely saw Art. He still spent days and evenings deep in his burrow. How could Nut be picking up these habits and traits if she didn't see them enough to know that *they were* habits and traits? At no point did I assume that these were Nut's idiosyncrasies – they were definitely ours. Since we spent our evenings together, I could get it if she was picking up my quirks through boredom or experimentation. But Art's?

I don't know if Art was thinking along the same lines as I was. He hardly looked up from his desk to talk about anything. His head was in the sand – not owning up to the truth at home, or even confessing to his publisher that he couldn't write anymore. I understand; it's soft and dark down there, and we've all done it. Even Mum, ignoring her own body as she succumbed to her cancer. I wanted to pull Art up by the hair and scream at him; *Nut has never existed in isolation. She has always been our past, our inheritance, our legacy. You know it now. We both do.* Her heart was warm with his blood, not just mine, and perhaps her charms were inherited from (this was the first time I used the word) parents? Hardwired into her being. And did this mean that she had an awareness of these quirks? Did Nut like herself? Did Nut like us? But I never said any of that to him. Never out loud. But I told Nut. I whispered it deep in her ear late each night, when the house groaned in the winter winds and the world slept.

That was when I felt safest, and, apart from Stokers, I hardly left the house at all. Why would I want to be anywhere else? My plan was for Art, Nut and I to spend Christmas alone, so there was plenty of time to press into the walls of my cocoon. Art had suggested we have another New Year's party, to mark everything that'd happened that year. It was such a change to hear Art suggest anything social, so I immediately agreed to it – thinking that it seemed like an age away. With almost three weeks booked off from work I was looking forward to switching off and maybe even teaching Nut a few more tricks. Perhaps how to stand on her back legs, or handle a spoon.

My final week at work dragged as I knew it would. On the last day I decided to leave a little early, so set to packing up my desk – Stokers' policy – to remove any trace of myself from my cubicle. When the office was closed, management liked the idea of the place being wiped clean. New Year, new start.

I was almost finished squeezing the last of my notebooks into a drawer when Markus appeared by the side of my desk. His face and neck were puce, his jaw locked tight against his words.

"Are you off, Norah?"

"Yep. I've tied everything up, not started anything new."

Markus laughed under his breath and began to pick at the fabric at the top of my divider wall.

"I'm glad I caught you then. Come for a minute, will you?"

I followed Markus through the mostly uninhabited cubes. A few faces peered over the top of cubicle walls, their brows furrowed. A middle-aged woman a few feet from Markus' office tilted her head as I approached, her tongue flicking off the edge of her incisors. A few seconds passed before I recognised her as Markus' PA. She'd been out of the office for most of the year, and in that time I'd overheard soft, sympathetic voices in the lunchroom discussing how she'd finally reached the top of the waiting list for an NHS hospital bed, and would finally receive treatment for her *greying*. Intensive chemotherapy. No mercy. The voices seemed to disagree about the cause of it, though. One thought it must be the city air and shoddy purifiers that Stokers was determined to never invest in, while the other thought it must be something in the PA's food – "She never ate anything organic."

I kept walking towards the woman, wearing what I hoped was a soft, encouraging smile. She looked well to me – thin, I suppose, but her blonde hair was voluminous, sticking out in curls that would normally belong to someone less than half her age. But as soon as our eyes met, the woman lowered her head and started scribbling blindly on a notepad with so much force that the paper was tearing beneath the nib. Her mouth was a tiny little knot now, pinned shut. My skin stung as if doused in cold water.

Something wasn't right.

Markus held the door open with his head down, and waited for me to enter. Against the wall adjacent to Markus's desk sat Fia, wearing a three-piece tweed suit, and next to her a face I hadn't ever wanted to see again. The man at our door, pressing his face in at our window. He was completely bald, his head shining under the brutal corporate fluorescence. He wore little round glasses and a vividly blue suit. A bright red handkerchief poked from a top pocket, and a battered flat cap lay across his lap. He peered up at me casually, as if I was simply squeezing past him on a train. Both he and Fia looked like they were dressed for a wedding, rather than the sterile grey of an insurance firm.

Fia looked up with a smile as the bald man stood up and offered me his hand. I shook it silently and sat in the steel chair opposite the desk. Markus sank into his executive chair, slouching low in the seat, his fingers stacked in a pyramid in front of his face. I held my breath and blinked slowly, demurely, waiting for one of them to speak. No way was I going first. Fia cleared her throat.

"It's lovely to see you in your domain, Norah. How long's it been now?"

I paused, for effect. "Four months or so. You weren't there when we brought Nut in."

Fia and the bald man looked at each other. "Nut?" Fia laughed, her forehead creased in confusion. "Goodness, yes. Five months. You've been very quiet."

"I didn't know I wasn't supposed to be quiet. Our next appointment with you isn't until February, isn't it?"

The bald man stared, perfectly still. Fia smiled to herself, her finger scrolling up on her tablet. "That's right. Though there's been home visits scheduled on a few occasions but you've cancelled each one. Is everything alright?"

I made sure my hands lay open on my knees, placid, and open. "Better than alright. We've just been finding it hard to book an evening when we're free together, and I thought you'd prefer to see both of us, rather than just me or Arthur on our own."

"But we have nothing scheduled yet. Have you not found a date?"

"I'm trying. Art's hugely focussed on his book, and I've been pulling quite long hours here." Excuses. They came readily to me, shrouding me like moths on bark.

"But your manager here tells us you usually finish at 5.30pm? And we've made lots of alternative dates for you…"

"I've had three letters, which I called you after."

"We've sent you *eight* letters, Norah. We've not heard from you after the first three. Mr Martin, my colleague here, has called round personally to your house four times to see you and there's no answer, though it seems like there's someone home. Can you explain that?"

Why couldn't they just step back? Why couldn't they just leave us alone? "The doorbell's broken. It's been like that for months." My voice croaked and betrayed my lies. Why, even now, did I want to see Fia smile?

She tipped her head. "We need to make sure you, Art and the ovum organi are working out. After what happened this summer, it's our responsibility to look out for signs of post-traumatic stress.

And we need to check your living arrangements. How would it make us look if the ovum organi was being neglected?"

"She's going from strength to strength."

"Then invite us in. Otherwise we'll access it another way."

"You don't have the right to come over without my permission, doctor."

Fia smiled. "We do, Norah. Ova organi are our property. Its function is our business. As are you."

I was struck between wanting to please the woman who held the keys to our happiness and wanting to slap her across her skinny and patronising face. A motherly embrace could quickly have turned to rage, my claws pulling tufts of fake, blonde hair from their roots.

The bald man was waiting for me to do something. He leant forward and pulled a notebook and pen from his pocket. He clicked the pen five times before speaking and something in my head lurched.

"So, if we send an appointment for just after New Year, you'll be there? And your manager will make sure you have the time off?" He peered at Markus over his glasses. Markus nodded, his eyes closed. He swallowed a lump.

"Brilliant news. I'll come along to that too. We can discuss any need for a residential stay at Easton Grove in January. Lots of members benefit from that. I'll bring a key, so we can let ourselves in, yes? We're family after all," Fia said, tapping on her tablet. "Speaking of family, how's Arthur doing?"

I wasn't stupid, Fia was leading me down some alley. The bald man was still staring at me, his face expressionless apart from the odd glance up at Markus, twitching in his seat.

"Why?" I said.

"Norah," Fia replied, her face all open with mock surprise. "You're not usually so abrupt – is something going on at home?"

What do you want?

"He's doing just fine. We're doing fine. All open, honest," I spat my last words, "like in the contract. Cut us and we bleed the same bronze."

Fia sat back in her chair and spoke slowly. "Do you need any tips from us on keeping everything nice and sweet? Perhaps for his Christmas gifts? When we spoke to him recently he didn't sound very–"

"No, Fia. Stop now." I stood up, my words loud, and I knew I'd made a mistake. In a split second, the bald man was on his feet too, towering almost a whole foot over me. For a mad moment, I actually had to stop myself from reaching out and touching his skull or even clasping that hot dome in my palm. I think I just wanted to remind myself of his vulnerability, his humanity. After all, like all of us, he was just blood, bones and a heart. He wasn't just a hired goon – he would have had a family, a home. But instead, I sat down again, my knees melting beneath my weight. Fia cleared her throat.

"Anyway," she breezed, as if the last minute hadn't just happened, "while we're here, we wanted to give you *your* Christmas gift. From Easton Grove, to you." She nodded at Markus, who caught her signal despite his eyes still being closed. Perhaps they weren't closed, but just appeared that way through puffiness? Markus began to speak, his voice hoarse and mechanical.

"An opportunity has come up, and it's perfect for you. It's about time you moved up the ladder. It's more responsibility. More pay. More prospects. Are you ready?"

Up the ladder? Here? *Up the ladder.* Up the ladder into the loft at Stokers. My own dark loft, with a hatch that opens at my keepers' bequest. Moving upstairs was moving into darkness, not the light.

Escape. Escape. Gush out honesty. For once, honesty.

"I- I don't know," I blurted. Fia was eyeing me up like a meal. "I've been thinking of something else," I said. "Something creative. My mum was a painter, she was really good. I think I'd like to do some classes. Maybe see how good I get, get some advice."

The three of them stared at me. Fia's eyebrows merged with her hairline. Dark patches ate Markus' shirt.

"But Norah," Fia laughed, "that doesn't sound very stable, does it? How far do you expect to get with that? It's too late for you to start again."

"I'll just do an evening class," I whispered. "This might be the thing I'm actually good at. Something creative, like Arthur." I tried to smile. "If anyone here has time, surely it's me."

I plucked the words I used like fish from a pond. But I could tell from their faces I'd gone too far, strayed too close to the deep waters. They knew me, what I was made of, what I tasted like.

Fia spoke slowly. "It might be that we can arrange a night class for you. A hobby class. But I think that's as far as that'll go. Norah, you're our shining example of what members of the Grove are capable of. We all want to be proud of you. Make us proud of you."

She reached across and placed her hand over my offered heart. It was almost… romantic. She stroked my knuckle with her thumb, back and forwards, back and forwards. Was it love?

"I'll try," I whispered.

"I- I think you'll like it." Markus stuttered, shuffling his papers with an eye on Fia and the man in blue. On top of the pile was a dull grey envelope with the bronze ankh and Markus' name on it. The paper looked wrinkled, damp, as if it'd been clenched in sweaty hands. Everyone was watching me, waiting for me to make my next move in the game.

"What is it you want me to do?"

"You'll be managing the staff on this floor, the clerks who process small claims. You've got enough experience of the day-to-day, anyway." Markus laughed, his face a shining ruby. The papers under his hands were softening in the damp, becoming waves on his desk.

"But Markus," I said. "Isn't that your job? Where are you going?"

"It's fine," he said, a bit too loudly. The blue envelope was in his hands now, shaking ever so slightly. "It's fine. I'll find something. It's a big world out there. It's exciting. Exciting."

Fia sighed, tutting under her breath. "Merry Christmas, Norah. We thought you deserved that. You're going places now. Setting down roots. Think of yourself. Just imagine where you might be in the years to come. This chair, this office. This could be *big*."

* * *

I stopped off on the drive home at a newsagent, one of those shops on a corner that specialises in paraphernalia to get you through the weekend. I went out of my way to find one I didn't pass every day. I scanned the shelves of sugary delights and creamy desserts, passing by the gossip magazines and beer and wine and gin. People came and went, pushing by me without a glance. People totally preoccupied with their own lives, the short pleasures they could afford for less than ten pounds.

Light-headed and empty-handed, I made my way to the front counter where a tired-looking man stood, framed by tall plastic stands slotted with scratch-cards and lottery tickets. He looked around the fifty-mark, though had probably seen more than fifty years' worth of trouble.

I handed over a twenty-pound note and pointed behind the counter to a row of old familiar packets. He picked one up and tossed it across the countertop with my change and a green lighter. I slid them towards me like a player in a saloon and let them fall into my handbag.

My bag sat on the passenger seat all the way home. I ignored it until I pulled up outside the house, the street glowing with the eerie half-light of amber lamps on frost. I pulled the box from my bag and removed the cellophane in one graceful twist and tug. The pack clicked open and the twenty foam tips shone pristine like white towers. I removed one, twiddling it between my fingers and letting that old smell take me back to when I was little. Funnily, those deathsticks reminded me of a time when I didn't worry. When doubts flitted by like leaves, coming and going on the wind.

I flicked the lighter with a thumb, enjoying the sharp gear working my skin. Beside me the house skulked darker than its neighbours, shrinking behind their garlanded walls. It looked overshadowed, a child between custodians. The runt. Or a convict, led to internment by two jailors. It was hard to believe that the house wasn't slowly being crushed by its neighbours, caving in on itself inch by inch.

When had Art spoken to Easton Grove? He hadn't said a word about it. What was he telling them? How could I ask him?

I slotted the cigarette and the lighter back into the pack and thrust them inside the glovebox. *The smell.* I rubbed my palms up and down my trousers to remove the scent, fluffed up my hair between my fingers, and stepped out of the car into the freezing night.

I held my breath as I entered the house, dropping my bag by the door like I always did.

"Art?" I kicked off my shoes, giving my fingers a subtle sniff while I searched for him. No reply. The house was cold, almost as cold as outside. A breeze from the kitchen licked my face with an icy tongue.

Still wrapped in my coat and hat, I ran to the kitchen to find the backdoor completely open, swinging slightly in the breeze. I went to lock it, but something stopped me. I didn't want to look. Such inexplicable fear of what I might see.

Art was standing in the middle of the garden with his back to the house. By a strange optical illusion, the light from next door's Christmas decorations flickered beneath his feet as if he stood on water.

"Art?"

He didn't turn or reply. I couldn't see what he was looking at in the darkness and was too afraid to step towards him and find out. I felt a brush by my ankles and leapt to the side. It was Nut, curling herself around my legs, seeking comfort in the cold dew. And she was outside, Art had let her outside. This wasn't right. What had he done? Why would he be so careless after last time?

"Arthur – Nut's here, help me!" I wrapped my arms around Nut's waist and tried to hoist her up but she was too heavy, her body too long for me to lift.

"Art, I can't do it on my own!"

He didn't move again but I wasn't about to let Nut go to see what was wrong with him – every second she was there she was buffing the lawn chemicals into her skin, and in a moment could disappear into the dark beneath that bastard bush at the end of the garden.

I managed to get her back to the house by dragging her, walking backwards with my spine bent. Nut didn't try to get away but didn't help much either. Her feet skated the lawn, her eyes on the clear sky and the stars above.

I got her into the kitchen and shut the door, brushing the blades of grass and dead leaves from her back. She'd lost the juvenile fur from her face completely now, and her skin was clear, beautiful, and white. But there, below her lip, was a definite dark smear, as if something black had trickled there and been wiped off. A stain. Perhaps she'd been eating insects or berries from the bush. Her eyes were bright; she seemed OK. Time to worry if the berries were toxic in a minute.

As Nut trotted off to the living room, I returned to the garden where Art still stood. I didn't say anything, and wrapped my arms around him from behind, placing my head on his shoulder. Perhaps Art had always been the more sensitive one after all. I felt his hands on mine, damp and freezing. His feet were bare and blue, swollen lumps of flesh in the grass.

I kissed his cheek and spun him around to face me. He looked right through me at the house, his eyes sunken into deep pits.

"Norah, they know. You need to be careful."

I squeezed his upper arms, holding him close to me. *Feel my heart*. "Did you tell them?"

He looked at me and then at the grass, his mouth pinched tight. After a ragged gasp of air he shook his head.

"Then they don't know anything," I said. Art's eyes were as wide as I'd ever seen them, and I unexpectedly remembered Mum's words about the moon being white as a pearl long ago. But was it as white as Art's eyes? No. Nothing could ever be as luminous, hovering in the green night-smog.

"Norah, I'm not quite myself."

"I know." So many problems that I couldn't help, so I tried to rub some warmth into his arms. What could I do? We were locked together in this now. "It's getting to me too. I don't know what we're going to do. *I didn't know.*"

Art shook his head and a little stream of blood, thin and mixed with spit, leaked from the side of his mouth. He looked like he was dying.

"Your lip…"

He brushed his mouth with the back of his hand and gave it only a glance before dropping his arm to his side. "That. That's nothing. It's fine. It's fine. But Norah, I can hear her. I can hear Nut, now more than ever. In my head." He clamped his hands over his ears. His voice sounded odd, slightly lisping, like his tongue was swollen.

A brush by my ankle and Nut was there again, walking around our ankles in a figure of eight, only stopping to lick the frost from Art's naked feet.

16

All Christmas, we kept ourselves locked in. Since Nut was now tall enough to reach up and use a door handle, we couldn't take any chances. A locked door meant no one would leave, but then no one would come in either.

Since that night in the garden, I'd been careful as to what I left lying around. I buried the cigarettes in the glovebox, and hardly left a room without carrying cups, plates or piles of papers. I vacuumed compulsively, emptying bag after bag of Nut's shed fur straight into the bin outside. I was clearing conversation-starters, triggers, mistakes. Every dirty smudge was a smudge on me, a clue to tell Easton Grove that I wasn't living my best life. I wasn't capable. That I needed them to intervene. That I was thinking against them. Christmas might be the only time left sacred and free. Fia had a key, but even that wouldn't let her in when the chain was on. Maybe that would be enough time to bundle Nut somewhere, perhaps back in the loft. Art would have to help, there'd be no way I could get her up the ladder on my own. Keeping on the double-lock would mean an extra few seconds to flatten my hair and pretend everything was fine. *It was fine.*

Swallowing a lump in my throat, I spent the weekend before Christmas cleaning out the red loft again, sweeping the floor of Nut's fallen fur, cleaning her beds, wiping clear the skylight. I plugged in the lamps and I filled a litter tray with white crystals. Art watched from his study as I carried up the cleaning supplies, his face blank, hands wrapped around the nape of his neck. I didn't want him to speak. This was beyond him now.

Outside was a dull, white watercolour. It hadn't snowed yet, but the sky weighed heavy with the expectancy of it, as if the cloud was a canopy filled with mud. One sharp thrust upward and all the weather would come pouring down, like it had built up over a thousand years.

So I prepared our Noah's Ark. Downstairs, I purged the kitchen of potted carcasses. Despite them all sitting in a row and sharing the same light, each plant had died in its own discrete way. Most had shrivelled back into a gnarled stump, and others had become mushy, sinking down like a creamy concertina. Aubrey's succulent had finally given up its last leaf, and the stalk stood obscenely naked, coiling towards the sun like an earthworm. I tossed them all into the composter and left the empty pots by the back door. I'd replace them with artificial plants later, once New Year had come and gone. I wiped down the windowsill and filled the empty space with Christmas cards from names I didn't know, signed in bronze ink.

I kept the lights in the house dim and everything in soft focus. I could stumble around, sherry in hand, eyes half-closed and still make it safely from room to room. Art said that it was as if I was preparing the house for hibernation, and maybe I was.

Even Nut seemed soothed by the semi-darkness. Her morning and afternoon runs around the ground floor took on a sluggish lilt, as if her body weighed more than her feet could handle, and her face scrunched with the effort of keeping up the pace. When she flopped, exhausted, by the sofa, she'd roll onto her back and expose her bald belly for a rub. I blew raspberries on it and she'd twist her spine left and right, her four legs kicking at empty air. *She should be wearing a Santa hat or something*, I thought.

I'd brought down Aubrey's patchwork blanket and folded it into a corner of the living room for Nut to nap on, like how we'd done with Art's fleece in the loft almost a year ago. But while she'd ignored his jacket, Nut rolled and twisted in the patchwork, gnawing the corners and rolling the bones of her fingers into the soft knit. It made my heart flutter.

I started to think about baking, cooking, all those extra hours in the kitchen spent preparing feasts that happen in most homes at Christmas. Maybe that's more for when there are kids running around hungry. It was a weight off my shoulders to know that I didn't have that to worry about, but maybe it would've been worth it to have the magic of the season brought back a little.

It was too late to make a Christmas pudding. Mum always made one – she called it a "rum dumpling", sodden with all the booze she could get her hands on. "If you're not drinking with every bite, it's not Christmas," she'd say. I wondered if she made one for her final Christmas, the year I didn't go back. I must've told Luke once about the rum dumplings, because I remember him attempting a Christmas pudding in secret, feeding it whisky, sherry and port until it bled. That ever-hungry beast must have cost him an absolute fortune. It quivered like a jelly. It also tasted awful, and I told him so, but not before he spat out a charred mouthful into the sink. I kept going back to it though over the next few days, letting a spoonful of that heavy pulp rest on my tongue.

I asked Art if he wanted me to go out and buy one but he pulled a face. I brought home a trifle, piled high with fruit and cream. I let Nut lick some from the tip of my finger, sending warm little sparks up my arm. She stood up on her hind legs for more, stretching her arms across the kitchen counter for treats to grab. Like that, her head was as high as my rib cage, her middle so thick that it obstructed her reach across the table top. We stood together like that while I made a batch of brownies for Christmas Eve. I narrated the baking process as I went along, "This is a whisk, to mix the egg and sugar, like this." My whisking flicked little droplets of egg in Nut's eyes and though she blinked furiously to protect her blues, she never wavered in wanting to take part, occasionally shuffling on her back legs to get a better view. I used to watch Mum bake in the same way, waiting for a finger-dip in the boozy batter. I dipped my finger in the chocolate cake mix and rolled it across Nut's lips.

After the half an hour in the oven was up, we bounded over to see the results – a soft and squidgy chocolate feast. I cut the hot sponge into even squares and four little cubes for Nut. After some gentle prodding to make sure they were cool enough, I placed one on the edge of the kitchen counter for her to reach up and grab. "You get the first taste, Nut. You made this cake yourself."

Nut stood up on her hind legs and swiped the cube into her waiting jaws. Her finger bones were so developed now that she could've picked up the cube if she'd wanted to. Instead, she batted it towards her like a cat, and after experiencing an odd spark of annoyance I remembered to be relieved. I let the feeling waft over me coolly, fanned by the wings of amnesty's butterfly.

Once the brownies had cooled, I brought Art a piece with a coffee. Though the curtains were open the study was dark, only lit by a little Tiffany table lamp. The walls looked black. Art was sitting on the floor in the corner by Nut's book-den, an open hardback across his lap.

I knelt beside him and closed the cover of the book, *Huckleberry Finn*. "It's Christmas Eve. Come downstairs."

Art looked up, and for a second, he was Mum looking back at me, how she would have looked at her last Christmas. Art and Mum looked absolutely nothing alike, but there was something in both their expressions that silently mourned something they'd lost and didn't know how to get back. Art's hands lay open across his thighs, palms up, as if still holding the book.

"Come downstairs, husband-to-be."

Arm in arm, I helped him to stand and he swayed a little. He lifted lightly, no heavier than a child.

We lay on the sofa together like a couple with nothing left to say. Art sat in front of me between my legs as if we were squished in a canoe or riding a horse. We half-watched *The Muppet Christmas Carol*, and then let the ads drift straight into *The Nightmare Before Christmas*. Art must have fallen asleep, as his chest began to rise and fall like waves on the sea. I wrapped my arms around him to keep him warm and kissed the top of that still-not-familiar head.

His hair smelled musty, like the loft when we first opened it up a year ago. His trousers hug loosely around his legs, his knitted maroon jumper engulfing him entirely. Art looked like he was in the process of being swallowed.

We went to bed together, hand-in-hand, and slept through the night, still clutching each other. Next year, I'd find more ways to touch him that he liked.

On waking, it was a shock to find us skin-on-skin, our bodies sticking together. Art was still asleep, the hollows beneath his eyes smudged like burst blackberries. His lips were moving just a fraction but he looked peaceful so I rose, wrapped myself in a dressing gown, and peeked through the blinds at the white-washed street. No signs of life. The sky was heavy and white, lighting the street like a wide fluorescent lamp.

I made sure the blinds were closed and then padded down to the kitchen. Nut was already there, her tail swishing behind her in excitement. She bounded over across the rug and I held her skull between my hands, rotating my fingertips behind her ears. Her cheekbones rose and she crooned a low, clucking mewl.

"Merry Christmas, little girl."

I kissed her forehead and held my lips there, savouring the soft, fragrant woodsmoke of her skin, changed so much since her early sweet talcum days. I dropped some artificial salmon into a dish for her and set it on the dining table so that she had to stretch up and stand to eat.

The kitchen was freezing, so I turned the heating on and set to scrambling some eggs for Art, brewing his favourite coffee on the side. Just as I was jostling our breakfast onto one vast tray Art appeared by the doorway, smiling that old warm smile, taking me back to the early days of party hats, of purple socks, of his old flat where he had seemed so exquisite.

"I love you, Norah."

Something inside me cracked. I didn't want to cry and I didn't even know what I was crying for, but those few words had opened up some vault inside of me. We held each other in silence like we were the only two people in the world. And we may well have been – there'd be no one knocking at our door that day – but I felt like I didn't care even if they did. Art. I had Art. I had him for life, and he had me, and he was fine with that. We would look after each other, and we'd have Nut. A little family of three. Nut was likely to be the only child I'd ever have, that *we'd* ever have. We could be happy, all three of us in love. This was what life was for, this was what it was all about. The three of us connected by more than ideas or ambition. This was biology.

I raised my head from Art's shoulder and looked deep into those wide blues. The lenses of his glasses distorted perspective, making them look further away than they actually were. He smiled.

"Do you love me too?"

I couldn't speak, and lowered my head with a gentle nod. He kissed me on the lips and like the snow it felt clean, cold, and pure. Stifling a sob, I gestured to the living room so we could eat in there, perhaps cuddling together on the sofa like the night before. Art carried the tray for me and I followed with only a brief glance behind me at Nut, who was sitting on one of the dining room chairs, tugging absent-mindedly at her ear lobe.

Art was quiet as we ate, and I couldn't figure out whether he was just relaxed or whether he'd drifted back to his own Christmas ghostlands. I spooned my mouth full with egg. Premium eggs meant celebrations.

"You chew with your mouth open, you know."

I laughed at that, and a gob of egg flew from my lips. He smirked and rubbed his ear. I bobbed my head to the rhythm of my chewing, and swallowed. "So do you."

"I know."

I ate the last few mouthfuls as delicately as I could manage and took the plates away. We hadn't planned anything, apart from that we wouldn't have plans. We huddled together under a blanket for most of the morning, only rising to bring more hot drinks, those little veggie sausages you get in a bucket, and other greasy nibbles from the overloaded fridge. I made sure Art kept eating, he needed it, but I avoided the unhealthiest snacks. I owed it to Nut to look after myself. Art nibbled on whatever I handed him and dozed, drifting away from me and back again, mumbling all the time under his breath.

I couldn't help him deal with this; he'd just have to see it through, like I had to. But despite how obviously wretched he felt, I relished the closeness of him, the way he'd fall asleep with his head on my shoulder like he'd known me for a hundred years. I held his hand and my insides bubbled. The air was warm and drowsy, a snug. I tucked his head in my neck, and jolted at any creak of a gate, or the shuffle of boots outside.

We waited until the evening for our gift-giving. Never really having done this before, we both promised to keep how much we spent to a limit. At first we'd not wanted to show each other up, but the truth is that presents just didn't seem so important anymore. Just having Art and Nut by my side made me feel stronger.

I sat on the floor by the Christmas tree with three small gifts tucked between my knees. One was a box of abstract design socks that I knew he'd love, one for every day of the week. I'd also booked us a weekend away by the sea, staying in a little B&B in Cornwall. It was more extravagant than the gifts we'd promised to each other but it was a present for both of us. And other couples did these weekends all the time. Maybe we could even bring Nut, though we'd have to hide her while on the road, burying her beneath blankets or a tarp.

Art came into the living room carrying two mugs of mulled wine, the steam curling behind him in question marks. He offered me the more colourful of the two. It was new, and painted with crude figures capped with corkscrew brown curls, all of them holding hands and dancing around the outer surface in a perpetual "Ring a Ring o' Roses". Each little figure was in the middle of a different activity. One was standing on what I supposed was grass, her ankles deep in weeds, one looking up at the sun overhead, and another was clad in black and white, which I think was meant to be a business suit.

"I broke the birthday rule," Art chuckled. Then he spluttered, the mulled wine catching his throat. All the little Norahs watched me with judging black eyes.

"Thanks. It's… weird."

"Think of it as an early birthday present. You can take it to your new job."

I mimed a "cheers" and raised my cup to him, smiling with all my gums.

Next he handed me a silk pouch, tied with a gold cord. I jingled it by my ear. He looked down at the floor, and the skin near his hairline flushed.

"Sorry it's not wrapped…"

He tailed off as I pulled open the bow and tipped the contents onto my palm. A little rock, partially polished, mounted on a pin. I was staring at it, trying to work out what to say, when Art said, "It's an ammonite."

It wasn't an ammonite. It was obvious that this was something else, definitely a fossil, but not an ammonite. My throat had constricted when I'd opened the pouch but it loosened a little when I realised that he'd got it wrong.

Art seemed to sense that I didn't know what to do. "It's just a little thing, it's fine if you don't like it. The Grove said you'd appreciate it."

"I do," I said, closing the pin in my fist and squeezing it tight. Art looked pleased.

"But anyway," Art leaned to the side, reaching into his pocket, "this is your main present. The others are crap."

He pulled out a velvet box. Like the pouch, it wasn't wrapped. He offered it to me on the flat of his hand, his doe-eyes peering at me below heavy brows. I took it, and it weighed nothing at all. I could have tossed it in the air and expected it never to have come down again.

The lid creaked open, and inside was planted a ring made of two loops – one gold and one silver, twisting around each other like rope. I didn't understand.

"It's an eternity ring. I know it's more usual to be married first, but we're not normal, are we? We're ultra-normal. And this is forever, isn't it? We're going to be together longer than any other couple we know. If that doesn't mean eternity, I don't know what does."

His eyes shone. He was either crying or just very, very tired. He wiped his eyes with one maroon cuff.

"Wear it now, you don't need to wait."

Art slipped it from the box and fed my ring-finger through its mouth. My heart was thudding in my chest, but if I closed my eyes I couldn't even feel the difference on my finger. How did I feel, really? I don't know. I was so happy that day with my head stuck deep in the sand, eating sand, drinking rainwater through the sand. Why was this ring, a symbol of love, now a shackle?

I kissed him. It seemed like something I could always do to answer without an answer. A key unlocking our next scene. Art smiled without parting his lips at the socks, giving me a knowing glance and pulling on a pair. He responded to the weekend in Cornwall with a similarly silent kiss.

By my knee there was one gift left, one little wrapped package tied with gold ribbon. Art clapped his hands together with a dull thump, both of them clad in another pair of fluorescent socks. "Oooh, one left for me, how exciting."

He pouted coyly, resting his pointed chin on his shoulder. I shook my head in defiance, holding my own chin aloft. "Well actually, no. This one is for Nut."

Art's face became blank. He looked at the package and then at me. "What do you mean?"

"I mean I bought her a little present of her own. For Christmas."

Art stared at me, his jaw snapped to the side. Something had changed, shifted, as if I'd told a lie, or a lie had been exposed and we both had to face the shame. We were dancing around a gaping chasm, both looking away, lest we turn to stone.

"Norah, what are you doing?"

I couldn't meet his eye. "What? How is this different to us buying her feed? Changing her litter tray?"

Art shook his head. "It's *very* different, you know it is. This isn't just about the Grove finding out – this is about *you* now. You're going too far."

"I'm doing things right."

"You've crossed so many lines, Norah. I've been protecting you, protecting us both. But at some point you're going to have to stop. You're going to drive yourself mad." His mouth twisted with each word, and all I wanted to do was slap my hands over it. How could he still pretend to pursue the same old course, as if he hadn't learned anything? As if he hadn't said himself that he'd heard her voice in his head? Whatever he said out loud – I wasn't alone in this. He was saying it for the sake of it, that's all. But why? My breath caught in my throat, and it occurred to me that Easton Grove might have bugged the house. Might be listening to everything we were doing. Would Art let them do that to me? To Nut?

I fingered the little parcel, wrapped lovingly in the iridescent silver paper I'd chosen because it looked like mackerel skin. I placed it between us on the floor.

"It's Christmas, and I was feeling giving. That's all. It's nothing really. She'll like it."

"Will she? Should she?"

"Yes!" I leaned towards him and brushed my lips against his ear. "She feels, she thinks. She thinks just like we do. She likes to be scratched behind the left ear and not the right. She hates the zest of lemons. She comes to us for warmth in the night."

Art leapt away, his eyes screwed shut. "Fuck. You can't say that–"

"I can. I see it all clearly, Arthur. You see that life in her too, don't make out that you don't. You've kept the den she made in your study. I saw it. Why shouldn't I make her happy? She's alive, alive now. Isn't it our responsibility right now to make her content?"

Art stared at the little package. As if she knew, Nut strolled through the open doorway and sidled up behind Art, scratching her flank on his back like a bear on bark.

"Would you rather she was just miserable?"

Art shook his head and covered his mouth with his fingers. "We need to be so careful now," he whispered. "You're skirting a fine line here."

"We are, Art. It's both of us. We're doing this together." Art looked at the floor, so I lifted his chin and gave him a soft, entreating smile. "I am being careful. I'm looking after us, don't worry."

Art took a deep breath and ran his hands over his scalp. I cast my lure. "Why don't you give it to her, if you're worried about me getting too close?"

A half-truth. A pacifier and a spotlight, all at once. If he did this, he'd see her happy face. *His own happy face.* I wanted him to see her as I did. He picked up the box and Nut immediately pushed her face into it, her nose twitching as she inspected it from all angles. She batted at it gently with a child-like hand, and turned her face up questioningly at Art.

"OK. I'll do it."

He lay his hand on her back and with cruel force, pushed her down into a seated position. He chuckled.

"I suppose it's only fair that I give her it really. She gave me a present too."

Art grimaced widely, his lips rolling back to reveal something shining like a new pearl. Past his canines, quite eye-catching – a new, slightly too small, porcelain white tooth.

I waited for Art to fall asleep on the sofa before suggesting that we head upstairs. Groggily, he succumbed, and dragged himself off to bed on heavy feet. As he headed up the stairs I called up to him that I'd turn all the downstairs lights off, and then follow him up. He might not have even heard me.

I turned off the TV, lamps, and fairy lights, and headed into the kitchen. Nut was standing by the dining table, pressing her face into the table top, licking up fake turkey slivers, the bloody smears of cranberry sauce. I stroked her temples, already frightened. My breath came out in fragments.

Wrapping my arms around her middle I tried to heave her frame on top of the table, but she was too long and too heavy, her skin too slippery. Every time I pulled she stretched out further like an accordion.

So instead, I cut a slice from the grey lump meant to look like a turkey leg, and wafted it in front of her face. She immediately went cross-eyed as she focused on it flapping in front of her. I pulled it from her slowly, coaxing her into the centre of the table. Using one of the dining chairs for leverage, she heaved her body onto the table, the old legs creaking beneath her. She settled down onto her haunches and I fed her the leg, which she chewed slowly before swallowing with a loud gulp.

I took a deep breath and stroked her cheeks with the heels of my hands. After a few moments, I pulled back the skin of her fleshy muzzle to expose her gums, moving slowly and gently so I didn't frighten her.

It only took me a second to find it, vast and black and horribly obvious. A gaping hole between her back molars. The gum stitched together neatly, and not quite yet healed.

17

I must have scrubbed every surface that could be scrubbed. The vacuum lay exhausted and steaming in the corner, its inner brush wrapped entirely in Nut's cast-off fur. Flip the vacuum over and you'd be excused for thinking that a mangy rat had died inside.

It was almost a year to the day since we'd last had people around to visit, and, again, it was entirely Art's idea. It had been in the back of my mind as something I didn't really need to worry about, almost like it'd been a dream I'd had. I was sure he'd forget or change his mind, but he'd actually perked up a little over the Christmas break. He had colour in his cheeks again, and even sometimes touched me like he used to. A finger on the neck, a hand on my waist. But these gestures were still intermittent. After Christmas Day, Art retreated to his study again, leaving me to down the leftover mulled wine and bin the increasingly stale pastries. Evenings were spent watching the TV with one hand holding my heart in, and the other spinning the eternity ring with my thumb.

I hadn't mentioned the tooth. I spent a little time massaging Nut's cheeks to ease any pain, and crushed paracetamol into her bowl each night. I coaxed her onto the sofa and held her body in my arms, holding it together in one vital piece. She would fall asleep with her head on my breast, cooing softly, and when she awoke she'd peer up at me with such vulnerability that it'd make my ribs open like wings, my heart exposed to the air in its most raw form.

That face.

I looked, but didn't look. I scooped as much of her up in my arms as I could to know her "wholeness", but she just reminded me of my weakness. When I stroked the soft swelling of her jaw, my stomach pitched, and my tongue rolled back to taste my own back tooth – sharp with bitterness, the cold tang of iron.

Though I needed to hold her, retell myself that I hadn't failed her, that she was still complete, I couldn't look at her without curling into the most fortified part of myself. She had the power to wind me with a single look, and when my turning away made her upset, she'd push against my thighs and clasp my ankles for love.

Failure.

Art emerged the evening before New Year's Eve to tell me that Adam and Margo would be here at 7pm the following night. At first I didn't know what he was talking about, and I let him ramble on about what they might like to eat without really listening. When I realised that he was serious, I pretended that I'd forgotten and that I was just disappointed that we weren't going to be spending the night together, just us two. Art waved his hand in mid-air as if swatting a fly, and then promised that New Year's Day would be just for us. Well, after all the party clean-up, of course.

That part hadn't even occurred to me. The idea that people I didn't know would be pressing their thumbs onto surfaces unseen, leaving foreign smudges which I might never find and that could be there forever caused my insides to squish up. It would seem only fair that Art could do the clean up, as they were his friends. His friends, his mess.

"Aren't Eleanor and Rosa coming? Didn't you invite anyone?" he asked.

What immediately followed was a rushed round of text messages to both of them, full of autocorrect errors, begging them to come to a party I didn't want to host. I had trouble reaching Eleanor at first. She wasn't reading the messages so I tried calling. My first few calls rang on and on, and then the next two went straight to voicemail.

I cursed under my breath and tackled Rosa. She picked up quickly, and after a few seconds of confusion as to why I was calling, I explained the situation. She seemed reluctant to come along, having arranged to spend the night in with Mike. With a hollow heart I begged her, promising that she could just drop by, she wouldn't have to stay late, and she could bring Mike. Her replies became increasingly blunt, and in the end she said she'd ask him what he wanted to do. So, I had to wait again.

I went back to trying Eleanor. This time she picked up, but she sounded strained, as if speaking to a stranger. When I laughed it off and told her it was me, she still didn't soften and in as few words as possible told me that she was in the airport, heading to Belfast to see her brother.

"Have I done something, Elle?"

There was a silence. "No," her voice was thin. "You've done nothing."

"OK," I said, not even trying to hide my frustration by this point. "Rosa's bringing Mike–"

Eleanor interrupted me. "Don't you want to ask me something?"

I held my breath. I didn't.

"Don't you want to ask me how my tests went?"

I swallowed. I knew that when I next spoke my voice would sound different, and I didn't know what to do to normalise it. "Has something happened?"

"Months ago, Norah. Months ago."

"I haven't heard from you."

"I tried contacting you. You weren't there."

The flurry of missed calls soon after the birthday meet-up. I could've pretended to not have seen them, I'd had a lot to do. She should know that. She should know the pressure I was under. The demands on me.

"Norah. There's nothing they can do. Nothing. Even though these private institutions can grow a new fucking spinal column from scratch, they can't help me do what I was born to do. *Ever*." She spat this last word at me *like it was my fault*.

"Surely there's some sort of treatment or–"

"Well, that's the thing, there's not. A year of dabbling for the NHS to tell me I can't, and there's nothing to be done. 'Not enough research', 'not enough funding'. Isn't it hilarious, Norah? Hilarious."

I didn't know what to say. Something had broken. We both felt it, I know we did.

"Maybe there's more to it all than kids," I whispered. "You can make your mark in other–"

"Shut up, Norah. I don't want to hear that shit. Especially from you."

I wanted to tell her. I wanted to tell her everything. That I understood, more than anyone. But I couldn't. That bridge would never be built.

Eleanor's final words were spoken more to herself than to me. They weighed heavy, as if etched in stone. History. Facts from a book.

"Decades of looking in a mirror. That's all this is. People who see only themselves. Don't look left or right. Licking their fucking chops. What a day it'll be when there are no faces left for mirrors to reflect." Silence, then, "I'm glad I'll not be here."

She ended the call shortly after that, already distracted, murmuring something about the storms in Belfast. I sat on the bed for a while afterwards on my own, wondering if there was something I should do for her. But anything I thought of seemed too trite, too trivial, and to tread further in would've been stamping my boots somewhere I shouldn't be. Either me or Eleanor was an alien, but I couldn't tell who'd changed.

You see, in her eyes I'd picked the wrong side, and maybe a year before this that might have been true. But things were different now. Eleanor couldn't possibly know how wrong she was to think that I didn't want to see something grow, nurture a living thing made from me. Someone that loved me.

But I had nothing to show her to prove it. Not yet. I could say the obvious, the idea that had been burning in me since the summer, but she wouldn't understand. She'd laugh at me. Tell me I was wrong.

And that's when I started to clean. Wipe and scrape and score.

Nut padded after me, stretching up to watch the sponge sweep across the kitchen counters, playfully tugging at the microfibre cloth as it squeaked over the window. When I came back in from taking out the recycling I found her sitting with an old shammy between her teeth, flailing her head backwards and forwards in front of the kitchen cupboards. Aghast, I took it from her and threw it in the sink. Who knows where that old thing had been, how many toxic substances it'd soaked in?

It was late and I was exhausted, but eradicating smudges and smears gave me a buzz. With every surface cleaned, a room in my head cleared too.

I checked my phone every few minutes until Rosa replied a few hours later, agreeing to bring Mike for a couple of hours but that they'd leave before the gongs. Fine. I suggested they come around for 7pm, and I called up to Art that Rosa would need to leave early, so maybe we could just put out snacks rather than prepare a sit-down meal. A muffled "OK" decided that.

I'd already started taking down some of the disintegrating Christmas decorations, but on New Year's Eve I revived our earlier merry-making with pursed lips. I re-hung whatever was in a fit state to be hung, stapling together broken paper chains and sellotaping some of Art's better origami stars, reindeer, and snowmen to surfaces in case the movement of guests sent them falling. I pieced myself back together temporarily much in the same way, with make-up, fine gold chains, and a wrap-around dress, finished with a tight black belt.

I was sitting in the bedroom gripping a glass of red when the doorbell rang at 7.12pm. I remember the time because my alarm clock screen was flashing, the batteries almost dead. Nut lay curled at the foot of the bed, her pale face scrunched deep into the shag-rug, her ears covered by her hands.

I heard the door open and the bellow of a man's voice,

"Helloooooo", followed by Art's drawling "Hey", and then hurried gushing and squeals. I'd have to go downstairs, but for now there was a fly skirting the surface of my Merlot, and I needed to get it out.

Art called up the stairs, and I surprised myself by calling back immediately. My voice sounded real, full-bodied, joyful. I gave Nut a little scratch on her forehead and floated down the stairs, almost giddy. I followed the voices into the living room, where a man and woman were sitting at either end of the grey sofa as if balancing the ends of a seesaw. Both were leaning heavily on the high cushioned arms and holding up a glass of wine in their opposite hand, a mirror image of each other. Together they focussed all their attention at Art, as if nothing else in the room mattered. As if Art was food.

Walking in was like interrupting a mating ritual. The man was wearing a red and white striped shirt that reminded me of those poles outside a barber's shop. He gave off the air of someone young yet his brow was pitted with deep furrows that sucked in the light. The woman looked me up and down in the fraction of a second when I walked in and raised her glass. Her white dress glowed, a luminescent moon sinking into a rain-cloud.

"Norah, honey."

She stood up and it was dawn, and I just stopped myself before I shielded my eyes. She looked flawless. "It's lovely to finally meet you."

She wrapped her arms around me, all elbows and shoulders protruding in a crude frame, like a coat-hanger. I didn't feel a thing. A drop of red streaked down my collarbone.

"Oh sweetie, I'm sorry, kitchen roll? Kitchen roll anyone?"

I dabbed away the wine with a finger. "I'll get some, it's fine."

As the woman sat down there was some movement by her ankles. Hair. Fists. Four socked feet. The woman bent down behind the arm of the chair, "Jasper. Georgie. Come and say hello." Two beautiful clean faces craned forwards, just as luminous as their mother. Both of them smiled and sucked their lips, then the boy sat back, politeness over. He must have been around ten, maybe. The little girl, much younger than her brother, looked up at her mother for reassurance.

I looked to Art, lost as to what to do. He reached across for my hand. "Norah, this is Adam and Margo. Their babysitter was a no-show, so the kids are here for the ride too."

I nodded stiffly. What would kids do in this house? I had nothing for them. Should I bring down some of Nut's toys, those safely stashed up in the loft? Would they like that? I was stocked in the style of a Greek Goddess, all I had was wine and sugar and fat. A whisper to Art, "Should we get them some juice or something?"

Margo sat back down in her chair with a heavy sigh, "Oh no don't worry about that. They've brought their stuff. They're fine here."

I looked down at them and, as if on cue, they'd both dispatched themselves mentally from the room. Jasper's index fingers were already tapping wildly on a tablet, while Georgie was scribbling in a book with a thick red crayon clutched in her fist. They knew the drill, so why didn't I?

I ushered myself off to the kitchen with the pretence of cleaning myself up, and tucked myself into the utility room, closing the door behind me.

It was cold. Dark. Quiet.

They weren't like I thought they'd be. Art had told me about Adam. Adam was another writer with the same publisher. They'd met when Art had only been in the country a month, and though they didn't see each other apart from at launches or meetings, I could tell that Art thought of him as a shadow-self, an alternative "Arthur" he could score himself against. It was perverse, really. He spoke about Adam as if he was a friend, but there was always a tight snap to his tone when he talked about how well Adam was doing, and a lush swoop if Adam was in a quiet phase. Art heard all Adam's news second-hand through his agent, and fleshed out all the detail with punishing imagination. I'd assumed that Adam would look just like Art, or at least give off the same vibes. But sitting there, his knees stood high above the sofa cushions, and his palm and fingers curled on the arm like wax dripping from a candle. He was spidery, cracked and crumpled, a crepe paper man in danger of tearing. He hadn't said a word while I'd stood there, just sipped his wine and watched Art over his little round glasses.

And he had a family. A real one.

Art hadn't told me anything about Margo. Art had winked at her conspiratorially across the living room just when I walked in. What was that?

In the dark, I licked my finger and stroked it along my collarbone. The solidity of it brought me back to the room, the blankness of it, lit only with flickers of grey from my eyes adjusting.

The bell rang again, and I followed its siren call.

I opened the front door before even checking the peephole. In that split second after turning the handle I had a momentary panic – what if it was the bald man – and I had to decide whether to keep opening it or close it. I considered just standing there until confusion drove them off. Maybe I was having a breakdown, maybe they'd be frightened. But propriety won, and hands that didn't belong to me guided the door wide in its unhurried arc.

Rosa stepped out of the night, her face obscured by her furry orange shawl. Behind her stood a behemoth, Mike it must be, a head like a planet, shoulders, and chest above Rosa. He wore a long leather jacket down to his knees and his scalp-skin shone under the streetlights.

I kept my eyes on him as Rosa gave me a curt hug. Rosa's boyfriends were normally stand-offish, but Mike reached out his hand straight away, his pink face softened by a disordered smile. His boots were dirty, the heel flapping, but his eyes were sparkling, his teeth straight and glacier-white. As I looked up from his feet something in my head tipped, and I gripped the bannister, jesting that I'd already drank too much and could he take his shoes off please.

Once I'd issued them with beer, the three of us returned to the living room, Rosa sitting on the floor between Mike's knees as he balanced himself on a kitchen stool. We didn't own enough chairs to entertain. Art and Adam were deep in conversation, and so he didn't notice that I'd left myself nowhere to sit. I leaned against the wall, trying to look as nonchalant as I could while standing in the middle of a room full of sitting people huddled in scrums.

"So what's happened then, you lanky streak of piss?" Adam laughed at his own joke. "Norah's blooming, but cohabiting looks like it's doing you in."

"Just a virus. Been a bit of bad timing," Art shrugged. "Give me a month, I'll be fine."

"Better be. Time stands still for no man. Not even you."

Georgie had laid her book on the carpet, and started scrawling the crayon backwards and forwards with her whole arm swinging like a metronome. Her eyes were on the blank TV in the corner. At the edges of the page, red hit carpet.

"You forget, love, this is exclusive real estate," Margo nodded at Art. "Time stands quite still for these two."

"Nothing stops time. It might be slower for them, but some of us don't need the cheat code," Adam kissed Margo on the nose, "We're cool."

Margo sipped at her wine and turned to me, "He hopes we are, anyway. We're very careful – we do the organic thing, less time in the city, a top of the range purifier. But we're saving for these two to join a Grove one day. It's the least we can do, you know? Give them a head start."

Adam peered at Mike and Rosa over his glasses, "Are you both members, too?"

Rosa shook her head and grasped Mike's knee before he had a chance to reply. "It's not for everyone. I'm not sure I'd want that."

Adam leant his head to one side, a nosy crow. "Why? Why *wouldn't* you want it?"

I watched Rosa from above. I could see her hair was parted neatly at the side to hide the patches where it was already thinning. Or was it her mousey roots, growing in the same shade as her skin? No, she wasn't a member herself, but it was only because of money, I'm sure. I expect what she said next, she said because she didn't want them to know how little she had. We're so proud, aren't we? We go out of our way to look like we're one thing, when really we're something else. But when we're taken at our word – the difference between the out and the in doesn't matter.

Rosa gave me a quick look before answering. "I don't think it's always ethical."

Adam leaned forwards, sniffing the air for blood. "Ohhh, do go on."

"Adam, stop." Margo's voice was a purr.

"No, let her speak. Free speech here. I want to know her problem."

Rosa's face was pale, her mouth a pursed navel. "It's everyone's problem. It's symptomatic of a worldwide fucking problem. It's a division of classes, all over again."

"Ah, you're a socialist."

Rosa glanced at Mike before glaring back at Adam. "I'm bloody not. Why should money mean more life, more opportunity? More more more. I have no problem with Norah or Arthur doing this," her wide eyes flicked over at me. "They're just people. People looking out for themselves. It's the world that's wrong. There shouldn't even *be* systems that divide people like this."

Adam's smile was of a puppeteer. "You mean every time I comb my hair, shave my beard, I'm making fun of those with alopecia?"

"Oh for God's sake Adam, it's New Year's," Margo interrupted. "Happy New Year everyone." She took a heavy swig from her wine glass and punched the empty into the air, eyes closed. "Happy fucking New Year."

Adam shifted and crossed his legs, still wearing his painted mask. While everyone still fed on what'd just happened, I saw the scene like a fresco. Mike kissing the top of Rosa's head and whispering cooling words. Margo swilling her glass to join the last droplets. Jasper leaning back on Nut's cushion, flicking his eyes from stranger to stranger, his jaw jutting. The cushion was squashed out of shape. He didn't know that was Nut's cushion. How could he?

No one was looking at me, so I excused myself to the kitchen and started to pour packets of nuts, crisps, and olives into bowls. I held a clutch of grapes under the cold tap until my fingers throbbed. Would the kids eat this? Would they say out loud if there was nothing for them here, and that I didn't know how to look after them?

In a single second it seemed that I'd prepared everything I possibly could and it was time to go back. I heard Margo's hushed voice from the living room, "Don't touch anything, don't go into any other room, and don't hurt your sister."

I carried the bowls into the living room on a tray shaped like a fish. As I placed the bowls on the table I asked, "Where are the kids?"

Adam waved his hand in the air. "Jasper's taken Georgie to the toilet. It's just at the top of the stairs, right?"

Something twisted, tight and deep.

Art was biting his lips, fighting soundlessly, his face white. I couldn't hear anything upstairs, the house was hushed. Even the music had stopped playing. Could I hear their muffled voices? Or was it thunder?

"Arthur, you were going to tell us about your piece de resistance?" Margo asked. "Should we expect something that'll change the world?"

His eyes were as white as snowballs. How would he be able to speak, with his mouth pinned closed between his teeth?

"Sure we should," Adam bellowed. "The Grove must believe he can do it. Did they make you do an IQ test or something?"

"You have to pass proficiencies. To prove you can make the most of a longer life." Mike's head was down by Rosa's neck. She turned her head towards him, nuzzling his cheek.

"It's more general testing," Art croaked. "They ask what we want from life."

Adam leant forwards. "Fuck. That's big. What did you say?"

Margo looked thoughtful. "I'm not sure how much of anything matters in the end."

"Shhh, Margo. What *did* you say?" Adam growled, insisting we bare our innards. The silence upstairs was setting my skin on fire.

"I want to be remembered for making something that moves people. I'm never going to be in the history books, but maybe something I write will. A parable."

"And what about your cash cows?"

"They'll keep going. People will keep buying them, forgetting them, buying them again."

"And what about you, Norah? You're different. What's your USP?"

There was no air left in the room. Already on my knees, the room was black and grey, grainy, filling in with white noise. Adam's lips were moving, first upturned, then downturned. I felt hot breath behind my ear, and Art's voice was underwater. "Norah has the world at her feet. She is goodness. She is kindness. She's exactly what the world needs."

A pair of ropes in green tweed around my neck. And then ticking, faster than a clock, right in my ear: *tick tick tick tick tick.*

A high voice, a woman: "But that's not what *she* wants. What did you tell them, Norah?"

Were my eyes closed or open? Art's breath, "It doesn't matter. That's for us."

Tick tick tick tick tick. Like a pen clicking. But no one there had a pen.

Take myself away from it. Oh, hot, sweet breeze through trees. I could smell almonds and peanuts and plum wine. If I rest my head back on Art, would that help me come back?

The sound of the sea, and then the squeal of a pig. It cut through me like glass.

"Georgie?" Margo stood up unsteadily, her colours coming back into focus. I was weightless, off-balance. I bit my tongue to resist laughing out loud.

"Go see what's going on, Adam. They've been too long."

Adam lifted his huge frame from the chair and headed doggedly towards the staircase. Margo stayed standing where she was, on the brink of staying and going. Adam had reached the doorway when Georgie flung herself at his thighs, reaching her tiny hands up his midriff. He picked her up and I caught a glimpse of a shining red face streaked with silver over his shoulder before it buried itself in his shirt.

"*Jasper*." Adam's voice was low, a lion. "What have you done? Why's she upset?"

Thump, thump, thump, went footsteps down the stairs. But Jasper didn't come into the living room.

"I didn't do anything."

"This isn't on, Jasper. You're showing us up. Apologise to your sister."

"No."

"You'll do it now."

"Dad–"

Adam drove forwards and grabbed Jasper's wrist. He rotated his grip, twisting the skin beneath.

"Dad, there's a thing up there. A monster. It scared Georgie, not me. It bit her."

He continued to twist and Jasper ducked, contorting his whole body to follow his skin.

Thump, thump, thump on the stairs again. And from between the bannisters watched Nut, her fleshy face pushed against the bars, one round, blue eye in each gap. Her mouth hung open as if she'd bitten something with sore gums, her hands bony waterfalls, pouring between the posts.

Something changed.

I saw her through Adam's eyes, through Georgie's eyes, through Jasper's eyes, and I understood. I understood Adam's stepping back into the living room, his face a mask of horror. Georgie's drawn-out moan. Nut was a whale out of water, her heavy breathing the heartbeat of the house.

"What the fuck?"

Margo broke the music and pulled Adam and Georgie back. Never taking her eyes off Nut, her open mouth dripped with disgust. Adam ran one hand through his hair like he didn't know what was happening.

Art was on his feet; I hadn't even felt the ropes slipping. "I'll put her away."

"Georgie. Georgie. Where did it get you?" Margo fumbled in Georgie's clothes for an injury. Georgie's face was still pushed into Adam's neck, so Margo lifted her arm. A blue sleeve, dampened with saliva in a semicircle as wide as a bowl. She wiggled Georgie's wrist and kissed her fingers, rolling up the sleeve to check her elbow. No blood.

Why? Why must we hide her away?

Margo turned on me, baring her teeth like a cat. "What the fuck is it doing out?"

She grabbed her progeny and crushed her into her breast. "Jasper. Jasper. Get here *now*."

I reached up a hand to stroke the low part of Georgie's back.

"It's OK, Georgie," I sang. "This is Nut. Like a walnut. She lives here, with us."

Georgie wailed and pushed her face hard into Margo's dress, her fists clenched over her ears. Margo started clicking her tongue in Georgie's ear, just like we used to do with Nut when she was newly-made and she didn't know language.

Margo stepped away from me, leaving my hand trailing in the air.

"You're disgusting. What are you both doing? What are you thinking of?"

"Did it escape or something?" Adam's voice was soft and slow, as if he addressed someone who might not understand him, someone who needed guiding to the light.

Or maybe Adam was afraid. Yes.

"I need to–" Art slipped by Adam through the doorway.

"Wait, Art." I folded my arms, cool as you like. "This is our home, Nut's home. There's nothing wrong with this."

"Yes, there fucking is!" Adam bellowed. "It's unnatural."

But now that Nut was out, so was I. I'd not felt this serene in months. All the layers were peeled back and I waved my stamen, flashed my golden pollen.

"She's the most natural thing in the world. How is this any different to you living as a family? How is Nut any less of a life, just because she wasn't born?"

Margo cackled, her face wild and flicking between Adam and I. She gasped, starting words but never getting them out. "You're mad. Mad."

Adam joined in, his voice high, harsh. "How can you compare it? It should be in a fucking institution. I didn't even think they let you keep them at home anymore."

Adam looked at Nut full in the face. "Jesus, Arthur. It even looks like you. How can you look at that every day?"

It even looks like you.

Of course she did. She had Art's eyes, his lips, his nervous grasp of the ear. She loved books and magic tricks. She'd inherited his assets and picked up his habits. She was as good as his daughter. We would never have children, that was in the contract. But he would have her. Our blood.

Art cleared his throat. "It's temporary. She got sick in the loft. She'll be put in an incubator when we can afford it."

Anger. I felt anger now. What did it have to do with them? With Adam, or Margo, or any of them? They didn't have an ovum organi, they didn't know. And how dare they say all this when Nut was sitting there, listening? They were invaders, unwelcome, unwanted, disgusting. Dirty. Smudging their dark ideas over white. Spoiling, staining, growing foul.

I lifted on pillars of hot air, sweeping them all up with arms glowing like iron red from the furnace. I could have gathered hundreds of people in those arms, and rushed them off the face of the earth.

"Get out. *GET OUT OF MY HOUSE.*"

Margo was already at the foot of the stairs, cramming on her stilettos and shoving Georgie's slippers in a tote bag. Jasper stood by the front door, staring at the top of the stairs where Art was attempting to drag Nut back onto the landing. I pushed them all aside and threw open the door onto the cold night. Bullets of rain swept in on a twisting wind. Margo flounced out without another look. Adam pushed Jasper out the door with a firm hand on his shoulder.

"Think about this, Arthur," Adam called up the stairs. The double bleep of a car unlocking. An engine. A sob.

Rosa stood behind me, held firm between Mike's hands. Her face was wet, shining like a mirror, her lips peeled back over her gums. Her cheeks were marked with little half-moon indentations. She was fixated on Nut between her fingers, blinking frantically, trying to clear away a nightmare.

"Oh Norah. It's so horrible. I never knew." Rosa let out a high whine. "*She's you.*"

A slight shake and Mike was directing her towards the door. She pressed the pad of her palm over her mouth, biting the flesh.

"How could you? How could you? How could you?"

And we were alone. And later the chimes were striking midnight. And the fireworks were filling the night's universe with fire and smoke.

18

How could you? How could you? How could you?

How *couldn't* I?

Art stood halfway up the stairs, bobbing his head towards the door, chewing the air. Behind him on the landing, Nut's face peeked around the bannister, her lips parted, her tongue tasting the icy draft.

I looped the chain through the eye and tested the handle, once, twice, thrice. I wanted to be with Nut, close her ears to the world. My first instinct was to make sure she wasn't upset, that she knew she was loved. She *did* understand language, I know she did. She replied to me, she muttered back.

I folded my legs beneath me a step or two before reaching Art and seized Nut's face between my palms. I closed my eyes and it became Art's face. I knew them both just as well as each other. Moving my fingers over the skin; it was smooth, a high arched nose, a prominent chin, seeded with bristling hairs. His cheekbones. My thumbs smoothed over lips, so soft they could have not existed at all, and above – Nut's eyes were open wide as if she heard more with the whites. I let out one long breath, and so did she, low and rattling.

Bones in a jar. Moths' wings against paper.

Her face was his face, yes, but it was broken. She was already missing a tooth. And I couldn't look at her without feeling utterly, utterly ashamed that I'd let this happen. No – that I hadn't even known that it'd happened.

Art was still standing beside us on the stairs, watching the door. I reached up, held his hand, squeezed. "Art, sit with me. It's just us again."

He looked at me, a complete blank. "I didn't want them to go. *I didn't want them to go.*"

I tugged at his hand, pulling him down to Nut and I. "Sit with us."

He sank to a crouch and let his hand be guided across her wide, white back.

"Why did they go? Are we really that terrible?" He mumbled the words under his breath, inside out. I could practically see his capillaries, everything slowing down. I stroked his cheek.

"Arthur. How could you take her tooth?"

"I didn't get to explain it to them. I didn't tell them I was sick."

"Do you feel her? In you?"

"I didn't tell them."

He was on a different plane; I couldn't reach him. I cupped his cheek in my hand.

"They knew, Art. I'm sure they knew."

But no, no. Not sick. *Not truly sick.* Not that type of sick. Not yet. It was too soon. *He would have told me.*

"Art, what's happening?" My voice trembled.

"You remember that we were bio-matched to share her?" he said, his hands clasping his elbows. "She's not just yours, she's mine too. And now I need her. I need you both."

Art had given up a lot – moving his entire life from Wisconsin to meet his closest biological match. He'd always said that his life in the US was a time he wanted to cut off, like a limb that wouldn't heal. And now he needed to slice more life away in order to save himself. All the time, Art had been raw, and I'd never noticed. He'd always looked eerily familiar. From the first time I saw him sitting across from me in the waiting room, and then when I saw him flitting along the corridors, bright as a bird, I knew it was him. He smiled a lot, and that made it all OK. Already he reassured me, and now he needed me to return the favour.

"I love you, Norah."

He wanted me to say it back. He looked like a child, but he wasn't. I was so aware that he was a grown man who was inching closer to a choice that we couldn't turn back from. I didn't say those three little words back to him. They weren't in me anymore.

Art let out a juddering sigh and squeezed his eyes shut. "It's booked for a few days' time. It's now," he whispered. "I won't be gone long. I'll be back before you know it, don't worry."

Cold lips pressed on my forehead, and my third eye peered down Art's throat for the fault, the failure. Was it *the greying*? Perhaps from his youth in the US? Had he played in his parents' overalls, never washing his hands after pressing them into the chemicals? I pulled Nut towards me, probably a little roughly because she let out a whimper and buried her head in the crook of my arm. Within seconds she was chewing the sleeve of my dress, placating the tension in her spine, her neck, with each rotation of her jaw.

I spoke with a fictional voice. "Have you spoken to Easton Grove?" I didn't sound like me. I was a canary, singing in a cage. An actor, reading a script. Art stroked his fingers down the joints of Nut's spine. Each lump was an onion bulb, pushing through a pigskin.

"She's a dinosaur, isn't she?" he muttered. "A fossil, already a fossil."

My heart high in my throat, I gave a dull thump of a word in reply. Art turned to Nut fully, exploring those ridges with his fingertips before rolling his hands around her expanse to her hips, straining under her weight. The lump of a knee, a foot, so like my own. Toenails.

In a second I could see it – Nut broken in two on a steel table, Art above with a sacrificial knife. He cuts deep, deep between the teats and yank, yank, yanks the blade towards him as if gutting a wriggling fish, then parts the wet lips of her belly. In he dives, his hands pressed together in prayer. Down to the waist in Nut, Art wriggles left and right before emerging, shining black, and holding a fist of beating red matter, just matter. And all the while Nut's legs are waving in the air and she's looking at him with his own face, his own eyes, that one gaping hole at the back of her jaw potent and wanting for a thumb to fill it.

But there on the stairs, Art was close enough to kiss her. "She's us, trapped in amber." He squeezed her middle, pressing probe-like thumbs into the thick layer of fat, "Already a fossil." Nut flicked her head back on her neck and croaked.

It sounded like "No."

19

Mum used to play a game. Whenever I was too sick to go to school, she'd make me eat fruit on the hour, every hour, from when she first arose to paint to the last hours of light.

At first I wouldn't care and savour the sugar, not minding when I wasted the peach-juice by letting it run down my chin because I knew another treat was coming soon. But by mid-afternoon I didn't want to eat any more. Every bite bit me back, and made my stomach burn with all the acids. Bitter replaced sweet.

"Come on, another piece and you'll be full of power-ups," she said, blowing out a stream of smoke like a wizard. "We're not stopping until you're bouncing off the walls."

It felt like a game, even when it hurt. Us against the virus. Mum was scared of the virus, she'd do anything she could to beat it quickly, while it was still weak. Even when I was faking it, she made me eat fruit. Even when she must've known that I just didn't want to go to school that day. But whether I was really sick or pretending, the quicker I got better, the more she made me swallow.

"We're winning! Another. Another!" Her red hair bobbed on her shoulders. "Another piece, Norah, and you'll live forever. I'll make sure of it."

Art stumbled to bed soon after our conversation, leaving me alone on the stairs. I called up to him that I'd follow him shortly.

After he'd switched off the upstairs light and there'd been a few minutes of silence, I headed to the airing cupboard and pulled out the spare duvet we'd bought for guests but had never used. I carried it to the living room, switching off all the lamps as I went.

Nut followed me, of course, and stretched out on the floor as I made myself a makeshift bed. I hadn't been able to find a pillow, so I rolled the patchwork blanket and squashed it by the arm of the sofa. Rain lashed against the window, sounding like someone whispering "hush, hush".

I tucked myself in as tightly as I could, burying myself beneath the cloud of cotton, but it didn't feel right, so I snaked one arm free and let it rest on Nut's head. She was still there, her breathing heavy and slow. I coaxed her onto the duvet with the dance of my fingers and she lay along my body, grounding me into the cushions. The patchwork smelled like Nut's smoky scent and matted fur, but I could also pick up Aubrey, the perfume of lilies.

I don't know how I slept, but I did. I wanted to be with Nut, and with my fingers on her neck I was connected to the whole world. Even years later, some nights I'd lie in bed and feel like anywhere anyone blinked, I'd be blinking too. Colours, wants, curses and swearing – everything everyone thought flashed across my retinas from left to right, and if I reached out to grab at them, hold them still, the ribbons would slip through my fingers. But I always slept eventually, lost in the chorus, all the noise bleaching itself out into nothingness, like switching off a lamp. There's the bright light of the day and then darkness, nothing. I wouldn't, and still won't, let myself digest what we did.

New Year's Day dragged me into the world without my agreement.

Even before opening my eyes, the morning poured its fire into my belly and burned, twisting my guts this way and that. To move, to open my eyes, meant accepting it so I lay there still, wasting time.

I reached down blindly for Nut and brushed my fingers against the carpet. Confusion, dread, and I bolted upright – scanning the room for signs of her. Art couldn't have gone, he couldn't have taken her already. He couldn't have. He wouldn't.

I stalked the downstairs rooms without breathing, quickly testing the front and back doors to make sure they were still locked. My head was swimming and took a few seconds to catch up with me as I bulleted up the stairs and tore into the bedroom.

I don't know what I expected to see. The bed left unmade, a sealed envelope on the pillow? Or signs of a struggle – pillows slashed with wild bloody stripes, finger-pinches of stuffing drifting on the up-draft. Maybe a fallen fingernail, a puddle of red and the edges rusting.

Instead, Art was folded beneath the covers, fully dressed, still wearing his glasses. His mouth hung open, consuming one unstuffed corner of the duvet. Nut was there, sleeping, stretched out behind Art's back. In that moment, the bed was split by a terrible mirror, both bodies totally unaware of how each life depended on the other. Take away the skins and together they formed one glutinous mass. The lump on the bed was both Art and Nut together, as it was meant to be.

I watched them for some time from the doorway before Nut raised her head, blinking at me in the light. It was still early, not yet past 6am. She'd be starting her territory-run soon and would wake Art. I had perhaps half an hour before I wasn't in control anymore. This was it.

I knelt down and smoothed the back of her head, lulling her to drowse a little more. At the same time, I slipped my arm under the bed and pulled out an old blue duffle-bag with a broken zip. It wasn't all that big, but the suitcases were stacked on top of the wardrobe and there was no way I'd get those down without waking him.

What could I grab? What could I take?

There was no plan. I hadn't thought anything through.

There was just this instinctual need to protect, protect, *protect* this creature as vital to me as a liver or beating heart. She was the closest thing I had to family, she was blood, and her life, though small, was just as valid as mine, if not more so because she was an innocent. How long do ova organi live? Does anyone even know? Do Easton Grove know? Would one live forever if we didn't consume it? How long had the oldest ovum organi lasted, before she was cracked open like an egg?

That was it – perhaps Nut deserved to be here more than we did. In the end.

All the wondering, lost in the metropolis of me. All that postmodern, existentialist, self-interested crap. *Maybe I'm not meant to create something. Maybe I'm meant to help her live on. Maybe I'm meant to save her. And maybe one day Art will understand and take me back.*

But this lie poured over me, black like oil. "You will save me?" he'd asked. "You promise to save me?" And I'd said "Yes". Always. To do what I was doing could kill him. He'd taken a tooth, but what next? A kidney. A liver. A heart. Bones. There would be nothing of her left. If he and Easton Grove were still going through with this, they couldn't understand the extent of their invention. But I did.

There wasn't a lot I could grab for myself; everything was in the wardrobes, and the more noise I made the greater the chance of Art trying to stop me. I so needed him to stay asleep. Doing this would mean I was breaking every contract, every law. I didn't for a second think that the Grove would just let us go. We might be hunted down. If Art wasn't involved then at least he'd be left out of it.

I didn't want to leave him, I didn't, so don't think I didn't care. We might have been matched by Easton Grove but we'd worked at this together. They couldn't have known the system would work so well. Art wasn't perfect but I liked him. I understood him. He'd be OK. No matter what I did, Art would still be a member of Easton Grove, he'd still be under their protection. If his book turned out to be everything he'd promised them it would be, they might make him his own ovum organi and he wouldn't need anyone to share it with. She would pump with his blood alone. Look at him with only his face. He could be better off.

But Nut only had this one chance. She was more than the sum of her parts.

She was Nut.

I carried some jeans and a dirty jumper downstairs, coaxing Nut behind me with a teasingly closed fist. Thinking I had inside there some piece of human food, she followed silently with saucer-eyes, absolutely on her best behaviour. When we reached the kitchen, I gave up the game and started pulling out tins of her food and shoving them into the holdall. Nut grunted in disappointment and leaned back into her haunches, flexing her fingers back before tapping them on the wooden floor impatiently.

What else would Nut want to bring? It didn't even cross my mind to grab photos of Mum, or her paintings, or anything else that was me before all this happened. Would Nut want her toys? Her own food bowl? Or would she be OK without the past? Would she adapt?

I grabbed them regardless and lifted the duffle bag onto the kitchen table, ready to go. The rain was still tipping against the windows, so I grabbed Art's jacket and snatched my keys from the windowsill, already mentally coordinating how I'd fit Nut in the back seat. She was too big for the footwell, maybe the boot would work…

And then there was a knock at the front door and I dropped my keys.

I froze. Acid cut the back of my throat.

The letterbox. "Norah?" A woman's voice.

I pressed myself back into the kitchen and out of sight. Silent.

"We can help, Norah. We have answers." A man. He sounded young. And then, silky smooth, like warm milk, *"It's going to be alright."*

I know that I could've gone through the back door with Nut. There was a gate at the side of the fence. There was an escape route right there, feet from where we stood. But in that second everything changed. I was a child, longing for the arms of those who would make everything better. Feed me sugar. Hold me tight in the dark.

A moment later, the key was in the lock and it slammed against the chain.

"Norah? We're here to help you. We know everything."

Deep in my head, *tick tick tick tick tick*, the pens clicking in those early assessments. The need to please. The desperate desire for someone to wrap me in their arms and tell me that everything would be alright. I clunked to the door on wooden feet. Perhaps part of me still thought I could deter them and smuggle Nut out when they'd gone. You'd think that's what it was, but I can't remember thinking that at all. The truth is that I didn't think a thing. I just wanted it to end. Ownership of myself had expired, the real owners were back in the house.

Small and indistinct, I unhooked the chain and flung the door wide, beaming my broadest grin. This was the first of January after all. *Happy New Year.*

"Hell-o Nor-ah," crooned Fia.

She stood on the step clad in a white puffer jacket which reached down to her ankles. Her round face was buried in a nest of black fur, and split by a tight-lipped smile. Behind her stood two other figures in the snow: the bald man, Mr Martin, and the young placement student from mine and Art's last check-up together during the summer. Nathan. Why was he still there? That was months ago.

"Happy New Year, Fia. And Nathan," I breathed. Light, light as air.

Fia clutched a briefcase close to her chest, "Will you let us come in?"

I showed them through to the living room, nudging closed the door to the kitchen with the tip of my toe and muttering, "Keep the warm air in." Thank God I wasn't already wearing my shoes. Or Art's coat.

Fia peeled off her parka and offered it to me in both arms, "Otherwise I won't feel the benefit, right?"

Why were they here? How did they know? Were they listening, had they bugged the house after all? I fingered my leather ID bracelet, flipping it over to see if there were any little holes or a catch for a battery or something. Nothing. It just looked like what it was, a piece of metal, a microchip, and a strip of blue leather. Besides, I hadn't said anything out loud, and I was still in the house. If I was being tracked, I hadn't done anything wrong yet.

I hung the sodden mound of fabric on the coat stand and quickly checked that Nut was still in the kitchen. She was, and she was starting to scratch the ground the way she always did before the territory-run.

When I returned to the living room – light as air, light as air – Art was there, already dressed in jeans and the same shirt as the day before. He was sitting on the chair and had been gesticulating with his left hand while rubbing his chin with the right. Leaning forward like that, the cotton hung from his middle and fell in folds around his waist. It never used to do that. He pushed his knuckles deep into his eye sockets, kneading them slowly behind his glasses.

"Art?"

He stopped speaking and looked up at me, checking me from a safe distance. He lifted himself slowly, uncurling his back and stretching himself as tall as he could.

My Art.

He wouldn't talk to them before he'd talk to me, surely? He stepped towards me, whispering so close to my nose that I wasn't sure what he'd said, and followed the bald man to the kitchen with one last look over his shoulder. He might have said "I love you," or it might've been "I have you."

"Sit down, Norah."

I stayed standing. "Why are you here so early?"

Fia sighed, smoothing the leather with iron-palms. "How're you doing, dear?"

"I'm alright. It's early, we had a party last night. I drank far too much."

"Oh dear. We'll get you in for a physical soon, how's that? There's a new research programme you're eligible for which ups your recovery time after alcohol. Would you like to try it? Shall I put you down for it? It's proving to be quite popular. We can sign you both up."

I didn't take the bait, but instead said, "How do I go back to the beginning?"

"Sorry?" She looked genuinely taken aback. "Back to when?"

"Back to the beginning of this whole thing. I want to know my rights. I've got this far and I don't even know what happens if I changed my mind."

"Changed your mind." Fia tipped her head. "Why would you do that?"

Full thrust. No more tiptoes.

"It's not your fault," I blurted, "but there's been a mistake. With our ovum organi. She's not like the others, what you said they'd be like. Something went wrong when you made her."

"Oh right… Have you reported it? We can take her in today and do an assessment."

"No, you can't. It's not right. I signed up for an ovum organi – a lump of skin, bone, and muscle that wouldn't engage, wouldn't talk. Would exist – just… exist. An organ-egg, right? But this one, *she's like us.*"

Fia narrowed her eyes. "OK. What's physically wrong with her?"

"You don't know?" I laughed, "I'll bring her in."

I must have looked mad. I felt mad. In the kitchen, Nut was tearing around the room, circling Art and Mr Martin who sat at the dining table with an open briefcase. I couldn't see inside it. Art looked grim. He fiddled with the zip of the duffle bag as the bald man scribbled into a notepad. I ignored them and tried to distract Nut from her hypnosis, grabbing at her on each lap. Both of them just watched me, didn't help, didn't interrupt. I was as wild as Nut then, and the expressions they wore said to me one thing – that I was on my own muscle-run and needed to get it out of my system. *Don't disturb it, let nature run its course.*

"Please, Nut," I begged. "Please."

Every time I placed my hands on her shoulders she twisted from my reach. Nothing could stop her running, fleeing from a predator, survival her only instinct. She galloped without sideways thoughts, driven by the need to grow, be strong.

I read later that it felt like electricity, building up around the sternum. The ovum organi's first instinct is to stretch, and then to release the charge by tensing the muscle groups one by one. But when this didn't work (and they were designed not to), this cup of electricity overflowed and caused the current to burn through the axons to the nerve-endings. The sensation would only end when the energy had been expended, the muscles exhausted. It sounded like torture.

The bald man stood up and handed me a mug. He'd made me tea. When? Art watched the cup warily, as if ready to launch himself out of the way if I threw it. The man had his head tilted down, peering up at me over his glasses. He wafted his hands up at me, like you do when you air a bedsheet, and I took a sip of the steaming brew.

I had to go back to face them. In the living room, Fia and Nathan were waiting in silence.

"She's running now, but you just need to see her for yourself. She's different."

Fia had already slipped her tablet from the leather folder and was scrolling. "We carried out a routine examination two weeks ago, and she seemed to be recovering well from the seizure this summer. She was well enough to donate to Arthur. A molar, I think."

The blood. I'd seen the blood. *That night in the garden.* The night Art had warned me. I imagined them all smuggling Nut out of the house or even worse – the dirty procedure happening within these very walls. Was Nut's blood on the carpet somewhere, trodden into the pile beneath my feet? Was I just as grubby as the act was?

"You shouldn't have done that," I said. "It didn't belong to him."

"It did, though," Fia responded. "He pays for it every month. Like you do."

Nathan leaned forward like it was his turn to sing. *All together now.*

"You both deserve this. The world's *so hard*, Norah. There's hardly a minute left in the day to work ourselves out. We need longer years. Would you give that up, now that it's genuinely owed?"

He didn't see. Neither of them knew. I had to whisper it in case Nut heard. I edged close, grasping Fia's arm in case she moved back. I had to make them understand before they took her away, before they drank her dry. "Nut knows things. She knows everything that's going on. She's alive."

Fia mouthed a silent "Ohhhh," and turned to Nathan. Maybe he knew more about this. Maybe this was what his research was all about? He smiled. "Of course she is. She's as living as you or me. She is alive. But she wasn't born, she was made. She was made of your matter, not of your mind. And we own that which we make, don't we?" He patted the leather folder on the coffee table. "It's in our code of ethics. A lamp lights *and* extinguishes."

Fia sat forward. "Norah, Nathan's been doing some work for us writing our new code of ethics. It's just been signed off, which means everything you're feeling is understood. Studied. It's acceptable. Natural, even. It's all part of the process. Once you've read the manifesto you'll see that everything we're doing is morally sound."

If Nathan knew the ethics, maybe I could make him see?

I shuffled across on my knees, ignoring the hot fire of pain on the coarse jute rug. "But a lamp is just an object. This is a soul. What happens to that when she's all used up? Does your code of ethics cover that?"

Nathan leaned into me and held my shoulders firmly, pinning my arms to my sides. It was intimate, and I felt *loved*, by a near perfect stranger – yes – but it was still beautiful. Like floating in a warm pool. A geyser, bubbling with kisses, scented with lavender. From Nathan's fingers poured golden honey to fill my bones. He lifted the mug of sweet tea to my lips again.

"If she has a soul then that belongs to you and Arthur. And won't that feel wonderful, to become one with it again?" He turned to the window, at the grey sludge of sky. "It's bad out there, Norah. She's not made for it. She's raw. Where safer for her to be than where she can be warm, loved, remembered?"

What was he saying? Did he mean here? In my house?

He looked back at me with soft eyes. "We took your stem cells to make her. All this is returning her to you. And think about it – when she returns to Art in body then he's taking on a part of your genetic material too."

"How amazing that'll feel," Fia hummed. "How together you'll be. So much love."

The ticking in my head had been replaced with cotton wool. I licked my lips. "What's in this tea?"

"So much love," Nathan whispered.

Unity. Love. The room was slipping in and out of focus. They were still missing the point. "But Nut will be dead. Where's the love in that?"

My voice was quiet. Nathan stroked my hair away from my face. His eyes were as green as sea glass. "We make another from the same material. Another 'Nut', you call her? Another one. Exactly the same. So you'll always have her with you until the day you die. She'll outlive you, Norah. She's not going anywhere."

"Really? Another Nut?" I daren't believe it. "The same?"

Fia smiled with her lips tight. "And newer and fresher and cleaner. All little again and covered in fur."

"The same," promised Nathan. "Born again. Whole and happy and unspoiled."

20

In my second year of university, when I was around nineteen, Aubrey would wake me up first thing with a shake of my shoulder, whispering, "The sun's out, let's go play." She never took stillness for an answer, and would jiggle the bits of me she could find to irritate me – first my arm, then my wrist, and finally rocking my body side to side under the covers until I, moaning, buried my head under the duvet and finally relented.

Even though I'd sit there sullen, squinting through sleep at my bowl of Crunchy Nut, I couldn't help but feel a spark of excitement. When Aubrey was in one of her good moods, only good things could happen. She grasped new people with fire in her belly and always made sure she pulled me into the mix. It didn't matter whether we drove to a new city or to a rural retreat for the day, it never took long before grey-faced flies were caught in Aubrey's web. Sometimes she brought her guitar and played on a park bench. Bees would swarm to the honey, and I – already drunk on nectar – would sip on an iced tea and drink in a share of her gold.

We achieved nothing, those days. We'd return to the flat with empty hands and empty pockets, the same way we'd left. But this was a cause for celebration. If we returned home without baggage then we were free and weightless for the next adventure, our internal worlds all the richer for memories.

Years earlier, if Mum had a prospector or a buyer visit she'd send me out into the garden to play, much in the same way. Our garden was long and splayed out at the far edges. You could follow a little gravel path around a small copse of trees in the centre, and if you didn't mind your shins getting scratched by the nettles you could follow the path all around the hawthorns until you ended up at the opposite side of the house, where an apt patch of dock leaves sprouted, ready for you to pick a fuzzy petal and rub where it stung.

"You don't need a toy, make your own fun," she'd say, propelling me through the back door with a glass of juice *"Make something good and bring it inside."*

If I'd gone out on my own whim, I'd have been stuck for what to do, but the fact that she'd *told me* there was fun to be had meant I had to find it. But every time I ventured out, I forgot my previous exploits and had to learn my mistakes again. I'd flip over stones to inspect the wrigglings beneath, forgetting that I found the curling woodlice repulsive or that a worm's squirming reminded me of the parts of a person that should be on the inside. I'd decide to look for sweeter creatures: minky mice with wrinkled noses, chocolate moles poking from the soil like a bristly flower bud. Maybe even a naked chick, fallen from a nest in the trees. My hunts always ended in disappointment.

My idea of the natural world was a fairy tale, based on the storybooks I read at school or the stretching cats in Mum's paintings. She captured wild things amidst the slow tide of extinction. She looked over her shoulder as the planet moved forward. And even now, I still see that garden in glorious technicolour. No roses are that violet, no trees are that ferociously green.

When Mum hollered for me to come in, usually hours later, she'd run her fingers through my hair, pulling out the tiny twigs and leaves. If I'd caught the sun, she'd stroke white lotion over my face with broad motions. It smelled like lavender, only slightly off. She'd ask me what adventures I'd had, what I'd seen and done, and when I told her I hadn't seen anything, I hadn't discovered anything, she tutted loudly, clicking her tongue, and held me across from her between those strong worldly arms.

"But you know more than you did this morning, so you've brought something back with you, haven't you?"

I woke up in an empty bed, too soon. It wasn't yet light.

The label on the bottle had said the pill would work for twelve hours, but here I was – awake and wearing the same prickling skin. I lay on my side, my hands pressed to my thighs, clutching myself as tightly as a life-raft.

Alone.

This was a new silence. The clock's tick was a meteor, the silence between was the swoop of an owl. The pause had a soft, wobbling quality. Above me the ceiling groaned, and swayed like the sail of a ship. Voices, ghosts, or neighbours – it didn't matter. I'd never heard the neighbours before. I didn't even know who they were.

This felt OK. Nothing burned or ached. Perhaps this was peace.

Alone, I had no one to answer to, no more questions. I could summon company at the stir of a memory, turning it to shadow with a flick of a fingertip. *If only I could live in there.*

I squeezed my sides with hands that would have normally sought out the firm mass of Nut or Art. If I listened hard enough, could I hear them still? Did they leave a part of them here, even when they were gone? I'm sure if I'd walked into Art's study I'd have been bombarded with what he heard every day – words and mantras and verses pasted on the walls. But I wasn't ready for that. It was enough to listen to the paintwork, and to the house for the thumps of its bleeding heart.

Would I be able to feel it, at the point one of them ended? And which would I feel the most?

For how long would Nut have lived out there if we'd left through the back door? How long before she'd become pink and raw, all light too bright, her lungs full up with smoke?

Cruelty. It would have been torture.

I looked at the clock and saw it was only 6.27am. They wouldn't be in surgery until 8am. I lay there, stranded between getting up to distract myself or reaching out to feel what Nut and Art were experiencing. Was Nut scared, in an unknown place? Art had promised to stay close to her for as long as he could, despite Fia's grimace. Despite not moving a muscle, my heart hammered against my chest. It might've been that no matter what I did I'd feel it – the draw of the knife, the heavy lift of hands.

When they made the new Nut, would they use the same stem cells as the first time? Would she fall asleep, lulled by drugs, and wake up anew? No ache in her jaw, no cut in her belly? There wasn't anything about it in the manuals. They made it sound like the end of one ovum organi and the beginning of the next just... happened. As if Easton Grove hadn't anticipated the question. No fuss. No confusion.

But now I needed to know what made up Nut, how much of her was love, and how much would be the same as before. Would she know me? Would she remember her last frightened moments? Quite possibly the original DNA samples were finite, but even then each sample would contain new cells, and so yield different results. Or are all ova organi cloned from one single perfect embryo? That must be it. Nathan said she'd be the same Nut, exactly the same. I had to believe that. They wouldn't say it without it being true. Caregivers don't take, do they?

I'd have liked to be there when they made her again, but I wouldn't ask that. Instead, I wrapped myself in one of the blankets they'd left behind, monogrammed in gold with "Property of E.G.", and thought solely of her when the clock struck 8am, as a way of saying goodbye. For the next hour, my hand held my heart in one piece as I imagined my second ovum organi being born and delivered to me in her vulnerable and dependent state. This would be my chance to do it right from the start. No dark time in the loft, no confinement. I'd need to make sure everything was ready for her here, from the softest beds to the juiciest toys. Maybe I'd give her toys from the beginning this time; she did love them. It'd be perfect. I'd learned so much, I could do it better than before. Give Nut a better start. My stomach fluttered with the delicious thrill of it all.

Art would be back in two days. He would be spending his thirty-ninth birthday recovering from Nut's birthday gift, a new piece of himself that was only one year old. I considered getting out the easel and carrying on our birthday tradition, now that it was Art's turn to be captured. But I couldn't remember his face well enough to copy it. So as I lay there, I imagined Art's body next to me, socks on the floor, his glasses on the bedside table. Scars spelling out a name. I tried to see him as he was when we met in the waiting room, or on that first date with the party hats. His wide grin, the gap between his front teeth. But aside from the mouth, I couldn't see him. His face was a lightbulb, blinding and featureless. I couldn't see his eyes – those windows inwards – so I drew them in my mind's eye, guessing where they belonged in his landscape.

I played with his face, fancying it might be different when he came back. It might be nice, I thought, if he did look different. A new start for us. All three of us. Because wherever Art goes now, there we are. The three of us. Woven into his being. Maybe he'll look more like me.

This silence was worth dancing in. I rose and floated through each room's harmonious note. Our bedroom was the chamber of a singing bowl. The bathroom was a whisper. The living room was the bellow of a didgeridoo. The kitchen – a symphony of white winter light. I didn't want to listen to Art's study, but I stuck my head in anyway. It sounded like a crowd of men and women, shouting.

I should have been back at work but the Grove had signed me off for two weeks. The form said that I'd developed "generalised anxiety disorder", triggered by Art's looming surgery. They'd assured Stokers that I'd be managing it in two weeks and ready to move into the new office, surrounded by things which weren't mine and that I didn't understand.

I sat up and pulled on an orange knitted jumper that lay beside the bed. The ribs sat high on my waist, and the cuffs dug into my forearms. I couldn't remember Art ever wearing it, but it must've been his. It didn't fit me. I heaved myself out of bed and tore through the wardrobe but all I found were tops and trousers that I didn't recognise. Clothes in shades I hadn't even seen before.

This was ridiculous. It didn't matter whose clothes I chose, I just needed to not be naked. I needed armour. I reached into the pile at the back of the wardrobe and zipped myself into the first pieces I picked up – some jeans, a checked black and white shirt, and a navy hoodie. The Heritage Museum opened at 9am, so I'd get there just as they were propping open the gates. I wouldn't use the main entrance though, I'd use the side door.

I wouldn't need anything else, so I grabbed my car keys from the kitchen counter on my way out. The keys had been thrown beside a messy pile of unread post and catalogues. Poking out from the heap was the top half of a photograph – me, looking vaguely happy at Art, while he, always with his attention on other things, sat captivated by something going on behind me, off-camera. Our studio session, over a year ago. I slid the photo out and held it up to the light. There, in the bottom half of the photo. Art's knuckles holding his knees so tightly that his trousers were bunching up in green waves. And my hands grasping Art's wrist so desperately that the skin on his arm burned red and angry under my embrace.

As I pulled up outside the museum, there were three other cars already there, two red and one bottle green. I parked on the bonnet-side of the red Polo, so my car couldn't be seen from the green one if its owner approached from the museum entrance.

I waited in the front seat, twisting my hands around the rim of the steering wheel. I was afraid. I wanted to walk in and be greeted with that same old smell, the smell of varnished wood and chemicals on fur. I wanted to pass the Anglo-Saxon gallery, see the same gold glint of riches behind inch-thick glass, smell the heady purple of frankincense, and step into the reconstructed Temple of Mithras, tomb-like, lit only by projections of flaming torches.

I hadn't been back in a year and a half. Was it too much to ask for time to have completely stopped within those brick walls? By their nature, museums shouldn't change. They're monuments to memory. If I peered into the Roman jewellery cabinet, the women who wore the trinkets would press their gold-looped fingers to the other side of the glass. It was a promise.

I slipped in through the side fire escape, propped ajar as ever it was by a plastic chair. I headed straight up the stairs to the natural history gallery, a labyrinth of lofty glass coffins, each one split into two halves by a glass shelf. The upper half would contain stuffed sparrows, falcons, robins, and underneath would be a staged display of moles burrowing beneath the earth, or rabbits in their warren, sniffing the air for danger coming. The gallery was always in semi-darkness, to protect the fur, feathers, and flesh.

Weaving my way through the cabinets, I tucked myself into the corner behind my favourite case – the seagulls. Three great white and grey sky-sharks, clutching bare rock with their bills open, their little clay tongues poking out and tasting the wind. One had its wings outstretched like two boundless kites, their edges sharp enough to slice through storms. They didn't look real, they looked designed, like what someone might paint if they were dreaming up a sky god, or anthropomorphising a luxury yacht. I could imagine them carrying souls from one land to another. Was it gulls that gave a sailor hope when lost without sight of the coast? Or was that the albatross?

And then, *he was there.*

Truly there. In the flesh. Surrounded by birds, and living, breathing, full of blood. He looked bigger somehow, and had grown his hair out so it curled under his ears in sandy coils. He carried a metal case and a small fold up stool, and took up residence at the other end of the gallery behind a cabinet of starlings. He unfolded the stool with a flick and undid the catch on the case, causing it to unfold upwards and outwards, like a doctor's medical bag.

I tucked in my legs beneath the bench and shrank into the wall. If I craned my head – just so – I could see him through the glass but he wouldn't be able to see me. From here the starlings looked like they rested on his blazer, on his shoulders, on his fingers. He undid the metal lock and swung the door open with a creak. How easy it would have been for him just to have crawled inside amongst the feathers and closed the door. I could have kept him, then.

And I split again.

The sight of Luke brought back that hot gush of want, and pain, and tearing of flesh from flesh. Skin sizzling on the hob.

Love.

If I hadn't joined Easton Grove, would we have still been one person?

When I was accepted onto the programme, I hadn't known what the real cost would be. They didn't disclose the personals until you passed the initial tests, I suppose because the results of the tests dictated the cost, and how you coped with the cost dictated the personals. It had been the genetic counsellor at the very beginning who'd given me my options and delivered the news that because of my limited funds the shared ovum organi route would be my only viable option. When Easton Grove first began, it had only offered one service, the exclusive ovum organi programme, and if you couldn't afford your own membership, you couldn't be part of it. It was as simple as that. For the first ten years or so, Easton Grove became synonymous with tailored suits, Cadillacs with tinted-windows, and an upper class who could afford to be anonymous. Mum was still here when the now-established Grove was in its earliest days, and I remember it being featured on the news from time to time when I came home from school. She'd watch the reports with one eye still on her work, painting grating strokes with a dry and brittle brush.

But at some point something happened, a shift in internal comms. Easton Grove decided that they needed to improve their image, and announced new, accessible, and more affordable options for regular people. They sold it as the perfect solution to glue together a splitting world. This secondary programme involved genetically matching individuals (across continents if necessary) who were biologically similar enough to share an ovum organi, and thereby almost entirely eradicating the risk of the body rejecting non-compatible ovum organi organs. This one ovum organi would sustain both members with donor parts, whilst they shared the financial burden. It was essentially one membership split into two, and so two lives would be combined as one.

Easton Grove spoke to the nation about how families could live longer together – cue the sultry spoken voiceovers over stock footage of young couples in wooden cabins, early-retiree ex-pats on a beach in Acapulco. Cue the first time they used the beautiful summer couple, gazing forever into the pool. It even looked *better* than the exclusive single membership, because of the togetherness. What a secret to share with someone, what a connection. In a way, it was like taking us back to the Bronze Age, when we worked together to survive. Community, but in this case, a community of two. Everyone was talking about it at work, the hope it gave, but no one ever mentioned the cost.

This was a few years after I'd sold the last of Mum's backlog. I was sitting in front of the TV eating dinner, and I asked the white walls out loud what I should do. My inheritance sat in the bank, every day reminding me of the fragility of life – even when it was lived to the full – just as Mum's was. It was her passion liquefied into cold cash and it needed to be used for something important. Looking around, my flat was empty of answers. The only light shone from Mum's paintings, those portrayals of life that would outlast her. In the hearts of her collectors she'd live forever. She'd achieved a kind of immortality that most people could only dream of. And what had I done to make her proud? I didn't even know who to be, never mind what to do. If her art was immortal, then perhaps the money earned from them was, too.

I registered my interest on the Easton Grove site the sam evening, and the young me in Mum's painting nodded her he sagely. It took seven years after that for them to contact me F And the rest is my history.

The contract with Easton Grove had said that Art and I had to appear functioning – *more* than functioning. They needed the good publicity; emotive stories about two people – brought together to share longevity – building their world around the Grove. A demonstration of an ovum organi partnership transforming into a blossoming love-match. And if the Grove could prove that membership enhanced your life professionally too, well, that just meant more kudos for the programme, more funding, and more interest in their latest experimental research.

I was still with Luke, the first time I met Art. We'd been together for two years, hardly forever in the scheme of things, but he felt like my forever. I didn't tell him I'd registered until I'd already graduated from phase one. This was my only secret, only shared with Mum's shadow in the quietest hours of the night. I had to share it with her; her body was part of what these institutes had become. Her blood trickled through their pipes every day.

When Luke and I were together, I pushed this secret out of my mind, and when it crept back in again (reminded by something on TV or by overhearing a conversation on the street) I kissed him and shook it out again.

It didn't feel like a betrayal because I never thought it'd actually happen.

We'd talked about Easton Grove of course, who hadn't? But I'd been careful not to gauge how he really felt about it because I didn't want to be wounded. When I once did ask him outright, brimming with wine and superciliousness, he twisted his face up and said he didn't think it'd last. "It doesn't have legs," was the phrase he used. "Hollow people."

I suppose I always hoped that he would be a member too, one We couldn't share an ovum organi but if we both shared with ~ple... No, I'm not sure how that would have worked out. ng.

a lot, before I told the truth.

nd to his flat for the night. He knew something soon as he opened the door and immediately wrapped soothing words around me in ribbons. I needed to do it quick, there was no time, so I cut him before we even sat down. He stared at me as if he didn't understand, so I went on, and on, talking about my "genetic weaknesses". It wasn't exactly a lie, it was just sleight of hand. Who's to say that I wasn't predisposed to the cancer that had carried Mum off? And I didn't even know what had happened to my father, whoever he was. But my real weaknesses were emotional.

Even then, I lied to tell the truth.

He didn't beg. I thought he would. I'd imagined him crying, hooking me back by my heart, but there was just a lot of silence, thin air, light-headedness. I even goaded him, asking didn't he care, didn't he want to save me. After a long pause in which he stared at his open hands laid across his knees, he said that he couldn't try to stop me saving my life, but that I had to leave. He didn't look at me, he just pointed at the exit and broke off a piece of me in the process. That's a hurt that can't be fixed. I told myself and him that I was within my rights to decide how I wanted to live my life, and anyone that didn't want a part of it wasn't worth my time. He never returned the piece of me he kept.

I didn't reach out to him again after that, what was the point? He made it clear that he didn't want me to, and he never reached out to me either. It would've been pointless anyway. How could I build a life with Art when I was in love with Luke? How would it have made me look – leaving him behind when I lived my best life? I would have had to watch him die.

Aubrey never forgave me for what I did to him. Maybe she cared for Luke more than she did for me. She smirked and squinted her eyes at me when I told her I'd ended it, as if she was waiting for the punchline of a terrible joke. She didn't speak for a few minutes, and neither did I. I waited, tasting my bitter coffee in tiny sips and strong-arming my mind back to when we lived together, and when silence meant peace.

Her first words said it all. She asked how Luke was. When I said he'd be OK, she clasped her hands to the back of her neck and glared at her knees. I was Prometheus on the rock, and already I could see her sharpening her eagle's beak. She knew I was split, hurting, with hardly a minute to stitch my wounds and yet she still flew at me full force – rising on a storm of contempt.

I'd confused her, I get that, she thought she knew me and I'd betrayed that.

Slowly she stood, and without a word picked up her rucksack and strode to the door, her red heels sitting on the folded backs of her shoes.

Initially I was speechless. She was turning her back when I was most alone. I had no one, no one, and she was walking away as if she was better than me. But then I got angry. In that split second, I remembered every time I'd seen her at her worst – twisting with jealousy or hawking cruelties, and before I realised what I was doing I was screaming and screaming and screaming at her. My throat burned and I spat blood.

I must have terrified her.

"I'm going to see him," she said, quietly. "I can't believe what you're doing."

If you have to chain someone to you, it's not worth them being too close. No trust. The two most important people in my life had left me behind, and both with the same last look over their shoulders. A glistening look, pale and perplexed, as if the me they'd known had died.

That day in the museum was the first time I'd seen Luke since that night in his flat, and in heart and soul I was right back there, self in shards. He might've even been wearing the same clothes. It was unbearably hot inside my layers, and though I longed to loosen them, find myself some air, I couldn't even shuffle an inch in case he saw me. His hands and face were all I could see, the rest of the gallery was all wavy, as if we stood on a griddle.

Remembering to breathe, I took long slow drags of air through my nose. I wondered if he'd help me if I fainted right here on the floor. Would I look the same to him now? Should I speak? Go up to him and face him through the case, a ghost incanted back?

All of his attention was on the display, the stuffed figures inches from his face. I watched as he wrapped little pieces of wire around the bird's tiny claws, strengthening their connections to the twigs and branches they called home. Occasionally he'd stop to fiddle in the metal case for a tool before looking up again, flicking aside his fringe and closing his right eye, just like he did when painting his little people.

I moved my hands along the bench and gripped the edge, leaving a trail of misted fingerprints. My heart was too loud. Surely he could hear me? Every word in my head banged on my skull like a drum. I shuffled forwards on the bench. As I drew closer to him, even by imperceptible fractions, I began to feed from the current between us in the air, and grew stronger with each draft. I would have guzzled forever in my attempt to satisfy the bottomless cavity inside. I began to feel giddy, and my legs tingled – desperate to spring, or leap or jump. I had no idea what I was going to say, but I needed to show him that he was still with me. Maybe he'd return my shard of heart.

I held my breath before moving, but just as I began to lurch forwards a figure walked up behind Luke. I sat back again, craning my head to see who it was. A woman, about my age, wearing a deep red front-of-house fleece. She leaned in close behind him and kissed him on the ear. He leaned back and said something quietly to her, his eyes still on the starlings. She pointed at something I couldn't see inside the case and he moved his hands there. Their two faces side by side peered into the case, cheek to cheek. His new curls coiling into her swinging ponytail.

You know, now I think maybe she hadn't kissed him. It could have been a whisper. He didn't look at her once, and when I think about it, she didn't look him in the eye, either. But the closeness of them drove me out, and I didn't wait to find out what Luke did next. I don't even remember the drive home. It's a miracle I made it back whole.

Once I returned to the house, I threw open the front door and strode straight through the hallway, the kitchen, and out through the back door. No need to lock doors behind me now.

I leaned into the shed and picked up the garden axe, testing the weight of its swing as I strode across the wet grass. When I reached the far edge, I got to work on the berry bush, hacking to pieces that persistent fucking bush that I'd never planted, that I'd never wanted, and that kept coming back, again and again and again, like a vampire rising from the grave.

21

What did I originally ask for? At the beginning? I haven't forgotten.

I never saw Mum die. I never saw her slow decay into *grey*. I never saw the end of her life because I wasn't there. After the last November I visited, I didn't go back. For all those months I let her wilt on her own, drowning in her own body. I only returned when she was already gone.

Maybe this is why I'm alone now. Why I have so little time left, but I'm still waiting with the hot taste of sweet milk on my tongue. Why I'm wearing my "hello" dress, my "I remember all of your sisters" dress. It's threadbare, thinning like the skin on my face, the last white hairs on my head. If I hold up the hem they're all still there, ghosts in the silk scent of talcum. My blue bracelet dangles from my wrist, many times mended, but never fully repaired. I'm no seamstress. One final time, I'm waiting for a white van, stamped with the bronze ankh and "E.G." on its side-doors. This is my last day, my last day of all, and I'm waiting for men whose faces I don't know to bring our daughter to me – in a box.

Where are they?

I've been waiting such a long time. They should be here.

Below the window an immaculate blanket smothers the road, houses, hedges. It won't stay pristine for long, it never does. Cars are white mountains now, but soon they'll be dusted with ash. You could draw your name in it. No one's passed by since dawn, when single figures clad in black marched against the blizzard. Their footprints are hidden under the drifts.

There's nothing coming yet.

The last moments of life are a room. I can't be in that space, that dying space where I know she's been. There've been times when I've opened the door just a crack, just to see, and I can taste her misery on the air. Yet a spark in the mire – I know she wants me there with her. In her swirling world of oils and watercolours, she centred me in its eye. Those racks of unfinished paintings, some still sticky with oil – most of them were of me. She didn't know who I was going to be in years to come, but she still tried countless times to capture a piece just for herself.

You see, I can't be with her in that room. The day I meet her there is the day I come face to face with the shame of it, the blame I placed on Mum for causing her own end when I have done so much worse.

Mum's end was an end through joy – and are there worse things? I now think there are. Her blood danced in her veins in all the vibrant shades she shaped into poetry. My own blood hardly runs at all, yet I feel the dull slick of it, all the time ticking towards the point when I slow so much that I stop. Stop thinking. Stop being anything that can make a difference or leave anything behind. I've become *grey*, without ever being sick.

We tell our stories to make sense of what we've done.

Can you still hear me, daughter?

I see a tree. A tree which once was a home to birds, beetles, bats – all taking the bit they need to survive, nothing more. The tree quivers with a multiverse of life, each species coming and going with hardly a twig snapped or leaf dropped.

But we don't do this. We take all that the tree will ever have to offer and zip it in a bag or lock it in the bank. And soon, no spiders. No birds. All the glorious greens we've sacrificed for the assurance of an empty hand. And always we eat, we drink, we bloat.

And now the earth is bitter. But here, inside, wrapped in each other's flesh, we can survive.

Nut didn't come home, Art did. He wrote his great novel. It took him fourteen years to do it, fourteen years when I hardly saw him at all. And everything he wanted happened. It was published to great acclaim, nominated for prizes here and across the sea – though it didn't win any. He thrived off the book tours, panels, and never ran out of words when it came to interviews. There was a point when people started to recognise him when we went out together. He'd be picking up a coffee and be prodded on the shoulder by a bashful fan, wanting his autograph. His face never wavered, and he always remained cool and crystalline. Afterwards, in private, he'd be grinning from ear to ear, his voice somehow louder *and* quieter than it had been before.

Bookshop windows were decorated just for the launch. Illustrators were commissioned to paint frescos of chalky bones and skulls entwined with ivy. Easton Grove issued a release to the press about his success, which hiked up the book pre-sales even further. I met its cover in every corner of life, from my lunchtime walks and the stacks of copies in our hallway, to folk in cafés – sipping on cappuccinos with their heads buried between the pages. Even shops that I didn't know sold books set up special displays near their entrances.

On my way to work one day, I passed a cardboard box of them outside a café with no one around, and I – as casual as you like – bent down, picked one up, and slipped it into my handbag. When I reached my desk, I pulled out the book and laid it on my lap. I liked the weight of it, how the physicality of it between my hands reminded me that it was done. It was over.

I didn't read it that day, and I've still never read what Art wrote. I used to wonder if I was in there somewhere or whether Nut appeared in some shape. Art's daughter. His first daughter. But how can we really know how we exist within each other's minds, really? Who were we to Art, when it all ended?

During that year of success he was away a lot, talking, talking, always talking, a cuckoo in a nest of wrens. But, as it turns out, no one records anything anymore, and words die off remarkably quickly. Art's come-down was a slower process, and he talked about the book's glory long after the cover was no longer gracing the bestseller shelves. Easton Grove had gone quiet, and no matter how many times he contacted them about doing another interview or seminar they kept putting him off. Eventually the consultants stopped replying entirely, and had the receptionists refer him to the date of our next joint appointment, when we'd discuss the future of "things like that".

And in all that time of triumph, he never picked up a pen or wrote so much as a shopping list. It took a few further years of sitting around the house waiting for offers that wouldn't come before he realised that it was over, and his great work had been buried beneath hundreds, or more likely thousands, of other great works published before and since.

I don't think Art ever accepted that his magnum opus was now simply one lost voice in an overcrowded chorus. He reluctantly returned to his study, picked up the pen again and tried to repeat the cycle. I can't blame him for a lack of conviction. He thought the world would be different after literary success, but it wasn't. Even if he wrote another great work that too would fade, and he'd be faced with the same blank space again. He never said this out loud, but I know it's what he thought. I told him so, again and again.

I tried to encourage him. I brought him food and hot tea, and rubbed his shoulders as he sat staring at the empty page. I needed him to keep writing, to help fund the programme, for both of us. Mum's lump sum would run out one day, and though my salary paid for some of the fees, it was never quite enough. So I spoke soft words in his ear, told him that readers still loved him, that he needed to keep going. My eyes though, they would be looking out to the garden, the berry bush, the sprawling ivy. Art never wrote anything else, not even his penny dreadfuls or pulp fiction. He got by, editing other people's books and occasionally teaching the storytelling craft at universities, colleges or conferences. He never went into why he couldn't write anymore, but I always thought it was because he'd tied himself up so much in his great novel that he was continuing to run a marathon even though he'd crossed the finish line. Art was in a phase of unnatural life. He used to say that he'd lost his voice, and as the years went by, whenever he tried to write or speak he could hear hundreds of different mutterings, grumblings, and incomprehensible mewlings all at the same time, translating his thoughts into a chorus of different languages, none of which he quite understood. If his own American drawl was amongst them he couldn't tell, and he couldn't hear it. Though he tried to be good-humoured about it he was never the same, and pottered about the place in a style much more senior than his years. By then we slept in separate rooms, Art living in a new little annex built into the back of the house. I still don't go in there, it's not my space. It's a foreign land and exploring such a thing is of no interest to me now.

But what did I ask for? In the beginning?

I asked for nothing.

Maybe this was the reason they chose me. When the doctors dug down, sure that I must harbour some deep-seated motive, some ambition I was scared to speak up about, I told them straight, "I'm not asking for anything, because I don't know if I have anything to give."

Despite what they tried to make me feel, I'm nothing special. I'm normal. I'm not driven or obsessive over success. No matter how many pastimes or sports I try, I've never expected to find one that I'm a secret genius at. I'm every day. I'm you. I'm me. I'm a world, complex and unstructured. Perhaps that was the point. I was a beta for Joe Public. This has been my purpose. I've always been a glass of water, poured back and forth whenever they tipped the wrist. They see right through me, know my insides.

But there was something I wanted. I just didn't know it then. And I got it.

I wanted somewhere safe. This house is part of my body, and without it I'm a thin and weedy thing, a tortoise without its shell. I'm never without my security.

I had Art, the longest marriage of all my friends. Art was my home just as much as the brickwork. Ours was a true partnership, and every time he needed to use our ovum organi I understood and gave him my blessing. Art has not been well over the years. By the time he died at ninety-eight, he housed a hundred different souls inside him. They said it was dementia, but I know it was just too many voices for him to cope with. He couldn't hear himself. He forgot who he was.

The Easton Grove programme gave Art exactly what he wanted, and me too. To live a life of few surprises. I needed protection and time to work myself out. It's not their fault that I've never worked out who I'm supposed to be.

But maybe none of us do. Maybe that's what we find out when we live.

I hit a low patch in my fifties, after we'd been together for twenty years or so. I remember it as the first time I stopped leaving the house, answering calls. I still hear Art's voice, clear as day:

"It's like we're on a cliff with a lake under us. You've got to jump, Norah, jump in and through the meniscus. I'll hold your hand. We'll pass through our reflections and see we were there all the time in the water."

I wonder if a lack of mistakes means I've never broken through the glass. I'm not myself.

The spring after Rosa saw Nut at the New Year's Eve party, a car Mike was driving went through a red light and hit the back of a transit van. It was late and they'd both been drinking. Mike was under the limit and walked away from the scene whereas Rosa had been broken in two. The bus was empty apart from the driver, so no one else was hurt.

I'd only seen her once after the New Year's Eve party, a month later when Eleanor had invited us both for a meal in an attempt to bring us back together. Eleanor looked thin, tired. Rosa was late, and she arrived drunk. She told us she'd been for a "few drinks" with Aubrey just around the corner, and when Eleanor asked Rosa why Aubrey hadn't come to say hi, Rosa just shrugged and said, "She's got places to be, people to see. *You know* how it is."

Mike read a passage at Rosa's funeral. He acted like he'd written it himself but the words seemed too familiar. I struggled to remember where I'd heard them and I still don't know, even now. I can still see him, unfolding those little pieces of paper, the sheets rattling between his hands.

"Rosa De Louise lived lightly," he called across the crematorium. "She hardly had a footprint at all."

He gasped, and his lips peeled back over his gums. I could see strings of saliva linking the rows of his teeth. The last few words were spat rather than spoken, but I think I heard them right.

"She knew what was important. We were going to do amazing fucking things. Amazing fucking things. And now she can't." The last bit he said to everyone. "They're saving the wrong ones."

Rosa's body was taken for its parts, just like everyone else's.

I didn't see Aubrey anywhere. I couldn't imagine her in black, only lying on a beach somewhere or climbing a snowy peak. A stock photo of health. But Aubrey was Rosa's best friend, so she'll have been there, maybe up at the front with Eleanor. I scanned the back of the congregation's heads, wondering if any of them were members of Easton Grove. Would an ovum organi have saved Rosa? I've heard incredible feats of medicine, where even the most broken body has been almost two thirds replaced with ovum organi organs. Some premium members have four or five ova organi ready for use all at once, allowing them to drink, overdose, whatever. Live how they like. Maybe Rosa could have still been here, with Mike, if she'd had enough to invest.

After Luke, I did find love again.

I've loved and cried with each ovum organi, each new Nut I've met. I've watched so many grow and saw my husband's face blossom beneath the fur in all of them even before he needed them. On the hardest days, locked in the bathroom, curled in the pit of the shower, I told myself that they weren't dying. Not really. They were going to be with Art, who they loved, and that there would be another one on the way soon to help *the good*.

With each fresh Nut, Art became more and more affectionate, to all appearances forgetting that at some point he would consume them. Perhaps this brought him closer to them, as he knew that one day each would be just as much a part of him as all the Nuts before. As for me, I held them close from the beginning, bestowing on them all the kisses and embraces I'd give to any pure, innocent being. The loft, no longer an ovum organi quarantine, became a space for all the excess stuff that life affords. One day someone will come and take it away. It's been so long since I went up there that I don't even know what's inside the boxes anymore. I don't know who will be left to do that for me, when I'm gone. Who will divide up my life into "Keep", "Donate", and "Bin"? Who will decide what ends up disposed of with the rotting food and dust?

I spend more and more time now thinking about what comes after. I live in silence, and this silence will last longer than I will. I don't know what else I could have done differently. I'm nearing the finish line but there's no one else in the race.

Only me.

Mum's binoculars are at home in my hands. I scan the horizon for a point of focus. My wrists ache from the weight of the leather and glass, so I push the viewfinders deep into my sockets, scanning the flurry of white for something dark, moving, feathered, but the sky is too bright. Too stark. The world is turning *grey*.

There are no birds left anyway. I know that now.

Beyond, the scatterers are still at work, parting the snow to sow the good numbers. Administering their long-term prescription. Is it hope, or is it duty? Their feet drag, their carts rattle and shake. They're never old, they never make it that far. They're probably no more than thirty. They look so tired.

There, there it is – a white van approaching with the ankh on its side. It slowly skirts the corners to avoid sliding on the ice and pulls up outside the house. The van leaves black tyre tracks tracing where it's been, and the young men unloading the cardboard crate from the side doors leave slushy, wet footprints. Looking at the marks, you might think they've been dancing, turning and waltzing together in the snow.

They bring the box in for me, setting it down on the sofa in the living room. I sign my acceptance with a prick of my finger and they leave, locking the front door behind them. They won't be back. That was their final visit, that's what the letter said. This is my last daughter. I'm yesterday, and tomorrow there's another way.

I secure the digital bolt and the ancient chain before returning to the living room, the old tattered blanket spread across the floor. The welcome patchwork that smells like all of her sisters, like family trees, like genetics, like love, like nurture, like the blood of all those who have been born and lost – and of me, still left, still remembering.

I lower myself slowly onto the chair opposite the crate, massaging my hands calmly with alcohol. They air dry on my lap, palms to the ceiling. I'm ready.

Nathan and Fia lied to me, you know. They're never the same.

The day my second arrived I swore the face in the box didn't belong to us. It was a mistake, they'd sent the wrong one. Where was the face I'd been dying to see? This one didn't look like Nut. It didn't move like her. She didn't know me.

I called Easton Grove, I told them that it'd gone wrong and they needed to come and collect her or bring the other Nut back. But they didn't. They sent around a member of staff to speak like Nathan and mix me up. Give me more tea.

I prayed for it to be a mistake. I prayed to whoever was listening to fix it all and bring back my daughter. I lay in bed and couldn't move. But the days passed and nothing changed, and then this Nut picked up Art's love of beef jerky, his fiddling with his ear when he was nervous. When she was five weeks old, she swallowed one of his pen lids and had to go back to the clinic, and after that we let her sleep in our room again. She was short-sighted, and would inspect her food up close for a few seconds before tasting it.

But beneath the face, her soul was the same. Nut was in there somewhere, expressing herself via a different flower. And when her time came to go and the next ovum organi arrived, I didn't know whose face I wanted to see most, which of my babies. But this one was different again, her fur almost white, flecked with black like a snowy owl. From the very first day, I picked her up in my arms and fed her milk from a bottle, stroking her cheek as she sucked on the rubber teat.

Perhaps the best thing I ever did in my life was produce innocents with the capacity for so much selflessness. I've always been so excited to meet the next one. To see who she looked like, and get to know who she'd be. Waiting for one with wild red hair.

My babies took up more and more of my care as the years went by, and I wanted to go out less and less. Luckily the Grove arranged it so that I could work from home, and still the promotions came, regular as clockwork. Maybe Easton Grove's development division put in a good word for me but I'm sure if it hadn't been for my own good qualities I wouldn't have got the new positions.

The problem was, by then I didn't want any of it. My eyes had turned inward, and eventually Easton Grove gave up on me. I stopped hearing from them, and they stopped pushing. I was a disgrace, and if I couldn't be the face that proved the programme was working then it was for the best that I stayed hidden. The press team could tell the world whatever they wanted about me and I wouldn't disagree. I calculated my own little victories by telling the truth. By counting our ova organi, by reminding Art of how many we've consumed. In rituals. By touching myself in secret places every day to feel the parts which weren't me and now are. By appreciating my ingredients. By reminding Art that we aren't *good* or *pure* anymore, that we're composite creatures.

A few weeks ago, I found an old magazine under the bed. It was nearly forty years old, from around the time when Easton Grove was in and out of the news for darker reasons. The magazine's headline article accused staff of selecting members for shadier criteria than they made public. For vulnerability, impressionability, pliability. It made me laugh. Not Fia, Nathan, or any of them could've made me do something I didn't want to do. I didn't want to scale the world. It took me longer than it should've to work it out, but really what I wanted all along was to bury myself deep where it's warm and never come out. I won, they didn't.

You never hear about the other members of the programme on the news anymore. After the Grove started to fragment, always apologising without actually apologising, they stopped taking on new members. They stopped inviting us back to the clinic, kept us all at a distance. Phone calls, and then letters. No one lives forever, but where have they all gone?

I take a pair of scissors and snip expertly at four safety tabs at the front of the box, unfolding the cardboard sleeves like the petals of a flower. Slowly, slowly, no hurry. Waiting is fine, I have all the time in the world to wait. Has she been listening to me telling her how she came to be? Why her whole world is here? *I'll tell her again when she's in my arms.*

It's night now, and the room is as dark as an underground warren. If I lower my head, in the back of the cave I can just about see a huddled ball of grey fuzz, curling in on itself like an ammonite. And looking over her shoulder, a little face with my brown eyes, my turned-up nose, and a nervous smile. This is my last ovum organi, and she looks like me.

There have been so many faces, and I outlive all my children.

ACKNOWLEDGEMENTS

Firstly (and this is a bit disturbing) I have to thank my cat, Juno, for being the most humanesque cat I could know, and for inspiring Nut's movements and characteristics in everything she does. If it hadn't been for Juno, Nut wouldn't have been born, and this book would never have existed. I owe you a lot of tuna. A lot.

And then secondly, onto some deserving humanesque humans. A huge thank you to my agent, Ed Wilson, for bei`ng an endless ball of energy and taking on this weird story in his whirlwind of a world. Ed, thank you for not only guiding me to be a better storyteller, but for embracing the style and words that make me, me. I appreciate it more than you could know.

A thank you to the Angry Robot crew for helping me transform *Composite Creatures* into something that works. To Eleanor Teasdale, for believing in this story from the very beginning, for the expert advice, and for the kitten pictures. To Rohan Eason, for lending your pen to such a gorgeous and atmospheric cover illustration. And to Sam McQueen, Gemma Creffield, Rose Green, and Paul Simpson for all playing such an important part in bringing this book to life and keeping me on the straight and narrow. A huge warm hug and thank you to the whole Angry Robot author community too, for welcoming me into the fold.

A thank you to my readers and constant critics; Alistair Leadbetter for being the world's speediest beta reader, to Anya Kiel for being a constant cheerleader and keeping my morale up when I questioned – oh – just about everything, and to Russell Jones for being the best writing and editing pal an author could have. Your endless feedback to my many projects has taught me so much over the years and I'll always be so, so thankful for that.

And then a few of my favourite humans. Thank you to my friends and family for listening to me waffle on with my strange and twisted ideas.

And finally, to Ben. Without you, I wouldn't have had the confidence to write anything like this. Every day, you've listened to me spin ideas or worry about tangled plot knots, and you've always listened and nodded sagely, even when I didn't make sense. Your patience and love has helped me learn and grow, and with you by my side I know I'll keep sprouting new buds and dark blooms. The biggest thanks go to you.

THE BATTLE OF THE TEACUP

It was a tiny place. A high street, a dozen or so houses on each side, a pub and a corner shop, a few other streets and lanes leading off the first but all in one direction only, and that was about it. A church at one end, a school at the other. Two street lamps. Nyquist stood at the head of the road, under one of the lamps, and he took an envelope from his suitcase. He drew out a set of photographs, and found one depicting the street. The edges of the image were faded and details were lost here and there, blurred over, but yes, it was the same location. In fact, the photograph had been taken from somewhere near this exact spot. And he was sure then, for the first time, that he had come to the right place: Hoxley-on-the-Hale.

He was nervous. What would he find here?

The rain had come and gone: a short but violent downpour, enough to soak him through and to drive people indoors. The street was deserted. He walked along, passing the shop and the pub, both closed, and the expanse of a village green with a circular pond and an oak tree that looked as old as the village itself. A maypole stood at the center of the green, its revelries long passed. The clock on the church tower crept towards six The cold set in deep and his breath silvered the air.

He crossed over a stone bridge. The waters of the river Hale

271

passed beneath, and the church and its graveyard waited for him on the other side. He walked around the building, left to right. It was a small church. The tombstones were laid out without pattern, many of them cracked or fallen over, pushed up by the roots of trees. The newest addition seemed to be *Gladys Coombes*. She'd died in the spring of this year, aged 38. A fresh bunch of flowers lay at her graveside. The doors to the church were locked. Beyond the church the woods took up again; no more houses. He walked back over the bridge onto the high street. The pub was called The Swan With Two Necks. It would probably open up soon and he could see if they had a room available. And a drink. He sat down on a bench. He was tired and dirty, having traveled all day to get here. What could he do next? Perhaps one of the customers in the pub would help him? Yes, that was it, he'd ask everyone about the person he had to find. But then he thought again: would such a move be wise? Maybe it was best to play it tight.

Across the way a light came on in the downstairs room of a house.

Nyquist examined the photographs by the glow of the street lamp. Each was dark in places, or spotted with white dots, or blurred.

A village street.

A church.

A corner shop.

A field with a tower visible in the distance.

Two people standing outside a house. Male, female. Talking to each other, their faces turned from the camera.

Another man, older, mid-fifties. The face as subject matter: a portrait of sorts. But his features were slightly distorted in parts, smeared across the surface.

Six images, each one taken through the same damaged lens.

The church was the same church he had walked round, and the shop across the street was identical to the one in the photo. *Featherstonehaugh's Store*. The letters were squashed and tiny, in order to fit on the board.

A pair of winter moths fluttered above his head: his thoughts taking flight.

Nyquist slid the photographs back into their envelope, all except for one, the image of the couple standing outside a house. Perhaps if he found this residence, it would give him a way forward. He stood up and walked from end of the high street to the other, checking each house in turn against the one in the image, but none of them matched.

He took the first of the side streets, nearest the school. It was called Hodgepodge Lane: just six houses and then open country, the meagre light of the village waning quickly into a gray landscape. None of the houses corresponded to the one in the photograph. He moved on, exploring each side street in turn. One of them, Pyke Road, was much longer than the others, allowing the village to continue up the gentle slopes of the valley. He walked up, looking into one tiny side street after another. He was about to give up and head back down to the village center, when at last he found the cottage he was looking for. He'd already passed it once. He held the photograph up to his eye line, to match each feature and decoration in turn. The house was called *Yew Tree Cottage*. Nyquist rapped the crow's head knocker against the door.

It took a while. It took a long while. Until at last he heard someone moving around inside and a voice calling out, "Go away. No visitors today."

Nyquist rapped again, louder this time. "Hello. I need to talk to you. It's important."

Minutes passed. He was tempted to knock a third time, but then the door opened and a man peered out at him through a gap. One eye was visible.

"Yes, what do you want?"

"I'm trying to find someone."

"There's no one here to find."

"You might be able to help. I was given this address." It wasn't quite true, but Nyquist needed to act.

The visible eye blinked a few times. "Who are you?"

"Can I come in, please? It's freezing out here, and I got caught in the rain."

"Quickly then, before someone sees you!"

The door opened wider and the man grabbed Nyquist by the arm and pulled him inside, dragging him roughly into the hallway. The door closed immediately. The man's face loomed close. "What were you doing out there? You shouldn't be outside, not today." He gestured to an inner doorway. "Well then, make yourself at home. I'll be with you in a minute."

The householder walked off towards the kitchen at the back of the house, where the kettle was already whistling. Nyquist entered the living room. It was softly lit by a standard lamp, and it took him a few moments to realize he wasn't alone. A woman was sitting in an armchair, facing the radio. He nodded to her. She remained as she was, perfectly still, staring at the radio's grille with eyes that never seemed to move. But the apparatus was silent: no voices, no music.

Nyquist coughed and looked around the room, taking in the sideboard complete with a set of decorative plates, a birdcage on a tall stand, a painting showing a dismal seascape. He went over to the fireplace and warmed his hands.

The woman sat in silence.

The clock on the mantel ticked gently.

He turned to the birdcage, peering through the bars at a blue and yellow budgerigar. He made a chirruping noise, but the bird was too busy examining itself in a small oval mirror.

He looked again at the woman: she was as still as before, staring, staring, staring.

The man who had let him in came into the room, carrying a teapot and cups on a tray. He put these down on a side table and poured Nyquist a cup of tea. Biscuits were offered. The woman in the chair was ignored. The two men sat adjacent to each other at a table and drank their tea and ate their custard creams.

Introductions were made: "We are the Bainbridges. Ian, and Hilda." He nodded to the woman in the armchair, but she didn't turn to look his way. "My wife." He said it with a heavy heart.

Nyquist gave his name in turn. Then he said, "I need your help." He knew of no other opening.

Bainbridge looked nervous and he spoke in a sudden rush, "As you might ascertain I am a man of some intelligence, but really, this is beyond my comprehension, that such a thing might happen on today of all days." He was in his forties, yet he seemed older in his speech patterns, his mannerisms, and the way he dressed: a brown jumper over a check shirt, cavalry twill trousers and polished brogues. His hair was shiny with brilliantine, a lot of it. He was healthy looking, well-bred, yet his eyes were the oldest part of him: all the pains of his life had collected here. He rubbed at them now, spreading tears on his cheeks, and he repeated: "Today of all days!"

"It's a Thursday," Nyquist said. "I don't understand."

"Not any old Thursday. It's Saint Switten's Day."

The very mention of the saint was enough to cause Bainbridge's head to bow down so low that his chin was tucked into his chest. He was mumbling a prayer, the words unheard until the final amen. The budgerigar sang sweetly in its cage.

Bainbridge looked up, a calmness on his face as he explained: "We're not supposed to go outside on Switten's Day, not until midnight."

"That's when the curfew ends?"

"It's not a curfew. It is time put aside for silent contemplation. Of course, not everyone follows this to the letter, darting from house to pub and back, thinking a few minutes here and there don't count. Or else they cover their heads with an umbrella, so the sunrays or the moonlight doesn't touch them." He tutted. "Ridiculous."

"What's the punishment?"

The man showed a set of yellowing teeth. "This is not a day for flippancy."

Nyquist was scrutinized. The table was cleared of crumbs. More tea was poured. The Queen's face smiled demurely from the curve of the cup, a souvenir of the coronation.

"Tell me about Saint Switten's Day."

"We have our traditions. Our ritual observances. This one goes back to when Switten himself walked these fields around, centuries past." Bainbridge tapped on the birdcage, causing the occupant to flap its wings uselessly. "Abel Switten was punished terribly for his beliefs, stripped bare and staked out in the dirt." He made a blessing, his hands descending from brow to stomach, tapping at five points in between in a serpentine curve. "We are beholden to our benefactors."

Nyquist felt the day was getting the better of him. He said, "I've been traveling by train since eight this morning. I haven't eaten, not properly. And then a long wait for a bus, and a ride across country. Another hour of that. And then I had to walk through the fields, through a wood! A goddamn wood! In the rain."

Bainbridge shook his head in wonder.

Nyquist cursed. "I've never stood in a field before, not one so large."

"Never?"

"The sky hurts me."

The budgerigar started pecking at the bars of its cage repeatedly, making a racket. Mr Bainbridge tried to calm the bird, rubbing fingers and thumb together and speaking softly: "Here, Bertie. Here, Bertie, Bertie." And so on. It had a suitable effect and the creature was quiet once more.

Nyquist placed the photograph of the house on the table. Bainbridge looked surprised. "That is my house. Yew Tree Cottage. Why do you have a picture of my house?"

"And this is you?" Nyquist tapped at one of the two people depicted. "It looks like you. And the other person looks very like your wife."

Bainbridge picked up the photograph and studied it more closely.

"I'm sorry, Mr Nyquist. I'm afraid I don't understand what you're asking–"

The radio crackled suddenly. Hilda Bainbridge bent forward slightly in response to the single burst of static.

Her husband held his breath.

Nyquist looked from one person to the other, expecting a deeper reaction or a speech. But none came.

The budgerigar sang the same few notes over and over, like a broken recording.

Nyquist decided to tell the truth. He took the other five photographs from the envelope and laid them out on the tablecloth so that each image was visible.

"I received these in the post a few days ago. There was no accompanying letter. So I don't know who sent them. Or why." He paused. "But I intend to find out."

Bainbridge looked at the photographs without speaking.

Nyquist carried on: "All of them show scenes from this village. Look." He showed the postmark on the envelope: "Hoxley. There are a number of villages called that, so I had to do a little detective work. The name of the church, and the shop, and this delivery van, here." He pointed to the photograph of the high street, to a parked van. "*Sutton's*. A bakers. You can make out the address painted on the side. I needed a magnifying glass to read it."

"The Suttons are well known around these parts," Mr Bainbridge said. He pointed out the brand name on the one remaining custard cream. "They're a local firm."

"Exactly. A *local* firm." Nyquist's eye passed over each photograph. "So I did a bit of digging, and I put it all together."

"I'm impressed."

"It's my job. How I make my living."

Bainbridge looked at him in a new way. "You're a police officer?"

"A private investigator."

"I see. So, this a case you're working on, for a client?"

Nyquist took a moment to answer. "This is for me. Entirely for me."

Bainbridge turned his attention to another image, the one showing the tower in a field. He said, "I've never seen this building before. I don't think it's from around here."

"It's not very clear in the shot."

"Still, I don't recognize it."

Nyquist turned one of the photographs over. "What about this? The photographer's mark. It's on all six pictures." It was small pale blue-inked rectangle, somewhat faded, the stamp damaged. "But I can't see the name properly. Nor the address."

Bainbridge squinted. "No. It's too faint."

"There aren't any photographers in the village, professional ones, I mean?"

"Oh, maybe, yes, but I don't believe they live here anymore. I think they left the village a little while ago."

"What were they called?"

"I really can't remember. I don't like having my photograph taken, neither does Hilda. We're very private people."

"But somebody took this picture of you and your wife."

Bainbridge looked puzzled. "As you can see, it was taken without our knowledge. Why would anyone do that? It scares me, to think of it."

"You've no idea?"

"Hilda and I, we lead ordinary lives. It sounds ridiculous to say it, but there is nothing to *spy* upon. Nothing at all."

There was an awkward moment. Neither man spoke. Nyquist glanced at the clock on the mantel: ten past seven.

"What I don't understand," Bainbridge said, "is why you've come all this way? I mean to say, why is this so important to you?"

Nyquist gathered up the photographs until only one was left on the table, the portrait of the middle-aged man.

"Tell me, do you know this person?"

Bainbridge glanced at the image and shook his head. "No."

"Take a closer look."

"I've told you. I don't know him."

There was a noise from the corner of the room and Nyquist looked that way, hoping the woman was alert now, that she might have something to offer. But she was sitting there as before, gazing intently at the now silent radio set. Perhaps her eyes moved slightly, perhaps they flickered?

Bainbridge picked up the photograph. "I can see a family resemblance."

"Yes. It's my father."

Nyquist could feel his heart being wound up tight, a fragile half-broken machine. "I haven't seen him since I was a child. A boy. Twenty-four years have passed. I thought he was dead. And now…" He looked at the photograph. "And now this."

Ian Bainbridge stared at his guest. This stranger, a wanderer, someone who didn't know the rules, a lost soul. He said, "I swear. I swear on Saint Switten's unmarked grave, in all my years I have never seen this man."

Nyquist frowned. He gazed at his father's face. Then he swallowed the last gulp of tea and said, "There's something in my cup."

"There is?"

"Christ. It's moving about."

Bainbridge was puzzled. "You know my mother used to read the shapes in tea leaves. She could view a person's future through them."

Nyquist was irritated. "What would she make of this?"

Bainbridge looked into the offered receptacle. "I cannot say." But his eyes widened, as Nyquist reached into the cup and made to pull out the worm or insect or whatever it was. The creature's squirming body stretched out, one end of it still clinging to the cup's interior.

"What the hell are you feeding me?"

"I'm really sorry about this," Bainbridge answered. "I don't know what to say."

The worm or whatever it was, was still clinging on, lengthening as Nyquist tried to pull it loose. He leaned forward to examine the foreign body.

"I don't think it's a worm. It's the wrong color. Unless you have green worms around here?"

"No, of course not. Green? No. Nothing like that. Just normal worms, nothing special."

"I think this is more like a plant."

"A plant? Really?"

"It's a tendril, or a piece of root." Nyquist turned the teacup this way and that under the light. He said, "But the way it moves, it's more like a living creature."

Bainbridge looked worried, terrified almost. His voice rose in pitch. "We only bring the coronation tea set out when we have guests, which is very rarely these days. And anyway, I keep a clean house!"

Now the two men were both looking at the strange fibrous substance held between cup, and Nyquist's forefinger and thumb. It had stretched to about a foot in length and was still clinging onto the china by its suckered end. Queen Elizabeth II continued to smile gracefully from the cup's outer surface.

"I can feel it pulling back at me," Nyquist said. He felt lightheaded. His eyes couldn't quite stay in focus. His tongue was thick in his mouth.

"I don't feel well."

The dark green fiber was wet and sticky. Tiny burrs hooked at his skin. He gave it a sharp tug, but instead of the sucker coming loose from the cup, the tendril extended itself even further and wrapped itself around his fingers.

"It's got you!"

"The thing's digging in." It was beginning to hurt. "It's tightening." Nyquist pulled with all his strength, watching in a kind of horrified fascination as the tendril stretched out, further and further.

"I think it likes you," Bainbridge whispered. The fear had left him. Now he had a look of wonder in his eyes. "It doesn't like me. And it doesn't like Hilda. It likes you."

"Hold the cup!"

Bainbridge did so, as Nyquist backed away from the table, until he reached the limits of the creature's physical hold. There was a bureau in the corner of the room, and his free hand scrabbled around until it closed on the handle of a paper knife.

Bainbridge gasped, and he whispered, "Don't hurt it." Nyquist swore at him. Or tried to. Nothing made sense, not a single thought or word. Had he been poisoned? Was he hallucinating? Only one thing mattered now. He placed the blade against the tendril and started to slice into it. It was awkward using his left hand, and the thing was resilient, but eventually the knife did its work and the tendril snapped in two. Bainbridge groaned aloud. His wife looked on, her eyes turned at last to the scene before her, a lone silent member of the audience at an absurdist drama.

One section of the tendril was still wrapped around Nyquist's fingers, but it was weaker now. He pulled it loose and threw it to the floor.

"I felt that." He could speak again, after a fashion.

"What? You're mumbling. I can't hear you."

Nyquist rubbed at the fingers of his hand. "When I cut into it, it really dug in. Holding on for dear life." He grabbed the cup from Bainbridge's hands, and examined the remaining half of the tendril. There was a green ooze seeping from the severed end.

"Is that blood?" Bainbridge asked.

"It's green. Like sap."

"So it is a plant then." Bainbridge's mood had changed again. He now looked like a man in a puzzle palace, trying to find his way out.

Nyquist put the cup down on the table. "I killed one half of it. But this section's still alive. It's like a worm that's been cut in two."

"You said it wasn't a worm."

"Well then, I don't know…" Nyquist couldn't finish the sentence. He tried to gather up the photographs, but his hands wouldn't quite do what he asked of them.

"I'm sorry I can't help you further," Bainbridge said.

"I can taste it."

"What?"

"That thing you put in my tea." He steadied himself against the table's edge.

"I didn't put–"

"It's nasty. Bitter. It tastes like…"

"Like what?"

"Like biting into a moth. Not that I've ever…"

Bainbridge grinned. "Oh, I'm sure the effects are temporary."

"I don't feel too good."

"You see, I'm just trying to…"

"Yes?"

"To live my life. And to look after Hilda, that's all."

Nyquist felt sick in his stomach. "All I need is… all is need is information… relating to my father." His body was slowing down.

"I've told you everything I know."

He looked into Bainbridge's face. "I've interviewed lots of men." He had put on an act, forcing the words out. "Tougher guys than you."

"You have?"

One last effort: "I know when someone's lying."

Hilda Bainbridge clapped her hands together, just the once.

The sound was shocking.

It set the budgerigar fluttering and chirping madly. It took Nyquist's every last ounce of strength, just to stay upright. He looked at the woman in the armchair. She was staring at him intently, without a flicker of her eyelids. The room trembled.

One shiver, a second shiver.

He placed a hand against the wall, holding on.

Like so. Concentrate. You can…

The third shiver.

The budgie started to ring its little silver bell, over and over and over.

Liked what you read? Good news!
There's a whole series to get
stuck into!

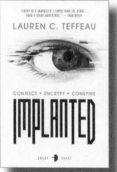

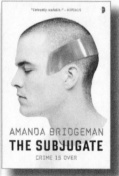

We are Angry Robot

angryrobotbooks.com

We are Angry Robot

angryrobotbooks.com